D0359320

THE AFTER PARTY

OTHER TITLES BY A. C. ARTHUR

Tempt the Dragon

Playing for Keeps

Play to Win

At Your Service

THE AFTER PARTY

A.C. ARTHUR

This is a work of fiction. Names, characters, organizations, places, events, and incidents are either products of the author's imagination or are used fictitiously.

Text copyright © 2021 by A. C. Arthur
All rights reserved.

No part of this book may be reproduced, or stored in a retrieval system, or transmitted in any form or by any means, electronic, mechanical, photocopying, recording, or otherwise, without express written permission of the publisher.

Published by Montlake, Seattle

www.apub.com

Amazon, the Amazon logo, and Montlake are trademarks of Amazon.com, Inc., or its affiliates.

ISBN-13: 9781542031127
ISBN-10: 1542031125

Cover design by Faceout Studio, Amanda Hudson

Cover illustration by Rachelle Baker

Printed in the United States of America

To "My Clerks," Vanessa Destime, Manti Bean, and Beatrice Thomas. Thanks for blessing me with something I never expected . . . friendship.

True friendship isn't about being there when it's convenient; it's about being there when it's not.

—Unknown

Chapter 1

Jackie

"His ass can kick rocks or die. I'd prefer the latter." Jackie tipped her head back and swallowed every drop of Henny from the glass.

Venus had just finished her drink and now rubbed her finger over the rim like she was contemplating pouring another shot. "I'd prefer he simply lose his job, but if that doesn't happen in the next fifteen minutes, I'd be okay if he croaked."

Draya shook her head. Shiny black curls bounced at her shoulders with the motion. "Death's too good for that petty motherfucka. He needs to suffer, like something painful and prolonged so he gets time to stare at the one he wronged, knowing that they finally got even with him."

Jackie glanced again at the prim and proper Venus McGee wearing a black velvet dress, Louboutin pumps, and a thick diamond tennis bracelet on her left wrist. In the four years she'd been at Billings Croft Construction, Jackie had never seen a hair out of place on Venus's head. Tonight was no exception; Venus was a natural beauty with her micro-mini braids pulled neatly into a bun at the back of her neck. As for Draya . . . Jackie poured herself another shot before pushing the bottle across the table, stopping it in front of Venus. Draya Carter had a high-yellow complexion with a round, pretty face highlighted by the makeup she expertly applied on a daily basis. She wore only the best weaves and wigs her six-figure salary could afford. Tonight's curly look was a win. And so were her ample breasts and juicy ass. But that's where all the good stopped, because Draya's tongue was as sharp as the tips of her manicured and designed nails. If she didn't like something someone said or even how they looked at her, she would cuss them so bad and so fast, they'd wish they never crossed paths with her. Sassy and smart—that's how Jackie classified her.

She was sitting at a table with these ladies again, similar to the way she sometimes did when they were in the lunchroom at work. Not that they were the types of acquaintances who agreed to meet up for lunch daily, because they weren't. Or at least she'd never really thought of them that way. It just seemed to work out that on a good number of days in the past year when they were each feeling the stress of working at BCC, they sort of migrated toward the same table all the way in the back of the lunchroom. That's where the commiserating about their homophobic and immature-ass boss had begun.

"Y'all don't even understand what I'm tryin' to tell you." They didn't, but Jackie was about to explain. Earlier today, she'd been pushed over the edge where Rufus, their petty and foul boss, was concerned.

"This man told Ellen to keep tabs on me," she began and sat back in the chair without touching her newly poured shot. "So Ellen is all up in everything I do. Every invoice I approve, every email I send. She even came down to the office today to tell me my vacation time for the summer wasn't being approved. Can you believe that shit? July is seven months away, but I can't take a week off in that month because they're projecting a busy summer. Bullshit! And she didn't have to deliver the news face-to-face; our email was working just fine today."

Dropping her hands into her lap, Jackie frowned down at her pants. While the memo had distinctly said "formal attire" for those attending the annual BCC holiday party, she'd opted for new black khakis with a black turtleneck and a cherry-red wool blazer. The gold watch on her right wrist gleamed.

"She doesn't even like Rufus." Draya slid the last olive off the cocktail pick in her drink and popped it into her mouth.

"But she does like to kiss ass," Venus added. She finally took the bottle and poured into her glass for her second shot of the night. "Her father was one of the first investors when Ted Billings decided to start this company. Ellen's been working here since she was thirty-one and her husband left her and their four kids for a nightclub singer."

"And now it's time for her wrinkled old ass to retire," Jackie snapped. "She gets on my nerves day in and day out."

"Have you ever thought of approaching Rufus about the situation?" Venus asked. "You know, to find out what his real problem with you is. Because she wouldn't be riding you so hard if he didn't approve it."

Venus was absolutely right. Even though Ellen was as old as the bricks that built this building, Rufus was the VP of operations, which meant that nothing happened in the Fells Point office that he didn't know about.

"Oh, that's obvious." Draya reached for the bottle and poured the golden-brown liquid into her empty martini glass. "Rufus doesn't like any woman who's not checkin' for him. Which you clearly are not."

With a you-know-what-I'm-talkin'-'bout nod in Jackie's direction, Draya returned the cap to the bottle of liquor and immediately lifted the glass to her lips.

"I don't wear a note on my forehead" was Jackie's reply. Because she didn't. While she'd dropped any shame of being a gay Black woman a long time ago, she didn't mess with anyone on the job on a personal basis. So to her way of thinking, that meant her sexual orientation wasn't any business of anyone at BCC.

Draya shrugged. "Yeah, but you've got a vibe."

Venus nodded. "She's right. Everybody knows. But I didn't think anybody cared."

Yeah, right, that wasn't how things worked. "Welcome to my world." Jackie took another swallow and let the liquor slip slowly down her throat. An hour ago, she'd been ordering Cokes with a splash of Henny. Then Rufus had arrived, and she and Venus agreed they didn't need a filter tonight. Draya had insisted on her pretty-girl drink until a few minutes ago.

"He approached me in the parking garage one night a couple months back. I was just getting into my car, about to close the door, when he came up on me. I told him I was off the clock, but he wasn't tryin' to hear that. This bastard leaned inside, put his hand between my legs, and asked point-blank if I'd ever tried dick, because if not, he'd be willing to give me a lesson." Jackie cleared her throat and wondered for a few seconds if she should continue. Did she trust these two enough? Hell, it wasn't like she had anyone else to share this type of shit with, so she might as well. "I grabbed my Glock outta the glove compartment and set it on my thigh, a few inches from where his hand was, and asked him if he'd ever tried hot lead up his ass. Those beady brown eyes of his bulged, and he jumped back like he'd been burned."

Venus's eyes went wide. "What? You pulled a gun on Rufus? He could've called the cops and told them you threatened him."

"You could sue him for touching you inappropriately," Draya said, totally ignoring Venus's panic-laced comment. Draya had slowly lowered her glass to the table while Jackie talked and was now looking at her, one elegant brow lifted. "He'd be fired for sure, and you'd get a good chunk in a civil suit."

"You a lawyer now?" Venus asked.

Draya rolled her eyes. "No, and neither are you. Just because your daddy used to be one doesn't mean you carry his degree by default. But"—Draya put a lot of emphasis on that word—"I know a lawyer, and he knows how to win these types of cases."

These two had known each other for a while, but judging by the low-key tension that always buzzed between them, Jackie wouldn't exactly call them friends. In fact, she might've thought they were enemies if it weren't for those impromptu meetups in the lunchroom. Almost like the three of them were drawn together for one reason or another. Truthfully, she figured the reason they continued to appear at that table on the same days was because the two of them were just like her—outsiders.

"Does your lawyer friend know how to get me another job as facilities manager, making what I make, in the city that I love? Because if not, I don't want any parts of suing anybody. I've worked hard for my life here. The last thing I want is some high-profile lawsuit dragging me for filth, because you know they always go after the so-called victim instead of the bastard committing the offense." Jackie sighed. "Plus, when I pulled out of the garage that night, I did think he was gonna send the cops to my house to arrest me. You know Rufus is a punk-ass. I was sure he would use my one slipup to have me fired and prosecuted, but he didn't. I don't know why; I just tried to act like it never happened, until Ellen started ridin' my ass."

"She's right about the lawsuit," Venus said. "And there's no doubt Rufus would play dirty. He'd definitely get the police involved the moment he found out you'd contacted a lawyer."

Jackie nodded. "Exactly, and I'm not tryin' to go to jail for him or anybody else. But I did get a kick out of how scared and pathetic he looked in those moments after I threatened to shoot his ass."

"Good!" Venus lifted her glass. "Let's toast to scaring the shit out of Rufus and bringing him down a notch, even if in private."

Draya rolled her eyes at Venus and then turned her attention back to Jackie. "He didn't call the police because he didn't want you to tell anybody that he hit on you and you turned his ass down. Rufus can't stand rejection. But now he's harassing you through human resources. That means they're probably building a case against you. Preparing for when they finally fire you."

"That's precisely what they were doing." Jackie had been thinking about that since the morning after she'd threatened Rufus, when Ellen appeared in her office. "She already got me with one complaint from Felix—you know, the maintenance guy that's been here forever."

Draya and Venus nodded.

"Supposedly, he told Ellen I was asleep in my office. Ellen calls me to her office and threatens to write me up, but I was like, nah, get Felix up here and call Rufus in on the meeting too. I wanted Felix to look me in the eye and tell that lie, 'cause there's no way I could sleep in that uncomfortable-ass chair in my office."

"Did she set up a full meeting? Because you do have the right to face your accuser." Venus frowned.

"Hell no. Two days later, Felix retired and moved to Florida to be with his daughter and grandchildren." And that write-up had gone into Jackie's personnel folder without her signature.

"Speak of the bitch," Draya mumbled seconds later. Then she lifted her glass to take another slow sip.

"Good evening, girls. Isn't this a fabulous party? Rufus really went all out this year. You three be sure to thank him for being so generous." Ellen stepped closer to the table wearing a too-tight black sequined dress with a white jacket and a necklace made of small Christmas lights. The dress made her look like a glow eel, and her high-pitched, sugary-sweet voice grated on Jackie's nerves the second she began to speak.

"The holiday party is a corporate function." Venus was the only one to meet Ellen's gaze.

Jackie gripped her glass and stared down into the liquid as if it were somehow going to save her from saying something she shouldn't say to the woman who circulated her paycheck.

Venus continued. "And Rufus actually hates it. He told me so two years ago."

Ellen didn't like to be corrected or, in this case, rebuked. "Times and people change, Venus."

Venus shrugged. "If you say so."

There was a quick huff, and Jackie imagined Ellen's cheeks turning bright red. Her cool gray eyes were probably narrowed by now, those spindly webs in the corners crinkling even more. Venus could get away with saying a little more to Ellen without repercussions because Venus's father, Councilman Donald McGee, represented the district, and thirty-five years ago he'd been instrumental in getting Ted Billings his first city contract, which, in turn, started this company.

"At any rate, I'm sure that bottle wasn't made available to you at the bar. And it's in bad taste to have it sitting out in the open while you guzzle it down." Ellen didn't quit, which was just another thing to hate about the woman.

She was well beyond retirement age and yet she still showed up every morning with the sole intent of making as many employees of the company as miserable as she possibly could.

"Why don't you have a drink with us, Ellen?" Draya asked.

Jackie wasn't sure when Draya had taken such a big gulp of her drink, but there was barely any left as she offered the glass to Ellen.

"Disgraceful. You're in a management position, Draya. You should be setting an example for the others," Ellen snapped.

"Others" meaning Jackie, because even though she was a manager in duties, title, and pay, Ellen continued to treat her as if she were at the bottom of the barrel at BCC. Draya worked in finance, and Venus worked directly with Rufus as a senior project manager.

"I should be enjoying this party like every other grown person in this room is entitled to do. So why don't you relax for a change and go on over to the bar to get yourself a drink." Draya's red-painted lips tilted at the corners as she continued to stare up at Ellen.

Jackie contemplated saying something or, at the very least, looking at the woman, but the Henny called to her, and she answered by tossing her head back and emptying her glass again.

"Merry Christmas!" Venus called after Ellen Scrooge when the woman had finally given up and walked away.

"I take it back," Jackie said when they were once again alone. "I wouldn't shoot him. I'd go for a more subtle takedown. Something he'd never see coming."

"What?" Draya asked and immediately shook her head. "Oh . . . Rufus. Look, I'm tired of talking about that man. Let's get over to the buffet before Taylor from the contracts department eats everything in sight."

Venus turned around to look across the room to where the tables full of food had been set up, and Jackie followed her gaze. Taylor was on her third run at the buffet. Jackie had snagged this table in the far corner of the ballroom at the waterfront hotel immediately upon entering. Venus had joined her after she'd made her rounds speaking to other management peeps, and then Draya had followed.

"I'm not hungry," Venus said. "And wasn't Taylor just telling you in the lunchroom the other day about how wide your ass looked in your pencil skirt?"

Draya pursed her lips. "Hmph, and you heard me tell that heffa I don't have any problems with my curves and don't get any complaints on my big ass."

"Maybe she's a stress eater," Jackie chimed in. "Working at BCC is stressful as hell."

"You ain't nevah lied about that," Venus agreed, and poured herself another glass.

The Henny was getting low, and it was the only bottle Jackie had brought with her. The bar was top-shelf and free, so they could easily head over and get more drinks. But no doubt Ellen would be policing the bar like she was personally paying for each drop of liquor being poured.

"Know what else I'm not lying about?" Jackie couldn't help the thoughts swirling through her mind, and since for some reason she felt extremely talkative tonight, she continued even when neither Draya nor Venus had asked her to. "How I'd kill Rufus."

Draya shook her head and used a napkin to dab at her lips. "You're drunk," she snapped.

"Nope," Jackie said and waved a hand in front of her face. "My mind's clear as a summer's day. I wouldn't waste a bullet on his trifling ass. Instead, I'd have one of my homies from the gym drive me out to that big ole house Rufus and his wife share in Columbia. It'd be one of those nights where they have to attend some fancy function. You know that's the only time he goes anywhere in public with fine-ass Pam."

"She's got a point there," Venus said. "Rufus isn't known for being seen with his wife on a regular. He's much too busy with . . . other . . . things." Venus's gaze went immediately to Draya, who only squared her shoulders and stared right back at Venus.

"He's the married one, not me," Draya quipped.

These two took jabs at each other all the time. They'd met in college, but it was obvious they hadn't been BFFs.

"Yeah, whatever, he's a pig; we all know that. So listen, once I get into his house, I'd head straight to the bathroom," Jackie continued.

"To piss out all the Henny you consumed while going on this chaotic joyride, no doubt," Venus added with a roll of her eyes.

"Shhhhhhhhh." Jackie tapped her finger to her lips. "When I get to his bathroom, I go straight for the toothpaste, and I snap that top off. But I hold on to it tight so it won't fall down the drain in the sink. Don't you hate when that shit happens?"

Draya and Venus glanced at each other and then back to her, but Jackie didn't stop.

"Then I pull out this little packet. It looks like it could be coke, but it's not. I don't want this bastard to get high. I want him dead as dirt." She leaned closer to the table, propping her elbows onto the glossy brown surface. "All I need is a little bit, so I take my time pouring it down into the tube of toothpaste. I got gloves on, so when it kind of piles up at the top, I use my finger to push it down. Then I put the cap back on and place the tube where I found it. Then I take a piss, 'cause you right, I had to go."

Draya shook her head again. "You're a goofball."

"No, listen. The next morning when Rufus gets up and goes into the bathroom to start the ritual that creates the monster that rolls up into the office every morning, he pulls out his toothbrush and opens that tube of toothpaste. He squeezes some onto his brush, then scrubs his pearly whites until his gums bleed. Spits, rinses, realizes something doesn't taste right, and then looks into the mirror the exact moment that poison slips into his system. Then bam! He collapses on the floor."

Jackie extended her arms and fell back in her chair, letting her head loll to the side.

"And that's how the paramedics find him—naked as a jaybird with his teeny-tiny dick exposed and his insides boiling from the anthrax."

Now Draya frowned. "That's sick!"

"But a little funny," Venus said with a chuckle. "Especially the teeny-tiny-dick part."

"I know, right?" Jackie laughed along with Venus until eventually Draya couldn't keep scowling at them and she started to chuckle too.

A few seconds later, Venus abruptly stopped laughing, and Jackie followed her gaze across the other side of the room. Rufus was standing with a few other tuxedo-wearing assholes.

"Hey, why don't we take this party up a notch?" she asked, reaching into her jacket pocket to pull out the blunt she'd rolled before climbing into a car and coming to this weak-ass holiday gig.

Draya folded her arms across her chest, an act that pushed the ample cleavage already on display to the point of possibly spilling over the top of the fitted green dress she wore. "Now, that's just classless. How do you come to an office function with weed in your pocket?"

Jackie shrugged. "Easy. Roll it and put it in your pocket, because like I said, working at BCC is stressful as hell. Look, we not gonna smoke it in here. We'll just go up a floor into one of those bathrooms and light up. Nobody from BCC will even miss us."

"Shit! He's motioning for me to come over there," Venus whispered.

Jackie and Draya forgot their conversation for a moment.

"Don't go," Jackie said.

"Go," Draya countered. "If you don't, he's just gonna come over here and make you feel small for not doing his bidding. And he's with Crenshaw, Mr. Billings's right-hand flunky. If you ever want to take Rufus's position, you have to chum it up with Crenshaw."

Draya was right. All executive positions were assigned by Mr. Billings, and Louis Crenshaw was in Billings's ear on a regular basis.

Venus huffed and stood slowly from her seat. "Lord, hold my tongue and give me strength."

"I'd give you my gun, but it's in the car," Jackie told her.

Venus rolled her eyes and walked away. When Jackie looked at Draya, it was to see her once again shaking her head before saying, "You're a hot mess."

Chapter 2

Venus

There wasn't enough Hennessy in the world to make her feel good about standing next to not one but two ass-kissing, backstabbing, less-experienced men with a cordial grin on her face. Unfortunately, this was a position Venus had become quite accustomed to.

Seven years ago—during her first internship—she had trained Rufus to manage his first project with BCC—even though he'd been working at the company before her in some entry-level position. Two years ago, he'd schmoozed his way into the director position, corner office, and salary she'd coveted. This morning, Rufus had once again betrayed her by announcing Mike Livingston as project manager for the $20 million Terrell Hopkins Sports Complex project to be built in Southwest Baltimore. Tonight, Rufus was smug and confident, dressed in his designer tuxedo with the waves in his short-cropped black hair poppin', his beard neatly trimmed, and diamond studs in both ears.

He was fine, there was no doubt, but Rufus Jackson was also a jerk of the highest caliber. From his arrogant attitude, to the numerous infidelities, to the way he treated the women on his staff, he was a pathetic excuse for a human being. He was also an integral part of her career, having always been in a position above her at BCC.

"I presume site selection and analysis have been researched and laid out for the client meeting on Monday," Louis said while raising his bushy eyebrows in question.

Mike didn't respond, and neither did Venus, because it wasn't her project to speak on. Until Rufus stepped closer, giving her arm a little bump with his. She didn't even have to look at him to know he expected her to bail him out yet again. For an instant, she considered leaving him hanging the way he always seemed to do where she was concerned. Then she thought about who was standing a couple of steps away from her.

"Yes, there's already a report for two prospective sites in the area Mr. Hopkins specified with complete analysis and a plan to work with many of our regular vendors who've proven to be dependable and budget-friendly. The final plans for the complex came in earlier this week, so the team has had a few days to familiarize themselves with them. The team should be ready to roll on Monday." She knew all of this because for the last four weeks, since they'd received the call from Terrell Hopkins's lawyer that he was interested in partnering with a local construction company on this project, she'd been working as if she would be handling the account. As senior project manager, she should've been the one to get it. Not Mike, who was only one year out of college and had no experience supervising a project of this size on his own.

Louis smiled, treating her to a view of his straight white teeth and the deep dimple in his right cheek. "Excellent! So the plan is to work through the winter to get this done by next fall. I hear there's a lot of promo in the works for the unveiling, and Terrell's being allowed to talk about the project in conjunction with his other endorsements, so that's some major exposure for BCC."

"It sure is, and we plan to take advantage of that, while also giving Mr. Hopkins our full attention to his project. We've come up with some pretty cutting-edge plans with one of the best architects in the city," Venus continued now that she had Louis's ear.

Talking about the positive work she'd been doing in the department was a hell of a lot better than contemplating the times she'd remained silent when Rufus was making decisions that could've been detrimental to the company. She couldn't go back to the past and undo the fact that she hadn't told Louis or anyone else about going behind Rufus to correct his mistakes with a few of their big customers.

As many times as she'd considered doing just that, especially after this morning's announcement, it was too late. Bringing it up now would make her look as if she'd been complicit in his intent to falsify the spending records on projects—even though she'd ultimately corrected them. Add to that the very truthful claim that she was angry about being passed over for a promotion, and remaining silent about the past was in her best interest. Which was precisely how Rufus had put it when they'd argued in her office earlier today.

"Excellent. We're sparing no manpower on this project; whatever Hopkins wants, he gets, and then some," Louis said. "Adding a former NBA player to our client list is invaluable, and his promised endorsement at the end of the project is something we want to be sure to maximize. We're thinking of a commercial featuring him after the project is complete."

"That's a wonderful idea, especially with Mr. Hopkins's desire to specifically focus on sports as rehabilitative therapy for the disabled and providing a safe haven for inner-city youth. BCC can capitalize on the community-services angle as well as showcasing our ability to snag high-end clients. This project is a win-win for us," Venus said, more enthusiastically than was probably necessary.

The two and a half glasses of Henny she'd had were starting to settle in.

"And that's precisely why I chose Mike to head up this project," Rufus interjected. "He began playing ball in middle school and ultimately received a full-ride sports scholarship to Michigan State, where he graduated with his degree in construction management."

He'd barely graduated with that degree, which was probably the reason he didn't pursue his master's. A severe knee injury during a bar fight in his junior year had ended his NBA dreams. None of which equated to Venus's education and work experience.

"Good. Good." Louis nodded. "All of this sounds good. Mr. Billings will be pleased. Now, if you'll excuse me, I hear the eggnog is spiked this year." With a wiggle of his too-thick eyebrows and a weird conspiratorial grin to Rufus, he walked away.

"Don't. Ever. Do. That. Again," Rufus said the moment Louis was out of earshot.

He was looking directly at her, and Venus tried valiantly not to roll her eyes. This man got on every last one of her nerves. He was jealous and spiteful and didn't deserve any of the accolades that came his way. She despised him and knew that as long as he was at BCC, her place would always be behind him, no matter how much she smiled in Louis's face. If it weren't for her father's connection to this company, she would quit and leave Rufus to fend for himself.

"Do what? Answer the question that you couldn't answer?" she snapped.

Rufus grabbed her elbow and walked away from Mike, attempting to pull her along with him, but she yanked out of his grasp.

"This is a team, Venus. That means no superstars with all the answers." He was speaking to her through clenched teeth, even though as loud as they were playing the Motown Christmas carols, nobody in the large ballroom was going to hear their conversation. "And if you don't know how to play on the team, then it might be time for you to take a rest on the bench."

"You sure that's what you want me to do?" Her voice trembled with all the pent-up rage she had toward him. All the times she'd wished she could just say to hell with the career she'd built for herself and any negativity that might come back on her parents' carefully cultivated reputations within the city. "Because if I sit on the bench and keep my mouth shut, who's going to keep your simple ass out of jail?"

Rufus wasn't the only one who could toss a threat around. They both knew she wasn't going to act on the threat, but she'd be damned if she were going to stand in front of a room full of people and let him push her around.

He stepped closer, grabbing her arm once more, this time with even more force. "Don't try to blackmail me, Venus. You know you're not built to run in my circles."

Was he serious?

Did this fool who hadn't possessed a response for the executive's questions about a multimillion-dollar project just insinuate that he was smarter than she was?

Her?

The one who knew every aspect of this project because she'd been the one to do all the research, consult with the architect, and compile the reports.

"Stay in the place I put you in, or you can explain why you waited so long to open your mouth about all those things you think will put me in jail. Do you understand what I'm saying to you?" he continued, even though she knew the look she was giving him said she didn't give a damn about the foolishness coming out of his mouth.

This time, she used her free hand to push him back as she yanked the other arm free of his grasp. He stumbled, and a hush fell over the room. "If you ever put your hands on me again, you'll regret it. Do *you* understand what I'm saying to you, Rufus?" Job and everything else be damned—there was only so much more she was going to take from this man.

And she was obviously louder than she thought the music had been, because seconds after the words fell from her mouth, she noticed that not only Mike but a few other people who'd been either walking by or standing there before were staring at her. Whatever—they could stare until their eyes bulged out; she'd had enough. At least for tonight.

Walking away and leaving Rufus to deal with the audience felt good, but not as good as finally stopping at the table where Draya and Jackie still sat, grabbing her purse, and saying, "Let's take this party to the next level."

The "next level" apparently meant Venus's apartment, because that's where they ended up half an hour later. Venus lived only ten minutes outside of downtown Baltimore, but it had taken her and Draya forever to get their cars from the valet and then cut through the traffic leaving the Inner Harbor area because of a convention that was in town. Jackie had taken an Uber to the party, which was actually good thinking, since despite the normal open bar at their holiday parties, she'd brought her own bottle and weed as reinforcements.

It wasn't until Venus was parked on the street in front of her building—with Jackie reclined in the passenger seat—that she wondered why she'd brought the party back to her house instead of suggesting Draya's or Jackie's place. These women weren't personal friends; they were coworkers, and before tonight she'd never even entertained the thought of spending personal time with them. Yet here they were. She convinced herself it was because she was too damn old to be smoking weed in a hotel bathroom, even if the waterfront hotel had the best bathrooms she'd ever seen.

"This is niiiice." Jackie had just about finished that bottle of Hennessy by the time Venus had returned to the table at the party. Her words had slurred as she'd stood and high-fived Venus on her idea to take the party elsewhere. Now she was still a bit wobbly on her feet as she surveyed the building where Venus lived. "Didn't they used to have offices in this building?"

"Yes, but they gutted it and turned it into apartments that they now get to advertise as being in a historic building, charging me almost double the amount of a standard apartment for rent," Venus replied when they stepped off the elevator and headed down the hallway toward her unit.

"That's why I moved to the suburbs," Draya chimed in. "If I'm gonna pay a grip for a place, I want peace and quiet and something other than the hospital and downtown buildings to look at."

She had a point. Venus's parents lived in a row house in West Baltimore, just along the county line. They had grass yards, a porch, and neighbors who had cookouts and played cards in the backyard on summer nights—not that Donald and Ilene McGee ever participated in such events. At her apartment, Venus had a balcony where she could extend both her arms and touch the walls. But she liked it and the proximity to the office.

Draya and Jackie followed her inside, and she flicked on the floor lamp closest to the door. The twinkle lights on her Christmas tree and in the windows were on a timer, so they'd already switched on, but that wasn't enough illumination. They all peeled off their gloves, scarves, and coats. Well, Jackie only wore a coat, with her gloves hanging out of the pockets.

"Have a seat. I've got Moscato and Tito's in the kitchen. Gotta pee first, but I'll get it when I come out," she told them.

Jackie grinned. "That sounds like a good start to the next-level party!"

"I can't do any more partying until I take these shoes off. They're cute as hell, but damn my toes are screaming for help," Draya grumbled.

Venus walked down the short hallway to her room. She kicked off her pumps before running into the bathroom. By the time she returned to the living room, Jackie had tossed her black overcoat and the blazer she wore beneath it on the arm of the couch and was lighting the blunt. Draya was checking her phone.

They looked comfortable, like they'd been here a million times before. Venus rarely had company, and it had been a very long time since she'd been out with friends, so this was foreign to her, but she brushed that thought aside. Today had been one hell of a day; she wasn't about to end it by overthinking every situation, as she was prone to do. She crossed the room and went into the kitchen to grab glasses and the bottles from the fridge. Ten minutes later, they were sipping and puffing while sitting around the glass-topped coffee table, staring at the nativity set Venus put out every year.

"I don't think I'd bother taking the time to poison Rufus and wait for him to come across the poison," she said after another puff of the best weed she'd ever had.

And yes, she'd had several different types of weed. Even though she was an only child, she had lots of cousins—mostly boys—and they'd believed in treating her just like she was one of the crew. So when they'd experimented with drugs, she'd been standing right beside them. Luckily, she'd decided quickly what was and wasn't her thing. Weed was okay here and there, but she preferred edibles, mainly because they were less likely to be discovered by her parents. All the other controlled substances they could keep.

"Don't have the patience, huh? You want him dead instantly." Draya laughed and finished her first glass of Moscato before accepting the blunt Venus passed her and having a puff.

"Nah, when it's his time, that's just it. And I don't need any weapons, although I'm a dead-ass shot and carry a blade in my purse. All I need is five minutes in the ring." By now, Venus was lying on the floor. Her body was flat on the cream-colored carpet, hands crossed over her stomach as if she were lying in a casket. This was the most relaxed she'd been in . . . she couldn't even recall.

Draya coughed, and Jackie lifted her head up off the couch. Jackie had switched positions too. Now she was lying on her stomach with one arm hanging down to the floor. She only lifted her head when it was time to take the blunt and puff or grab her glass of Tito's and drink.

"The ring? What, you gonna give him a gift that'll kill 'im?" Jackie asked.

Venus turned her head so she could see Jackie through the bottom half of the table. "No, girl. I would beat his ass to death in the boxing ring. My eighth-grade teacher taught me and my cousins how to box. All I'd need with Rufus is two rounds—three, tops. By the time I get finished punchin' on him, he'd fall to the ground and beg to be put out of his misery."

"That's a little primitive," Draya said with a frown. "But I think I like it." She laughed, that full-bodied sound that was obviously contagious because Jackie started laughing too. Venus followed but continued with the path her imagination was taking.

"He'd bop into the ring wearing some god-awful shorts that probably cost half his salary, bragging and showboatin'."

"Yessss, he loves to showboat, especially when he's naked. I mean, he's got a good body, but damn, man, your dick ain't gold, and I certainly don't have to keep staring at it all night. You know what I mean?"

Jackie and Venus looked at each other after Draya's question and said in unison, "No."

Never, not even drunk and well on her way to being high, had Venus ever thought of seeing Rufus naked. Even if she could allow that he was a handsome Black man moving up in the world, he would never be her type.

"Jesus don't need to hear nothin' 'bout Rufus Jackson's dick," Jackie said and reached out her arm so that her fingers could grab the little manger on the table. She pulled her hand back and tucked the manger with the baby inside beneath the couch cushions.

Venus frowned, not wanting to burst her bubble with the fact that Jesus was well aware of what they were doing and everything they were saying. Instead, she continued.

"The minute they ring that bell, I'd be on him like flies on shit. Punching with my left and right, dancing around so he can't land a punch on me. And when he finally falls to the mat, I'd jump on him and pound away some more." Before she realized it, Venus was punching the air, making the motions of a right, then a left, then an uppercut and jab to the kidneys.

"By the time I finish, he'd be a bloody mess. Then I'd stand up and pull off my gloves, drop them to the mat, and leave his conniving ass there to die." She flipped her middle fingers on both hands as if Rufus were there to see her.

"Die, bastard! Die!" Jackie yelled.

The blunt made its way back to Venus, and she took a deep puff, holding the smoke inside for a few seconds before releasing it slowly through a slit in her lips. "Yeah, die," she echoed and watched the waves of smoke floating over her face.

"What about you, Dray? You wanna kill 'im or just screw 'im again?" Jackie asked.

Draya took another swallow from her glass. Venus could see that her eyes had gone a little glossy, but other than that, she was talking just fine and still sitting in the chair with her thick legs tucked beneath her.

Venus watched as Draya lifted her hands and plucked at her hair. They'd gone to college together but hadn't dealt with each other a lot in those years. Draya's outspoken, gregarious, and flamboyant personality was the polar opposite of Venus's conservative, introverted style. Those very basic differences weren't compatible with a personal relationship, yet here they were.

"I'm definitely not sleeping with him again. I got my promotion now, so that's done. Plus, I felt some kind of way about knowing he'd slept with other women in the building while he'd been with me. I wasn't tryin' to marry the man, but I at least expected to be the only one in the office building he was fuckin'," Draya said.

She should've felt some kind of way about sleeping with a man who was already married, but Venus didn't say that. Jackie was wasted, but to her credit, she didn't do more than crinkle her nose at Draya's statement.

"That's one of the reasons I cut that off. He served his purpose and I was ready to move on, but that is one petty, jealous, and controlling sonofabitch!" Draya leaned forward and picked up her glass again. She tossed her head back to drink from it, but there wasn't that much liquor left inside, so she ended up frowning into the empty glass seconds later.

Venus sat up and handed her the blunt. Draya accepted it and put her glass on the table before taking a deep drag, holding the smoke in her puffed cheeks before blowing it out in a perfectly straight stream. The colorful twinkle lights from the Christmas tree that stood in the corner behind where Draya sat made the moment seem magical, like Draya was a cheery elf dressed in green about to start pulling gifts out of Santa's bag . . . after she took another hit of weed.

"That boxing is too messy for me. And while I'd love to see his ass suffer, I'm really not trying to exert any more energy than absolutely necessary on that man. No, sir, I'm going the classy mobster route and hiring a hit man to take care of my dirty work." She shook her head as if reconsidering. "Or no, I'd hire a woman. Since Rufus thinks he's God's gift to every woman in this world." Draya's lipstick had faded, but her long, fake lashes were still holding strong as she blinked innocently.

"I'd find someone who would do it for a reasonable price, 'cause I'm not tryin' to go broke for him either. Something quick and clean. A bullet to his head just like John Shaft would do—Samuel L. Jackson, not Richard Roundtree. An in-and-out job leaving no fingerprints and no other clues. Rufus would be dead after one shot, and I could live the rest of my glorious life in peace." Draya shook her head. She looked as if she wanted to say more, but she didn't.

"That's it? Hire a killer and keep your hands clean?" Jackie asked.

Draya's head snapped in her direction. "Well, you're just gonna break into his bathroom and poison his toothpaste. Either way, somebody's finding his dead body lying on the floor!"

"At least he'd be ass out when they found him in the bathroom. Your guy's just gonna walk up and blast 'im on the street like any other random shooting," Jackie snapped back.

"That's why I opted to beat his ass instead," Venus interjected. "When he feels like his insides are exploding and his eyes are swollen shut, he's gonna peek through them and see me standing right there. He'll know exactly who served the last blow after all these years of him taking jabs at me."

The twinkle lights were dancing all over the room now, casting the place in a colorful glow that was making Venus's lids feel heavier. She lay down again and now turned her head to the side, looking at the nativity scene without its Baby Jesus.

Get yo' ass up off the floor and go to bed. You've had enough for the night.

That directive came from one of the Wise Men, and she blinked rapidly to see if she could figure out which one.

"Long as that mofo ends up dead, I don't really care how he gets there," Jackie mumbled. "Sick of his shit!"

She reached out to take the blunt from Draya but rolled off the couch instead, bumping into the table and knocking the Wise Men down.

Venus frowned because she'd never figure out which one was talking to her now.

"Who are we kidding? This was some grand wishful thinking. Rufus is gonna outlive us all and make our lives even more miserable each day. The two-minute bastard," Draya said.

She pushed herself up from the chair and bent down to put the blunt in Jackie's hand. "I'm going home. I got a massage appointment at nine tomorrow morning, and I'm not going to be late because I stayed up drinking and smoking with you two."

"She leavin' our next-level party," Jackie said before puffing on the last bit of the blunt.

Venus rolled over onto her knees, then slowly pushed herself up off the floor. She was more than a little wobbly, which meant she was agreeing with Draya . . . and the Wise Man—it was time to end this party and go to bed.

"Yeah, you're right," she said when she was finally standing.

Draya was already collecting her coat from the back of the dining-room chair where she'd draped it when she came in. The wool ankle-length red coat fit Draya nicely, but Venus would've never worn it with a green dress, not even to a Christmas party. The green and red together was a little too festive for her tastes.

"Thanks for the joyous time. It was the best BCC holiday party I've ever attended," Draya said when she stood at the door.

Venus hurried around her and opened the door, because it was the hospitable thing to do. "It was, wasn't it? I really didn't want to go, but now I'm kinda glad I did. Even if Rufus tried to use me again."

"That old dog ain't changin' his stripes." Draya's words might've been slightly confused, but she was still speaking more coherently than Jackie when she walked out the door. "See y'all at the place bright and early Monday mornin'."

"Yeah, see ya. Text me to let me know you got in safely," Venus hollered down the hall because Draya was already walking toward the elevator.

Draya's response was a lift of her hand as she waved fingers with those long painted nails. Venus turned from the door, expecting to see Jackie getting her coat on as well, but that one was still lying on the floor.

"Jackie?"

No response.

This time a little louder. "Jackie?"

With a sigh, Venus closed the door and walked over to her, kneeling down to tap her on the shoulder. "Jackie, get up."

The woman jumped up then and sat on the couch. "I'm good."

"Okay, it's time to go. Call your Uber and I'll get your coat."

"Nah, I'm fucked up. I can't drive."

Venus turned back to see that Jackie had returned to her stretched-out position on the couch.

"You told me you once drank a bottle of Henny before you came to work in the morning. So how are you too drunk to drive now?" She shook her head in an attempt to clear the fuzziness from her mind. "Plus, you took an Uber to the party. All you gotta do is call one now to come and pick you up."

Jackie shrugged and turned her face away from Venus. Seconds later, she was snoring. Venus folded her arms over her chest, staring at the woman with her black boots on the couch, the top part of her hair that she wore in long locs now splayed over one of the pillows at the other end. Her hair was cropped very low on the sides, but the locs would come down past her shoulders if she wore them out, which Jackie never did at work.

Jacqueline Benson was younger than Venus by a couple of years and, as far as Venus could tell, kept to herself at work, except for the last few months, when she'd been easing over to the lunch table with Venus. It wasn't a big deal to Venus; they agreed on one thing—that Rufus was a bastard—so she'd been fine with the occasions they'd had lunch together. She'd sensed a hint of sadness in Jackie's tone some days but had opted not to pry into the woman's personal life because she expected the same courtesy. None of that meant she could ease her ass onto Venus's couch and crash there for the night. Venus opened her mouth to yell for her to get out but stopped when she could've sworn that same Wise Man was now standing on the table again, giving her a warning glare.

What if the Uber driver realized how drunk Jackie was and took advantage of the situation? Or worse, since it was a Friday night, what if the Uber driver had a bad week at work and decided to wash his sorrows away with liquor, too, wrapping his car, with Jackie inside, around a pole? Venus would never forgive herself. The fact that she hadn't considered Draya driving home drunk was something she'd have to pray about later.

"Damn, girl," Venus muttered and turned back to lock her door.

It was almost one in the morning. The Christmas lights were timed to turn off at one, so she switched off the lamp and made her way to the bedroom. She was undressed and beneath the sheets in minutes, falling asleep with visions of all three Wise Men watching her as she beat the crap out of Rufus in a boxing ring.

Chapter 3

Draya

I'm home.

Draya sent the simple text to Venus. She had her phone number because all executives, senior-level employees, and department heads of BCC were required to have an office and cell number listed in the company's private database. That listing was designed for emergency work-related issues. Since it was nearing one thirty in the morning and she was just returning to her condo with a raging headache after attending the company holiday party, she figured that qualified.

Dropping her keys into the bowl on the table by the door, she set her purse down beside it and kept her phone in hand.

Glad you made it safely. Good night.

After reading the text, Draya shrugged. It surprised her that Venus would actually wait up to hear from her. The coat came off next, and she once again stepped out of her shoes. Those things landed on the floor while she continued her trek to the bedroom. Moonlight pouring in from the large curtainless windows on one side illuminated the space, and she went to the nightstand. After plugging her phone into the charger, she grabbed the remote that controlled the electric blinds.

When it was dark, she peeled off her dress and the bodysuit shaper she'd worn beneath it, breathing a welcome sigh of relief at the freedom. Moments later, she climbed into bed, burrowed under the warmth of the blankets, and closed her eyes. Only to have them pop open seconds later when a replay of her conversation with Venus and Jackie rolled through her mind like movie credits.

Had she actually talked about killing Rufus? With Venus and Jackie, coworkers with whom she'd previously only shared a few lunch hours? What the entire hell was wrong with her?

She sighed, blowing air through her partially opened lips, and got a whiff of the liquor. That's what was wrong. Loose Lips, that's what her oldest brother, Bo, used to call her whenever she got drunk.

"You'd snitch on Momma and Granny if somebody got you drunk enough." With a groan, she swore she heard Bo's deep, raspy voice right here in her bedroom.

"I'm not a snitch." That comment immediately followed into the quiet space.

And she prayed Venus and Jackie weren't either. She didn't know them very well, so she couldn't expect loyalty. The fact that they'd both been talking about killing him, too, would have to be enough of a shared secret to hold their tongues. It probably didn't matter anyway; they'd all be so hungover in the morning that they most likely wouldn't remember a damn thing any of them had said.

She turned onto her side, pulling the blankets with her.

Sleep didn't readily come, which was abnormal for her. There were few things in this world Draya coveted, and sleep was definitely one of them. Yet right now, even with the help of the liquor, it seemed to evade her. Too many thoughts were rolling through her mind. Snatches of conversations from earlier today, mingled with her run-in with Rufus as soon as she'd arrived at the hotel.

"Meet me after the party," he'd said while his hands smoothed down the lapels of his tuxedo. Somebody walked past and he'd nodded, giving them one of his cocky-ass grins as he spoke.

"No." She'd snapped the answer and attempted to walk away. His hand on her wrist in a soft and subtle move stopped her cold. Pulling away from him and stalking off were options she briefly entertained, but doing so would give a man like Rufus the upper hand.

Draya was familiar with Rufus's type—she'd been dealing with controlling people all her life. From the time she was a young girl growing up in a city neighborhood touted for its poverty and crime, she'd been judged by teachers, doctors, and social workers who claimed their hurtful words or actions were an attempt to help her out of her circumstances. In the months she'd been sleeping with Rufus, he'd felt the same way—that he was doing her a favor.

"You want your wife to see you touching me like this? Or perhaps the execs who I'm sure are here tonight?"

Rufus had only grinned. "You want those pictures to hit social media?"

She'd swallowed and bit back a curse. "Begging and blackmailing don't become you, Rufus. You know we've run our course, so just let it go." She did take a casual step away from him then, because more people were heading toward the party. She and Rufus stood near the doors of the ballroom, and everyone walking by would notice them together.

He'd lifted a hand, running his fingers over his goatee as he shook his head. "I say when it's over."

She hadn't had the opportunity to respond before he'd walked away, an act he believed proved—just in case his words weren't enough—that he was still in control.

"I should've never fucked with his petty ass," she whispered into the silence of her bedroom, the words ringing especially true now that he was blackmailing her with the tits-and-ass shots she'd taken.

Rufus had requested the pictures on more than one occasion, but she'd always declined. Despite a childhood of being teased about her weight by other kids and those supposed leaders who'd disappointed her, Draya had learned to be proud of her bodacious body. After spending her elementary-school years being depressed and hating herself, she'd decided on her first day of middle school that the only way to beat those who disliked her or insisted on predicting her future based on her present circumstances was to prove them wrong. Taking those pictures had seemed empowering at the time.

"Mistake number one hundred and fifty-two," she mumbled, keeping a tally of all her fuckups.

If Rufus put those pictures on social media, everything she'd worked for up to this point would be ruined. After all she'd been through, Draya had been determined to get to a place where she had the power and resources to help young Black girls in similar situations. The promotion at work and the increase in her salary would do that.

Those pictures, however, could undermine the respect she'd earned in her community. Who was going to take her seriously after seeing her naked? Sure, there were women who'd overcome that stigma or had just taken it all in stride, but she didn't want to have to be one of them.

With those pictures on social media, every click and/or view would chip away at Draya's liberation, and her confidence would no doubt vanish. She'd be that overweight elementary-school student again, succumbing to the judgment and degradation from people who should've been supporting her instead of trying to tear her down.

"Dammit!" she screamed into the darkness of her bedroom.

"What the hell do you want at this ungodly hour in the morning?"

"I want you," Rufus whispered through the phone, and Draya sighed. "I need you to come over to work on something for me."

"Rufus, it is . . ." She paused and pulled her phone away from her ear so she could see the screen. Seconds later, she was pushing the phone back to her ear. "It's six thirty on a Saturday morning. Whatever you need me to work on—that better involve actual work for the company—will have to wait until Monday."

"We can't do this at work. I mean, the paperwork we need to go over is here at my home office, and I need you to come and make sure that paperwork reconciles with the company's general ledgers."

Draya sat up in bed now, rubbing her eyes with her free hand. "What are you talking about? My department handles all reconciliations during the last and first weeks of the month. Is there a problem with a particular account?"

If there was, that could wait until Monday as well, but something in Rufus's tone had Draya on alert. After sleeping with him for six months, she knew all his moods and what to do to make most of them better. This morning, Rufus sounded worried, almost panicked, and that wasn't a good sign.

She heard shuffling through the phone, as if he were covering the speaker or moving the phone away from his face.

"Rufus?" She called to him, but for a few seconds he didn't reply. She was about to hang up when he seemed to remember she was on the line.

"Look, I don't want to talk about this over the phone. Just get over here so we can fix this."

His voice was a little louder this time, but she still got the impression he was trying to be quiet.

"Are you out of your mind? I'm not coming to your house at six thirty in the morning. And why are you whispering?"

"Dammit, Draya! If you don't get your ass over here, there are six very enticing pictures that I'm sure your sorority sisters and anyone else following you on social media would love to see."

This was Rufus's bitch-ass mood.

"You sorry, lying, cheating piece of crap. You really plan to hold that over my head, don't you? Just because I've moved on. You're a married man, Rufus; you can't keep a chick on the side forever." Well, he could, but Draya had decided she wouldn't be that chick.

"If you're not here in twenty minutes, Draya. Twenty minutes is all the time I'm giving you!"

It dawned on her then that his wife must be home because he was still whispering. She'd been to his house many times before, but obviously never when Pam was there. This early in the morning, of course the woman would be home in her bed, just like Draya was. So what in the world was Rufus up to now? She couldn't ask him again because he'd already disconnected the call.

"Rufus? Rufus?" She called his name anyway, frowning before finally dropping her phone onto the bed.

"Dammit!" Cursing wasn't going to make it better. She fell back onto the pillows, dropping an arm over her eyes.

That didn't make it better either.

She wasn't going to this man's house at the crack of dawn on a weekend. There was no need, because they still had another week before it was time to reconcile company accounts in preparation for their billing cycle and then the second reconciliation proofs that came with their bank statements.

But if she didn't go, he'd post those pictures. He hadn't mentioned her not meeting him at the hotel last night like he'd requested. Could she take that as a sign that he was only bluffing with this blackmail scheme? More important, was she willing to call his bluff by not showing up today too?

With a groan, she rolled over onto her stomach and bunched the pillow up under her face to stifle the sound of the scream she let loose.

How had she gotten herself into this position?

By being attracted to a man who looked like an Idris Elba wannabe and matched her expensive tastes in clothes and shoes, that's how. She'd known Rufus was married. Everybody in Baltimore City knew that, since his wife, Pam, was a deputy state's attorney. But Draya hadn't cared. Rufus was the VP of operations, and with that title, Louis had given him authority over not just the projects department but management over client accounts as well as the facilities management department. That's how he'd been in a position to orchestrate the harassment Jackie was now receiving. It was also how he'd been able to promote Draya from accounts supervisor to finance manager three months ago.

"He does not control me!" It was a bold statement, one she'd been reciting for the past two weeks since Rufus had made his intent to blackmail her perfectly clear.

"I'm not bowing to his will."

But she was climbing out of bed and heading into the bathroom.

Because she had to pee. That was the only reason.

She knew it was best not to give in to a blackmailer. He would never stop if she did. He'd give her one command after another after another until she was back in bed with him. Or rather, in the office. Rufus loved fucking in his office. It made him feel powerful and daring. It was a pain for Draya because she had to use the women's bathroom to get cleaned up afterward instead of a more comfortable hotel or home bathroom.

"Rufus Jackson is a no-good bastard, and as soon as I get my holiday bonus, I'm gonna hire me that hit woman to take his sorry ass out."

She talked to herself as she climbed into the shower, knowing everything she said was a lie. That lump sum was already earmarked as a down payment for the lease on a building that would serve as the headquarters for her foundation. Focusing was key here. She couldn't let Rufus hamper her efforts to give back to her community.

Her personal conversation continued after the shower as she returned to her bedroom and grabbed some clothes from her closet. Cursing Rufus and the air he breathed lasted until she was sitting in her driver's seat waiting for her car to warm up.

◆ ◆ ◆

At seven fifteen—she'd texted him to let him know she was running late—Draya walked up the stone pathway to Rufus's stately home. It was a stunning redbrick-front Colonial with a bold red door and matching shutters. Inside was a two-story foyer, five bedrooms, four bathrooms, and a gourmet kitchen. Granny would've loved cooking their big family dinners in a kitchen like that.

It was much colder today than it had been last night, but she'd pulled her leather jacket out of her closet before quickly leaving her condo. Her gloves were on the passenger seat in her car, so she clenched her fists as she stepped up to ring the doorbell. As soon as she extended her arm and was about to press the button, she noticed that the door wasn't closed all the way.

Looking around on this chilly morning, she saw nothing across the street but a wooded area. To her left, where she'd just pulled her car into the driveway, there was nothing else. Rufus always parked in the garage, but Pam didn't because she left for the office earlier than he did, and Rufus didn't like the sound of the garage waking him up in the morning. Pam's gold Mercedes wasn't in the driveway. If it had been, Draya wouldn't be standing here right now.

Maybe Rufus had left too. She reached into her jacket pocket and pulled out her phone to check her text messages. Nothing. Rufus hadn't even responded when she'd texted to tell him she was running late. The fact that Rufus had been so insistent on her getting here in exactly twenty minutes but then ignored her when she said she was running late was odd. Standing in front of his house wondering about the call, the blackmail, and the open door was also foolish, since it was damn near freezing outside. Stuffing her phone back into her pocket, she shrugged and pushed the door open before stepping inside.

Her heart stopped, arms frozen at her sides, and her eyes wouldn't shut. They should have. She should've been screaming and running so damn far away from what she saw, but she couldn't move, couldn't breathe, and could barely think.

Rufus was lying on the lovely gray-and-white marble floor, a circle of blood pooled around his head.

Scream, genius!

Run!

Do something, dammit!

Draya did nothing but stare while thoughts ran quickly through her mind. Was he dead? Who had killed him? Was the killer still here?

Wait . . . "Shit!" Her thoughts finally made it to her throat, and the word rolled out in a panicked timbre.

"Shit. Shit. Shit!" She pushed a hand into her pocket and found her phone again. Her fingers shook as she scrolled through her contacts for a number she'd only texted once before. Why she chose that number on this morning, she had no clue. Perhaps her mind was still in a hangover haze and the only other person to understand that was . . . Shit, why wasn't she answering?

"Hello?" The groggy voice finally rang out on the other end of the phone.

"Venus! Listen to me—we got a problem. A big problem!"

"Draya? Is that you? Are you still drunk?"

Now her mind was reeling, and her heart had finally caught up to her mind, so it was pounding in her chest.

"No! But he's dead! Rufus is dead!"

"What?" Venus was yelling now, but Draya was whispering.

Just like Rufus had been when he'd called her, and now he was . . . She should've called the police instead of Venus. This was a murder scene, and she was just an accountant. No, she was a Black woman standing in her dead boss's house at the crack of dawn. Closing her eyes, she realized how badly she'd messed up again. If she called the cops, they'd ask what she was doing here, and she'd have to tell them that Rufus had called her to come over when his wife wasn't home. She was his mistress, or at least she used to be, and he was dead. Would they assume she'd done it? Probably, because way too often, the color of her skin was the deciding factor.

"Draya! Draya! You still there?"

Venus's shrill voice snapped her out of those fretful thoughts.

"You gotta get over here to his house quick. Somebody shot Rufus," she told Venus. "Somebody shot him, and I don't know what to do."

"Call the police!" Venus yelled back. "Where are you? Never mind, just call the police!"

"No! I can't," she said. "Somebody shot him in the head, just like I said last night that I'd hire somebody to do."

And this morning. Just a half hour ago, she'd been thinking again about hiring a hit woman to take him out. Dammit!

"But you didn't . . . did you?"

Venus's question both irritated and frightened Draya, because it was exactly what she thought the police would say.

She was already shaking her head when more of her brother's words of wisdom rambled in her mind: *Keep your fuckin' mouth shut!*

Between Bo's warnings and Venus's yelling, Draya wanted to scream, but that might alert somebody that she was in the house. Holding the phone closer to her ear, she continued. "He called me on his cell phone. Damn, I'm probably the last person he called. Perhaps the last person to hear him alive, and now I'm here and he's dead. You gotta come quick—we gotta get rid of this body!" It was her only option. If nobody knew he was dead, nobody would think to search his phone and see that she was his last call. Somewhere in the deep recesses of her brain, she knew that didn't entirely make sense, but her thumping heart and the panic spreading throughout her body like a disease easily overruled common sense.

"What? No. No and definitely no!" Venus yelled through the phone. "You call the police, Draya. Right now!"

"I can't, and either you're gonna come and help me or you're not." Draya disconnected the call because her mind was moving too fast now to carry on two conversations. Her heart was still beating frantically, but now her shock had turned to adrenaline, and she was filled with the urge to move, to fix this, to save herself because nobody was ever going to believe she'd found him like this. She was his ex-lover, which, next to his wife, usually turned out to be the top suspect in a murder case. Not to mention the fact that he was blackmailing her, something they would definitely uncover if there was a murder investigation. No, she had to do something—and quick—to salvage whatever parts she could of this huge mistake she'd made by getting involved with Rufus.

She pushed the front door closed and ran through the house, searching each room to make sure she was the only one breathing in there. In the living room, it occurred to her that if there *was* someone else here, she had no way of defending herself, so she grabbed the sharpest thing she could find out of a stand near the fireplace and continued her search. When the house seemed clear and a thin sheen of sweat dotted her forehead, Draya walked into Rufus's office. She had no idea how long she was in there, but she cursed the second she heard the screech of tires outside.

Chapter 4

Venus

"She's out of control," Venus grumbled after taking the Columbia exit off I-95.

"He's dead? That's what she said—he's dead?"

Jackie had been repeating that question every few minutes since Venus had shaken her awake. Her first thought was that Draya's call was ridiculous, that Rufus couldn't be dead. Then she'd thought of their party, after the party, last night and cringed. They'd all been talking about ways to kill him. But none of them had actually meant to do it. Right? Was Draya that damn reckless that she'd actually hired someone to kill Rufus?

In the years Venus had known Draya, she'd heard some pretty wild stories about her partying and promiscuity. Although she knew that every story that traveled through the rumor mill on any college campus needed to be taken with a grain, or perhaps a couple of teaspoons, of salt, Draya's unapologetic attitude had led Venus to assume that most of the stories must've been true. After all, if she were innocent, wouldn't she have said so? Venus certainly would've if it had been her, which it was never going to be, because she knew the repercussions of making bad decisions.

So why was she on her way to a murder scene right now? Every fiber of her being knew that was a bad decision. But wouldn't not going have been worse? Just like last night when she'd decided to let Jackie sleep on her couch to possibly save her from a disgruntled Uber driver getting into an accident and killing her. What would happen if she left Draya there alone? Would she really try to get rid of the body, only to have it turn up later with some evidence that pointed to her moving it in the first place? Shaking her head because she was certain that was a scenario she'd seen on a television show, she tried to get her thoughts in order.

Two seconds later, she was screaming at a guy driving a green pickup truck like he was in a funeral procession. "Dammit! Get outta my way!" The irony between that comparison and the reason she was using the highway as a racecourse early on a Saturday morning had her gritting her teeth as she pressed her palm heavily on the horn. When that didn't jolt the grandpa driver, she whipped her black Jaguar around the damn truck.

Jackie swayed with the motion of the car, leaning over until her head smacked against Venus's shoulder and then back again so her opposite shoulder slammed into the door.

"You're gonna kill us trying to get to the dead man," Jackie spat. "I mean, if he's really dead."

Venus rolled her eyes and entered another lane, focusing her mind on the last time she'd been to Rufus's house. It was last New Year's Day, when Pam had hosted a brunch for her coworkers at the state's attorney's office and some of the BCC executives. Venus's father had been invited because he was a huge supporter of Pam's boss, State's Attorney Leslie Drake, and was looking for the same support from her in next year's election. Don had insisted Venus come with him to show her support of his upcoming reelection bid and on behalf of BCC. Rufus hadn't bothered to tell her anything about the shindig and had the audacity to act as if he'd invited her when she arrived.

"She couldn't have done this. Right? I mean, you don't believe she actually hired somebody to kill him, do you?" Jackie repeated the questions circling in Venus's mind while drumming her fingers on her knees and staring straight ahead with wide eyes, as if she expected Rufus's body to bounce off the hood of the car at any moment.

"She was talking about it last night like she had it all planned out," Venus replied.

"We were *all* talking about it last night like we had it all planned out, because we do. I mean, we did. Each of us wished he were dead. And now he is."

The last of Jackie's words echoed throughout the silent interior of the car. Venus gripped the steering wheel tighter, the boxing scenario she'd conjured replaying in her mind. Her chest felt tight as she imagined actually killing someone, even if it was just Rufus.

"But you and I didn't end up at Rufus's house at seven in the morning."

"No. We didn't." Jackie looked out the side window. "Why are we going there now? Draya's at the house with a dead body, so that sucks for her. But why should we join her? 'Cause I don't know about you, but this ain't my idea of another party."

"Mine either," Venus agreed as she turned down the road toward Rufus's house. "But the moment I picked up that phone and listened to her talk about Rufus being dead but didn't hang up and immediately call the cops, I became an accessory to murder, or at the very least, I obstructed justice."

"And you just had to tell me." Jackie sighed as they turned into the driveway. "I wish you'd have kept that to yourself."

"Then you should've carried your drunk ass home last night," Venus said, put the car in park, and yanked her keys out of the ignition.

Just as she'd been when Venus had pushed her arms into a jacket and run out of her apartment twenty minutes ago, Jackie was right behind her as they approached the front door.

Venus stopped, stared at the door, and then looked over her shoulder. "Put your gloves on," she told Jackie while she reached into her pocket to get hers out.

It was a good thing she kept a pair of gloves in the pocket of each of her winter coats. She hated for her hands to get cold and found this was the best remedy against forgetting to transfer gloves from one coat to the other.

"Maybe we should call her and tell her to let us in," Jackie suggested when they stood in front of the door for another few seconds.

"No." Venus shook her head. "No more phone trail. Phone records can be subpoenaed. I'm going to try and open the door, see if it's unlocked. Then we're going in to get Draya and dragging her ass out of there."

"And then what? We head on over to Jimmy's for breakfast?"

Had Jackie been this talkative last night? If so, why hadn't it grated on her nerves enough to make her want to leave the party without her or Draya? Because dammit, these two were really being pains in the ass!

"No, we're not going to breakfast," she snapped. "Just be quiet and let's get this over with."

She didn't wait another second but put her hand on the doorknob and turned. There was a clicking sound, and when she pushed, the door opened. They stepped inside. Venus slapped a hand over her mouth to keep from screaming.

"Dayyummm! He's really dead," Jackie said while Venus felt as if everything she'd eaten for the last week was churning in her stomach and ready to stage a revolt.

"It's about time y'all got here," Draya said.

Venus thankfully tore her eyes away from Rufus to see Draya coming down the winding staircase. She was walking slowly, like she was some type of royalty and this was her castle. Her curly hair had been pulled back into a ponytail, her face was made up as usual, and she wore a burgundy velour sweat suit with black UGG boots.

"What the hell are you doing? Why were you upstairs? Did you disable that alarm?" Venus asked, unable to hide the disbelief from her tone as she pointed to the wall where the security panel was left open.

"And why do you look like this was a very personal visit you were paying to your lover instead of rushed and thrown together like Venus is?" was Jackie's follow-up question.

Venus shot a heated glare to Jackie, who was squatting next to Rufus. Jackie didn't meet her gaze because she'd turned to look at Draya.

"Excuse me?" she asked, but then looked down at the old black sweatpants and wrinkled green T-shirt she'd worn to the gym the day before yesterday. She'd pushed her feet into black tennis shoes but had forgotten socks. "To hell with both of you—this isn't a beauty contest; it's a damn crime scene. Now let's go!"

"This was definitely a hit," Jackie continued. "They probably rang the doorbell. He answered. Then bam . . . right in the head. Looks like they put the gun directly to his temple."

"You've been watching way too much *Law & Order*," Venus said and headed back toward the door. "We need to get out of here before somebody shows up. Where's Pam?"

"To answer one of your first questions, no. I didn't touch that alarm, so it must've already been disabled. And Pam is in Virginia for the weekend. Girls' holiday shopping trip." Draya walked over to join them near the body, giving Pam's whereabouts as simply as if she were giving the time of day.

Venus had no idea how the two of them were remaining so calm. While normally she was even-tempered and levelheaded, in the time since she'd sat at the table with these two last night, she'd been doing all sorts of things that were out of character. There was blood on the floor—a big pool of dark blood—and the smell made her stomach roil again. This time she lifted her arm and turned her face into the inside of her jacket.

"You know her schedule? Is that something you had to memorize so you wouldn't show up here when she was home?" Jackie continued with the interrogation. Venus half expected her to whip out a notepad and pen.

The look Draya gave Jackie was the equivalent of *mind your business*, but Jackie pressed on. She stood and looked around.

"This is a great house. Damn, look at that painting." Jackie walked across to the other side of the foyer, pointing up at the Baltimore cityscape in what looked like different hues of blue watercolors. "It's a Nanda Lynch original. That's gotta be worth at least ten Gs."

Jackie lifted her hands, touching the side of the frame.

"Don't touch anything!" Draya yelled. "I made that mistake already, but I went back and wiped everything down."

"You've been walking around this house touching stuff? Draya, how simpleminded are you?" Venus asked.

Now she was the recipient of a sharp Draya look.

"Not at all, for your information. In fact, while I waited for you to get here, I worked out a plan," Draya told them.

"I got a plan too," Jackie chimed in. "If we take this painting and those two that I can see over there in the living room, it'll look like a robbery, and we can make a cool fifty grand to split. That's a nice Christmas present, right?"

"What?" Venus shook her head, incredulous at the nonsense coming from both of them. "No, that's not a nice Christmas present. And I don't wanna hear about any plan! There's a dead guy on the floor, and we're standing around like we were invited to his place for a housewarming party and he's gonna jump up and greet us at any moment," she snapped.

"Fuck that, I hope not," Jackie—who was trying to lift the frame off the wall—said with a frown.

"Put that back," Draya instructed. "Rufus told me one time that they've got everything in this place insured, and some of the really expensive stuff is tagged with a GPS chip, so taking anything is only going to get us caught."

"Finally a bit of sense coming from you. But standing here chit-chatting is also going to get us caught," Venus told them. She'd had enough of the smell and took a few steps back so that she was now closer to the door.

"Right, so Jackie, you leave that painting alone and get on the phone," Draya said.

Jackie looked confused. "On the phone? Who am I calling? The cops?"

"Absolutely not!" Draya yelled. "Call one of your little homies and have them come over here, get the body, and then dump it in Leakin Park. Or no, have them drive it out farther, maybe to Carroll County. I'll pay whatever price they name to take care of this."

Jackie's brows furrowed, her thick lips turning up at the sides. "Homies? Who in the world do you think I hang out with? And if I'm not mistaken, wasn't that your cousin involved in the high-speed chase on the eleven o'clock news? He seemed to enjoy running from the cops; why don't you call him and see if he also likes getting rid of dead bodies?"

Draya put a hand on her hip. "Because involving my family might connect this back to me. You, on the other hand, don't have to worry about them finding out if you slept with Rufus."

"Oh, so you weren't assuming you know a better class of people than I do, since you moved to the county and I'm still living in the city. It's more like you know better people because you're straight and I'm not." Jackie shook her head. "You trippin'."

"What?" The befuddled look on Draya's face added to Venus's confusion on the turn this conversation had taken.

She needed to breathe some common sense into this highly uncommon situation. Options for getting out of this without anyone knowing they'd been here had been volleying back and forth in her mind since the moment Draya called.

"Look!" Venus's stern tone put an end to their uncomfortable exchange. "We're not stealing any pictures, and we're definitely not arranging a pickup and drop-off of this dead body. What we're going to do is go outside and get into those cars and drive the hell off. Hopefully nobody has seen us out here."

"On the phone, you kept yelling for me to call the cops. Now you want us to just leave him here?" Draya asked.

"Yes," Venus snapped. "And don't give me any excuses or other great plans you've come up with. Right now, the bottom line is, we're all accessories to murder because even though we weren't here when the murder was being committed, we know about it now. To make that even worse, by not calling the police, we're obstructing justice."

"The police don't give a damn about justice where a Black man is concerned," Jackie countered.

Venus exhaled a breath, hating that since her father had been a defense attorney for years before going into politics, she knew all too well how the justice system in Baltimore City worked. And that meant that Jackie's comment was accurate as hell.

"If we call the police, they won't believe I just found him like this," Draya said. She was shaking her head slowly as if hating the truth of those words.

Venus sighed. "I know." This didn't look good. Not for any of them. "We each have motives for wanting Rufus dead."

"Yeah, but nobody knows about our motives but us, right?" Jackie asked.

Draya stared at Venus, and Venus wondered if Draya knew about the cover-ups she'd done for Rufus. After all, Draya was the finance manager. All financial records pertaining to individual accounts eventually ended up on Draya's desk. But why would Rufus have shared that type of information with her? If he didn't want the world to find out he was a lying, cheating scum in business as well as in his marriage, he certainly wouldn't tell his mistress about his missteps.

"It doesn't matter," she continued. "Us being here at this time of morning without a really good reason—that somebody else can vouch for—is a problem. The cops are never going to believe this is just some coincidence. So again, we're gonna get the hell out of this house and go somewhere to get our stories straight because when the cops come—and they will because they always question the people who knew the victim—the last thing we're going to tell them is that we were all sitting around last night doing a puff-puff-pass and talking about how to kill this man lying here with a hole in his head!"

Draya opened her mouth to speak, but Venus held up a hand. "Not another word until we get out of here. Unless you want to stay and wait for the Howard County cops to roll up in here and cuff you."

Jackie was standing with her feet planted, arms folded across her chest, still dressed in the khakis and turtleneck she'd worn to the party last night. She'd left her red blazer at Venus's place but had her black ankle-length coat and boots on, looking like a wannabe gangsta . . . who wanted to steal the paintings off a dead guy's wall.

Venus didn't wait for their responses but walked to the door, turned the knob with her gloved hand, and stepped outside. She inhaled gulps of fresh air, praying that, too, didn't make her want to hurl. Two minutes later she was backing out of the driveway with Jackie once again in the passenger seat.

"We could go to Jimmy's and talk about our alibis," Jackie suggested.

Venus stopped at the bottom of the driveway and shifted the car out of reverse while cutting her eyes at the woman.

Jackie shrugged. "What? Dead people make me hungry."

Chapter 5

Draya

She canceled her massage and leaned against Venus's bathroom door with a heavy sigh. Last night, she'd been in this apartment having a few sips and puffs and a marginally good time. This morning, her pressure was up and she had a USB drive stuck down her bra.

"Y'all want cheese in your eggs?" she heard Jackie yell, and imagined Venus frowning at the question. Jackie had been talking about food since they all got out of the cars and walked into Venus's building ten minutes ago. That girl's bout with the munchies obviously had a delayed effect.

With a shake of her head, Draya pushed away from the door and moved to the sink. *How the hell did all this happen? Why did it happen?* Her heart pounded like she'd run a few hours on the treadmill instead of taking a leisurely stroll like she was prone to do whenever she made her way to the gym. That wasn't nearly as frequently as she walked into the Silken Hands Spa, but she digressed.

What the hell am I gonna do?

The face staring back at her through the mirror over the vanity had zero answers.

"It's gonna be fine," she whispered, since one of them had to take control. "Nobody saw you there, and you got what you needed."

That comment could go two ways, since she had gotten a promotion out of Rufus and now, thanks to his early-morning call, she'd found the USB drive that she prayed contained all her nude pictures. Still operating on the adrenaline pumping through her veins, she'd gone straight to his office after hanging up with Venus earlier and searched high and low for it; then she'd made sure there were no other copies on his computer's hard drive.

That had been a little tricky, since she'd almost gotten locked out for putting in the wrong password too many times. It should've been obvious, given that she knew what Rufus considered his best asset. Typing in "MRDICKLY"—no punctuation and all caps, the same way he used to sign his written notes to her—on the third try had been like striking gold. That would've been a first where Rufus was concerned, because while he was a fine-ass brotha, his performance in the bedroom didn't rate in her top five. Or top ten, if she was being brutally honest. Being in his office was also how she'd learned of Pam's whereabouts. Rufus had it written on his desk blotter. No doubt as a reminder of the free time he'd have to slink his trifling ass into some other woman's bed.

But she shouldn't have been in his office. A heavy sigh followed that thought. She shouldn't have been in his house. None of this would've happened if she'd just stayed in her nice warm bed this morning. But she couldn't have done that; it would've been risking too much.

Glancing down at her breasts, where the drive was presently stuffed, she sent up a silent thank-you that Rufus was finally out of her life. But before she could feel the wash of relief from that piece of good fortune, the memory of his dead body flashed in her mind. Her legs wobbled as if she were standing in his foyer once again, staring down at his legs twisted in an unnatural fashion, eyes wide open. She gasped, slapping a hand to her chest, as if that action would keep her heart from thumping right through her rib cage, and then groaned.

"Every damn time." She swore and moved away from the vanity, toward the toilet. Pushing down her pants and panties, she swore again as the same thing that happened whenever she got nervous came like clockwork.

Damn, she hoped the cops didn't dust for fingerprints in Rufus's upstairs bathroom, because she'd had to run in there and take her customary nervous pee after seeing all that blood leaking from the hole in his head.

"Don't die in my bathroom, Draya." That was Venus's raspy, condescending voice.

Draya rolled her eyes and finished her business before returning to stand in front of the vanity. This time, she turned on the faucet and washed her hands, looking up into the mirror again as she scrubbed them together.

"It's gonna be fine," she repeated. "This'll all blow over and life will go on."

By the time she finished in the bathroom and stepped out into the short hallway, she could smell bacon frying and hear cabinets being slammed shut as Jackie acted like this was a normal Saturday-morning breakfast with friends. Which it was not. Venus wasn't Draya's friend. As the daughter of a city councilman, Venus had always thought she was better than Draya. Even when they'd both claimed top honors in their graduating class at Morgan.

The McGee family lived on the west side of Baltimore in a four-bedroom row house that had everything but the proverbial white picket fence. In addition to her father's clout in the community, Venus's mother used to be a high school principal, but when they were in college, she'd come out of the school and had taken a job in the administration. They also belonged to one of the biggest Baptist churches in the city. While Draya was the fourth of seven children being raised by her mother and grandmother and sharing two bedrooms in a three-story row house across town. But those were just logistics. She and Venus were both successful women now, and Draya wasn't above reminding Venus of that fact.

Leaving the bathroom and walking into the living room, she saw Venus sitting with one leg crossed over the other, the laces to her relatively new Chuck Taylor tennis shoes untied and her shirt wrinkled. This was about as unkempt as Draya had ever seen Little Miss Perfect. That meant this shit was really happening. Rufus was really dead, and for the moment, the three of them were the only ones who knew about it. Well, besides the one who shot him.

Jackie came into the room behind Draya. She had a red-and-white-checkered dish towel slung over her left shoulder and the sleeves of her black shirt rolled up to her elbows. "So nobody's gonna answer me, huh?"

"Nobody's tryin' to eat at a time like this, Jackie. We have to figure out what our plan is," Venus said with a roll of her eyes.

"Just a little while ago, you didn't want to hear any plans," Jackie told Venus. When Venus only frowned in response, Jackie shrugged. "Anyway, I do my best thinking on a full stomach. So everybody's gettin' cheesy eggs and bacon. If you had something other than wheat bread in here, I'd make toast, but no amount of stress is gonna make me eat that dry shit."

Draya moved to the chair she'd sat in last night, hoping her stomach didn't growl loud enough for Venus to hear it. She could totally understand where Jackie was coming from. Her family ate at all times. When somebody announced they were pregnant, they had a big-ass baby shower, inviting half the neighborhood, feeding them a buffet in exchange for gifts. Weddings were the same, even though they were usually somewhat limited with the standard unseasoned banquet food caterers tended to provide. But funerals and holidays—those were the real smorgasbord in the Carter family. They had food for days and usually at multiple houses so relatives could visit with one family, then hop on over to another family member's house and grab a plate there too.

"It's not that deep, Venus," Draya said when she'd watched Venus's foot wiggling uneasily for a few minutes. "I mean, he's dead, and there's nothing we can do about that now." At least that's what she was telling herself in order to keep her heart rate at a normal pace.

"That's not the problem," Venus replied, her head whipping in Draya's direction. "Or rather, it's not our most pressing problem. The issue I'm more concerned about is, what if our cars were seen in his driveway? You said he called you this morning—you know as soon as the murder investigation jumps off, they're gonna dump his phone records and see your number."

She did know that, but she was trying like hell not to let it freak her out. The key to dealing with any situation was to stay calm—nothing good came from overreacting or running back and forth to the bathroom.

"I work for him; it's not uncommon for him to call me. Besides, they'd still have to get a warrant or a subpoena for my phone records, right?" She wasn't the daughter of a lawyer like Venus, but a number of her family members had firsthand knowledge of the criminal legal system in Baltimore. Still, there was no good reason for Rufus to be calling her at six thirty on a Saturday morning. The obvious conclusions that she was sure a good detective would draw were: he was calling to invite her over or to tell her he was on his way to her place. One of which was true and would obviously put a big ole check mark by her name as a suspect.

"It should've been uncommon for him to call you at this time of morning. He damn sure wouldn't have called me at that time."

Draya sighed. She couldn't really blame Venus for stating the obvious, but that didn't mean she was going to keep quiet while the woman judged her.

"Look, you've already made your feelings about me sleeping with a married man very clear. You're definitely entitled to your opinion, but

I don't have to hear it every ten seconds." Especially not when she'd already been regretting the affair with him.

She drummed her fingers on the arm of the chair when she looked over to see Venus giving her a get-the-fuck-outta-here-with-that-BS look. Draya rolled her eyes this time. "Well, what do you want me to do? I can't go back in time and not accept the call. And I had no idea somebody was gonna roll up on him as soon as he hung up with me and shoot him in the head."

But maybe Rufus knew.

"He was whispering on the phone," she said before she thought about stopping herself. Last night, she and Venus may've been kickin' it like they were old friends, but they'd also been pretty drunk. This morning, they were what? She inhaled and flattened a hand over her stomach as she caught another whiff of bacon. Well, considering Venus had been the first person she'd thought to call when she was standing over Rufus's body and they were obviously about to have breakfast together, she guessed they could at least be considered friendly coworkers.

"Whispering?" Venus asked. "While he was asking you to come over? And you didn't think that was odd?"

"Of course I thought it was odd, Venus. What, do you think I'm stupid?"

When there was no response, Draya sat forward in her chair, ready to pounce on this bitch if she fixed her mouth to call her stupid to her face.

"I think we're all in a pretty fucked-up situation because you decided to one, accept his call, and two, go over to his house. I mean, what the hell? Were you used to going to his house at that time of morning?"

"Don't judge me," Draya snapped and stood, propping one hand on her hip. "You're not better than any of us, Venus. You may think you are, but you're running around kissing Rufus's ass just like everybody else who works at BCC."

For an instant, she saw a flicker of shock in Venus's eyes; then Venus popped up off the couch. "No, that's where you've got this twisted. I work at BCC, and Rufus just happens to be my immediate supervisor, but I sure wasn't fuckin' him, and I don't run around behind him like Mike and Ellen do."

Draya closed the space between them, getting right up in Venus's face. "You don't know every damn thing either."

"I know what you did to get a promotion, and that's enough," Venus replied, her lips turning up at the corners as she leaned in closer to Draya.

Draya's fingers itched to smack her. It'd been a long time since she fought a bitch, but that was because most everybody in her family knew not to come at her wrong. Venus obviously needed to learn that lesson.

But before she could talk herself out of slapping this woman in her own living room, a high-pitched beeping filled the air. Draya turned around, looking toward the ceiling, because it sounded like a smoke alarm going off. Streams of smoke came from the kitchen, and Venus pushed past her, heading that way. Still ready to put her hands on Little Miss Perfect, Draya shook her head and followed the smoke.

"Damn this cheap-ass pan," Jackie was saying when they walked into the smoke-filled room. She tossed the pan into the trash can, but when she turned, the dish towel fell from her shoulder onto the stove.

The open flame immediately licked at the material, and Venus reached for it, grabbing it with the tips of her fingers, trying to wave away the flames. In an effort to keep her nonfriend's apartment from burning down, Draya grabbed the first thing she saw—the mop leaning against the wall inside a bucket—and began swinging it at the dish towel in an attempt to put out the flames.

"Oh shit!" Jackie's delayed reaction to the flame show Draya and Venus were now performing was followed by more cursing and Jackie running from one end of the kitchen to the other. "911! 911! Call the fire department!"

"Who the hell you think is gonna call the fire department? Grab the damn phone!" Draya yelled.

Venus finally dropped the dish towel into the sink, just as Draya swung the mop again, this time smacking Venus against the back of her head.

"I got it! I got it!" Jackie yelled just as Venus turned her angry gaze toward Draya.

Their almost physical collision was once again thwarted when cold water splashed on them. Now the duo turned to see Jackie standing in front of the refrigerator, an empty water jug in one hand, a slice of burned bacon in the other.

Chapter 6

Jackie

"So basically, we're gonna just go on like none of this ever happened," she said fifteen minutes later when they all sat in Venus's living room, teeth chattering because of all the open windows.

The burned smell clung to the cold air, and Draya sat in that same chair she had last night, but now with her jacket on. "We can't act like it never happened, since I might wake up tomorrow with pneumonia thanks to you."

Draya was referring to her wet hair, of course, but what the hell had she expected Jackie to do when the flames going between her and Venus were getting out of hand?

"It's a wig, Draya. The water didn't even touch your scalp, so I'm sure you'll be fine," she said.

"A hundred-and-fifty-dollar wig that's ruined thanks to you," Draya snapped.

"You have way too much money to spend," Jackie replied, but then held up her hands in surrender. She knew better than to insult a Black woman's hair—even the kind she paid for—but this situation they were in was tense as fuck. "My bad. If it's really messed up, I'll pay for it."

"She could've let it catch fire," Venus said before resting her elbows on her knees and leaning forward. She wasn't wearing a coat, and the water hadn't damaged her braids at all, but she was sportin' a pretty mean frown that filled Jackie with guilt. After all, she had almost burned the woman's kitchen down.

"Anyway," Venus continued, cutting off Draya just as she'd opened her mouth to reply to Venus's previous comment, "yes, that's exactly what we're going to do. We'll go to work on Monday and go about our business as usual."

"Meaning none of us says a word about Rufus," Draya added.

"Nah." Jackie shook her head. "That's not normal for me at all. And what am I supposed to do if Ellen brings her nosy ass into my office again?" From the moment Venus had awakened her and relayed the phone conversation with Draya, Jackie had been thinking about how Rufus's death would ultimately affect her.

Had he told Ellen about her pulling a gun on him? Was Ellen going to go to the police with that information as soon as she learned Rufus was dead?

"We do exactly what we would normally do," Venus continued. "If that's sit at your desk and bitch about Rufus, then that's what you do. If you do something else where Rufus is concerned, it's probably better that you do that too." Venus looked from Jackie to Draya.

Draya only blinked before replying, "Or if you spend your time running in Rufus's office to complain about not getting a promotion, you should keep right on doing that too."

These two and their bickering were giving her a headache.

Venus huffed. "My point is, nobody knows what we know unless we tell them. And we're not going to tell anybody anything."

"What if Ellen already knows about me pulling a gun on him? What if she tells the police? They'll consider me a suspect without even knowing I was at that house this morning." She hadn't realized how very real that fear was inside her until she said the words out loud.

When nobody replied, Jackie rubbed her hands together, lifted them to her mouth, and blew into them. "I'm sayin' his body's not going to just lay there for the next two days and nobody will find it. By Monday, the news is gonna be out that somebody killed him."

"She's right," Draya added.

"That's fine. The news will be out, but my point is the same—nobody knows what we know. If Ellen tells the police about you pulling a gun on Rufus, it's just hearsay because she didn't witness it herself. You can always deny it." Venus's hands were clenched in front of her. "If somebody says something to you about Rufus's death, act shocked, express your condolences, and get on with your day. We have to stick together in this, or it all falls apart and we'll get caught."

"We didn't do anything," Jackie reminded them, or rather she wanted to remind herself. "He was dead when we got there."

She hadn't shot him in the balls in that parking lot even though he deserved it, and Draya hadn't hired someone to shoot him in the head. Jackie wasn't sure whether Venus was really doubting that last fact or not, but Jackie was certain Draya wasn't a killer. None of them was.

"But we didn't tell anybody. That's a crime," Venus stated evenly.

Draya sighed. "She's right—not telling is a crime. And it's probably not the morally correct thing to do. But it's a decision we all made together because we realized it was in our best interests. Which means at this point, we all have something to lose by telling. So we keep our mouths shut and let this blow over. Case closed."

At that moment, Jackie felt like she might have a little more at stake than they did, but she was thankful for the group approach they agreed to take.

"I'm going home," Draya said when nobody else had spoken. "You want a ride?"

"You sure?" Draya's place was in the opposite direction from Jackie's, and after the morning they'd had, she didn't want to impose.

"Come on," was Draya's response as she stood.

Ten minutes later, they were pulling away from Venus's apartment building in Draya's Audi A5.

"How angry do you think Venus is about her kitchen towels? Should I buy her a new set?" They'd just passed a linen store that Jackie was certain her mother had shopped in when she was a little girl.

"I don't know. Venus is always so uptight, it's easy to annoy her. But if it were me, yeah, I'd want you to replace my kitchen towels." Draya made a left turn and then added, "You're lucky I can just blow-dry and recurl this wig."

Jackie glanced over to see the straight ends of the wig and held back a sigh. "I told you I'd get you a new one."

"And if I wanted you to do that, I'd have told you so. Stop being so agreeable."

Jackie frowned. "I thought I was being considerate."

Draya shrugged. "Whatever. You can stop it now because it's all settled. Buy Venus some towels and give them to her for Christmas and she'll be fine."

Jackie hadn't thought about them exchanging Christmas gifts. It hadn't seemed necessary for sporadic lunch buddies, but now that they all shared a secret, she wondered how the dynamic of their tentative acquaintance would change.

"What about you? What do you want for Christmas?"

The loud burst of laughter coming from Draya instead of an answer made Jackie feel a little unsteady. Friendships weren't her strong point. Not since she'd graduated college and come out as being gay to her family and those she'd thought were her friends.

"Girl, I haven't given a Christmas list to anybody in years," Draya finally replied.

"And that was funny?"

"Yeah, because some things in life you have to laugh about to keep from crying."

That was pure fact, and Jackie could only shake her head at how much those words hit home.

"Well, anyway, if we're gonna do a gift exchange, we should all list maybe three things we want, and then each of us can pick from those things." She was already thinking of the three things she was going to put on her list.

"Wait, now it's a gift-exchange thing? I thought you were just trying to make amends for almost burning Venus's house down."

Jackie shrugged. "We need something to keep our minds off the negative. I'm gonna start a group text thread about the exchange, so you get to thinking about the three items you want to put on your list."

"We pick names for Christmas gifts in my family," Draya said. "Ten-dollar limit, one gift, because there're so many of us. Then on Christmas Eve, we gather at Momma's house and exchange our gifts."

"Not on Christmas Day?"

"No, Christmas Day is just for eating, and at my momma's house, that's an all-day affair." When Draya laughed heartily again, Jackie thought about Christmas dinners at her parents' house.

It'd been six years since she'd been welcomed into the house where she'd grown up. Almost an eternity in Jackie's mind. "We used to do everything on Christmas. My parents always invited their friends from the church over after we'd opened our gifts and then we sang carols, ate, and talked until it was too late to do either anymore."

"Used to? Y'all don't do that anymore?" Draya glanced over at her, and Jackie went back to staring out the window.

"Nah, they do, I guess. I'm just not invited."

If Draya wanted to ask why, she didn't. Jackie was surprisingly relieved by that fact. When her parents had first disowned her for what they called her defamation of the child they'd raised and loved, Jackie had craved comfort and peace. She'd found that in a queer couple she'd met at school. And as if the Lord were answering another one of her prayers, that couple had introduced her to Alicia, who'd quickly become her best friend and lover. Five years after they'd met, Alicia left to find a better life without Jackie—taking their small circle of friends with her. In the last year, Jackie had grown accustomed to not talking about any of that painful shit, and she wasn't ready to change that now.

The conversation dwindled to a few comments about whatever was playing on the radio, and then, as a saving grace, they pulled up in front of the row-house-turned-apartment-building where she lived.

"Thanks for the lift," Jackie said and got out before there could be any uncomfortable looks or exchanges.

Pulling her coat close, she ran up the steps and used her key to open the first-floor door. Her place was on the third floor, so she took the stairs two at a time until she was letting herself into her apartment.

Heading straight to her bedroom, she shrugged out of her coat and dropped it on the bed. Going to her dresser, she placed her keys on the glossed wood surface. Her wallet and watch landed next to them. She was walking toward her nightstand when her head started to throb. It wasn't a hangover, 'cause Jackie never got those. She'd been drinking since she was ten and her father began sending her to the fridge to grab him a beer when he came home from work. Taking the first swig after opening the bottle for Clive Benson had become a daily act, until the taste for liquor sat on her tongue the way casino lights called to a gambler.

Nah, this headache was from something—or rather, someone—else. Two someones, to be correct. Venus and Draya had hella tension brewing. They either needed to get laid or get high—probably both.

Not that she liked to rely on either one, but Jackie wasn't as uptight or on edge as Draya and Venus were. She also wasn't trying to live the showboat-all-your-success lifestyle either. Venus and Draya competed for that shit. Last Christmas when Venus had gotten that big bonus, she'd bought a fly-ass black Jaguar that she looked damn sexy pulling up in. But when Draya got her promotion in September, she bought one of those new half-a-million-dollar condos they'd built in Baltimore County. Both of them tryin' to show everybody they were on the come up.

Jackie rubbed her temples, thinking that wasn't her style. Sure, she was proud of her accomplishments—graduating with honors from high school and college, obtaining her associate's degree in business administration, and mostly staying out of trouble. Landing a job in BCC's mailroom hadn't been what she'd expected after working her ass off to get that college degree, but she'd remained patient and worked her way up, until her first promotion to shift supervisor in the mailroom led to another move to the facilities department. From there, she'd found her niche and had worked hard to utilize all the skills she'd learned in school, until it landed her in a top management position. Alicia would've been proud. Her parents *should've* been proud.

Those thoughts had her sitting down heavily on the bed. Why the fuck was she still thinking about any of them? They'd made it clear they didn't want her in their lives, and begging was another thing that wasn't Jackie's style.

Her phone vibrating in her pocket pulled her thoughts away from that dismal shit she had no control over, and she breathed a sigh of relief. Pulling the phone out, she swiped a finger over the screen to reveal the full message. After reading it, a grim weight rested on her shoulders.

Still waiting for that callback. K

Shit. Karlie.

The sweet Puerto Rican honey she'd met at Jazzy's Lounge, her favorite hangout, a month ago had been calling or texting her weekly ever since. Staring down at the phone screen, she envisioned Karlie when she'd first approached Jackie that night. Bold as fuck, she'd walked right up to where Jackie sat back in her favorite booth, one arm across the back of the curved bench seat.

"Dance with me," Karlie'd said.

Jackie had been busy watching her approach, the easy confidence in her stride commanding attention. The black dress she wore that clung to her like a second skin wasn't easy to dismiss either. She couldn't see her thighs but imagined them to be soft. Her waist was slim, breasts full, creamy honey-hued cleavage peeking above the tight fit of her dress. Long, curly black hair hung over one shoulder and her voice . . . damn . . . it'd been almost as smooth as that Apple Crown Royal Jackie had been sipping on.

"Nah, I don't feel like dancing right now" had been Jackie's response. She'd gone to Jazzy's after a long day at work and another run-in with Ellen. Her goal had been to just unwind and relax, not meet anybody, not dance the night away or whatever.

Karlie had slid onto the bench, easing over until her side bumped against Jackie's. "Then what do you feel like doing?"

She smelled good. That was another thing Jackie had noticed about Karlie. Her perfume was soft, something floral that didn't burn her nostrils like most perfumes did. And her voice—she was back at that again—had made Jackie's pulse jump.

"Drinkin'," she'd replied stoically. "You down for that?"

Karlie had reached over and picked up Jackie's glass, bringing it to her lips while keeping eye contact. Jackie's pulse danced then, her throat going dry as she watched Karlie's lips touch the glass.

"Yeah." Karlie put the glass down. "I'm down for that."

Jackie groaned and tried to shake away the memory. The action was unsuccessful, as her body now ached with need. She plugged the phone into the charger on her nightstand and stood. Minutes later, she was naked in the shower. Closing her eyes, she let the warm water splash over her face, praying it would wash away all the pain and regret that filled her at this moment.

Alicia wasn't coming back; she'd told Jackie that the day she walked out, and Jackie had believed her. But Karlie definitely wanted into

Jackie's space. Shaking her head and turning so the water streamed down her back, Jackie tried to push that thought aside. She wasn't ready for another girlfriend, and Karlie was definitely the girlfriend type. If she was just looking for a quick lay, she wouldn't still be calling and texting Jackie who, despite having given Karlie her number, had been ghosting her since that night. Nah, Karlie wanted more, and Jackie didn't have a damn thing to give.

She grabbed the soap, bringing it to a thick lather in her hands before putting it back in the dish. Then her hands were moving over her body, her mind volleying between how sweet she knew Karlie would taste and how desperately she didn't want to go to jail. Both issues had her muscles tense, her body strung so tight, she thought she might break into pieces at any moment. She needed relief, and unfortunately, neither drinking nor lighting another blunt was an option at the moment. No, now, more than ever, her mind needed to remain clear. They all had to focus on appearing as normal as possible come Monday morning.

Normal was something Jackie hadn't felt in a long time. Too damn long. As the soap rinsed from her body, her hands moved over her breasts, scraping past the pebble-hard nipples, easing down her tight abs to her pulsing mound. She groaned the second her fingers inched farther, pushing deep. Then her mind went blank. Unhappy exes, out-of-control bosses, holiday-party smack talkin', and even dead bodies slipped from her thoughts. And then there was only pleasure, only peace.

At least for the moment.

Chapter 7

Venus

She was going straight to hell. Sitting in the sanctuary of New Visionary Baptist Church on Sunday morning with her legs crossed, purse and Bible on the pew next to her like she was the same person she'd been last Sunday. That lie almost trumped all the others Venus had become accustomed to telling herself.

Folding her arms across her chest, she stared straight ahead to the front of the church where the organist, Mr. Ray, whom she'd known since she was a little girl, played some unknown tune while they waited for the eleven o'clock service to begin. The tune sounded familiar, but no matter how hard she tried, she couldn't latch on to the lyrics that went with it. Normally she knew most of the gospel songs she heard either on the radio or during any church service. That came from growing up in the church and maintaining a spiritual link through music as an adult.

After an hour of local news on Sunday mornings, she always turned on the gospel station and let the songs blast through her apartment as she got ready for church. She'd done the same this morning, singing along with some songs and letting the lyrics to others sift through her mind. But now that she was in church, she couldn't make a connection.

Perhaps because the Lord wasn't pleased with her right now. For that matter, she wasn't pleased with herself. How in the world had she gotten herself into this mess? More important, how was she going to get out of it? Those questions had kept her pacing her apartment all day yesterday.

The possibility of being charged with obstruction of justice or any other criminal act stood front and center in her mind, creating a dull ache across her forehead and at the back of her neck. Linking her fingers together, she mentally recounted each mistake she'd made in the last two years and frowned when she realized they all involved Rufus.

The two accounts she'd noticed his excessive billing on were the first pitfall and coincidentally were now connected to her desire to keep her involvement in Rufus's death a secret. Both were errors in judgment that she had been fully aware of yet powerless to stop. Again, it boiled down to keeping her mouth shut about things that would adversely affect her or others. On the one hand, that might seem noble, but on the other, it could be construed as foolish as hell. "If you see something, say something" was just as catchy a phrase as "snitches get stitches."

Both options paled in comparison to what would happen when—if—her parents ever found out. Panic soared across her chest in the form of a sharp pain that had her gasping and slamming a palm over the area. They couldn't find out. After a few deep breaths, she could only shake her head at how odd it seemed that she was more afraid of her parents finding out what she'd done than being prosecuted for doing those things.

Don and Ilene McGee were pillars of their West Baltimore community—they put not only their time into supporting various groups within the neighborhood but a good portion of their money as well. There was a plaque at the Rising Star Community Center with their names on it because they'd funded complete renovations of the kitchen and theater area last year. Within this very church, her father had been a trustee for thirty years, and her mother had held various positions with the Women's and Sunday School Ministries. Everybody knew the McGees, and to know them was to know how upstanding and commendable they were.

Learning that their daughter was a party to two crimes—even if only by default—wasn't going to go over well with them. When Venus had been suspended from school for fighting in the fifth grade, her parents had lectured her like she had one foot inside a jail cell. And years later, when they smelled marijuana on her clothes, her father had interrogated her as if she were on the witness stand. Everything about the McGees had to be above reproach, especially when her father had entered politics.

"We're not only expected to be better than everyone else, Venus, we're *required* to be. *You* are required to be."

Her father had told her that more times than she could remember, until the words were practically imprinted in her mind. She had to get the best grades, perform the best on any team, run the fastest, debate the strongest. Date the right men, hang out with the right girls, wear the right clothes, do the right thing. Every hour of every day, without fail.

Bringing her fingers to her temples, she rubbed as a dull throbbing began.

"Mornin'. Mornin'." A voice yanked her from her troubling thoughts, but before she could reply, "Scoot over" followed.

Looking up, she almost cursed when she saw Jackie and Draya standing next to her pew.

Yes, this pew was hers, or at least this corner of it was, because it was where she sat every Sunday while receiving the spiritual word to carry her through the week. These two were never here on Sundays or any other day. That didn't mean they didn't go to church. Venus had no idea what their relationship with God was. What she knew was that they weren't fostering that relationship here at New Visionary Baptist.

"What are y'all doing here?" She spoke in her hushed church voice as she turned sideways on the pew so they could squeeze past her.

"Yesterday you said we had to stick together," Jackie answered as she took the seat right beside Venus.

Draya, who'd sat on the other side of Jackie, leaned forward so she could see Venus. "She texted me this morning, suggesting we get right with God." The shrug confirmed Draya hadn't given that a thought before.

Venus wasn't surprised. Draya's morals didn't exactly align with the church. Nor did hers lately, if she wanted to be specific about it, which she didn't. Draya just irked her. It had been one thing to feel they didn't have anything in common except for working at the same place and dealing with her strictly on those terms, but now thanks to Draya's twisted morals, they were illegally connected.

"This place is huge," Jackie said. "I've only ever seen it on TV."

"You watch the televised worship services?" Venus couldn't help her surprised tone. Jackie always seemed so irritated with everything about the world; Venus just assumed church was included.

Jackie shrugged. "Sometimes it's safer that way. You know religious folk have definite feelings about gay people. And I have definite feelings about punching homophobes in their hypocritical mouths."

Venus didn't reply. She remembered how Jackie had dealt with Rufus's unwanted advances, and she felt bad that Jackie probably faced a lot of unnecessary adversity because of her sexual orientation.

Mr. Ray changed the song to something Venus immediately recognized. The intro to "We Lift Our Hands in the Sanctuary" started, and the worship leader stood behind the podium in the pulpit and motioned for the congregation to rise. Venus stood first; Jackie and Draya followed. The moment the choir began to sing, Draya started clapping and swaying to the rhythm. She wore a honey-mustard-colored sweater dress with a bold purple belt. Venus didn't have to lean back to see if Draya's shoes matched her outfit—they always did. If there was one thing she could say to Draya's credit, it was that the girl could dress her ass off.

Deciding it was best to not worry about whether what Draya was wearing was appropriate for church or why the woman was actually here, Venus clapped her hands and sang along with the choir as they marched toward the choir stand. She let the lyrics and the spiritual energy that was finally moving seep into her, focusing her mind on the reason she was here and nothing else.

"Dayum, she fine!"

Venus turned her head so fast she could've sworn she heard a cracking sound. Jackie slapped a hand over her mouth as she drew her gaze away from the choir member marching down the aisle. Draya shook her head but continued clapping and singing. It was a good thing New Visionary's congregation was about 250 deep at the eleven o'clock service. There was another service at eight in the morning and sometimes a third service at four in the afternoon, and they each had approximately 125 in attendance. Anyway, Venus was positive nobody heard Jackie's outburst, since everybody was still standing, swaying, and singing.

When they sat, she reached over and pinched Jackie's arm. "Get yourself together." The act and the words made her feel like her mother, and she hurriedly pulled her arm back and stared forward.

"Ouch!" Jackie frowned, and the woman sitting in front of them turned around, giving her a mean face.

Venus knew that scolding look. How many times had her mother yanked her up in this sanctuary when she wasn't behaving the way she'd instructed her to? She sighed as she recalled the many conversations her mother'd had with her about school behavior, church behavior, and any other thing she dared Venus to do that might embarrass the McGees in any way. She knew better, and so there was never any question that she would do better.

The service progressed, and Jackie managed to sit quietly even though she gave the woman in front of her an equally stank face the next time she turned to glare at her. Draya chuckled at that, and Venus, even though she didn't show it, felt the woman got what she deserved.

If nothing else, Jackie was a whole adult whom the woman didn't know, and therefore she had no business turning around to chastise or judge her. Venus, on the other hand, had to shush both her Sunday-morning guests when they asked for candy and gum just as Reverend Henderson was about to begin his sermon.

"Y'all act like you've never been to church before," she said while digging into her purse and pulling out a pack of chewing gum.

Jackie quickly took that, and when Venus also retrieved a handful of mints she'd swiped out of her mother's candy dish last week, Draya reached over and snagged two of those. If she hadn't been feeling motherly earlier, she certainly was now.

It wasn't until the three of them had listened to the sermon, shouted their amens and hallelujahs, and then stood to leave the church that Venus felt she could breathe a sigh of relief.

She had no idea what she'd thought was going to happen as they sat in the sanctuary—the pits of hell would've opened and swallowed their lying souls or something equally as painful and dismal—but a heavy weight had rested on her shoulders when she'd first arrived at church this morning. Now, as they stepped through the front doors and walked down the steps, that weight seemed to have lifted. Breathing in the crisp air, she pulled her coat together and tied the belt at her waist before turning to them. "Hope you enjoyed the service."

She did hope both of them had heard or felt something that would help get them through the week. It was the whole purpose of going to church for her, and even though she hadn't invited Jackie or Draya, she hoped they could both take away a sense of spiritual comfort as well.

"I did, despite Miss Lady, who kept minding my business," Jackie said. "I might try coming back. I used to go to church every Sunday when I was younger." She was standing with her leather jacket zipped, hands stuffed into the front pockets of the dark-brown slacks she wore.

Draya had buttoned her coat and was adjusting her black-and-white-checkered scarf when she said, "My family's never been big on religion, but we were faithful CME members—you know, Christmas, Mother's Day, and Easter." Draya and Jackie chuckled, and Venus couldn't help but join in.

She knew plenty of CME members.

"I visited this church a long time ago," Draya continued. "I'm still not an every-Sunday churchgoer, but when I do go, I usually prefer the smaller churches."

Venus tried not to take that as a slap toward her church. Religion was very personal, and she had no business judging who chose to go where or do what with their lives. She was about to say something like that but refrained when she noticed Draya's hands had stilled on her scarf. Venus followed her gaze to see that she was staring in the direction of where her parents stood.

"What are you looking at?" Venus asked.

Draya cleared her throat and finished with her scarf. "That woman talking to your parents is Leslie Drake. She's the state's attorney."

"I know who she is. She's a member of the church," Venus said, staring at the petite woman with her honey-blonde hair pulled back from her face.

Jackie nodded. "She's up for reelection next year. Channel forty-five did an exposé on her and her husband's financials a couple weeks ago. They're in trouble."

"She used to sleep with Rufus," Draya added.

Venus and Jackie turned to stare at her. "How do you know?" Venus asked.

Draya tilted her head and arched a brow. "I was never fool enough to believe I was the first person Rufus stepped out with."

Jackie frowned. "But wait a minute—Rufus's wife, Pam, works for Drake. She's a deputy state's attorney so, like, she works really closely with the woman."

Draya nodded. "Rufus was fine and smart about his business, but he was a low-down dirty dog when it came to women. He and Leslie were creeping around a couple years ago when Pam was still working at Legal Aid."

"Again," Venus said, unable to hide the confusion in her tone, "how do you know all this?"

Draya sighed. "I saw her coming out of his office one night when I was going in. Well, I hadn't gotten there yet. I was at the other end of the hallway when his door opened and she stepped out. He came out with her. The tight hug and kiss—minus the tongue but still a little too long with the touching of lips—told me all I needed to know."

"You asked him about it as soon as you got into his office, didn't you?" Jackie nodded, probably assuming she already knew the answer.

"You damn right I did, and the smug bastard answered with pride. He didn't care how many women in this city he slept with; he thought he was invincible," Draya said.

Jackie gave a wry chuckle. "Well, we know that's not true now."

Venus hadn't realized they'd all shifted their gazes in Leslie's direction again until her father began waving for her to come over.

"Shit! My father saw me," she whispered. That same wave of panic that had seared her chest a couple of hours ago when she'd been thinking about her parents reappeared. It wasn't that she didn't like seeing her parents . . . Well, okay, seeing her parents was stressful even when she wasn't hiding something from them.

"He sure did, and he wants you to come over there," Jackie said, waving back to Donald like she knew him.

Draya smiled in Donald's direction while speaking through clenched teeth. "You should go. And remember—act normal."

Draya seemed mighty pleased to be tossing Venus's words back at her, but she didn't have time to address that with her. She was too busy trying to figure out how exactly she was supposed to act normal while hiding the fact that a man was dead, and the only other people who knew about it were wearing goofy-as-hell smiles and following behind her like a schoolgirl clique.

Chapter 8

Draya

Okay, Venus's father was fine as hell.

He was much taller than her five-foot-four stature. Even with her four-inch heels on, Draya looked up at him as they approached. His wife was standing beside him, accepting Venus's hug and kiss while Draya kept her gaze on Donald McGee.

"It's lovely to see you and your friends in church this morning," Donald was saying.

Draya watched his mouth move. He was a stately man she'd seen more on television than in person. With gray at his temples and sprinkled throughout his low-cut beard, he appeared distinguished and spoke like he could be a Baptist preacher himself. And he was looking at her with just as much interest as she knew she was tossing his way. He had no idea her easy smile was actually because he was just as predictable as all the other older, established men who had looked at her with lascivious thoughts while condemning her with their unfounded judgments. When she was younger, she'd been disgusted by every one of them. Now she played the game just as well as they did, knowing that what they thought of her meant absolutely nothing, and they'd be touching her only if she allowed it.

"It was a wonderful service," she said, and out of the corner of her eye saw Jackie frown.

Venus had been leaning in to hug her father, so she didn't have time to react to Draya's words. Draya could easily tell each of them that neither her words nor her smile meant anything, but why bother? Women tended to judge just as quickly and probably more harshly than men.

"I don't think we've met before," Venus's mother said to her.

That was code for *back up off my man*. Draya almost chuckled when she let her gaze shift to Mrs. McGee. "No, ma'am, we haven't met. I work with Venus at BCC. My name's Draya."

"Oooohh, these are your coworkers." Mrs. McGee drew that word out like it made up for the fact that her husband had been staring at Draya like she was on the dessert buffet.

"Yes, ma'am, I'm Jackie."

"Okay, hello, Jackie," Mrs. McGee said.

Donald shook both their hands. Draya let hers slip away slowly, wanting to see if he tried to hold on longer.

"You work for BCC?" Leslie's question and its haughty tone pulled her attention away from Donald, as well as Venus's scowl that she'd seen out of the corner of her eye.

"Yes. I'm the fiscal director," Draya answered proudly because Leslie looked like she couldn't fathom that notion. "Jackie's the facilities manager."

Leslie pursed her lips. "Did you know your boss was found murdered this morning?" Those words immediately stopped Draya's gloating. Jackie began coughing, and Venus pounded on her back.

"What?" Venus asked while still trying to clear Jackie's lungs.

"Oh my, that's horrible. Are you sure?" Mrs. McGee brought shaking fingers up to her neck to emphasize her shock.

"I received a text alert about it during the service," Donald said. "I was going to call you when I got home, Venus."

"I didn't know," Draya said. "I guess there's a reason why I was in church this morning." She turned and gazed in the direction of the building. "God bless his sweet soul." That was probably a bit over the top of "normal," but whatever, she was doing her best.

"Was it a robbery or carjacking?" Mrs. McGee asked, her eyes still wide with shock. "Have they caught the killer?"

Leslie opened her mouth to respond when Jackie coughed even louder.

"Is she okay?" Donald asked.

"She's fine," Venus started. "I mean, she'll be fine. She's had this tickle in her throat all service."

Venus was wrapping an arm around Jackie's shoulders then, as if she were trying to steer them away from this little group.

"We should get her home. Come on, Draya." Venus was too damn bossy, but Draya didn't like the way Leslie was looking at Jackie. Her pert little nose had crinkled, and she'd taken a step back as if she thought she might catch something from Jackie's cough. Plus, Draya hadn't missed the dismissive way she'd looked when Draya told her what Jackie's position was at the company.

"It might be something in the air that's making her choke," Draya offered. "Something foul."

Venus bumped her as she moved with Jackie. "Right. Sure. Let's go."

"It was nice meeting you, Councilman McGee." Draya paused. "And Mrs. McGee."

She left Leslie out because she was certain the woman had seen her that night at Rufus's office. After the kiss she'd witnessed, Rufus had ducked back into the office without glancing in Draya's direction. But Leslie had taken a few steps, then turned back. She and Draya had locked gazes, each woman silently assessing the other. She had known Draya was Rufus's mistress during that time, and Draya hadn't cared. Her knowledge that Leslie and Rufus had something illicit going was far more damaging, considering Leslie's position and the fact that her husband was trying to become chief of police.

Draya turned without saying another word to Leslie. By the time they got down to the end of the block where Draya's and Jackie's cars were parked, Venus was cursing.

"Well, what happened to 'act normal'?" Draya asked. She dug into her purse for her keys. "You damn near coughed up a lung, and your stuttering and excuse making were pitiful."

"I said act normal when we get to work tomorrow. Not at my church," Venus argued and then huffed. "They found his body. So it's probably all over the news."

Draya watched Venus pull her phone out of her purse, while Jackie used the back of her hand to wipe her forehead.

"Man, that shit caught me off guard. I think I swallowed my gum." Jackie rubbed her throat, and Draya frowned.

"Look, we knew this moment was going to come. Now it's here. They know, so that's that," she said and actually felt a bit of relief.

All last night, she'd tossed and turned, wondering how she would feel the moment the world found out what she already knew. Rufus was dead. Try as she might, she still couldn't muster up a tear or even a smidgen of sorrow for that fact.

"It's all over social media. All the news outlets are reporting it. They say Pam's on her way back from Virginia. Reporters are already making speculations." Venus scrolled through her phone, and Jackie leaned in to look.

"They're thinking gang-related or some other organized-type hit, looking into his business dealings and . . ." Venus's words drifted off, and her hands shook as she held her phone.

"Okay." Draya held up a hand, as if that action would stop their yapping. Her keys jiggled with the action, and that caught their attention. "I don't need to know who killed him or why. He's gone, and now we can all get on with our lives without the stress of knowing his bitch ass is lurking around the corner."

"I don't think it's that simple," Venus sighed.

"I don't wanna hear it, Venus. I'm not standing here going over all this worrying and replaying again. The news is out, and all we gotta do is keep on steppin'. It is just that simple." Her voice was too loud, her heart beating slightly faster than it had been just a few moments ago, but Draya didn't care. "Look, if y'all wanna stand here and look guilty as hell for no reason at all, go right ahead. I'm going to my mother's for Sunday dinner."

Jackie nodded. "I could eat."

Draya had already stepped into the street and was heading to the driver's-side door. "Come on," she said with a frown. "My momma has so many people going in and out of that house, she calls everybody a cousin anyway."

Jackie rubbed her hands together and dug into her pocket to get her keys. "You comin', Venus?"

Draya held her door open and stood there staring at Venus, who was still holding her phone and looking like she'd seen Rufus's dead body for a second time. She would've never thought to extend the invitation to Venus, but something told her that if Venus went home alone and her father called her to talk about Rufus's death, Venus's perfect ass would crumble and tell him everything.

"Come on, we need to get there early. My brother Bo and his friends'll be waking up right about now, and once they realize it's Sunday, they'll head straight to Momma's house." She slid into the car and kept right on mumbling. "They eat like a bunch of starvin' animals, and some of them look like it too. I don't want them even breathing on my food."

Chapter 9

Jackie

The second she walked through the front door and stepped up from the vestibule into the living room, a wave of nostalgia hit her, and Jackie swayed with the force. It smelled delicious in here—a mixture of the food being prepared and the fresh pine-cone centerpiece on the coffee table. Heat immediately warmed her cheeks as her booted feet moved over the clear plastic runner that covered the dark-blue carpeted floor.

"Mmmm, is that roast beef?" She paused, inhaled deeply, and let the breath out slowly, her mouth watering with the thought.

As this was Draya's mother's house, Draya had entered first and had already removed her coat and dropped it over the back of a floral-print love seat. She turned to Jackie and grinned. "Girl, if you don't know nothing else, you know about food, don't you?"

Jackie may have grinned in return, but the swirling emotion in the pit of her stomach was anything but happy. She unzipped her jacket and shrugged out of it before replying, "I just know when something smells good."

She put her jacket right next to Draya's, figuring if Ms. Carter had a fit about coats not being hung up—the way Jackie's mother would've—her excuse would be that she was following Draya's lead. Venus was right behind Jackie, but she wasn't removing her coat as quickly.

"Is there somewhere we can talk in private?" Venus asked them, worry etched along her face like some sort of cosmetic.

"You gotta relax," Jackie told her. "If we're supposed to be playin' this cool, you have to fix your face."

That brought a frown to Venus's normally cute features, and Jackie sighed.

"The local news sites are buzzing with this investigation. I don't want to be caught off guard. We should talk about alibis; we didn't get to that yesterday." Venus pulled roughly at the belt of her coat as if it, too, had somehow angered her. "And besides that, playin' it cool doesn't mean being unprepared. We should definitely be ready for the questions that may come at us."

Draya smoothed down the front of her dress and, to Jackie's shock, agreed with Venus. "That's not a bad idea. I mean, I was thinking about this on the drive over here. Without them somehow knowing that we were at Rufus's house, there's really no reason for the police to single us out right off the bat. Our only connection to Rufus is through work. At least that's where it stops for the two of you. And there are plenty of people at the office who hated him enough to kill his sorry ass. As for me, like I said before, I know I wasn't Rufus's only dalliance, and we've been over for three months. Still, it's always better to be prepared."

When Venus was still taking a long time with her coat, Jackie reached over to help. "It's hot as hell in here; you're making me sweat keeping this coat on," she explained when Venus looked at her in question.

Draya chuckled. "Momma says an electric bill is gonna hit her doorstep every month until she dies, so she ain't freezing in the winter or sweating in the summer."

Jackie was laying Venus's coat on the chair beside hers when that yearning in her stomach started to grow. It wasn't simply hunger, as Draya or even Venus would've probably thought if Jackie had mentioned the feeling to them. No, it was something totally different. Something she'd tried like hell to get over but had obviously failed—homesickness.

Maiselle Benson had a similar thought pattern. She believed in paying the household bills on time to avoid bill collectors calling and being a pain in the ass. By that same token, she believed in taking full advantage of everything she paid for, without an inch of guilt. *Damn.* Jackie sighed. She really missed her mother. What she didn't miss was the curt and painful words her parents had spoken to her the day she announced she was a lesbian.

"Okay, so we all left the party together on Friday. That can be proven by anyone at the party and the valet guy who you insisted on tipping with a kiss." Venus's last comment was directed at Draya, who only smiled in return.

"Honey was fine as hell and you know it. Plus, he and I had already done all the preliminary flirting when I stayed in the car while he drove to the parking garage," Draya replied.

Venus narrowed her eyes. "Are you really that ratchet? You just hop on any fine man that suits you?"

Draya took a step toward Venus, and Jackie inched her way between them.

"When the attraction is mutual, yes. Why the hell not? You walkin' around here with your panties in a bunch all the damn time waiting for what? Mr. Right?" Draya laughed, but it wasn't an amused sound at all. "So tell me this: When Mr. Right shows up, what do you plan to do, get married and have a bunch of kids? Settle down in a house like your parents' and be the next generation of the respectable McGees of Baltimore?"

Frowning, Jackie intervened. "Come on, y'all, we're supposed to be talking about our alibis."

Draya stepped back, waving a dismissive hand in Venus's direction. "Whatever. You don't have to answer. I know all about Black folk like you."

"What's that supposed to mean?" Venus asked.

"Ah, alibis," Jackie said a little louder. "We left the hotel together and went straight to Venus's place, where I stayed all night, and you . . ." Her words drifted off as she stared at Draya, who now stood with hands propped on her plentiful hips.

Draya must have spent just as much on her shapewear as she did her hair, because she always had a smooth, voluptuous, hourglass figure that reminded Jackie how long it'd been since she'd had a woman.

"I went right home, undressed, and climbed into bed, where I slept until Rufus called me at six thirty on Saturday morning." Draya's tone was crisp, her heated gaze resting on Venus.

"Okay, they'll no doubt dump Rufus's phone records immediately, so they'll see the time he called you and how long that call lasted. If they really want to, that might be enough for them to convince a judge to give them a warrant for your phone records too. In which case, that call will be proof that you were at your place at that time. The pings from the cell towers will also confirm you were at his house when you called me," Venus said.

Last night, Jackie had thought about everything Venus just said. "But once they pinpoint his time of death, won't that also prove that she arrived at his house after he was already dead?"

"That doesn't mean I couldn't have hired the hit woman I talked about." Draya's arms dropped to her sides, and she turned away from them. "I didn't, if either of you was thinking that."

"Of course we're not thinking that," Jackie said. She didn't glance at Venus but hoped she was in agreement with her.

"Draya? Is that you?"

They heard the voice before the woman, who looked like she could be Draya's twin sister, appeared. The woman's slipper-clad feet made a slapping sound against the linoleum floor in the dining room, going silent when she stood at the opening to the living room.

"I thought I heard the door and then your loud mouth. Never did find your inside voice," the woman said, then looked to where Jackie stood beside Venus. "And you brought company?"

"Momma, these are my coworkers Jackie and Venus. We went to church, and then I invited them for dinner."

"If that's okay, Ms. Carter." Venus spoke before Jackie could. "If you haven't prepared enough for us, we can leave. It was rude of us to intrude anyway."

Ms. Carter was shaking her head—shiny black curls bouncing on her shoulders—before Venus could finish speaking. "Nonsense. I always got enough to feed a hungry soul."

Jackie almost sighed. Her soul sure was hungry for home-cooked food, as well as for the warm feeling of family this woman and this house were projecting.

"Thank you, ma'am," she said and smiled at Ms. Carter.

The woman waved her hand, similar to the way Draya had done moments ago. "Now, you can just stop with that 'ma'am' nonsense. Call me Aunt Dot, just like everybody else. And since you're all here, you can come on into the kitchen and help me finish up with the cooking."

Dot had already turned and walked away by the time Draya gave them an apologetic look. "Momma thinks everybody should pull their weight, even company."

"Oh no, it's fine. I don't mind helping. It's the least we can do," Venus said.

Jackie agreed, and when Draya started for the dining room ahead of them, Jackie grabbed her elbow and whispered, "Your alibi is that you stayed at Venus's all night, just like I did. You were just getting back to your apartment at six thirty when Rufus called you."

Draya didn't say anything at first but looked over Jackie's shoulder to where Venus stood behind her. Jackie thought she was gonna have to elbow Venus or slap some sense into her when Venus spoke. "Right. Both of you spent the night at my place."

There were a few moments after Venus's statement that the three of them just stood staring at each other. It felt like a silent oath was being taken. They were once again agreeing that they were in this together, and that made Jackie feel good. It made her even more nostalgic than the scents and the warmth of this house did, and she tried like hell to fight the tears that threatened to form in her eyes.

It was stupid anyway. This wasn't her family. This was Draya's family home, and she'd only been invited here for dinner. Yet she couldn't put away the feelings it all evoked, especially not when they walked through the dining room and into the large kitchen at the back of the house.

Her parents' home had a similar layout to most inner-city Baltimore row houses. A long table was pushed up against the left wall, four chairs around the open areas. Beyond the table were two trash cans and then the back door, which was held open a couple of inches by the chain lock so that the heat from the oven and the pots simmering on the stove could ventilate. A large washer and dryer were on the wall with the door, a window above them. On the right wall was the stove and refrigerator, and pushed into the corner was a deep freezer. If she'd closed her eyes, she could've visualized this exact space without ever stepping foot in this house. It was so similar to the home she'd grown up in that she wondered if she took three steps across the linoleum floor, it would squeak. That's how her mother always knew she'd snuck into the kitchen for a late-night snack.

"Well, hello." An older woman who'd been sitting at the table peeling potatoes looked up over wire-rimmed glasses.

Jackie knew that look. It went from her feet to the top of her head and then back down again, assessing every part of her and figuring out how to proceed. It didn't make her as uncomfortable as the way Miss Lady had looked at her at the church this morning, and since she was a guest in this house, she put on a smile and said, "Hi, how you doin' today, ma'am?"

The woman's thin lips pressed together. "I'm alive. How 'bout you?"

"Happy to be breathing too." Jackie grinned, but it was the truth. Rufus being here one day and gone the next had her considering her own mortality. Maybe that's why everything was making her feel homesick. Well, more homesick than she'd felt over the past six years.

"Granny, these are my coworkers. This is Venus and this is Jackie." Draya went straight to the sink and turned on the water to wash her hands.

"You can call her Granny too," Aunt Dot said.

"Hello, uh . . . Granny." Venus cleared her throat and then went to the sink where Draya stood.

She seemed uncomfortable, but Jackie felt the exact opposite. After nodding at Granny and smiling again, she waited for Venus and Draya to finish at the sink and then went to wash her hands. The lemon-scented dish liquid wasn't the same brand her mother used. This wasn't her mother's house. She had to remind herself of that fact. Maiselle had told her that as long as she liked girls in a carnal way, she wasn't allowed to step foot in her home. The fist that seemed to squeeze her heart until Jackie thought it might burst through her chest was intentional and left her gasping.

"You all right over there, Jackie?" Aunt Dot asked. "I got some blocks of cheese here that need to be shredded for the macaroni and cheese."

"Yes, ma'am, I'm fine," Jackie lied. Then she rolled her shoulders back and grabbed the dish towel to dry her hands.

She sat at the table next to Venus, who was using a cookie cutter to make neat circles in the dough that would later become biscuits.

"You young ladies went to church this mornin'?" Granny asked.

"Yes, ma'am, we did," Venus answered. "I go to New Visionary Baptist, and Draya and Jackie decided to join me today."

"Dray, you went to church and it ain't even Christmas yet," Granny laughed. "Must've been some man there. Dray likes the men."

After that last sentence, Granny looked over to Jackie. "You're right handsome yourself."

Jackie didn't know whether to smile or be offended. When Venus chuckled, she decided to go with laughter as well and muttered a quick "Thanks."

"There's no man at Venus's church for me, Granny. I was just there visiting," Draya replied. She was back at the sink, washing the chicken Aunt Dot had taken from the refrigerator.

"You too old to be trying to ask Jesus to save your soul," Aunt Dot said.

"No," Venus said with a shake of her head. "You're never too old to come to Christ."

"You a preacher too?" Granny asked her, and it was Jackie's turn to laugh at Venus.

Venus cut a glare at her, but there was no heat in it. In fact, Venus had relaxed significantly while working on those biscuits. "No. I'm not a preacher, just been in church all my life."

"Oh, well, we've believed all our lives that Jesus makes house calls," Aunt Dot said.

"I believe that too," Jackie chimed in, because it was true—otherwise she'd have missed a whole lot of blessings. "It was a good service, though. Me and Draya are thinking about going back."

"We are?" Draya asked.

"Absolutely," Jackie continued. "We can all use a little more religion." Especially considering all the madness that seemed to be going on in their lives right now. "We also gotta get our Christmas lists together for the gift exchange. I texted both of you last night, but neither of you have responded."

"Oh, y'all buying each other gifts? I want one," Granny said, her eyes wide with excitement.

"You wanna get in on the exchange? We can have a group of just the five of us." Jackie hoped she didn't sound too excited, but she would love to go out Christmas shopping for Granny and Aunt Dot. It would feel great to have people to shop for again.

"Granny, we already do a name exchange with the family, remember?" Draya told her grandmother. "This one is just for me and my friends."

When Jackie noticed Granny's frown, she spoke up. "But we can let them in, Dray. Just the two of them, nobody else." She desperately wanted to buy Christmas gifts this year and to watch Granny's face light up, the way it had moments ago, when she opened it.

Sure, she'd just met the woman, but the same way this house felt like home, Granny felt that way to her too. Like family.

"I'm in," Venus said. "I'll text my list when I get finished."

"When you finish, I want you to put those green beans on the stove," Aunt Dot said. "And then you can get that notebook from on top of the refrigerator and a pen from the drawer over there and write a list for all of us. Granny and I don't do those text messages like y'all."

Venus grinned and shook her head when she caught Jackie looking at her in triumph. Jackie couldn't see what Draya's expression was, and it didn't matter; she was in the Christmas gift exchange with all of them whether she liked it or not.

Two and a half hours later, they were seated at the old dark-wood table in the center of Aunt Dot's dining room.

"Pass me the potatoes," Bo, one of Draya's older brothers, said before smiling at Venus for the billionth time. "You want some potatoes, sweetness?"

He'd been following her around since he came into the house. One of his three friends who had come in with him, Levi, was too busy staring at Jackie's breasts to hear Bo's request, so Jackie reached across him. He grinned, licking his lips as he watched her pick up the bowl and extend her arm across the table to Bo.

"You sure got some fine friends, Draya." Levi's voice was a gravelly whisper that was grating on Jackie's nerves.

Apart from his annoying ass, this entire day had been like a flashback to a former life, one she'd missed more than she should. How long had it been since she'd been seated at a table for a family dinner? Sure, Dot and Granny—who, as it turned out, had even less of a filter on her mouth than Draya did—were sitting in the kitchen with Uncle Andrew, who'd just come in from working at the post office. But with Bo and his friends, Venus, Draya, and her, the dining-room table was full. Andrew's son, who'd been dropped off by his mother just seconds after Andrew walked through the door, was sitting on the steps, a TV tray holding his plate of food in front of him.

"I didn't want any more potatoes," Venus was saying as Bo spooned a heaping pile onto her plate.

"You cute an' all, but I like a little more meat on my honeys." Bo moved to his plate, giving himself another pile of potatoes, then sticking the spoon into his mouth to lick it clean before jabbing it back into the bowl.

Jackie and Venus frowned, and Draya rolled her eyes when he set that bowl with the now- contaminated spoon in the center of the table. "You're gross, and you're too old to be drooling over a woman who don't want you no matter how much food you give her."

Jackie guessed Bo was probably close to forty, since Draya was thirty-one and there were two more siblings between them. She'd gotten some of the family-tree breakdown from Granny.

"She wants me," Bo said. "You know how y'all high-maintenance chicks be tryna play hard to get. But I promise you I can keep you happy."

"I can keep you happy too," Levi said, dropping a hand to Jackie's thigh. "We can be like one big happy family."

Jackie picked up her fork and used it to spear some carrots and bits of beef. She brought the fork to her mouth but paused to glance at him. "I told you before you're not my type. Now, you've got three seconds to get your hand off me or I'm—"

"Stop pushin' up on her, Levi. Damn, she already told you she's into women. I can't bring nobody over here without y'all actin' up." Draya hadn't quite yelled, but like Aunt Dot said, she struggled with an inside voice. The rise in tone brought Bo's and Levi's attention to her. Jackie eased the fork into her mouth and chewed her vegetables.

Then Granny came into the room.

"What's going on in here? Y'all ain't smokin' those funny cigarettes, are you?"

Draya groaned and rolled her eyes toward the ceiling. "No. We're not smoking. We're just trying to eat, but your grandson and his goons can't keep their hands to themselves."

As if to magnify her words, Jackie jabbed her fork into the back of Levi's hand, which, despite her warning, was still on her thigh. Now he was jumping up, knocking his chair over, and yelling expletives as he waved his hand back and forth. He called her everything but a child of God and then whined to Granny that his hand was bleeding.

Jackie looked across the table to make sure Draya wasn't pissed at her for stabbing somebody in her mother's house, but the grin on her face said she was not.

"Y'all chicks don't know how to act!" Bo yelled and grabbed a napkin to toss at Levi.

Venus eased a hunk of potatoes into her mouth and hummed happily.

"I thought I smelled some of them funny cigarettes," Granny mumbled and headed back into the kitchen.

Jackie wished she had one of those cigarettes too. But for now, she was content to finish her second plate of food. There was a pineapple upside-down cake on the small card table in the corner that she couldn't wait to get a piece of. Just as she was chewing the last bite of her food, her phone vibrated in her pocket. Dropping her fork and wiping her hands on a napkin, she reached for it and froze.

It continued to vibrate until Draya said, "Answer or decline, girl—it ain't that hard to decide."

Venus nodded as she finished taking a sip from her glass.

Jackie stared down at the name on the screen and then up to them. "It's Ellen."

Chapter 10

Venus

Yesterday, Jackie had declined Ellen's call. This morning, Venus repeatedly slapped the "Close" button on the elevator door when she saw Ellen hustling down the hallway to catch it.

It wasn't working as quickly as she needed it to, and Ellen yelled out her name. "Venus! Venus! Hold on—I need to speak with you."

"Not today, Satan," Venus whispered and slammed her palm on that button again. The doors finally closed seconds before Ellen could step inside, her cutoff expletives music to Venus's ears.

Slumping back against the wall of the car, Venus tried to get her mind right. Last night had been another fretful sleep after hours of watching the news and scrolling social media for any tidbits on Rufus's murder. He wasn't a celebrity, so there really wasn't much coverage except for what she found on the local TV-station websites and social media accounts. Even they didn't have a lot of facts, just that the prominent businessman had been shot and killed. The body had been discovered by a neighbor, and Pam was on her way home.

Shot and killed. Rufus. The man she despised. To be fair, a man *so* many people despised. It didn't escape her that there could literally be any number of suspects in this murder. Unfortunately, because of circumstances she couldn't go back in time and change, she could eventually end up at the top of that list. But she couldn't think about that right now. As she'd told Draya and Jackie, it was Monday, and she planned on acting totally normal. That meant going straight to her office and getting to work. Focusing on business would be the only thing that kept all other issues from her mind. That's how it'd always been.

She suspected it was because work was the one thing she knew she was good at without any help or misguided encouragement from her parents. Deciding to major in construction management hadn't been her parents' choice for her, but she'd insisted. It had been one of the few times she'd pushed back against them, but after she'd expressed how important it was for her to study what she wanted, they'd reluctantly backed down. It wasn't until after her first-semester grades came in—straight As—that Don and Ilene began to accept her career path a little more.

The elevator door opened, and she pushed away from the wall, walking off and down the hallway toward her office. She made it halfway there before being stopped by Mike.

"Did you hear? Rufus is dead. Hopkins wants to meet today to discuss how we move forward. What are we going to do?"

He said all that in one breath, his face ashen, hands moving around like he was a bundle of nerves. She held her briefcase in one hand, her purse on the opposite shoulder, and simply stared at him for a few moments after he was finished. The time was used to gather her thoughts and give him a second to breathe. Even though from the sickly look on his face, she wasn't sure breathing was really going to keep him from keeling over at any second.

"We can talk in my office" is what she finally said to him before continuing her walk down the hallway.

She passed a bay of cubicles, and a couple of administrative assistants who liked to get into the office early looked up from their computers as she walked by. They, no doubt, had questions just like Mike's. Everyone would want to know what to do, and they'd all look to her. This had been another thing weighing heavily on her mind last night. For years, she'd done her job and Rufus's behind the scenes. Now he was out of the picture.

Mike followed her into her office, closing the door loudly behind them. Venus didn't stop until she was on the other side of her desk, pushing her leather chair out and dropping her briefcase on the floor. After taking her phone out of her purse and setting it on the desk, she pulled out the drawer to her left and placed her purse inside. When that was done, she sat.

"What exactly did he say?" Without looking at Mike, she turned on her computer and waited for the screen to wake up so she could type in her password.

"I didn't talk to him."

Her gaze immediately shifted to him. He'd sat in one of the guest chairs across from her and was now drumming his fingers against the arms.

"What do you mean you didn't talk to him? You said he called and asked to meet today."

"He called and left a message. My assistant isn't in yet, but I listened to the message."

"And you didn't call him back? What time did he call?" She was an early bird, so she was normally up by six and in the office by eight. It was now eight fifteen.

"Maybe twenty minutes ago or something like that. Look, I need you to figure out what we're going to do. We can't meet with him today when we don't know what's happening. I mean, damn, doesn't the guy know our boss just died?"

"*Your* boss just died." She clamped her lips closed, realizing that biting remark may've come too quickly. Reminding herself to be calm, she decided not to take it back. On a normal day, she probably would've made the same distinction. "Rufus was the director of operations, but that doesn't mean this department—or this company, for that matter—cannot function without him."

Her fingers moved over the keyboard while she ignored Mike's glare.

"So you just don't care that the man was killed? Are you really that cold?" Mike's forehead wrinkled, his eyes narrowing.

"I'm really that professional," she replied in what she knew was a cool and even tone. "I'll send my condolences to Pam and support whatever efforts the company comes up with by way of paying tribute to him, but the most pressing issue right now remains this deal. Rufus would've felt the same way." He *had* felt the same, which was why he'd been such a dick to her Friday night at the party.

Mike sighed. He rubbed a hand over his face and sat back heavily in the chair. "Well, what're we going to do about the deal?"

Resisting the urge to roll her eyes, she chose instead to look away from him and scroll through her Outlook address book. Seconds later, she found the number she was looking for and then glanced over to Mike again. He was such a pitiful man. Handsome, yeah, she guessed, in a basic light-skinned-dude type of way. And he could dress a little, but really, she didn't pay that much attention to him because she couldn't stand that he had no backbone, had no personality, and preferred to kiss ass rather than at least try to fake like he was learning this job.

"I'm going to call Hopkins and set up a time for us to meet with him today."

"What? Are you serious? We can't do that. We're not ready to do that!"

"If you're not ready, then you can stay here," she replied, picking up the phone and putting it to her ear. "I'm meeting with the client and moving forward with this deal."

◆ ◆ ◆

And that's precisely what she did when, an hour and a half later, she was stepping out of the back seat of the company's Lincoln Town Car and starting toward Terrell Hopkins's mansion in Monkton. Her steps made a crunching sound as she walked over the gravel-lined driveway. She silently thanked the heavens that she'd worn her platform-heel boots today or else she may've toppled over from the unsteady ground.

That was probably the only part of this magnificent estate that baffled her, or perhaps it was just the first part, since she hadn't yet made it into the house. Inside the Hopkins client folder on her laptop, she'd stored pictures of this estate. It was only one of four properties Terrell owned and the one he occupied whenever he was in his hometown: 127 acres of dynamic landscape that included a stream and a secluded swimming hole. Of course, she should've expected nothing less from the four-time league MVP and star forward right up until he'd retired at thirty-six last year.

"You didn't tell me what the game plan is. This is my account, so you have to keep me in the loop," Mike said, coming up behind her as she climbed the two redbrick steps toward the door. "Rufus warned me that you weren't a team player. Even when we stopped at Goldfinger after the party, he was still talking about how I had to make sure you knew I was in charge."

She stopped, taking a slow breath to keep from slapping this fool who sounded like a petulant child instead of the "boss" he was trying to mimic. During the entire ride out here, Mike had talked about Rufus.

"He was such a great guy." "My mentor." "I can't believe this happened to someone like him." "This world is so cruel."

She'd wanted to scream *Shut the fuck up!* at least twenty times but had kept her lips shut so tight, they felt like they'd been superglued together.

"Stop it," she snapped through clenched teeth. "Stop it right now. From the moment I ring this doorbell, I want you to stop all talking unless you can figure out something to say that remotely matches a college graduate with an ounce of experience in the construction industry."

Before he could mumble a response, she reached out and pressed the doorbell, then yanked her arm back while keeping her gaze glued on him. The door opened almost immediately, and she turned with a smile in place.

"Hello. I'm Venus McGee, and I'm with the Billings Croft Construction company. Mr. Hopkins is expecting us." It didn't matter if she introduced Mike or not; he was grinning like a hyena now, ready to pour on the charm he was known for, no doubt, since the person who'd answered the door was a woman.

"Yes, Ms. McGee, I'm Chantel, Mr. Hopkins's assistant. Come right in."

Chantel stepped aside, opening the door wider, and Venus entered the house. Of course it was spectacular—a grand entryway complete with a double curving staircase, a huge crystal chandelier hanging in the center, and numerous gleaming gold picture frames with black-and-white portraits paying homage to Black history that stretched along both side walls.

"Hello."

Venus turned at the deep voice that snatched her away from her breathless perusal of the house. It was a wonder she didn't gasp or otherwise make a fool of herself. If she thought Terrell Hopkins was fine as hell on television running up and down that court, giving interviews, or appearing in commercials, up close and personal he was like a freakin' god. She gulped in as subtle a way as she could manage and took a step toward him, extending her hand for a shake.

Mike, with his simple ass, decided it was more important for Terrell to notice him first, so he attempted to step between Venus and the few feet of space that separated her and Terrell. He was wearing an expensive-looking pair of tie-up dress shoes that obviously didn't agree with the gleaming marble floor, so he skidded and stumbled just as he began saying, "I'm Mike Living . . ."

The rest of his name was lost as he tried to keep his face from slamming into the floor and Venus did her best not to burst into laughter.

"Whoa, take ya time, Mike." Terrell's smile was everything. He reached out and grabbed Mike's arm just in case Mike and his slippery-ass shoes couldn't manage to stand upright on his own.

"I'm good. I'm good." Mike eased out of Terrell's grasp and extended his hand to the man instead. "Just lost my balance for a bit. I'm Mike Livingston, your project manager."

Terrell continued to smile, and Venus continued to stare at the spread of his semithick lips and gleaming white teeth. She wasn't a groupie, and she definitely wasn't getting wet from some basketball player's smile. It'd been a minute since she'd been with a man, so this hint of physical attraction was normal.

"It's cool," Terrell told him and shook Mike's hand. "And you must be Ms. McGee."

"I am," she replied when Terrell turned his attention to her, stepping closer.

He was tall, and she loved a tall man. But he was really tall. Like, she was five feet eight and she had to tilt her head back to keep eye contact. And he was built. On television, he looked slimmer, or perhaps that was due to the baggy uniform or the slim-fit suits he wore. Standing close enough to take her hand—even though she'd let it fall back to her side after Mike's near tumble—Terrell was wearing a tight-fitting gray T-shirt that made his shoulders seem broader, his chest and biceps much more defined.

She shook his hand and again reminded herself to push whatever personal reaction she may have been having toward him to the side. He was her client and that was it. "It's a pleasure to finally meet you in person." If she was talking, then she couldn't be thinking about touching the biceps that her gaze kept wanting to shift to. "I've been working on the plans for your project so long, I feel like I already know you."

"Really? Well, then, I guess I've gotta catch up, because all I know is your name." His smile was slow and mesmerizing.

She squared her shoulders and kept her resolve, even while a part of her felt that wave of satisfaction at knowing he was having some type of personal reaction to her as well. Then again, a man like Terrell probably had this act of impressing a woman and capturing her full attention down to a science. He was rich, famous, and good-looking, three prime attributes for any woman looking for a man. Which Venus was not. What she was here to do was to get this project started. With that in mind, she slipped her hand out of his grasp and took a step back.

"I'm glad you called this morning and suggested a meeting. If we could just have a seat somewhere, I'd like to reassure you that BCC is still ready to handle this project for you."

"Yes," Mike interjected. "We have the plans all laid out and are certain that we can continue with our proposed timeline. The fact that Rufus is dead isn't a big deal at all."

Except you just made it a big deal by bringing it up, asshole. Hadn't she told this fool to shut up?

◆ ◆ ◆

It felt like someone was jabbing ice picks into Venus's temples four hours later when the car finally pulled up in front of the BCC office building. Getting out of the car and going into her office, alone, was the goal she'd been aiming for since the moment they'd sat down in Terrell's living room. Mike was on every last one of her nerves, and the second she heard the other passenger door slam, she groaned.

"We need to make a statement." He came around and stepped up on the curb quickly.

She hadn't stopped moving, so she was still a few steps ahead of him, but he easily closed that space, inching in front of her to block her path to the glass front doors.

"Stop," he said, a frown marring his face.

She did, but not because he told her so. The debate over whether she should push him out of her way or just cuss him all the way out and get it over with raged in her mind.

"Stop ignoring me, and stop acting like you're the lead on this project, because we both know that's not true. You wanna act like it's fine that Rufus is gone, cool, I don't have time to navigate around whatever womanly thing you might be going through today. But this is my project, and we're going to handle it my way." When she didn't immediately respond, he seemed both shocked and empowered.

Mike continued. "Now, we're going to go in here, take a few minutes to get our bearings after this meeting, and then we're going to come together to develop a statement regarding Rufus's death, because that's what Louis wants done by close of business today."

She'd read Louis's email, too, while they'd been in the car, but coming up with something positive to say about Rufus after spending hours trying to save the deal he'd put Mike's ignorant ass in charge of wasn't high on her list of priorities. It was two thirty in the afternoon, and a blustery wind was blowing while cars drove up and down the street behind them and people walked along the sidewalk just a few feet away from them.

"Are you done?" she asked after waiting another five seconds, regardless of starting to get cold.

He huffed. "Yeah, I'm done."

"Good. Your fly's down." She watched his head drop and his gaze go to his crotch before stepping around him and pushing her way through the doors.

Chapter 11

Draya

Pacing was better than smoking. But smoking would be better than panicking. Almost anything would be better than being in Venus's office with the door closed, waiting for her to show up so they could figure out what to do. Since when did she need Venus's help with anything? Since they'd decided they were all in this together and had sealed that deal by submitting their list for the Christmas gift exchange Jackie was intent on hosting.

Her mother had already called her four times about the lists and what gifts she and Granny were planning on buying. Initially, when Jackie had suggested the idea during the ride, Draya had pushed the thought aside, chalking it up to the rise and fall of adrenaline they'd all experienced on Saturday. Draya hadn't brought many friends home when she was growing up. She loved her family, quirks and all, but she was well aware of how others saw them as just another poor Black family with kids who would amount to nothing. As she'd grown and focused on proving her haters wrong, she'd also become fiercely protective of her family.

Surveying her day as a whole, talking to the most important women in her life numerous times about a gift exchange was the least of her worries. It was all the other phone calls that had been driving her crazy, and as if to make its presence known once more, her phone rang, and she bit back the urge to scream.

She squeezed the device in the palm of her hand, closing her eyes and counting down from five, because ten was going to take too long and she might toss the damn thing out the window in that time.

"Hey," she answered finally, searching for a semblance of calm.

"Hey, beautiful. I've been calling and texting you all day. We still good for later tonight?"

On any other day, the smooth, sexy timbre of the voice of her new, fresh-out-of-law-school bae, Travis, would've traveled over her skin like warm oil, inciting instant arousal. Right now, it slightly grated on the already frayed nerves she'd been coddling all damn day.

"I thought you were gonna be tied up in depositions or something." Her personal schedule was a vague memory, as she'd spent the bulk of her day ignoring calls and text messages from Franklin Gifford, Rufus's private attorney.

"Well, if you'd read any of my texts, you would know that two of them were canceled, so I'll probably be done here around seven instead of later. I want to see you."

Travis always wanted to see her, and she'd already dodged him Saturday and Sunday. In the six weeks she'd been dealing with him, there hadn't been a day that passed when he hadn't suggested they do something together. Dinner on Monday, a visit to a museum on a Sunday afternoon, drinks at The Bygone after work, a movie on a Saturday night. He was all about spending every free second he had with her. Hell, he'd even been happy with a quickie in the back seat of his truck in the building's garage—which was where Ellen had seen her leaving from a few weeks ago and then promptly reported it to Rufus. That little tryst had kicked off Rufus's plot to blackmail Draya. Breaking up with him had been one thing, but her screwing the rookie lawyer who rented office space in their building was something Rufus's larger-than-life ego couldn't stand.

"Sorry about missing your calls and texts." She wasn't, but it was the polite thing to say. Even though it was obvious Travis wanted more out of this dating situation than she did, it wasn't necessary to be rude, or dismissive of him. "I have to work." The lie slipped easily from her lips. "Things are a bit chaotic around here today."

"Yeah, I heard about Rufus. That's wild, right? Getting shot in his house and a neighbor finding his body."

"What? How do you know who found his body?"

"It was on the news this morning. A lady from across the street said she heard tires screeching down the road in their normally quiet and very nice neighborhood where nothing criminal ever happens." His sarcastic tone was clear, and she imagined just the type of woman who'd say such a thing—the nosy and privileged type. "The sound alarmed her, so she went to the door to see what was going on and saw Rufus's front door was open."

The winding driveway in front of Rufus's house was at least thirty-five feet long. From the end of it, there was a sidewalk, a wide roadway, and another thirty-five-foot-long driveway to the front of the house that wasn't even directly across from his. This woman heard vehicles outside at seven in the morning and saw a door open seventy feet away? Draya supposed it was possible, except she was certain they'd closed the door when they left Rufus lying on that floor. She remembered because she'd cursed when she got into her car, wondering if she should've left it ajar the way it had been when she'd first arrived.

"Draya? You still there? Draya?"

Travis yelling her name through the phone jolted her from her thoughts just as Venus walked in.

"Yeah. I'm here, but I gotta go. I'll call you later tonight." She disconnected the call before he could say another word and sighed at Venus's questioning gaze. "We got a problem."

Venus closed the door and walked past her. "Yeah, we do. You obviously forgot your office was downstairs."

Ignoring her biting remark, Draya followed Venus over to her desk. "Franklin's been calling me all morning."

"Franklin?" Venus was behind her desk now, setting her bag and purse down before shrugging out of her coat.

"Rufus's private attorney. He's been blowin' up my phone, and I don't know why."

"What is it with people not knowing how to deal with phone calls today?" She shook her head while unbuttoning the jacket to her black pantsuit. Then she took her seat. "Did you consider calling him back?"

Frowning, Draya again bit back a snappy retort. The last thing she had time for today was verbally sparring with Little Miss Perfect. "I've never talked to this guy before, Venus. Why would I just call him back now? On today of all days? What the hell does he even want with me?"

Venus sat back in her chair, rubbing the heels of her hands over her eyes. When she dropped her hands, she asked, "Did he call the office or your cell phone?"

Draya sat down slowly in one of the guest chairs. "My cell. That's how I know who it is, because each time he calls, he leaves a message, and then he starts sending me text messages to call him back ASAP."

Venus held her gaze. "How did he get your personal cell-phone number?"

Her tone was suspicious, and Draya instinctively thought it was because Venus assumed she'd slept with Franklin too. That was probably still part of it, but she'd also noticed Venus's quick blinking. She'd done that yesterday outside of the church while she'd searched her phone for news about Rufus and then again while they'd talked about alibis at her mother's house. Draya took that as a sign that she was worried.

"That's exactly what I've been trying to figure out." Now that they were both in agreement that there was something to be concerned about, Draya crossed one leg over the other.

Frowning, Venus continued. "Besides that, what's it been like around here? Anybody else say anything to you about Rufus?"

"I've had my door locked all day. Told my staff I was working on reports and couldn't be disturbed. I saw the company emails announcing Rufus's death and Ellen's emails about keeping us informed on funeral arrangements." She'd read each email, then closed out of them, refusing to reply or address any of the directives included. "Where've you been? I tried calling you a couple times."

Venus groaned. "As soon as I got here this morning, Mike was on my ass about the Hopkins complex. Of course that idiot didn't know what to do, so before I had a chance to get a cup of coffee, I was scheduling a meeting at Hopkins's estate."

"Really? But you aren't supposed to be on that project? Did Louis tell you to go to the meeting?"

"No." Venus shrugged. "I arranged the meeting and I went."

When Draya didn't reply but only raised a brow, Venus rushed to continue.

"Mike wouldn't even call the guy back, and when I called, Terrell was like, 'Come on out here and we can talk this morning.' What was I supposed to say—*Ah, no, sir, I have to wait for somebody to give me the okay*? Or better, *Sir, I'm not allowed to be on your account, but I'll send the dumbass with a dick and a failed basketball scholarship instead.*"

Draya couldn't help it—she chuckled. "You did not call him a dumbass with a dick."

Venus's lips quivered as she tried, but failed, to hide her smile. "Girl, he's the worst. I swear, I wanted to punch him in his throat at that meeting."

"I bet you did. So what'd Hopkins say? Is he going to keep you on the account with Mike? Did he mention anything about Rufus?" The latter was the bigger issue, but Draya knew how important this project was. She'd seen and approved some of the preliminary projected revenue reports, and at Rufus's direction had personally prepared additional analysis for this complex and all media resources. That was something she would've normally delegated to her staff to work on with the project manager, but Rufus had wanted her to handle it personally.

"Mike brought up Rufus, even though Terrell had already heard the news, which is why he called bright and early this morning in the first place." Venus moved just enough to have her chair swerving lightly. "He also didn't miss an opportunity to tell Terrell he was the project manager. I just didn't mention that I wasn't supposed to be on the project at all."

Draya nodded. "I wouldn't have either. Especially since you're the one who did all the legwork. Let Mike have the title and you do the job—Louis will know the difference in the end, believe me. His head's not as far up his ass as Rufus's was."

"You mean, his ego's not as fragile," Venus said with another grin.

"Right!"

They were sharing another rare chuckle when there was a quick knock on the door . . . seconds before it opened without receiving a response.

"I'm gonna strangle her," Jackie said through clenched teeth after closing the door behind her.

Neither Draya nor Venus moved or said a word, while Jackie growled and came to drop down into the chair beside Draya.

"This bitch just took my executive parking space." Jackie sat back in the chair, then lurched forward, pointing a finger at no one in particular. "Then she wants a total reconfiguration of the executive floor and, in light of Rufus's death, the office should have its own memorial service, so who's handling the logistics for that? Me! That's the fuck who! Now I get to plan the funeral for a guy I couldn't fuckin' stand."

"Lower your voice," Venus said.

"Calm the hell down," Draya followed up.

"What?" Jackie looked from Draya to Venus and then back to Draya again. "You two been smokin' in here without me? You wouldn't be calmly whispering if you had Ellen on your heels all day. Every time I moved, she was either calling my cell or having me paged. Even when I was on the toilet!" Jackie dragged her hands down her face. "They had tuna in the café today, and you know how that shit makes me go."

Venus shook her head. "I told you to stop ordering that."

"Hey, I got an idea," Draya said. "We've all had a rough day. Let's get out of here and go for a massage."

Thanks to Rufus, she'd missed her appointment Saturday, and after church and dinner at her momma's yesterday, she'd only wanted to go home and get some sleep. Now she was still tense as hell and sitting in this office with questions steadily running through her mind about the mysterious phone calls from Franklin. She desperately needed some relief.

"I just told you this woman has me wanting to kill her and you wanna get a massage?" Jackie asked.

"First, stop talking about killing people. That's the last type of conversation we need to be having right now," Venus said. "And second, hell yeah, let's get a massage. These last few days have been stressful as hell."

Shocked and amused by the way Venus immediately stood from her chair and grabbed her coat, Draya grinned. "Well, all righty, then. Let's go!"

Chapter 12

Jackie

This woman's hands were magic. Moving up and down Jackie's bare back, applying just enough pressure to the spots on her shoulders that needed it most. With the side of her face pressed on the towel beneath it, Jackie closed her eyes and focused solely on the wonderful release of tension.

What she didn't concentrate on too deeply was the text from Karlie this morning that she'd finally responded to. It had simply said: Good morning. To which she'd immediately replied: Good morning.

It wasn't a big deal, just a simple pleasantry. But Karlie's reply smiley emoji had elicited a grin and the barest movement of something that felt akin to butterflies in the pit of Jackie's stomach. Of course, that had been seven o'clock this morning. Now, at some time after four in the afternoon—because that was the earliest appointment they could get—so many other things had happened that this was the first time she'd let her mind really linger on those texts.

The masseuse's oiled hands moved over her skin, the woman's knuckles rubbing along her spine. Jackie moaned and then grimaced at the very sexual sound.

"Feels good, doesn't it?" Draya asked from the table six feet away from her.

"Hell yeah," she replied but kept her eyes closed.

Venus was on the table on the other side of Draya and for the past fifteen minutes since they'd been here, neither of them had said a word. This was Jackie's first massage, but she was certain it wouldn't be her last.

"After this, we can go sit in the steam room. You're gonna feel so loose tonight, you'll melt right into bed." It was Draya's turn to sigh heavily then.

"That's exactly what I need," Venus chimed in. "I haven't had a good night's sleep since Friday."

"Well, Friday night we all probably had a good rest with the help of Tito, Hennessy, and Rick, my weed guy." Jackie chuckled and remembered how good it had felt just kickin' it at Venus's place.

It had been a long time since she'd just hung out with friends. Jackie had been wildly popular in high school, playing on the girls' basketball team and running track. It seemed she was always doing something after school and then either going to someone's house to study or they were coming over to her house. Her mother loved having Jackie's core group of four friends at the house. The girls Jackie had known since middle school had called Maiselle Mom too. But most childhood friendships weren't meant to last. That hadn't occurred to her in the beginning, not even when they graduated from high school and two of her closest friends had gone away to college. The other two were still here, one opting to be done with school and get a job, the other going to hair school. For a while, the three of them continued to hang out on weekends or whenever they were all free.

Jackie hadn't been free often. In fact, she hadn't totally been free until she'd accepted what she'd tried to fight for far too long. Deciding to finally be honest with herself and with those closest to her had been the hardest thing she'd ever had to do, but in the first few minutes after she'd made the announcement, she knew she'd never felt prouder. In the weeks that followed, as her parents had cast her aside and her friends conveniently stopped answering her calls, she'd realized that freedom often came with a price.

"It's always been my motto that finding a guy whose sex could put you to sleep right was a blessing," Draya said.

It took Jackie a minute to clear her thoughts of the past and focus on what Draya was saying. Her slow speech said the massage was relaxing the hell out of her too.

Venus groaned. "I don't recall how long it's been since I was put to sleep by that method."

"Me either," Jackie added. "And that means however long it was, it's been too damn long."

They chuckled.

"That's 'cause y'all probably have too many standards," Draya said. "See, all I need is a handsome face, a nice body, clean teeth, good breath, and of course, great dick."

"Really? That's all you need?" Venus didn't sound as sarcastic as she normally did whenever Draya's love life was discussed. "I like to know a guy a little better. What's he do for a living? What're his goals? How's his credit?"

"That's absolutely all I need," Draya replied. "I don't need him to have a high-paying job, 'cause I've got one of my own. He doesn't have to own a big ole house because I don't plan on living with him. I've got my own place too. Now, I do like to go out from time to time, and even though I can pay my own way, a brotha has to pull his wallet out for all outings. I can take my damn self to the movies without having him tag along if I have to buy my own popcorn."

Jackie chuckled. "I don't mind spending money on my lady. But I'm all for commitment. I'm not about to put myself all the way out there for a quickie with some chick I barely know. And you really be worrying about a dude's credit just to go on a date with him?" she asked Venus.

"Not all the time," Venus said. "I mean, I don't actually ask him to sign an authorization so I can pull a credit report. I just like to talk to him about basic stuff to get an idea of how responsible he is." She paused, and Jackie figured that was because that woman's fingers were working their magic on her.

"Relationships are like an investment to me," Venus continued. "They require careful planning and attention to reap all the benefits."

Draya did one of those explosive laughs, and Jackie grinned because she knew it would piss Venus off.

"Girl, gettin' some dick is not like a business deal. You make everything so damn serious. That's why you're alone. If you just relax and let things flow naturally for once, you might find a little bit of happiness." Draya had opened her eyes and turned her head to face Venus while giving that nugget of advice.

And before Jackie could close her eyes, she saw Draya turn her head in Jackie's direction.

"You too. Physical pleasure doesn't come to those who overthink it. You gotta relax to receive that bomb-ass release." Draya settled her head down again and closed her eyes as the masseuse kneaded her shoulders and the back of her neck.

"Take the guy I'm seeing now, Travis Millhouse. He's an attorney with his own firm. His office is in our building; that's how I met him on the elevator one day." Draya paused and sighed heavily when the masseuse moved her hands up to her temples. "He's six feet three inches of hot chocolate sweetness, you hear me? I've never seen a man rock a suit the way he did that day in the elevator. He even made that slim-fit look seem sexy. He's got those thick lips and that bald head and his hands, whew, chile, lemme tell you about his hands—"

"Let you not tell us about his hands while these other women are in here trying to do their job," Venus interrupted and then chuckled.

Jackie grinned too. She was enjoying this afternoon respite much more than she'd thought she would. There was something cathartic about hanging out with people you liked, honestly sharing shit that you all were thinking.

There were a few moments of silence before Venus blurted out, "I think our new client is fine."

Draya lifted her head up again. "Who? *The* Hopkins complex?"

"Yeah," Venus replied.

"He holds the record as one of the league's top scorers," Jackie said.

"Oh no, I think she's considering having him score some points with her. What else happened at that meeting this morning?" Draya sounded like she was more than interested in those details, but Venus blushed.

"It was probably nothing, but I think I picked up some signals from him. Like maybe he was more interested than he should've been for just a business associate." Venus shook her head. "But I don't mix business with pleasure. Plus, I'm not into that groupie-chasing-a-baller scenario either."

"See, that's what I mean by overthinking it," Draya said. "I'm sure he's not thinking you're a groupie. He probably just saw a good-looking woman he wants to get his hands on."

"It's unethical," Venus said.

"You're too uptight," Draya replied.

Jackie figured she'd better jump in before these two started to get serious. "Does he have good hands? That's the question, 'cause good hands and of course the mouth is important," she said, her thoughts going back to the night she'd met Karlie.

She remembered her palms had tingled with the urge to touch Karlie's smooth, honey-hued skin.

"Hmm, you sound like you got somebody on your mind over there," Draya said.

"Do you?" Venus asked.

They were both staring at her now. Venus had lifted her head up, so Jackie could see her clearly.

"Nah," she said on impulse. "I mean, there's this one lady I met a while ago. But it's nothing."

"It's nothing because you want it to be nothing or because you're too afraid to accept that it's actually something?"

"What?" Jackie and Venus asked Draya in unison, and then all three of them laughed.

They were still laughing when Jackie heard the footsteps.

"Good afternoon, ladies." At the sound of a man's deep voice, she turned slightly until she could see the tops of a pair of brown leather lace-up dress shoes.

Those butterflies she'd been trying to ignore in the pit of her stomach each time she'd thought of Karlie were quickly replaced with a heaviness that had her shifting. Coming up on her elbows, she glimpsed the dude standing in front of the three tables.

He was a dark-skinned brother with close-cut, wavy black hair and matching beard. His suit was russet brown, a crisp white dress shirt without the tie beneath it. Reaching into his inside jacket pocket, he pulled out a badge and flashed it before saying, "I'm Detective Jennings. Do you think you could give me a few minutes to speak to these ladies in private?"

His question was directed to the masseuses, but Jackie entertained the option of getting up off this table and walking out the door too. The other women left silently without even asking if Jackie, Draya, or Venus wanted to be in this room alone with this slick-ass-looking cop.

"I hope you plan on paying for the portion of this session you're interrupting," she said, unable to tamp down the uncomfortable feelings spreading in her gut.

Detective Jennings glanced in her direction. "Jacqueline Benson?"

"That's me." 'Cause there was really no point in denying it. Plus, cops always looked for the second somebody started lying to them. And since she knew she was about to start some pretty serious storytelling, she decided to begin on a good foot.

"Draya Carter." This was said with a nod as he shifted his gaze to Draya.

This chick sat all the way up, pulling the big towel the masseuse had pushed down to her waist around her body. She dropped her legs over the side of the table and gave one of her dazzling smiles to the detective. "Yes?"

If that wasn't enough of a show, the sickly look on Venus's face when the detective went to stand in front of her table had Jackie frowning.

"Venus," he said, his voice noticeably deeper and quieter than it had been before.

Venus licked her lips slowly—not in a sexy way, but more like an I'm-dying-of-thirst-and-this-man-might-not-offer-me-a-drink-before-I-croak kind of way. Then she spoke in the barest whisper. "Malik."

Shit! Venus knew him.

"I've got some questions about your boss, Rufus Jackson," the detective said.

"He's dead," Jackie offered and had the pleasure of three sets of eyes looking her way. "I mean, that's the news, right? You've come here to tell us that Rufus is dead."

Malik continued to stare at her while putting his badge away. "When was the last time you saw him?"

"Why are you here?" Venus asked in response. "How did you know we were here?"

"That's an excellent question." Draya eased off the table and walked barefoot toward Malik.

He gave her a cursory glance, keeping his gaze above her neck, which Jackie knew wasn't what Draya was aiming for.

"My partner and I have been talking to all of Rufus's acquaintances. Today, we moved on to coworkers." He was looking at Venus again now. "You weren't in your office."

"So?" Venus shrugged. "You could've waited until tomorrow and come back."

There was something here, a vibe Jackie was picking up even if Draya was oblivious.

"That still doesn't tell us why you came all this way just to see . . . who?" Draya now stood close enough that she used the hand not holding the towel around her to run her fingers along the lapel of Malik's jacket. "All of us or just one of us?"

Malik looked down at Draya. "Your assistant overheard you making the appointment for three massages. She also knew the spa you preferred visiting."

When Draya didn't immediately respond, Malik took an easy step to the side before going to stand in front of Venus again.

"I was surprised to learn you were working in the construction industry." He was looking at her like he wanted to say something else . . . or quite possibly *do* something else.

Venus stayed in her position, but her body had gone totally tense as she stared up at him. "I've been at BCC for seven years. Rufus was the director of my department."

Malik nodded. "And you were seen having a heated argument with him at a holiday party on Friday. Witnesses overheard you telling Rufus he'd regret something."

Venus didn't reply; she only blinked quickly.

"Lots of people argued with Rufus," Jackie added. "At parties. At work. At the football game last season when he knocked that Steelers fan's beer out of his hand." She nodded. "He was about to get his jaw rocked when that security guard stepped in and saved his ass."

Her comment caught Malik's attention, as she'd known it would. He walked away from Venus and stopped at the table where Jackie was still propped up on her elbows. Now, she figured she should get up so she could really look this dude in the eye, 'cause unlike Draya, she wasn't hoping the guy liked what he saw if her naked body were on display.

"Do you mind?" she asked him when he was still staring at her. And when he didn't seem to get her drift, she moved a finger in a circular motion, telling him to turn around.

He did and continued talking at the same time. "How'd you know about the incident at the football game? Were you there?"

"Sure was. In the skybox," she said while getting up from the table and wrapping her towel securely around her body. "You can turn around. They were company tickets, and the guy was a cousin of one of BCC's other employees. Once Rufus learned that, the other employee was mysteriously demoted."

When he turned around again, Malik had a notepad and pen in his hand. "So in your opinion, Rufus was vindictive?"

"In my opinion, Rufus was an ass," she said and then cleared her throat, as she could see Venus easing off the table to stare at her. "There were lots of people who thought that way. I'm sure you and your partner will figure that out by the time you talk to everyone at the office."

"I talked to someone at the office who relayed a situation with you and Rufus. She said you pulled a gun on him."

It felt like all the air had been sucked out of the room, and Jackie struggled to keep her gaze level with the detective's. She wanted to take a deep breath, to release it slowly while she considered how to reply to this. This being what she'd feared all along.

"There are four hundred and sixty-seven employees in our downtown office." Draya had tucked her towel down securely so she could fold both arms over her chest. She was glaring at Malik now, the flirtatious tone gone from her voice. "You came all the way over here to see us. Why?"

Venus had come to stand beside Draya, and Jackie moved until she was next to them as well. Malik scribbled something on his notepad and raised his gaze to them slowly.

"Because after Venus argued with Rufus at the party, the three of you were seen leaving together. The next morning, Rufus was dead. Today, I learned that Jacqueline pulled a gun on him." When none of them commented, he continued, staring directly at Draya. "And because several people at the office mentioned you were sleeping with Rufus."

Jackie and Venus remained silent as Draya smiled.

Chapter 13

Draya

"And?" she said with a raise of her brow.

"And I just think it's pretty interesting that the three of you left the party together Friday night and you're all here today. Together, again. Instead of at work, where it seems most of the employees are pretty broken up about their boss's death," Malik said.

Venus stepped up then, moving so that she was between Malik and Draya. "We're friends outside of work who left an hour early to get a massage. That's not interesting enough for you to follow us here."

"My job is to take note of all the interesting details to see if any of them form pieces that'll complete the bigger puzzle," he told her.

"Then you should head back out there and go find yourself some more details, 'cause there's nothing for you here." Jackie was serious in her stance and her tone.

Now Malik raised a brow. "Really? Then how about you tell me more about the gun you pulled on Rufus. Where is it now, and where were you on Saturday morning between the hours of six and noon?"

Jackie immediately shook her head. "Nah, you can call my lawyer. He's got all the answers."

Venus tilted her head, staring at Malik like she couldn't believe he'd just about called them suspects. She smirked before replying, "Same."

"I'm going to request you contact my attorney as well," Draya said, offering him a sugary-sweet smile.

He hadn't looked at all interested in her, which was fine—she'd only done the flirting thing to try and throw him off his game. Meaning she'd much rather him think about the possibility of fucking her than arresting her.

"I'll do that," he told them. "It was good seeing you again, Venus."

Venus didn't look as if she liked him very much. Then again, Venus gave everybody that stank face.

"Have a good evening, Detective," Draya told him when Venus didn't say a word.

He looked at the three of them once more before turning and walking out of the room. Jackie went off the second he was out of earshot.

"Oh fuck! What're we gonna do? He wants to question us." All her words ran together as she said them in one breath, and Draya walked toward the locker-room doors.

Thankfully, they took the hint and followed her, Venus closing the door and slipping the lock in place behind them.

"You know him?" Suspicion slid along her spine as she watched for Venus's reaction to her question.

"We went to school together" was her tight response. Then she went to her locker and opened it, pulling out her clothes.

"That's a good thing, right?" Jackie had gone to her locker too, but she hadn't opened it yet. "I mean, if he knows you, then he knows you're not a killer. So he'll back off if you tell him to."

Venus removed her towel and began getting dressed. "I'm not telling him anything."

"But what if you can use the personal connection to our advantage?" It was a long shot, Draya knew, but it didn't hurt to ask. Just as there were asshole cops who couldn't be trusted no matter what, there were cops who had grown up around the way who sometimes looked out for their own. She had no idea which one Malik Jennings was, but suspected Venus did. "I mean, at the very least, you can just tell him that none of us was anywhere near Rufus on Saturday and he'll believe you because you know each other."

"Or wait, were you two not friends in school?" Jackie finally opened her locker.

Draya did the same, taking out her clothes and preparing to get dressed as well.

Venus huffed. "We were . . . friendly."

When Draya and Jackie both looked at her, she sighed again. "It was high school, okay? We had an on-and-off thing, but nobody really knew about it because my parents didn't like him. I haven't seen him since graduation." Their questioning gazes must've annoyed her, because she rolled her eyes. "And I'm not telling him anything. None of us is. Remember, they don't know what we don't tell them. Our lawyers can give them the alibi we came up with. If they don't come up with anything more substantial on us, then they should move on."

She didn't sound too convinced about that.

"Yeah, but you need to tell us if there's something going on between you and the cop." Because the last thing Draya wanted to deal with was Venus turning on them.

Venus had on her pants and blouse when she looked over to Draya. "I told you I haven't seen him since high school. There's nothing going on between us. And to answer the unspoken question, you don't have anything to worry about where we're concerned. If one of us talks, it incriminates all of us."

Jackie nodded. "She's right. Y'all really got attorneys? Because I know a guy. Everybody in my old neighborhood used to call him when they got in trouble."

"My father knows a ton of attorneys," Venus said. "But I hadn't planned on telling him anything about this."

"If he can get you the hookup on an attorney, maybe you should," Jackie said. "I mean, just about the detective asking you questions and your argument with Rufus at the party. Nothing else."

Venus shook her head. "I don't even want him to know that much. Any negativity could be catastrophic for his campaign."

"Well, the police aren't trying to question him. They want you. That has nothing to do with your dad's campaign," Jackie said.

"I'm his daughter—everything I do reflects on him."

Venus's words sounded rehearsed, her expression sad, and Draya felt sorry for her.

"First, you're an adult and responsible for your own actions, just like your father is responsible for his. Thinking that your every move plays out in his world is silly," Draya told her.

"Not in politics," Venus countered. "You know everything is fair game in politics."

She was right about that, and again, it made Draya feel sorry for her. No wonder she walked around being so uptight; she couldn't relax and do whatever she wanted for fear of causing a negative result for her father.

"Well, anyway, I'm sleeping with my attorney. If you want him to represent you too, just let me know." It was a simple and truthful statement that had her thinking she should probably stop ignoring Travis. She might actually need something else from him other than his good looks, big dick, and fresh breath.

◆ ◆ ◆

An hour and a half later, Draya was riding Travis's dick like he owed her money. Bouncing on top of him until her heavy breasts swayed and jiggled, her ass cheeks clapping against his bare thighs.

"I wasn't expecting to hear from you again tonight. Thought you were too busy for me." He spoke through gritted teeth, his hands moving down from her hips until he could cup her ass.

She leaned forward, grabbing the lobe of his ear between her teeth before whispering, "Stop talking; you're fuckin' up my flow."

He stopped talking and she eased back, steadying herself on her knees so she could circle her hips. This was her favorite position because she was in complete control. Staring down at Travis, she could tell he liked that shit too. He'd pulled his bottom lip between his teeth, his strong arms extended, fingers grabbing hold of her hips tightly.

This was exactly what she'd come here for. Well, it was the first thing—the second was to figure out a way to tell him she needed his representation because some fine-ass detective thought she might be a suspect in Rufus's murder. That thought irritated her, and she reached up to grab her tits, squeezing them in her hands until she gasped from the pressure.

"So damn fine," Travis whispered.

He loved to talk during sex. Sometimes she liked that, but tonight, not so much. There were too many things going through her mind right now. Too many issues she needed to get ahold on. This thing with Rufus was messing up her plans for the future. She had been counting on that bonus and already had a meeting scheduled with the real estate agent about leasing that building the first of the year. She also had shopping to do for her family, and now, thanks to Jackie, the gift exchange as well. Then there was BCC work, all the first-of-the-year reports that would need to be prepared, checked, and finalized.

"You look like you've got something on your mind besides me." Travis didn't wait for her to respond but sat up on the bed, holding her hips tightly before lifting her off him.

He was right, of course, but she wasn't trying to tell him that just yet. Normally sex was a fantastic de-stressor for her. It was the time she could be the most at ease, not having to worry about proving any points to anybody, because she was damn good at sex. Uninhibited, clear about her wants and needs, ready to give as well as she took, some had called her the perfect sex partner. She'd taken the compliment at face value because men often lied during sex, but instead focused on how good the physical act made her feel. Tonight, that was more of a struggle. Damn Rufus and all this drama he'd brought into her life!

"I've got this on my mind," she whispered and reached out to grab Travis's dick. Apparently that wasn't meant to be, as he eased away and stood from the bed.

"Prove it," he said through gritted teeth and turned her so that her ass faced him and she was on her knees.

There wasn't a moment for her to answer, not that she planned to. She knew what he wanted, and she was ready to give it to him. This had been one long-ass day—losing herself in a mind-blowing climax was exactly what the doctor ordered. Or in her case, the lawyer who was now pumping in and out of her like he was trying to litigate his way out of a multimillion-dollar lawsuit.

With her fingers grabbing the sheets, Draya closed her eyes and let the pleasure overtake her. In moments, she was yelling his name, her body trembling beneath his while he smacked her ass and begged her to repeat his name again. She did, and she came with an intensity that had her almost blacking out. Travis followed her lead, grunting and cursing through his release until moments later, they were both collapsing on the bed.

Draya got up first and headed to the bathroom, where she completed her aftercare. Looking into the mirror while washing her hands, she asked herself, *Is there a law against sleeping with your lawyer?* With a shrug, she figured it didn't matter. She could either find another lawyer or another playmate, which one didn't matter to her much.

"Come here and tell me what's on your mind," Travis said as soon as she walked out of the bathroom.

He'd probably used the powder room in the hallway to do whatever he needed to do after sex. She'd never been much of a snuggler, deciding it was too intimate. Sex was meant to fill a physical, not an emotional, need. Now he was lying on the bed, pillows propped up behind him. He'd pulled on his boxers but was otherwise naked. When she didn't move, he patted the mattress beside him. "Come here, Draya."

This man was fine as hell, and the instant pulsing in her pussy as she stared at his gorgeous body told her she wasn't finished with him tonight. So for the time being, she'd humor him and sit on this bed like she was gonna pour out her soul to him. Draya didn't give anybody that much access to herself, not even people she was related to—the chances of being let down were far too great.

Taking her hand when she was finally on the bed beside him, he asked, "What happened today?"

Where the hell did she begin? Not at the beginning, that was for damn sure. While she was certain she could trust Travis to the extent of them having a physical relationship together and if or when he was formally retained as her attorney, telling him all that had actually happened from the night of the party wasn't an option.

"You don't find out every day that your boss has been murdered." That was the safest place to start.

"Yeah, I guess not. You and Rufus worked closely together?"

That was an understatement. "Sure. I ran the financials for all the projects in the company. He ran all the projects."

He'd also run up inside her for nine months, time she couldn't erase if she wanted to, and she didn't want to, because without that time, she wouldn't be doing the job she was now.

"So it makes sense you'd be feeling some type of loss. I understand."

She shook her head because Travis had no clue about the losses she'd endured in her life. Nobody did, and she'd rather forget about them, because rehashing the past would have no effect on the future.

"The cops were at the office today, asking everybody questions."

Travis held her hand tight, bringing his other hand across his lap to rub those fingers along her arm. "They're trying to get a full picture of who he was in the office, who his enemies were, etcetera."

"The detective on the case followed me to the spa. He had questions he wanted to ask me."

"What?" Travis sat up straighter, looking at her with his brow furrowed.

His eyes were amber. In the weeks she'd been sleeping with him, this was the first time she'd noticed that.

"He followed the office rumor mill and the story about Rufus and me sleeping together. Then my assistant blabbed about me being at the spa, so that's where he showed up."

"And what did he ask you?"

"Where I was on Saturday morning between six and noon." To be exact, Detective Jennings had asked Jackie that question, but Draya was certain he wanted to know where they all were.

Travis wouldn't ask her where she was. But that quick muscle twitch in his jaw said he wanted to know if she'd slept with her married boss. For some odd reason, she didn't want to tell him.

"It was long before you, and I broke it off with him. I wasn't trying to marry the guy, just having a good time." Did that make her sound like a ho?

To women like Venus and probably a whole lot of other folks, the answer to that question would be yes.

"Did you answer the detective?"

"No." She licked her lips and took a gamble on how good her skills in bed were. "I told him to call you, my attorney."

The longest seconds seemed to tick by before he replied, "You did the right thing."

Draya sighed, and when he wrapped his arms around her, she went into them willingly. Feeling him hug her so tightly without giving her one judgmental word was a relief, and she closed her eyes to the surprising sensation.

She could only pray that getting Detective Jennings off her back would be this easy.

Chapter 14

Venus

The tensing of her shoulders came seconds after Venus stepped into her parents' house.

"Hey, Babygirl, surprised to see you out this late," Don said from the black leather recliner where he always sat in the living room.

A few feet away, tucked regally into the corner, was the eight-foot-tall artificial Christmas tree Ilene had decorated in the traditional red, green, and gold ensemble.

"Hey, Daddy." She closed the door and removed her coat, going to the closet to hang it up.

It was a little after eight, and she hadn't been home from work yet. After leaving the spa, she'd gone for a drive to clear her mind. That drive had lasted a few hours and ended with her decision to come here.

"I meant to call you yesterday after church, but I got caught up in an emergency meeting, and today was just as hectic," her father said. "Carol was in most of the meetings today, and she wanted me to tell you hello."

"It's okay; I had a pretty eventful day as well. And tell Aunt Carol I said hello when you see her again." Her godmother worked with her father and was very close to both her parents. Venus had seen her a lot when she was young and still living at home, but as an adult, she didn't often have time to meet up. "There's something I want to talk to you about, Daddy," she continued with the more pressing issue. Moving farther into the room, she pushed one of the three decorative pillows on the beige couch to the side before taking a seat.

Her father's graying eyebrows rose as he watched her. He still had on the pink dress shirt he'd most likely worn to the office this morning, but now with the sleeves rolled up to his elbows. The gray slacks that were no doubt also a part of the day's outfit were still on, but his dress shoes would've been removed minutes after he'd arrived home, to be replaced by brown leather slippers.

"You doing all right?" As if just realizing she was going to be staying awhile, he took the tablet that he'd been working on from his lap and put it on the side table next to the chair. "I saw a little more about Rufus's death on the local news tonight."

"I'm okay." That wasn't a lie—she was okay now.

Seeing Malik again had been more than a little disturbing. The reason for their reunion even more so. It had been one thing to worry about being considered a suspect in a murder or even just the possibility of being questioned in connection with a murder. It was something else entirely different when those things stared her directly in the face.

"I guess they'll have some type of memorial for him at the company, right? You know Rufus's father was close friends with Ted Billings. That's how Rufus got in over there right out of college," he said.

Seemed she and Rufus had more in common than Venus had ever wanted to accept. Both their fathers had pulled strings to get them the job they'd each coveted. She doubted the older men had any idea of the competitive atmosphere they were fostering at the time and hated that it was because of those jobs that she found herself in the middle of a mess.

"A homicide detective came to see me today. He wanted to know where I was the morning that Rufus was killed." With her hands in her lap, she recited the words she'd been rehearsing in the car for the last couple of hours.

It had taken her a while after leaving the spa to decide what she was going to do. The parking lot of a business complex forty minutes outside the city had been the place where she'd finally stopped and gotten out of the car to get some air.

Her father didn't give a quick reaction. Don liked to chew on his words, as he used to tell her. That way, he was always certain that his response was exactly what he wanted to say and in the tone he planned to say it. He did sit up straighter in his chair, staring from her to the television that was now on a national news channel.

"What was your reply?"

"I told him to contact my lawyer."

Don nodded. "Good. Never talk to the police without a lawyer."

That was one of the earliest lessons he'd given her when she was a teenager. Not because he thought she'd someday be in trouble with the law but because he had been a defense attorney at the time, and he said it was a rule everyone needed to practice.

"I didn't kill Rufus." She felt like she had to say that, to get it out in the universe just in case her father was thinking otherwise.

He shook his head briefly. "Don't be foolish; I know you're not capable of such a thing."

The comment was more dismissive than reassuring, but she accepted it.

"The question is why they came to you in the first place. What probable cause did he have to ask that question?"

She rubbed her palms over her thighs, then suddenly stopped when she noticed he turned to look at her. "I got into an argument with Rufus at the office party on Friday. The detective said witnesses told him it was a *'heated'* argument, but really I just told Rufus not to touch me again."

"He touched you?"

Again, there was no hint of alarm like one might expect if a daughter told her father that a man had touched her. He hadn't immediately clenched his fist and shifted into a defender status but instead looked at her as if she were simply a client whom he needed to retrieve facts from.

"Not in a sexual way." While there were waves of relief to her own peace of mind at that fact, her father only continued to watch her. "He grabbed my arm as I tried to walk away from him. I told him if he put his hands on me again, he'd regret it."

He raised a brow. "A threat, Venus."

"Yes, a threat, Daddy, because he shouldn't have put his hands on me. I don't care what we disagree about regarding work. I didn't like the way he was using me for information and then demeaning me at the same time, so I was angry and I shouted at him." She shrugged. "Now, I guess that's enough motive for a detective to question me about killing him."

"They have to follow every lead."

Her heart had begun to hammer in her chest as she volleyed between being used to her father's blasé attitude about things that concerned her—until those things concerned him—and the pricks of pain from wanting him to have a bit more of an impassioned reaction to all she'd just told him. She'd been feeling emotional as hell for the past few days.

"I already called a lawyer," she replied.

Taking care of business was always her mantra, whether it pertained to her schoolwork or whatever she needed to do at work to get the job done—that's what she was known for. It was what had gotten her to where she was today, not simply her father making a call to an old friend. No matter what Don's relationship was with Ted Billings, Venus was certain that if she hadn't shown up at BCC every day giving them 110 percent of her effort and skills, she wouldn't be in the senior project manager position. The past few days, however, had made her second-guess that, but in the hours she'd been driving around, she'd begun to get her mind right.

Her father turned to her with a strained expression. "I wish you would've come to me first. Who'd you call?"

"Tabitha Sloan."

He sighed and then nodded. "Good. She's really good and trustworthy. I'll give her a call in the morning, and we'll get this taken care of."

"I can handle this, Daddy. I only came to tell you because I wanted you to know what was going on."

As if what she'd just said was preposterous, he stood and walked over to where she sat. "Nonsense. You don't have any experience in these matters. Tabitha and I will take care of it. All you need to do is return to work and act normal."

Venus knew his words were meant to end the conversation, and as if he'd silently summoned her, her mother appeared seconds after he'd spoken them.

Ilene circled around her father like he was a piece of furniture, not touching or even looking at him. She stopped in front of Venus and reached for her hand. "You look tired. You should head home and get some rest."

There was no doubt that her mother had been eavesdropping on the conversation, and Venus briefly wondered if that was something Aunt Dot would've done. No, yesterday, Draya's mother had walked right into the living room when they'd been talking, bringing her bold personality and spreading warmth to the two strangers who were in her house. Sitting here tonight in the living room where she'd grown up, Venus felt cold and alone. Weary from the events of the day and not in the mood to further analyze her parents, she ignored her mother's outstretched hand but stood anyway.

"You're right. I'm going to leave."

"And listen to your father. He knows what he's doing, and he'll handle everything."

There was no point in repeating that she didn't need Don to *"handle everything."* She supposed by coming here, she'd given the impression that she required his help, because it really didn't matter that she'd said she didn't. They rarely listened to what she had to say; they simply told her what they expected her to do.

Thirty minutes later, Venus was in her apartment. She'd changed into her pajamas and had the television on the HGTV channel while a frozen dinner cooked in the microwave. The moment she sat on the couch with her meal and drink in hand, her phone chirped. Setting the two things on the coffee table—where her nativity scene had been neatly reassembled—she picked up her phone and read the text.

Lunch tomorrow at 1? Not in the lunchroom!

With a slow grin, she replied to Jackie's text with agreement and put the phone back on the couch beside her. A moment or so later, when she chewed the first bite of her food and tried to get into the couple on the screen searching for their dream home, it occurred to her that this was the first time Jackie had officially invited her and Draya to lunch. All their prior meetups in the lunchroom had been impromptu, fueled by the camaraderie they no doubt felt at each hating Rufus's guts. And while there was no denying he was their initial connection—especially not considering the present circumstances—this invite felt different.

She finished her meal and eventually began commenting on the couple on the screen's poor choices, determined not to think about her parents, Rufus, and especially not Malik, for the rest of the night.

Two days later, plans to formally say goodbye to Rufus—the family funeral and the memorial service Ellen was spearheading—had been announced. Venus had been dropping all the emails about both into an Outlook folder marked "Stuff." It was stuff she didn't want to deal with from people she didn't like being bothered by, and after just a couple of days, she was more than sick of it.

Sitting back in her desk chair, she picked up her phone and scrolled through the last few text messages. One from her lawyer thanking her for paying the retainer fee and promising to let her know when or if she heard from the cops on her behalf. Groaning, rolling her eyes, or even cursing the part of her life that revolved around that message was pointless. She'd been doing too much of that in the past few days, and the stress was keeping her up at night.

Who was she kidding? Insomnia had always been in the top five of her life ailments. When she was a teen, her doctor had chalked it up to an anxious mind. As an adult, she called it a pain in the ass, as it meant that caffeinated beverages became her daytime partners in crime. Case in point, the larger-than-life blue mug containing hot black tea with lemon and extra sugar sitting on the right-hand side of her desk. As she glared at the mug now, a half smile tugged at her lips—Lucy from *Peanuts* making a statement about being the boss paraded around the mug. It was her favorite, and not just because she preferred blue but more so because she *was* Lucy, running the show even when people didn't want or expect her to.

The phone buzzing in her hand startled her, saving her from going down the pity-party road, so she answered the unfamiliar number after only one ring.

"Venus McGee."

"Good morning, Venus McGee."

It was a familiar and sexy voice.

"This is Terrell Hopkins. I wanted to call you personally and give you the good news."

Well, she could certainly use some good news, and hearing it from fine-as-hell Terrell Hopkins was even better.

She cleared her throat and sat up straighter in her chair, as if he could see her slouching and would possibly take that as a sign she wasn't up to working on this project.

"Hi, Mr. Hopkins. It's good to hear from you. Should I try to link Mike in on this call?" Lord knows she didn't want to talk to that silly man this morning, but this was business and it always came first.

"I don't think we need Mike at this meeting."

Those words were music to her ears. "Well, then, what's this good news you'd like to share?"

"I've decided that moving forward on this project, I'd prefer to work with you. Alone." Spoken in the tone of a man used to getting what he wanted. She squared her shoulders and tried like hell to keep a cheesy-ass grin from her face.

"That's not usually how it works here at BCC. There's a team assigned to each project, a lead and then their assistant," she began, hating that Rufus's and Mike's comments about her not being a team player still echoed in her head. "But our ultimate goal is to provide you with the best experience possible."

"And that would be working with you, I'm sure."

Now she was grinning because he sounded too good, saying all the right things, on this phone at eight thirty in the morning.

"Listen, I gotta run, but I'll definitely be in touch with you again real soon. In the meantime, I'm trusting you to do what you do and make this happen."

She'd barely had a chance to agree before he'd disconnected the call. For a few startled moments, she stared at the phone in her hand, wondering what the hell had happened. Did Terrell Hopkins just give her the project she'd wanted to spearhead from the start? And did he just say he wanted to work with her alone?

The answer to both those questions was yes and was unfortunately punctuated by a stern knock on her office door. Dropping the phone to her desk, she yelled, "Come in."

Mike opened the door, stepped inside, and immediately started toward her desk. The happy air that had just filled the space because of Terrell's call dissipated instantly.

"What the hell do you think you're doing?"

With a raised brow, she gazed up at where he now stood, hands planted firmly on the edge of her desk. "Excuse me?"

"Don't play with me, Venus. I just saw the same interview on *Morning Baltimore* that half the city, including Louis and the other BCC executives, probably saw. What kind of underhanded stunt are you trying to pull?"

Venus always prided herself on being professional, but Mike's tone, the angry look on his face, and the foul shit spewing from his mouth were taking her out of character.

"Perhaps you should start by lowering your voice. Then you can tell me what you're talking about." She busied herself with pulling up her schedule to make sure she had time to evaluate the plan for the Hopkins complex once more before making the necessary calls to get started.

He pushed back from the desk, dragging one hand down the back of his head as he turned away from her. Seconds later, he was whirling around again, this time pointing a finger at her—something that annoyed the hell out of her. "You know exactly what this is about. It's about Terrell Hopkins officially announcing that he's building a sports complex and that you're heading up the project for him."

Standing and pushing her chair back, she spoke in what she hoped could be construed as a neutral voice. "I've told you once about your tone. Now I'm telling you not to point at me." She said this while moving around her desk and past him to shut her office door.

"And for the record, I didn't know anything about an interview on *Morning Baltimore*." Just like she hadn't expected Terrell to call her seconds ago and announce that he wanted her to work on his project alone.

"Please, don't give me that crap. You couldn't wait to call him the other day, inserting yourself into my project. Then you were all over him at his house. Smiling up at him like you had some kind of schoolgirl crush."

Oh, Mike was certainly feeling himself this morning, coming into her office and saying all kinds of shit because he thought he could. The nervous chuckle that erupted from her chest was only a prelude.

"No, what you watched at his house the other day was an experienced project manager getting the job done." She stepped closer so he knew without a doubt that she wasn't backing down from him just because he'd raised his voice. She could get loud too. "And if you had any real experience, you would've chimed in to help save this project, but no, you're so used to riding on Rufus's jock that you're floundering now that he's gone. Well, let me tell you something—I'm not carrying your ass around here. You either step up and earn your paycheck or you can crawl your simple ass out of my office and don't come back."

Telling him to leave actually wasn't an option.

"You're not the boss." He stepped closer to her as well, until there was no more space between them. "And if you want to pick up where your friend left off and start sleeping your way to the top, fine by me. But Louis is gonna hear about how you stabbed me in the back on this deal, and when Terrell Hopkins is tired of your piece of no-class ass and drops you like he does every other groupie he's met, I'll be right there, laughing at how pathetic and predictable you are."

Only the grace of God kept her from punching him in the face. That and the fact that she was in the office and didn't want to lose the respect of the other employees of this company. Still, her blood boiled while watching Mike walk out of her office. He was an asshole in a designer suit, Rufus's pathetic little understudy, and the current bane of her professional existence. The punk ass wasn't lying; he was going directly to Louis, and how exactly that was going to turn out, she didn't know, but she didn't have time to figure it out because she had another visitor.

On a heavy sigh, she glared at Ellen, who eased her way into the office, giving a slow and slithery smile as she approached.

"Well, I guess that meeting didn't go well."

Rolling her eyes, Venus turned away from Ellen and went back to sit behind her desk. "What can I do for you, Ellen?"

The woman wore a red pantsuit and cream-colored blouse. Her snow-white hair was styled in a severely short manner.

"You can stop this little act you've got going on, for starters."

Giving her a what-the-fuck look was all Venus could manage.

"I've seen the memos you sent to the other project managers in this department, telling them to send all their status reports to you, and I just heard how you were speaking to Mike. It's disgraceful." The disdain in Ellen's voice was simultaneously obvious and annoying as hell.

"It's necessary. The show must go on." Without a care for how curt or possibly cold she may sound, she continued. "With Rufus gone, I'm the next highest in authority in this department."

Ellen's lips thinned as she shook her head. "How dare you. It's as if you wished this on him so you could step up and take his place."

She eased back down into her chair, telling herself to take it slow with this one. Ellen had already told the police about Jackie's run-in with Rufus, and she'd still been doing shady things to Jackie in the meantime. Draya had even said she'd walked by Ellen's office and the woman had been crying at her desk.

"That's an unkind thing for you to say, Ellen." Unfortunately, it wasn't as untruthful as Venus would've liked to pretend. "I recognize that Rufus was an essential part of this department."

"He *was* this department, and this company wouldn't be where it is today without him. Rufus brought a fresh edge to BCC, and he had plans to take us further into what promised to be a highly successful future. You've always been jealous of that fact."

Okay, this bitch was downright delusional.

"I promise you that I've never been jealous of Rufus. Now, if you'd like to lodge a formal complaint as to how I'm handling the transition in this department, you can take it straight to Louis."

"Oh, I plan to." She pointed to Venus, shaking her head as if it would help make her point. "And you can bet I'm going to tell him all the funny business that's been going on the last few days. Like you stealing Mike's project right from under him, and you and those other two skipping out of the office whenever you feel like it. What you've been doing doesn't look good to the other staff, and I'm going to put a stop to it."

"Do what you need to do," Venus told her, not even bothering to question why Ellen was apparently keeping tabs on her, Jackie, and Draya now. "But if you can take it out of my office, I'd appreciate it."

Ellen huffed and turned to leave, but Venus couldn't be that lucky. The woman whirled around as soon as she got to the door and glared at her. "Mike made a good point—if you're going to start sleeping your way to the top like your friend Draya did, you'd better be prepared for the backlash."

Despite all her normal rantings about decorum and professionalism, Ellen slammed the door when she left, and Venus sighed with relief. Letting her head fall back against her chair, she closed her eyes for a few moments and tried to focus her thoughts. She really didn't have time to deal with Mike or Ellen. And so what if she'd sent out management emails? She was in a management position, and nobody else in this department had stepped up to take care of business, so she'd done it. Surely Louis would be proud of her taking initiative, especially since he hadn't done anything besides send emails about wanting a written tribute to Rufus before the memorial service, which was scheduled for next Friday.

Speaking of writing something, she sat up in her chair and reached for her cell phone. Finding the group-text thread among Draya, Jackie, and her that had been going steadily since their first out-of-the-office lunch date a couple of days ago, she sent a message: Guess what just happened?

Jackie replied first: I just left the police station. Meet at Maisy's @1130

Chapter 15

Jackie

"I've never been to a police station before," she said and picked up her glass to take a drink of the ginger ale she'd ordered. "Sitting outside in a car while my high school friend waited for her boyfriend to be released doesn't count."

"I have," Draya replied. She sat across the table from Jackie, the crab cake sandwich and fries she'd ordered halfway finished. "Too many times to count. But not for the purpose people think I would've."

"You know people who think you would end up at a police station?" Venus asked Draya.

Venus sat on the side of the table next to Jackie. She'd ordered french onion soup and a Caesar salad that she'd barely touched. Today's lunch meeting was earlier than the ones they'd had previously, but this was also a special circumstance. Jackie hadn't wanted to be alone.

Draya took an abnormally long time to respond, wiping the sides of her mouth with the napkin and then her hands with ridiculous slowness. "Yes," she eventually said. "Apparently, teachers and community leaders are allowed to voice their opinions to children regardless of how mean and hurtful they are."

"That's ridiculous." Venus frowned.

"You mean to tell me nobody at your church ever made a comment about something you were wearing possibly leading you to a teenage pregnancy?" Draya asked with mock surprise. "Or nobody told you that based on where you grew up, you'd end up addicted to drugs or on welfare?"

Jackie hadn't personally been told either of those things, but she knew they were said about lots of kids in the inner city. Her parents and their friends often talked about the unfairness of the stereotype. It wasn't until recent years that she'd come to the conclusion that her parents were hypocrites. They were totally against any children or young adults in the neighborhood being judged solely because of their address and income status, but apparently sexuality was a totally different story.

"Come on, Venus, even I know you can't be surprised by that."

Venus shook her head. "No, I'm not surprised. I'm well aware of those types of conversations being had by ignorant people. I just didn't think an adult would actually say that to a child."

"Well, anyway, those types of conversations can also serve as motivation for children to succeed." Draya cleared her throat and picked up another fry to stuff into her mouth. "What happened after you made your statement?"

This wasn't the first time Jackie noticed that Draya didn't really like talking about herself. While it appeared on the outside that she was self-absorbed and a little cocky, there'd been more than one occasion where Jackie thought there was something in Draya's past that had hurt her deeply. Perhaps instead of the saying "game recognized game" where the two of them were concerned, "pain recognized pain" was more accurate.

"My lawyer actually made the statement; I took that whole 'You have the right to remain silent' thing to heart." She gave a wry chuckle but immediately realized even that didn't take away from the seriousness of the discussion. "Not that they could arrest me—they couldn't because they didn't have enough evidence. But my lawyer thought it was better for us to voluntarily meet with the detectives. He did all the talking, explaining only that I went to the holiday party, left with you two, and spent the night at Venus's."

"So they can come to us to verify your alibi," Venus said. Her hair was pulled over one shoulder today, a dark contrast against the cream-colored turtleneck she wore with brown slacks and boots.

"And we'll confirm by making the exact same statement." Draya took a drink from her glass of soda.

"Exactly," Jackie replied with a nod. "My lawyer also gave them my gun to be tested and a copy of my registration."

Venus's eyes widened. "What? Without a warrant?"

"Yeah, that was my initial reaction when he said that's what he wanted to do. But then he explained that it would give the impression that I was cooperating with the police instead of actively working against them, which would undoubtedly cause more suspicion."

"I don't know anybody who would've done that. You sure your lawyer is used to representing criminals?" Draya asked.

Venus still looked shocked, which meant she agreed with Draya's statement.

"Denying I have a gun and then having them get a search warrant and finding said gun would only make me look guiltier. And before you say it, I know it was Ellen's word against mine, but you know that bitch is out for my blood. She was going to keep pushing the narrative that I threatened Rufus and I had a gun, so my lawyer said it was better to just let them test the gun, since we know it's not the murder weapon. The hope that it would clear me of suspicion outweighed the risk of it giving the cops more ammunition to dig even further into my connection with the murder." At least that's how she prayed it would turn out.

Her lawyer seemed certain of the outcome, and she'd decided she was going to think positively too. "Plus, Detective Jennings looked like he believed me."

Draya smirked. "Because he didn't arrest you?"

"No, because he thanked me for coming down and making a statement. He urged me to tell you two to do the same."

"Absolutely not," Draya replied first. "Not until he gets more on me than a rumor that I slept with Rufus. My lawyer doesn't think that's enough and advises we sit tight and see if they come up with something else."

Venus had gotten unusually quiet.

"How 'bout you? Did you talk to your lawyer?" Jackie asked her.

"Uh, yeah, we've talked on the phone, and she doesn't think there's a reason for me to do or say anything at this point either. If the cops really thought the argument Rufus and I had at the party was a motive, they'd be pushing harder to get me to talk." Venus didn't look convinced by those words, but she sat up straighter and gave that look of combined confidence and nonchalance she had perfected.

"Good, then we're all clear." Jackie breathed a sigh of relief. From the start, she'd realized she was the only one of them who had a tangible motive against Rufus. If the bastard hadn't told Ellen about their altercation in the garage, that wouldn't have been an issue. But even once she'd explained the situation to her attorney, he'd agreed it was self-defense against Rufus's sexual assault, which they'd gladly point out and if need be go public with. Jackie had prayed that last part didn't come to fruition. If she thought Ellen was out to get her now, telling the world that the womanizing Rufus Jackson had made a pass at her—a known gay woman—wouldn't go over well at all.

"And since we can finally breathe a sigh of relief, I say we celebrate by hitting the mall for some Christmas shopping. Two of the things on Granny's list are hard as hell to find online. Plus, I already took a personal day from work." She hadn't been sure how things at the police station were going to turn out, but she'd known the last person she wanted to deal with afterward was going to be Ellen, so she'd gone through the necessary protocol to officially be absent from work for the entire day.

Venus folded her arms over her chest. "I don't know if I can. Terrell Hopkins called me this morning to say he wanted me to oversee his project alone. Then Mike stormed into my office, accusing me of flirting with Terrell to get him to go on television and make the public announcement that I was heading up the project."

"Wait. Slow down and say that again. It sounds like you said you got the promotion you wanted after all." And if that were the case, she was even more ready to go out and celebrate.

"That's what I heard too," Draya added.

The tentative smile that spread across Venus's face made Jackie happy. She knew Venus worked hard and that she was the best project manager at the company. Rufus definitely should've given her that promotion over Mike.

"Well, not exactly. I mean, Louis did call after I got Mike and that irritating ass Ellen out of my office. He'd already spoken to Mr. Billings, and they both agreed that I was experienced enough to spearhead the project. Besides that, they want to keep Terrell happy."

"Obviously," Draya said. "This project is bringing major money and exposure to the company. And you're in charge of it. Jackie's right—we need to celebrate."

"I agree a celebration is in order, but I'm not going to take the rest of the day off. First, because I've got a lot of work to do, and second, because Ellen's apparently started keeping tabs on all of us now. The last thing I want her telling the cops is that we all mysteriously took the day off, just a couple days after we all left work early." Venus rolled her eyes and picked up her glass of water to take a drink.

Draya nodded. "That's a good point. Plus, I've gotta leave early today anyway. I have a meeting at the bank about this loan."

Jackie probably wouldn't have thought twice about what Draya had said if Draya hadn't looked guilty as hell seconds after she said it.

"You're getting another loan?" Venus asked. "You just settled on your condo a couple months ago."

Draya's frown had Jackie thinking she was about to pop off at Venus for being in her business, so Jackie spoke up. "I mean, you did just tell us you're going to get a loan, so you might as well tell us what it's for."

The logic seemed clear, but that didn't stop Draya from frowning. She huffed and tossed her napkin on top of her plate. "I'm trying to lease a building to open a foundation that'll help young girls in the community. It would provide counseling services as well as resources to assist every girl in reaching her highest potential. Enforcing positivity and support instead of feeding them with doubt and disappointment."

Draya clamped her lips shut again and this time looked at them like she was expecting laughter or criticism in return.

"That's amazing," Venus replied without hiding the shock and awe that Jackie was feeling too.

"Yeah," Jackie said. "It is."

With a quick shake of her head, Draya sighed. "But we should definitely celebrate. So let's go out tonight."

"That sounds good. Dinner at The Bygone?" Venus suggested.

"Oh no, I mean a real celebration. Let's go to a club—I feel like dancin'." Draya's smile was bright now as she waved to the server to bring them their check.

"I do too!" Jackie agreed. "So, seven tonight. We can go to Chino's." She hadn't been there in years, preferring to frequent Jazzy's because it was quieter and more secluded, but tonight, she wasn't thinking about not being in a crowd or having people staring at her with questions. They each had something to celebrate, and that was important to her, more important than any hauntings from her past.

Chapter 16

Draya

It was ladies' night, so admission to Chino's was free, and drinks were five dollars until ten thirty. It was a little after nine, and Draya was on her second martini. They weren't playing the heavy dance music yet, but she'd watched a new DJ step into the booth as she finished off the nachos they'd ordered. Venus had wanted a nicer dinner, so they'd gone to The Bygone as soon as they met up at Venus's apartment at seven and had a quick dinner. But Draya loved Chino's nachos loaded with cheese, jalapeños, bacon, and scallions.

"I'm gonna have heartburn tomorrow," Venus moaned as she leaned against the leather-backed booth where they sat.

"Girl, I keep a pack of Tums in my purse, my nightstand, and in the medicine cabinet," Draya told her and drank from her glass of water this time. Her chest felt a little fiery now after all those jalapeños, but it wasn't bad enough to start medicating.

"This place is poppin' for a weeknight." Jackie had been looking around since they got there, like she thought she might see somebody she didn't want to see. She'd ordered a White Hennessy classic gold margarita and now ran a finger over the rim of the half-empty lowball glass.

"You okay over there?" she asked because this was supposed to be a celebration, and Jackie looked a little somber.

Jackie moved her hand from the glass and ran it down the back of her head. Her locs were twisted in a neat knot on top of her head, and the sides had been freshly shaped up. Her eyes were a pale golden color that blended smoothly with her tawny complexion, and they lit up when she smiled, which was normally a lot. After their lunch today, Draya had gone back to the office. She'd wondered how having to give an official statement to the police had felt. Would she have been in as good spirits as Jackie had seemed earlier, if she'd had to do it? What if it did turn out that she'd have to talk to the police about her affair with Rufus and his blackmail scheme against her, because that was a possibility she couldn't totally dismiss. But she didn't have to think about it tonight.

"I'm cool. Just haven't been here in a while," Jackie replied with a shrug.

Venus wore black leggings, an oversize off-the-shoulder gray sweater, and knee-high boots. She sat with one leg tucked beneath her, rocking a little to the beat of the music. "Me either. I mean, like freshman year of college, I think."

Draya wouldn't have thought Venus was the club type, which would explain why she'd never seen her here during their college years. "Well, I love dancing, so this has always been my spot," she told them. "Plus, ladies' night is without fail a draw."

"Discounts are inevitably a plus. One of the reasons I stopped clubbin' was because drinks can put a serious dent in your bank account," Jackie added.

"Ain't that the damn truth." Draya chuckled. "But you can meet some cuties in the club, and sometimes they're nice enough to buy you a drink."

"You've got a point there," Venus chimed in. "I used to go to more clubs in DC, but there's really nothing like a Baltimore club."

Draya was shaking her head. "See, I can't do DC's nightlife. I don't know if it's the music or the people or the combo that just turns me off."

"I went to a DC club last year." Jackie was staring somewhere over Draya's shoulder as she said that.

Now normally, Draya wasn't one to pry. If somebody wanted to tell you something, they told you. If they didn't, that was fine with her too. There'd never been a point that she didn't have enough going on in her own life to need the addition of anybody else's baggage. She'd even refrained from asking for more detail when Jackie had made that off comment about not knowing if her family had Christmas dinners. Tonight, however, Draya wanted to know what was going on.

"Really? How'd you like it?" she asked.

Jackie shook her head. "Truthfully, I didn't pay much attention. I went there to see somebody I used to know."

"Oh." Draya let that word hang as she glanced at Venus.

"So you don't know this person anymore?" Venus asked, obviously homing in on Draya's want-to-know-what's-going-on vibe.

Picking up her glass, Jackie stared down at it for a few seconds before taking another gulp. She set the glass down hard on the table and sighed. "Nah, I thought I knew her real well, but then one day she just said she wasn't happy. The life we'd built here wasn't what she wanted anymore. She still sings like an angel, though. I watched both her sets that night at the club in DC; then I left, 'cause I didn't want to seem like some creepy ex stalking her."

"But you *were* kind of a creepy ex stalking her," Draya said with a grin.

Venus nudged Jackie, who really seemed sad after that admission. "Yeah, just a little bit."

Jackie chuckled. "You right, you right. But I had to see her. You know what I mean? I had to see for myself if she was happier without me." Another look of sadness crossed Jackie's face, but then her lips tilted in a slight smile. "But it's cool. I always want her to be happy."

Even if that woman's being happy broke Jackie's heart. Draya didn't say those words, but she understood. She'd never felt a love like that before and truthfully didn't plan to. She'd seen how love could hurt and leave the women who'd given in to it bitter, her mother and grandmother being prime examples. Still, she didn't begrudge anyone for wanting to experience it.

"Fuck this!" Jackie finished her drink and stood. "We're supposed to be celebrating tonight. Get up and let's hit the dance floor."

Draya didn't need to be told twice. She finished her martini and stood too. Running a hand down the front of the burnt-orange sweater dress she wore, she glanced over at Venus. "You comin', or are you gonna continue babysitting that drink?"

Venus had a mojito that she'd barely touched and a big-ass glass of water like she was trying to keep from getting drunk. Only she would've had to actually drink the alcoholic beverage for that to happen. She seemed a little off tonight, too, but Draya was tired of feeling down. And she didn't want either of them feeling down anymore either.

"C'mon, girl. Get up!" she said and reached for Venus's arm, pulling her until she started to slide along the seat and finally stood.

"I want to be home by eleven," Venus said just as the song changed to a bumpin' hip-hop beat.

"Yes, Mother," Draya said, imitating a creaky old voice. She didn't wait for Venus's response but instead lifted her hands and started dance-walking to the center of the club.

Everybody got on the floor as the new DJ yelled into the mic about getting the party started. Draya was more than ready for that. Jackie and Venus were right beside her, dancing until they were still laughing and swaying three songs later. That's when the three guys approached them. Draya immediately went to the tall one, who was built like a linebacker and had a dimple in his left cheek. His hands were on her hips ten seconds after she told him her name, and the temperature on the dance floor grew ten degrees hotter.

From the corner of her eye, she could see that Venus had been persuaded to dance with one of the other guys, even though she wasn't even as close up on him as Draya was. Well, Venus had turned around, and dude had come up on her ass like he was surely planning to hit it from behind before the song was over. Jackie, on the other hand, must've let guy number three down gently, but she didn't leave the dance floor. She found herself a cute girl with goddess braids that almost touched the floor and was currently bumping and grinding until those braids were moving in the wind.

"Heeeeyyyy!" Draya yelled, enjoying the music and the company.

Dancing always made her feel free, and when she couldn't make it out to a club, she had no problem blasting the music and dancing along in her condo. In addition to feeling free, moving her body to the rhythm cleared her mind like nothing else could. All those worries that she'd valiantly tried to push aside throughout the workday vanished until all she could focus on was the bass in the music and the way she was now tossing her ass back at the guy—Gerald, she thought his name was. His dick was rock-hard, poking into her as he matched her dance moves. She loved a guy who could keep up with her on the dance floor. His rhythm was flawless and, her most important point, his breath was minty fresh. But she didn't intend to do anything more than dance with him.

A persistent tapping on her shoulder pulled Draya from the bliss she was riding high on, and she frowned before turning to see Jackie at her side.

"We got company." Jackie jerked her head toward the door, and Draya followed her movement.

"Shit!"

Detective Jennings stood close to the door, two other guys at his sides.

"That your man?" Gerald asked from behind her. He couldn't have been serious about the question because he hadn't backed up off her ass.

"No," she replied and stepped away from him. "But I'm done dancing."

Gerald looked like he was about to say something else, but he wisely shook his head and walked away, leaving Jackie and Draya to continue staring at the detective.

"What's he doing here?" Jackie asked.

"It's a free country," Draya said. "And it seems like he's here with his boys. Those two definitely aren't cops."

"How do you know?"

"Because I just know," Draya said. "Where's Venus?" She'd been so lost in her dancing cleanse, she'd stopped watching what Venus and Jackie were doing. Now they both scanned the room for her.

"I don't see her," Jackie said.

"Neither do I." A tingle of dread wiggled down Draya's spine at the admission.

"Let's find her and get out of here. I've answered all the questions I plan to answer of his, and I don't really feel like coming face-to-face with the guy again." Jackie was already on the move, and Draya fell into step behind her.

She didn't think they should pick up and leave just because Detective Jennings had also decided to hang out at this club tonight, but she did want to find Venus, just to make sure she was all right.

Ten minutes later, they realized Venus was more than all right. Chino's had a pool room in the back, and that's where Venus had obviously migrated to.

"She must've been tired of dancing," Draya said as they watched Venus sitting on a pool table, her legs wrapped around the waist of some dude who was kissing on her neck.

"But not tired of doing whatever it is she's doing now," Jackie replied.

They continued watching while Venus tilted her head back and the dude's hand cupped her breast.

"This is probably inappropriate," Jackie whispered.

"What? Her gettin' busy on a pool table or us watching her get busy on a pool table?" Draya didn't think either was out-of-bounds, considering she wasn't the one who started any of this.

"Stop it." Jackie nudged her. "Let's go get her."

Again, Draya followed her, even though she wasn't totally in agreement with stopping anything. Venus was a grown woman, and it was nice to see her letting loose for a change. Jackie, on the other hand, reached for the arm Venus had around dude's head, holding his face to her neck, and pulled on it.

"Hey, c'mon, we gotta go," Jackie told her.

Venus's eyes popped open, and she pushed dude away from her so fast and hard, he stumbled back, bumping into Jackie and almost knocking her down.

"Whoa there, buddy," Jackie said when she caught him and then tried to step away.

But dude was apparently not having the interruption. "What? Get the fuck off me!" he yelled at Jackie, who wasn't about to let his tone or foul language go.

"She's leaving, so you can go too," Jackie told him, but he wasn't trying to hear anything she said.

He was obviously twisted, as evidenced by the way he swayed on his feet before moving toward Venus again with his arms out. "C'mon, baby, let me take you out of here."

Venus had already jumped down off the pool table and was straightening her clothes when she easily dodged his grasp. "No. Uh, she's right—I'm about to go."

"Yeah. You 'bout to go home with me." His words slurred as he reached for her. This time he grabbed her arm, pulling her toward him.

And that's when all hell broke loose.

Draya stepped close enough to grab Venus's other arm and pull her away from dude just as Jackie pushed him square in his chest and yelled, "Back off!"

Dude stumbled back a couple of steps, looking at Jackie with his head tilted. They'd drawn the attention of the other dozen or so people in the pool room, and Draya knew that wasn't going to be good.

"So you really tryin' to be that guy, huh?" dude asked Jackie. "You think 'cause you in here pullin' chicks tonight like the rest of us with dicks, you tough enough to come at me?"

"Jackie, let's just go," Venus said.

Draya knew that wasn't going to happen, but she tried as well, moving past Draya to touch Jackie's shoulder. "She's right. Let's just leave."

"I'm cool if he's cool with her leavin'," Jackie said. "No means no, dumbass!"

Dude lunged at her at that moment, but he was stupid drunk, and all Jackie had to do was step to the side and he fell flat on the floor. Somebody must've called his boys from the front of the club, because the next thing Draya knew, there was a rush of movement, twenty to thirty people coming toward them, yelling over the music.

"Shit!" Draya winced.

"We gotta get out of here," Venus said. "This is about to get bad."

Draya knew Venus had no idea how real her words were, not until they heard a deep voice yelling, "Break it up! Move back! Police!"

Dude was getting up off the floor, and as soon as he did, he took a swipe at Jackie but missed again. This time Jackie wasn't just dodging the blow—she punched him once, and blood quickly spewed from his nose. He yelled in a high-pitched voice and grabbed his face. "Arrest this bitch! Assault! Assault!" he continued screaming like he was really the injured party here.

Well, Jackie had probably broken his nose, so that could technically be true. She heard Detective Jennings's voice again and grabbed Jackie's arm. "Let's go!" she shouted over the growing noise and turned to leave the room.

Venus was in front, pushing through the crowd, trying to lead them out of the melee. They made a quick stop at the booth for their coats before joining a crowd of people rushing toward the front door. They made it outside, the brisk night air slapping against their faces. Draya held her coat up under her arms and tried to run as best she could in the five-inch-heel snakeskin boots she wore. Jackie and Venus were in front of her, but not that far, because the sidewalk was still crowded with people rushing to get away as well.

"Stop!"

Draya knew who that was without turning around, but she was determined to keep going. If the detective wanted her, he was going to have to catch her. But Venus stopped and turned around, so Draya crashed into her and would've tumbled to the ground if Jackie hadn't appeared on her other side to keep her upright.

"Malik?" Venus whispered while Draya still fumbled for leverage, holding tight to Venus's shoulder on one side and Jackie's arm on the other.

"What's he doing here?" Venus asked them, but Draya was too irritated and out of breath to respond.

Jackie only frowned.

Detective Jennings caught up to them, the intense glare in his dark eyes almost lethal. "What the hell happened back there?"

Jackie sighed. She'd said she wasn't in the mood to answer any more of his questions, but she was the first to speak. "We were ready to leave, so we went to get Venus, but Drunk and Stupid back there didn't want to let her leave. He came at me, and I defended myself."

Just like she'd defended herself with Rufus. Being a dumbass must run through men like testosterone.

Detective Jennings looked like he believed Jackie. He was also looking at Venus like he was torn between wanting to kiss her or shake some sense into her. "Did he touch you?" His question was directed to Venus, who was pushing her arms into her leather jacket.

She cleared her throat before responding. "Not after I moved away from him."

"So you were letting him touch you? Do you know this guy?" He looked equal parts confused and pissed the fuck off.

Draya didn't like how this was going. "Look, we were all having a good time; he just got a little carried away. But it's over now, so we'll be leaving. Good night, Detective Jennings."

"What are you even doing here?" Venus asked him. "You're a Howard County cop."

"Doesn't mean I can't party in Baltimore, Venus," he told her. "And obviously the three of you can't either, without getting into trouble."

Jackie opened her mouth to say something, but Venus spoke again.

"So you're here for pleasure, not business? You're not following us around, trying to find out what we're doing or how it could be connected to your murder case?" Venus asked him.

Oh, hell no, they weren't going there. Not out here in these frigid temps with her feet and thighs screaming after the run and almost fall. "Let's just go, Venus," she told her while Jackie nodded her agreement.

Detective Jennings finally tore his gaze away from Venus to stare at Jackie and then Draya. "Yeah, you . . . I mean, all of you should just go. Now."

When Venus looked like she was going to say something else, Draya grabbed her arm and pulled her down the street toward her parked car.

"I don't know what happened between the two of you in the past," Draya said when they made it to the car and Venus unlocked the doors so they could get in. "But that shit ain't over. I don't care what you say."

Chapter 17

Jackie

It was past time for her to get the hell out of this office. She'd been here since seven this morning—even after being out late last night with Venus and Draya—and now it was almost seven in the evening. There'd been so many things for her to scratch off her to-do list today, and she'd been determined to do them all. Giving Ellen one more reason to bounce her nuisance ass into her office wasn't something Jackie wanted to do. Instead, she was making sure to stay on top of every email and phone-call complaint received in her department for the past few days. Even the minor ones like, "The wheel on my chair is sticking—can someone from facilities bring me a new one?" Jackie made sure to put in the order for a new chair immediately and then personally took it up to the seventh floor and pushed it into the office of the marketing exec who had requested it.

She did a personal sweep of each floor, stopping by each office to make sure all was functioning well. Her staff was instructed to answer every call or email immediately, and they knew that anything they couldn't handle should come directly to her. There were no unread messages in her in-box, and only a few with tasks still outstanding because she was waiting for deliveries or further instruction from the requester.

She hadn't taken an official lunch, and not just because Venus had told them she was going on a lunch date but also because she didn't want Ellen to see her in the café. Since it seemed that any second she wasn't working, Ellen had a personal problem with it, she planned to solve that by steering clear of the spiteful witch.

It was while she was running around doing all those things that a thought started eating its way into her head. Was she thinking of Ellen as her mother? Comparing Ellen to Maiselle in the way that they both seemed to be disappointed in her for reasons that baffled her and they both ultimately wanted her to become something she couldn't? *Hell naw!* That would be giving Ellen way too much status in her life, and she'd be damned if she gave that woman anything.

Shit, she was tired. Last night had been a trip. After leaving the club, they'd gone back to Venus's place, sitting in her living room, trying to get a grip on everything that had happened.

"So not only do you pull guns on assholes, you apparently break their noses too. Girl, you out here actin' like Creed and shit," Draya had said and then chuckled as she sat in her favorite chair.

"Nah, that's not my normal," Jackie had replied easily and truthfully. "I'm just always prepared to defend myself and the people I care about. Besides, dude was drunk and stupid."

"I'm sorry," Venus said. "I shouldn't have been with him."

It'd been the third time she'd apologized since they'd left the club.

"I really wish you'd stop apologizing for something he did," Jackie had told her.

Venus had continued to shake her head. "No. If I hadn't given him the impression he could do it—"

"Stop!" Draya had interrupted. "If you're about to say you gave him the impression that he could touch and feel on you whenever he wanted, I need you to just stop."

"No. That's not what I was about to say, because of course he can't touch me unless I give him permission." Venus had sounded annoyed, but Jackie was almost positive it was more with herself than with either of them. "I shouldn't have put myself in that position. I never do that. Not in public and certainly not with guys I don't know."

"You're an adult—you can do what you want when you want," Draya had told her. "He should've backed up when you said you were done. Period."

"She's right," Jackie had said. "And he shouldn't have come for me just for reminding him of the rules." She'd really wished he hadn't; then she wouldn't have had to hit him, but like she'd told Draya, she had no problem defending herself or anybody else she cared about.

For the duration of the time they'd sat in her living room, Venus had seemed distant and agitated. And when Draya had brought up Detective Jennings and how irritated he'd seemed when he learned the guy was touching Venus, there'd been no discussion, because Venus had gone into the kitchen to get a bottle of water. When she came back, she'd talked about the gift exchange and how many more gifts she needed to buy.

Jackie hadn't spoken to her or Draya today, so she didn't know what was going on with them right now. Sitting back in her chair, she moved so it swayed slowly from side to side, taking a second just to breathe. And also to think about what she was eating for dinner, 'cause she was hungry as fuck. Maybe she'd call in an order to Friday's and pick it up before heading home. No, Chipotle would be better. She hadn't had a steak burrito bowl with fajita mix, mild salsa, sour cream, cheese, and two vinaigrette salad dressings in a long-ass time. Yeah, that's what she was getting, and she could place her order online so it'd be ready when she got there; then her trip home could be expedited.

Reaching into her pocket, she grabbed her phone and pulled up the Chipotle website. Just as she was about to type in her order, a text notification appeared—Karlie.

The grin that immediately spread across her face was instinctual, not because she liked Karlie or had expected to hear from her. But more so because of the feeling that sparked the moment she saw her name. It was like that first flicker of a flame but in the center of her chest. Shaking her head because she had no clue what that even meant, she swiped a finger over the notification so she could see the full message.

Thinking of you.

The words were accompanied by a picture of two drinks.

Her tongue slid over her lips as she stared at both, thinking she could sure use one after the day she'd had.

Should I respond?

Yeah, she'd been replying to those good-morning texts, but that was no biggie. Every day she said good morning to the homeless guy who made his bed outside the building. She even said it to Rufus's assistant, Lynette, who she knew had a problem with anyone in the LGBTQ community. It was the polite thing to do, and if there was nothing else she'd done right as Clive and Maiselle's child, she'd mastered the art of good manners.

But she had ghosted Karlie for about a month. That was rude and probably why she was poised to respond at this moment.

I could use a drink right about now.

It was true, but it wasn't an acceptance to any invitation. *Was Karlie inviting me to have a drink?* Nah, she'd just been saying something, kinda like all her texts were just saying something. She never asked for anything, like a date or even a phone call. She just sent the text and then smiled when Jackie responded. It was wild and sorta cool at the same time.

Rough day?

Jackie nodded her head at that response.

That's an understatement. But I'm 'bout to get outta here and go home to get some rest.

Now, that sounded like she was an eighty-year-old woman, and she grinned 'cause it was too late—she'd already hit "Send."

Rest is good. You need to take care of yourself. Or perhaps have someone at home to take care of you.

Her hands were shaking now as she held the phone and read the words. This definitely felt like Karlie was inviting her to something or proposing something. Question was, did she want to accept?

A loud thump sounded outside her door, and Jackie almost jumped out of her skin. Her office was on the ground floor of the building, and mostly everybody there normally checked out promptly at five. Security guards at the front desk locked the doors from the outside at six and required identification and a call to the person the visitor was attempting to see after hours. So who the hell was out in the hallway?

Tightening her grip on the phone, she sat perfectly still, wondering if there'd either be another sound or the visitor would just come into the office like a normal person would. Neither happened, and that freaked her out a little more. Willing herself to get it together, she pushed the phone into her pocket and stood from her chair. It was probably nothing. Perhaps one of the cleaning staff had dropped something. They were permitted into the buildings after hours to go through the offices on every floor to do their nightly cleaning—although there had been more than a few complaints about real cleaning not being done. Anyway, thinking about the cleaning crew relaxed her a little, until there was another thumping and the sound of somebody cursing.

A split-second thought to the possibility that Venus and Draya would insist she was overreacting came to mind, but she pushed it away. It had already been established that she was the impulsive one of their threesome. Moving stealthily now, Jackie inched her way to the door, grabbing the full-size umbrella she'd used when it had been pouring down rain this morning. Somebody was definitely outside her door, and for whatever reason, they weren't trying to come in. It seemed they only wanted to sneak around. Well, she had something for their ass. It wasn't the invitation to stare down the barrel of her licensed and registered Glock because the cops still had it, but the way she was holding the umbrella as if she were the star hitter for the Baltimore Orioles, the intruder would still regret sneaking up on her.

Rolling her neck on her shoulders, she reached out to touch the doorknob and yanked the door open. The intruder tumbled in as if they'd been leaning right up against the door, and Jackie immediately put her hand to the umbrella again, prepared to swing. Not moving nearly fast enough, she realized the umbrella was still raised above her head when a cool mist splashed over her face, stinging like the devil.

"Shit! Fuck! Dammit!" She cursed, closed her eyes tight, dropped the umbrella, and stumbled back. "What the entire hell?"

"Security! Security! There's an intruder in the building!"

She heard the voice yelling but couldn't see where it was coming from because her eyeballs felt like they were swelling and about to pop out of her head. Her cheeks and nose burned, and she feared the flesh would peel right off her face. "Ah, dammit! This shit burns like hell!"

There didn't seem to be enough cuss words in the universe, and they certainly weren't falling from her lips fast enough. Or rather, not in any way that would kill this fire-ass pain. She backed into the wall, bringing her hands up to cup her face. Something fell, and she banged her leg against a file cabinet.

"Security! I want you to call the police. Right now!"

The person was still yelling in a shrill voice that Jackie knew all too well.

"Bitch!" she grumbled and yanked her hands away from her face. Opening her eyes was a special type of torture that she would yell about later. For now, she needed to see Ellen's shriveled-up face. "What the hell are you doing?"

Three security guards came busting through the door at that moment. Robyn, the only woman in the group, came farther into the office to stand near Jackie.

"You okay? What happened?" she asked, touching Jackie's arm to get her attention.

"No, I'm not okay. This chick was sneaking around outside my office, and when I opened the door, she sprayed me with mace." Which felt like it may've been spiked with something like acid, the way her face burned.

Through blurred vision, she saw Ellen folding her arms across her chest. "How was I supposed to know it was her? It's dark down here. Why're all the lights out? Better yet, it's past time for everyone to be out of the office."

"You're still here, ma'am," Ebay, another guard, replied before clearing his throat. "As are a number of other employees on other floors. The building doesn't totally clear out until around eight."

"Then there should've been some lights on," Ellen huffed.

"What were you doing skulking around outside my door?" There were witnesses here now, so Jackie felt a little braver about confronting the annoying-as-hell HR lady.

Ellen's thin lips curved into a smirk. "Checking on issues you should've handled earlier today."

Translation: trying to set her up again. Jackie wanted to punch her right in her lying-ass mouth.

As if possibly reading her mind, Robyn grabbed her arm and led her toward the door. "Let's get you a wet cloth."

Ebay and the other guard, Tip, smothered smirks and turned away from Ellen, who was still standing in the center of the room.

"I need to speak with you about these outstanding issues, Jacqueline!" Ellen yelled to her.

"Nah, I'm out. It's past time for everyone to be out of the building, remember?" She didn't wait for a response and ignored the prick of irritation at Ellen calling her by her full name, just like her mother sometimes did. Following Robyn down the hall to the restroom made much more sense.

"That was wild," Robyn said as she yanked paper towels from the dispenser and moved to the sink to wet them.

Jackie stood a few feet from her, looking in the mirror. Her eyes were bloodshot, her face red as shit. "This whole year has been wild, dealing with her. I swear I'mma go off on her and God help me, I'mma probably lose my job. I thought she'd stop messin' with me after Rufus's death, but dayum." Shaking her head, she cursed again. Giving somebody this type of control over her wasn't something Jackie was used to doing. Not after all she'd been through in the past few years. But her job was important to her; it was basically all she had at this point.

"Here." Robyn put the cool paper towels over her eyes. "Just relax. You've got witnesses this time."

It was no secret that Ellen was evil walking in heels. Those in the building either knew and accepted it or denied it and kissed her ass. Jackie didn't tend to converse with the ones who did the latter. It was her practice to steer clear of unintelligent folks on all levels.

"This shit just gotta stop. I can't keep looking over my shoulder to see what she's gonna come up with next." *She's gotta go.* Jackie didn't say that part out loud, because it sounded too much like wishing Ellen dead. And like Venus had said a couple of days ago, that's the last conversation that needed to be taking place.

"Girl, everybody's looking over their shoulders around here lately. The cops keep coming back, asking more and more questions."

That comment got Jackie's full attention. "What do you mean? I haven't seen any cops around here."

"Oh, they've been here. Those two detectives from Howard County and some uniformed officers who were here to search Rufus's office the other day," Robyn told her.

Jackie hadn't talked to anybody at the office about the murder, except Venus and Draya, of course. That was part of their "act normal" strategy. But since Robyn had brought it up, she figured it might be safe to ask her more questions. Plus, her eyes were still stinging too much to consider walking away at this moment. "You think they have a suspect? Somebody here at the office?" She kept the towels pressed to her eyes so she couldn't see Robyn's reaction to the question.

"Me and Ebay were talking, and we think they're focusing on the job an awful lot. Ebay has friends down at BCPD, and they've been hearing rumblings about Rufus's business associates too. So I guess they think it's somebody here."

"Really?" She waited a beat. "After what I heard on the news, I was thinking maybe it was a burglar."

"That would make sense too, but I don't know. Rufus was into a lot of foul shit. I could tell you some stories. But I better get back out there before Ellen sends a search party for me."

Jackie didn't press for more information—she'd heard enough. The police thought Rufus's killer was a business associate. Damn.

Forty-five minutes later, Jackie had thanked Robyn for her help and gathered her things from her office. She walked into her apartment, closed and locked the door behind her, then cursed again. "Forgot my fuckin' Chipotle."

Removing her coat and dropping it on the couch, she headed straight back to her bedroom. There had to be something left over in her fridge, or a frozen meal, or whatever—she wouldn't starve. But she wouldn't have that steak bowl either. Still frowning, she pulled her phone out of her pocket and looked down at it to see she'd never replied to Karlie's last text, and Karlie hadn't sent her a new one. Sighing heavily, she was about to exit her text messages when one came through from Venus on their group chat.

Don't forget the funeral Saturday at 7.

Groaning because this night was already fucked, Jackie dropped the phone on her bed and headed for the shower. At least she'd be clean and fed if another bombshell dropped tonight.

Chapter 18

Venus

On the second Saturday after his death, Rufus Arnes Jackson Jr. lay in a maroon-colored casket with gold handles and a gold satin interior. If there was one thing Black folk didn't rush, it was a funeral. His body had been dressed in a black suit, white shirt, and gold tie. A picture of him with his father at his college graduation was fastened to the inside top half of the casket. They'd called his father Rudy—at least that's what Venus's father had told her. She hadn't cared to know too much about the Jackson family; knowing and being in constant contact with Rufus had been enough for her.

She walked away from the casket, intending to continue straight around the room to find herself a seat on one of the back rows. The service was being held in the funeral home, which was as big as most of the churches in the city, but not as big as New Visionary. Rufus had come to her church on a few occasions, mostly during the time her father was nearing reelection. She kept her gaze forward, not wishing to see or speak to anyone, but the sound of her name being called stopped her.

What was wrong with her? She knew it was customary for everyone who walked down that center aisle to view the body in the casket, then turn to the right where the family was seated on the first row and pay their condolences. But hell, she'd signed the card Lynette had passed around in their department. She'd also sent a separate card because she knew her father was doing the same. And she'd attended the job's memorial service yesterday. As far as she was concerned, her condolences had been paid in full.

"Venus. It's so good to see you." Deputy State's Attorney Pamela Jackson stood and walked toward her, because Venus hadn't moved an inch.

"Always a pleasure, Pam. Although I certainly wish it were under different circumstances." Those were the correct words, and Venus felt a wave of relief that she'd been able to say them without hesitation.

"Of course." Pam touched Venus's arm and then guided them to the corner about twenty feet away from the casket. "But I did want to speak with you privately."

"Is there something I can do for you or the family? Anything BCC can handle, you know it would be our pleasure." She wasn't sure where this was going.

It wasn't unusual for people to die without having any, or sufficient, insurance coverage. There'd been so many people in her family who fell into that category, she could almost recite her parents' harsh and judgmental comments on why they weren't donating a dime to anybody's funeral fund. Being prepared was another sticking point for them, which was why Venus had the policy offered from BCC as well as another, larger policy of her own.

"No, it's nothing like that." Pam obviously had those same types of folks in her family. She shook her head, but the classy short-cut hairdo she wore wasn't affected. Her black skirt suit wasn't wrinkled, nor was the white blouse she wore beneath the jacket, despite the up-and-down sitting and hugging she was doing to greet each attendee.

Venus wasn't surprised—there was never anything out of place where Pam was concerned. She was the epitome of a successful Black woman, from the way she dressed and spoke to the way she walked. On the day of her husband's funeral, Pam looked to be the pillar of strength, standing there with her shoulders squared and makeup intact because she'd probably threatened the tears that wanted to fall.

"I wanted to thank you for never giving in to Rufus."

Now, that wasn't a turn Venus saw coming. She cleared her throat. "I'm sure there's no thanks necessary." That seemed to be a safe-enough response, considering she wasn't totally sure what Pam was talking about.

The quick lift of Pam's lips into what appeared to be a conspiratorial smile caused Venus's stomach to drop.

"I knew my husband better than anyone in this room." Pam looked around. "Dare I say, anyone in this world. That's why our marriage worked. I never lied to myself about what our union was based on."

And Venus didn't give a damn what that was. All she wanted at this moment was to get the hell away from this woman, her dead husband, and the rest of the people who'd started to fill this room.

"Rufus was happy to be married to you." Lies. If he were happy, he wouldn't have been trying to fuck everything with tits and an ass.

Pam continued with that polite smile. "Rufus needed me as much as I needed him. We both benefited from the leverage of his position and mine. It was a business deal, nothing more. But I think you already knew that."

Venus didn't know anything. That was the safe answer.

"I'm still sorry for your loss," she said quietly.

"Thank you." Pam lifted a hand, smoothing it over the side of her hair, again not disturbing the style at all, just another natural movement while her mind calculated something.

Now Venus wondered what the hell was really going on here. Pam wasn't acting like a grieving widow, because she wasn't one. Fine, whatever their marriage was, it was none of Venus's business. So why did Pam have her hemmed up in this corner like they were planning a world war?

"I want you to tell me who his latest side chick was."

Damn, she hadn't expected that either. Taking a deep breath, Venus hoped she was masking her surprise well enough. "Excuse me?"

"You heard me. Who was he messing with in the office? And don't bother with denial; I know there was someone new, and I know she had to work there, because his late nights at the office had increased. Normally he took his tricks to a hotel, but with this one, he preferred the office. I've paid thousands of dollars to the private investigator to give me that information." Pam arched a brow as she waited for Venus to respond.

"As you've already stated, I wasn't the one sleeping with your husband. And I don't know who was. I tended to pay more attention to my job than who Rufus's flavor of the month was."

If Pam wasn't pulling any punches, then Venus didn't need to either.

"Listen, I'm not trying to do the cops' job. They're not telling me much about their investigation. I'd just like to talk to her before they get to her."

They were probably still considering Pam as a suspect—the spouse was always the first suspect.

Pam continued. "Surely there's a gossip mill at the office. There's always someone running their mouth about everything that's going on. We have it at the SAO, and I doubt your office is any different."

"When you keep busy with your own work and your own personal life, you don't hear as much." That's a philosophy Venus really did try to live by, but that didn't mean juicy tidbits of gossip never made their way to her.

"I want her name, Venus."

"Why? Are you planning some kind of meetup for all his past flings? Wouldn't it be better to just put the way he treated your marriage behind you?"

"No," she said simply, and Venus didn't know which one of her questions that response was to. "What I want is to know who was pissed off at him enough to finally have his ass killed. My thought is it must have been over something serious. Perhaps she's pregnant or, Lord forbid, she actually fancied herself in love with him and grew angry when he wouldn't give her what she wanted."

"Because he was never leaving you." Venus couldn't mask the incredulous tone. Pam was even colder than she'd heard.

She shook her head slowly. "No. He was never leaving me. And I was never leaving him. Except now he's dead, so that's that. Now tell me her name."

"I don't know it."

"Would you know it if I told you I could make sure your little project with Terrell Hopkins gets buried in permits and tax issues?"

Taking that as if Pam had physically attacked her, Venus stepped back and took a steadying breath this time. "Are you threatening me?"

"Not at all," Pam replied and touched the lapel of Venus's navy-blue suit jacket. "I'm asking you a question and requiring you to answer, if you want to continue with the job that I presume will ease you into Rufus's position."

"Hey, Pam. The mayor's here." Leslie began talking as soon as she approached, looking over to Venus as if she were an afterthought. "Oh, hello, Venus. Is your father here with you tonight? I need to speak with him."

"He'll be here soon, and I'll let him know you're looking for him." She glanced at Pam once more. "Again, I'm very sorry for your loss. I'll keep you and your family in my prayers during this time of grieving." *And I'm never telling you a damn thing, you silly, conniving wench.*

Those last words rolled through her mind as she hastily walked to the back of the room, slamming herself down onto the first empty pew and releasing a heavy breath.

"Oh no, girl, you look like death," Draya said, pushing Venus to the side as she slid onto the pew beside her.

"We're at a funeral. How else am I supposed to look?"

"Not like you're the one who should be in the casket." Draya was always ready with a snapback. She was also wearing a red dress that dipped low in the front and hugged her hips. Today's hair was smoothed into a side bun with a trio of red roses over her left ear. She looked like a modern-day Billie Holiday.

"And you shouldn't look like the dead guy's former mistress," she huffed. "Or his wife might figure out who you are."

Draya didn't speak immediately, and Venus wondered if she was offended or worried.

"You've been talking to Pam about me?"

Okay, she was worried. And she obviously didn't trust Venus, but then, Venus already knew that. She'd heard it in Draya's tone the other night at the club when she'd made her comment about Venus and Malik not being over. Which was precisely why when Draya brought up Malik again later that night, Venus had changed the subject.

"No. Pam asked me who Rufus's flavor of the month was, and I told her I didn't know."

Settling back on the pew, Draya set her purse between them and stared toward where Pam and Leslie stood at the front of the room.

"There's probably a long list. She should be careful about wanting to obtain that information."

Venus recalled Draya telling them she'd seen Leslie leaving Rufus's office. Pam was huddled close with her boss like they were thick as thieves. If only she knew.

"Yeah, be careful of the company you keep," she whispered.

"I don't think that's the meaning of that phrase. We should probably be singing 'Back Stabbers' by The O'Jays."

The lyrics to that song instantly popped into Venus's mind, and she started to hum the tune. A few seconds later, Draya joined in, until they were both humming and rocking to the rhythm in their heads when Jackie joined them.

"Okay, rocking to music that's not playing is the equivalent of talking to yourself." Jackie sat down next to Draya, giving them a questioning glare.

Venus immediately stopped, but Draya kept right on rocking as if she hadn't heard Jackie's words. Or she'd probably just ignored them.

"Why y'all sitting all the way back here? We can't see anything." Jackie shrugged out of her coat and placed it over the back of the pew.

Draya had carried her coat on her arm and had laid it on the pew. Jackie picked it up now and placed it over the back beside hers.

"I've seen all I need to see," Venus said, turning her attention to the other side of the room, where more people were coming in. They either went straight to a seat or made their way down that center aisle so they could view the body.

"What happened?" Jackie's tone was full of dread.

Venus didn't blame her. In the past week, it had seemed to be one thing after another. Earlier today, Jackie had connected them on a three-way call to share the mace incident with Ellen. All that coupled with her own parents basically ignoring her since that night she'd visited her father, and things weren't going as wonderfully as they could.

Draya finally stopped moving to the nonexistent beat. "Pam asked her who Rufus's latest mistress was."

"Oh snap!" Jackie was loud and she knew it, because she slapped a hand over her mouth, wide eyes still staring at Venus. "Did you tell her?" she asked in a much softer tone after easing her hand away from her mouth.

"What? Do neither of you trust me? Of course I didn't tell her. In fact, I basically called her bananas for wanting to know that information."

"Bananas with a capital *B*," Draya said.

Jackie shook her head. "It must be something in the water, 'cause I thought Ellen held that title for herself. Anyway, nobody said anything about not trusting you. Just trying to make sure we're all on the same page, that we all know the same stuff. You know, so we can keep our stories straight."

It occurred to Venus, and not for the first time, that they didn't all know the same things. As she'd pondered how annoyed she'd been with Draya the other night for acting like Venus hadn't been truthful with her about where things stood with her and Malik, she'd also realized she hadn't told them about the cover-up she'd done for Rufus. To be honest, she didn't know if that even mattered now. If Jackie had given her alibi statement that included them, then didn't that mean none of them was a suspect anymore? They hadn't heard from Malik or any other detectives investigating Rufus's murder.

"If you don't lower your voice, everyone in this room is gonna know we have a story to keep straight in the first place." Draya looked at her like an annoyed mother who was about to slap her even more annoying child.

Jackie sucked her teeth. "Nobody's close enough to hear us."

"Hello, ladies."

Speak of the sexy-ass devil.

They each turned to see Malik stepping closer to their pew. Draya cursed under her breath, and Jackie frowned. Venus fought the weird stirring she recalled feeling the other night at the club when she'd seen Malik. It was the exact same feeling she'd experienced when he walked into the spa to announce he wanted to question them. And it was the feeling she desperately wanted to ignore because, as she'd told Draya and Jackie before, things between her and Malik had been over and done with a long time ago.

"Hello, Detective," Draya finally replied. "You just keep popping up in places where we are, don't you?"

Malik kept his stern look. "This is my partner, Detective Sharae Gibson." He looked directly at Venus as he made the introduction.

She swallowed and sat up straighter. "Good evening." A cordial and stoic response. Never mind that Malik's glare was making her uncomfortable.

"Ms. McGee, I intend to call your attorney on Monday to schedule a time for you to come to the station to chat with us. We just have a few points we want to clear up about your interactions with Mr. Jackson." Sharae Gibson got straight to the point. She was a pretty woman with mocha-hued skin and curly black hair styled in a short bob and was dressed in a black pantsuit beneath her black leather jacket. She looked badass and sounded like she'd just as soon slap the cuffs on Venus than have an official interview.

An official interview. The words repeated in her mind, and she fought the waves of panic that threatened to surface.

"Then I'm sure my attorney will let me know the date and time." Her words sounded much more aloof and unconcerned than she felt. Hadn't she just been thinking this bullshit was over? Deep down, she'd known it wasn't.

Jackie cleared her throat loudly. "Um, the music's starting. That's code for *sit yo' ass down; this thing is about to get started.*"

Draya chuckled while Malik and Sharae both looked at Jackie with irritation. Venus looked away from all of them and stared forward just in time to see her father making his way to Pam. And he wasn't alone. Carol Benning was at his side.

Chapter 19

Draya

"I thought you said they were about to get started," Draya complained.

"Well, that guy started playing music. How was I supposed to know it was just for the family hour? Anyway, come on, let's get up here and see this body."

"Yeah, so we can get back to our seats," Venus said.

"We should've never left our seats. I don't need to see Rufus's dead body again."

They were walking down that center aisle side by side, and Venus elbowed her seconds after she'd spoken. She didn't take the words back because they were true. She. Did. Not. Want. To. See. Rufus's. Dead. Body. Again.

And yet here she was, stepping up to the casket like it was a prominent display at the National Museum of African American History and Culture. Shifting her weight from one foot to the other, she tried to look away, because Rufus wasn't anybody's role model, nor had he made any substantial contribution to the Black culture in her book. He was a jealous, lying, cheating bastard, and she would hate him until she took her last breath.

"Why's this casket all the way open?" Jackie asked, bringing Draya's gaze to the casket, not necessarily the man lying in it. "Who does that?"

"Who cares?" Draya snapped. "Can we just get this over with?"

"They have to pay for this," Venus said. "The family, I mean. Funeral homes charge to have the full casket open like this."

"With his pompous ass, he probably had it all written down how he wanted to be laid out. With his shoes shined and on display." Disgust was clear in her tone, but at least she hadn't yelled for all the room to hear.

"Those cuff links are boss," Venus noted.

"Right," Jackie agreed with a nod. She ran her fingers over the gold satin tucked along the corner of the casket. "He was a sharp dude, no doubt. Homophobic asshole."

"Y'all are ratchet as hell, critiquing this man in his casket. It's morbid too." Draya couldn't wait to get back to her seat. She'd never liked funerals.

Ever since her sister Ayanna had sworn she'd seen Great-grandma Jane's hand move while she was lying in her casket. Ayanna had taken off running and screaming throughout the church sanctuary like Freddy Krueger and Jason were chasing her ass. Draya hadn't seen the movement, but just the fear in her sister's voice was enough for her not to ever want to stand close to a casket again. Whenever she had no choice but to attend a funeral, she did so from the very back of the room.

"This suit looks Italian." Jackie eased a hand forward and touched the lapel of the black suit Rufus wore.

"You don't know a thing about Italian suits. Stop touching him!" she hush-yelled and reached out to slap Jackie's hand away.

"Ouch!" Jackie yanked her hand back and glared at Draya.

But as Draya pulled her arm back, the clasp to her bracelet must've come loose, because the thin gold charm bracelet opened, and two of the charms dropped into the casket.

"Shit!"

"Dayyyum, your charms fell on dead Rufus." Jackie clapped a hand over her mouth when Draya glared at her.

"What are you two doing? You can't put stuff in the casket. Funeral homes do not like that shit. Get it! Get it out now!"

Venus didn't have to say that in her church-mother, I'm-chastising-the-hell-out-of-you voice, but she did. Draya rolled her eyes and grabbed the rest of the bracelet before any more of the charms could fall off. Then she sucked in a breath and stuck her hand into the casket to grab the others. One was easy to find, the lucky horseshoe—it had dropped onto the edge of the gold tie Rufus wore. But the other one, dammit, she didn't see it.

"It's right there! Right. There!" Jackie was jumping up and down like she had to pee, which, by the way, Draya had to do now as well.

Gritting her teeth, she followed Jackie's pointing and almost moaned when she saw the charm resting on the zipper of Rufus's pants.

The last thing she wanted was to touch this man's dick again, especially now that there was absolutely no chance of it getting hard.

"Hurry up," Venus urged. "People are lining up behind us."

Of course they were, because all these damn people were morbid and creepy as hell. Well, she might as well count herself as one of them now, since she had to reach out and touch a dead man's dick. Trying to move as quickly as possible, Draya reached for the starfish charm. She had it between her fingers and was about to breathe a sigh of relief when her wrist got stuck.

"What the hell?"

"Who still wears a bunch of gold bracelets? Wasn't that a nineties thing?" Jackie asked.

Draya wanted to strangle her, but no, she really wanted to scream as she tried to pull away, but the clasp of another bracelet was definitely stuck on the tiny exposed part of the zipper on Rufus's pants.

"Don't you say it, Venus!" Draya hush-yelled the moment she saw Venus's perfectly arched brows raise and her mouth open to discipline her again. "Fuck it." Draya leaned into the casket this time, because it was the only way she could see the clasp to work it loose.

"Oh my heavens, what are you doing?" Venus asked.

Jackie giggled. "Tryin' to give him head one last time."

The clasp came loose at that second, and Draya backed away from the casket, giving them both a death glare.

"I'm going back to my seat now," she said and turned, only to find multiple sets of eyes on her.

Rufus's wife; Leslie, his ex-lover; and the two detectives were among the group watching her like she'd just performed a sexual act in front of a room full of people. Which, according to Jackie, she kinda had.

Lifting her chin, Draya stared straight ahead and walked as if she were taking a stroll down the Inner Harbor. This wasn't the first time people had stared at her, judging her in their minds, condemning her even though they didn't know a damn thing about her. And she was certain it wasn't going to be the last. They could go straight to hell for all she cared. None of them did a damn thing for her, and they weren't bold enough to come at her with any of their foolish thoughts either. That made them nothing to her, absolutely fuckin' nothing, and she showed it by dismissing them and going to sit on the pew in the back. Acting totally unbothered, she pulled out her cell phone.

Seconds later, Venus and Jackie came sliding onto the pew beside her.

"Girl, they're all staring at us now," Jackie said.

Venus fixed her braids over her shoulder and sat back. "They were staring at us before. I don't know why, but they were, and it's all starting to be way too annoying."

"What is? Being stared at or having your daddy walking toward us with his sidechick?" Draya asked dryly as she dropped her phone back into her purse. She was so tired of these people pretending to be something they weren't and simultaneously treating her like she wasn't shit.

"She's not his . . . Hi, Daddy!" Venus hopped up out of her seat like a jack-in-the-box and hugged her fine-ass father while the woman beside him gave a fake smile.

"Hey, Venus. I thought we'd see you here. Why aren't you sitting with the other employees from BCC toward the front?" Don asked her.

"I'm sitting with my coworkers," Venus answered and looked back at Jackie and Draya.

Jackie waved and smiled.

"Hi," Draya said, directing her statement to Don only.

"Hello, ladies. You should all be sitting up front with the company. Not back here like you don't belong," he said.

Well, wasn't that nice of the city councilman, trying to include all his constituents.

"We're okay back here, sir. Why don't you join us?" To emphasize her point, Draya slid away from Jackie to make space for Venus's sexy-as-hell father.

"No, thank you, we're offering remarks, so we have to sit up front," the woman who was standing beside him but was not his wife told them.

"Hey, Aunt Carol, I didn't mean to ignore you," Venus said and then hugged the woman standing beside her father. "These are my coworkers Jackie and Draya. Y'all, this is Councilwoman Carol Benning."

The way Venus said the woman's name and looked pointedly at Draya was almost comical. Probably not as much as Draya with her face in dead Rufus's crotch a few minutes ago, but that was another story.

"It's nice to meet you." Aunt Carol had that politician's tone and the smile down, but Draya wasn't fooled. There was something else there, and she said so the moment Aunt Carol and Fine Don walked away. "Is she a blood aunt?"

Venus narrowed her gaze at her. "No. She's actually my godmother. And stop it before you even ask. My father did not have an affair with her."

Draya smirked. If Venus was so quick to defend that shit, then it most likely had happened. Her perfect ass just wasn't trying to hear it. But that was cool. Draya was hip to the game all these people played. Just because they had money and titles, they thought their shit didn't stink. But all the while, the same things they frowned at her for doing, without feeling an ounce of guilt, they were doing in the dark. Lying to themselves and the world.

The funeral did finally start with a preacher leading in prayer. Somebody read a scripture, a woman sang "Amazing Grace," Jackie asked for gum, and Venus dug into her purse to find her a piece. Draya tried not to fall asleep. This funeral hadn't started until almost eight in the evening, and she'd already had a long-ass day of Christmas shopping and gift wrapping. She wanted to go home, grab a hot bath, and climb into her bed.

All those thoughts disappeared from her mind as she looked to her left and saw the man staring at her. She knew him from the picture on his website, and dammit, she knew what he wanted. And unlike the dealings she tried to keep with the opposite sex, this wasn't going to be good.

He crocked a finger, beckoning her to come to him. She almost turned her head and ignored the hell out of him, but something told her that wasn't going to go over too well either. The last thing she wanted was to make another scene here, especially not just as Leslie was getting up to read Rufus's eulogy.

"I gotta pee," she whispered and stood from her seat. That wasn't a lie—she'd been sitting there, shaking her leg, trying to ignore the nagging sensation for the last twenty minutes. All because she hadn't wanted to get up and draw more attention to herself. Well, now she had no choice.

"You need Pampers," Jackie said.

"And you need Jesus, so pay attention," Draya clapped back and eased out of the pew.

She was two steps into the hallway, about four feet from the ladies' room door, when he grabbed her arm.

"Not so fast, Ms. Carter. I've been trying to get ahold of you."

Huffing out a breath, she turned around and stared into the beady gray eyes of Franklin Gifford, Rufus's personal attorney. "What do you want, Mr. Gifford? I need to use the facilities."

"You need to come with me." He started fast-walking toward the back door, and Draya's heart began beating wildly.

There were people at the front desk, all the way toward the entrance of the funeral home. If she screamed, they'd hear her, but she wasn't going to scream. Instead, she stopped walking and jerked her arm from Franklin's grasp.

"Hold up—I'm not going anywhere with you."

He arched a brow with an annoyed look. "I need to speak to you privately."

She looked around to the mauve-painted walls and the too-large and slightly gaudy plastic floral arrangements on glossed dark-wood tables. "There's nobody here, so talk."

They were about thirty feet from the entrance and too far from the back door for her to make a run for it. Folding her arms over her chest, she stared at him with a whatchu-gonna-do look.

"I'm looking for something that belonged to Rufus, and I believe you have it."

"I don't have anything of his." If her answer came too fast, she didn't care. She also had no idea what this man was talking about.

He stepped closer to her. "Don't play with me. I know you were sleeping with him. You know that saying about men telling hookers all their secrets."

She knew the saying about punching a disrespectful bastard in the face, but she digressed. "No. I don't, because I'm not a hooker."

Franklin laughed. He tossed back his scrawny neck so she saw his nasty Adam's apple bobbing up and down with the action. "He may not have left the money on your nightstand when he was done, but you got paid big-time for having sex with him. Now, all I'm asking for is whatever he gave you that wasn't money."

"For your information, Rufus never saw my nightstand. And I'll tell you again, he never gave me anything." Okay, that wasn't totally true. He sent her flowers all the time and Edible Arrangements, both things he could charge to the corporate account and not have it seem like he was giving his mistress gifts.

Draya hadn't needed Rufus's gifts, and he knew that. He'd given her what she wanted—good sex and a promotion—they'd agreed on that from the very beginning.

"I think you're lying."

"I think you're obnoxious. So we're even." She turned to walk away and almost lost her footing as he grabbed her again.

"I'm going to find what I'm looking for, and if you're keeping it from me, you'll be sorry."

She pulled out of his grasp for the second and last time. "If you put your hands on me again, you'll be sorry."

His lips thinned into a straight line, and she turned away, leaving him to stare at her ass as she walked—which she knew he did. All men stared at ass, especially a big, round ass like hers. They couldn't help it, the sorry, basic creatures that they were.

Chapter 20

Jackie

"What the hell? You've been in here so long, I thought you fell in." Jackie walked into the ladies' room the second Draya stepped out of the stall closest to the back wall.

Venus came in behind her, pushing past her to get to a stall.

"Y'all got some weak bladders," she said, shaking her head.

Draya stepped up to the sink to wash her hands. Jackie came to stand beside her, staring in the mirror when Draya looked up. "What?" she asked.

Draya frowned. "What do you mean, what? I'm washing my hands. Don't you wash your hands after you go to the bathroom?"

Jackie waved a hand at her. "Not that. What's going on? Why were you out here so long?"

"Is there a time limit on peeing?" She reached for the paper towels first, drying her hands and then covering the faucet with one of them to turn it off.

"Who was that guy who came out right behind you?"

A toilet flushed, and Venus came out of the stall. "Yeah, we saw him leave right after you, and then when you took a long time coming back, we decided to come see what's up."

Draya closed her eyes and tried to do that deep inhale-exhale thing, but that shit ain't work, 'cause she still looked stressed the hell out when she opened her eyes again.

"Wait." Jackie put her hand up to stop any words Draya was about to say. "Anybody check under the stalls?" Leaning over at the waist, she walked down the stretch of the bathroom.

"We're not in high school." Venus tore off some paper towels and began to dry her hands.

"Doesn't matter—people are nosy as hell at any age." She pushed each stall door open until it slammed against the side wall with a bang.

"Okay, nobody's there," Venus said and then looked to Draya. "Who was he and what did he want?"

"I've got a sick feeling this whole situation is bigger than we thought." The words came fast from Draya, and the worried look on her face sparked concern in Jackie.

She rubbed her fingers over her forehead. "How?"

"What'd he say to you, Dray?" Venus touched her arm, and Draya looked down to see what they all saw—her hands were shaking.

"Let's not talk here. Not tonight. I want to think about it some more."

"Think about what? And shouldn't we all be thinking at the same time?" For better or worse, they were in this together. If Draya was getting scared, then they all needed to fear something was about to pop off.

"Maybe we should get out of here. Go someplace private," Venus suggested.

"Your place." It was the first place Jackie thought of, the place where all this began, and the place where, for whatever reason, she felt safe.

Venus frowned. "No. You're still a hazard to my place."

"What are you talkin' about? I was just there the other night after the club and I didn't set anything on fire."

"Only because your hand was still throbbing from punching that fool," Draya chimed in.

"All right, whatever. You come up with a place and time where we can talk," Jackie demanded. She knew they were talking about the dead-Rufus thing, but she had no idea what had happened between the time Draya said she had to pee and now. She'd watched that dude dressed in the cheap pinstripe suit leave the room right after Draya and at first hadn't thought anything of it, but the longer Draya had been gone, the stronger that uneasy feeling in the pit of her stomach had gotten.

Venus and Draya continued to stare at each other until Venus sighed. "We'll go out to eat tomorrow. Brunch after church."

Then they both looked at her like she was a little kid and they'd just offered her a lollipop. "Oh, okay, I see what's happening here. Cool. Bet. Teavolve or Miss Shirley's? They both have the bomb-ass brunch on Sundays."

Venus didn't hesitate. "Teavolve."

"Miss Shirley's," Draya said at the same time.

Jackie grinned. "I'll break the deadlock, and I'll be at Miss Shirley's at one, 'cause y'all know I do my best thinking on a full stomach."

"Yeah, we know," Draya said with a chuckle.

They all left the bathroom smiling and talking about what they planned to eat at tomorrow's brunch, but each of their smiles slipped simultaneously when they saw the two homicide detectives talking to Ellen.

"Let's just go back inside, get our stuff, and leave," she said. "They don't know anything unless we tell them."

Venus nodded. "You're right."

They walked right past the group of three, knowing that each one of them stared at the women as they passed by. Draya and Venus had carried their purses into the bathroom with them, so after they all grabbed their coats, they came out of the room once more and this time headed straight for the front door.

"Text when you get home!" Venus yelled to them as she turned to walk down the left side of the parking lot where she was parked.

"Right. Text when you get home," Draya repeated and walked in the opposite direction.

Jackie's car was parked the closest, and she yelled "Bet!" to them and crossed the parking lot to get into her ride.

Her phone rang the minute she was belted into the driver's seat, getting ready to start the engine. Pulling it from her pocket, she smiled at the name. How'd she know this was the perfect moment to call? Why was it so perfect? Because Jackie desperately needed to hear a friendly voice right now. One that wasn't talking about a dead guy.

"Hey, you," she answered on the third ring.

"Hi. It's good to finally hear your voice again," Karlie said.

Jackie grinned. "Yeah, it's good to hear yours too."

"Really? I couldn't tell if you wanted to hear from me or not, since you've spent most of the time ignoring me."

"Nah, never that. I've just been kinda busy." Not a total lie. She had been busy trying to keep her job intact thanks to Ellen's and Rufus's scheming asses. "But I'm glad you were persistent."

Karlie chuckled, and Jackie sat back against the seat, running her tongue over her lips. The sound of Karlie's laughter was sweet and like a balm to the rough edges of her life right now.

"So what're you doing on this Saturday night? Heading out to the lounge, or are you in for the night?"

"Actually, I'm just leaving a funeral."

"At this time of night on a Saturday? Most funerals I've been to have been early on Saturday mornings."

"Yeah, I was thinking the same thing. But it's just some dude I worked with. Anyway, I'm 'bouta head home."

"Want some company?"

She'd known that question was coming. Karlie didn't seem like the type to beat around the bush. And normally, Jackie wasn't either. Life was too short not to go after what you wanted. But did she really want Karlie? She'd gone through this before. Karlie didn't seem like a hit-it-and-quit-it type of woman, and Jackie really wasn't in the mood for that type of connection either. But the sound of Karlie's voice, her laughter, the way Jackie could hear her breathing on the other end of the phone, waiting for Jackie to respond, was more than a little appealing.

"Meet me at Jazzy's in twenty minutes."

"Bet." Karlie disconnected the call before Jackie could change her mind.

For the first few minutes, all Jackie could do was stare at the phone in her hand. Had she just set up a date—no, it wasn't a date; it was a time and place to meet—with a woman who made her smile? Seemed like a date. She shrugged and tucked the phone back into her pocket. Seconds later, she started the engine and was pulling out of the parking lot.

Twenty-five minutes later, a white car pulled up next to hers in Jazzy's side parking lot. Jackie hadn't gotten out of her car since pulling up here a few minutes ago. She watched Karlie get out, wearing tight-ass jeans and a brown leather jacket that skimmed her waist. Her hair was pulled back into a smooth ponytail that swished when she walked. Jackie was so busy thinking of how that ponytail would look brushing over Karlie's bare back while she bent her over and licked . . .

"Hi!" Karlie knocked on the window to punctuate the word, and Jackie jumped.

Shaking her head to clear those sexy thoughts, she pushed the button to lower the window.

"Sorry I startled you."

"It's okay. Thought I was alone, that's all." She shrugged and tried like hell to act like she wasn't having a very physical reaction to this woman.

"Well, you did ask me to meet you here."

Yeah, but she didn't ask her to look so fuckin' hot or to smell so damn good. There was a light, chilly-ass breeze that blew into the interior of the car, carrying with it the fresh floral scent of whatever perfume Karlie was wearing.

Karlie looked around the parking lot and then back to her. "Should we go in?"

Jackie clenched the steering wheel while considering that question. "Nah, not feeling up to a lot of people right now. Get in." The sound of the locks disengaging was loud in the otherwise quiet night.

Karlie walked around to the passenger side and got in. "I'm so glad you wanted to meet up. I've been thinking about you a lot."

"I can tell by the way you keep texting and calling." That felt abrupt, but Karlie didn't seem to mind—she just kept smiling.

Her lips weren't thick, but they were covered in this peach-looking gloss Jackie wanted to lick.

"When I want something, I go for it," Karlie said.

"And what do you want, Karlie? 'Cause I gotta be honest, I don't have much to give."

Not much surprised Jackie after all she'd been through, but when Karlie reached over to take her hand, she felt a little bewildered. She'd never admit that to a living soul, but she did. Like, what in the world did this pretty honey see in her, or rather, why'd she think there was something here she had to fight so hard to get? Jackie just couldn't figure it out.

"I like what I've seen of you," Karlie said, threading her fingers through Jackie's.

"Looks be deceiving people all the damn time," she replied with a dry chuckle. "Seriously, though, you don't know shit about me. For all you know, I could be some kind of perv. Got you in my car and will drive off with your ass to do whatever I want with you."

Karlie tilted her head. Her eyes were like this hazel-brown color, and they kinda glittered or shimmered with tiny gold flecks that made Jackie feel like this whole interlude was some fairy-tale-type shit.

"That's not who you are," she said. "Besides, I'm a pretty good judge of character, and I think you're nice."

All that sounded good, but Jackie had to make her point clear. "I'm not trying to be in no relationship." Not ever again, she'd sworn that to herself the day Alicia walked out on her. "Been there, done that, got the war scars to prove it. And I don't believe in making the same mistake twice."

"I'm not her." That's it. That's all Karlie said before lifting Jackie's hand to her mouth and softly kissing the back of it.

No, she definitely wasn't Alicia, 'cause there's no way Alicia would be sitting out in this cold-ass car with her when they could be inside getting a drink and their dance on.

"You're prettier than her." *Shit.* Jackie cleared her throat. "Sorry. That probably wasn't the right thing to say."

"It's cool. I don't want you to see her when you look at me."

"What do you want me to see?"

"Possibilities." The one word was spoken on a whisper as she used her grip on Jackie's hand to pull her closer. "We don't have to put a title on what we do. Not if you don't want to. But just think of all the possibilities for us."

Jackie leaned over the console, more than happy to get closer to Karlie. "I can think of a few."

Karlie grinned when Jackie's face was closer to hers. "Only a few? Then come on over here with me, Jackie. Let me show you all I've got to offer you."

Jackie normally liked to be in control. She made the first move, set the dates, pulled out the chairs, brought the flowers. Wooing her ladies was her thing—loving them until they couldn't imagine being loved by anyone else had been a strongpoint. Until she'd been told all her efforts were futile, that what she had to give wasn't good enough. That shit had stung like nobody's business.

But now here was this sweet-smelling, lovely woman telling her to think of the possibilities. Well, shit, it was very possible that Jackie might've met her match tonight.

She eased into the kiss with Karlie, touching her lips softly to hers at first, then following Karlie's lead when she parted hers and slipped her tongue inside Jackie's mouth. That flame she'd felt flickering inside her all those times Karlie had sent her text messages was a full-on combustion right about now, and Jackie reached her free hand around to cup the back of Karlie's neck.

The silkiness of her hair rubbed against Jackie's fingers, and the soft moan that escaped her mouth spurred Jackie on. If Karlie wanted to explore the possibilities with her, then Jackie damn sure wasn't going to stop her. Hell naw, she was going to ride this sweet-as-honey wave until they got to the end, and then . . . Karlie whispered her name and slid her hand down to unzip Jackie's jacket. When her fingers smoothed over Jackie's chest, Jackie sucked in a breath, groaned, and deepened the kiss. Fuck the end—right now, Jackie planned to just enjoy the hell out of this amazing beginning.

Chapter 21

Venus

Jackie text you yet?

Venus shook her head as if Draya were there and could see her; then she replied to her text.

No. You?

No.

Shit.

Should we go out to look for her?

Venus had been thinking that same thing. But where would they look? They'd all left the funeral home at the same time. At least she thought they had. She'd had to take her coat off as soon as she got into the car because she hated driving with her bulky winter coat on. When she'd pulled out of the parking lot, she hadn't seen any other headlights, so she'd presumed that Draya and Jackie had both pulled off before her.

She typed another reply. I don't know. It hasn't been that long, maybe she stopped to get something to eat???

That girl is always hungry lol

Venus replied with a laughing emoji just as her doorbell rang. Setting her phone on the table next to the couch, she walked to the door and looked through the peephole.

Shit. Damn. Shit!

"I can hear you breathing."

She frowned, unlocked the door, and opened it. "Is that some special type of training they give you at the police academy?"

Malik Jennings walked his six-foot-tall muscularly built body into her apartment as if he'd just been there yesterday. He hadn't, of course. He'd never been to her place. In fact, she wondered how he knew where she lived but didn't ask as the obvious answer—*he's a cop*—came to mind.

"No, just good hearing. Your footsteps and then you were breathing against the door as you looked through the peephole and considered what to do next."

Closing the door, she leaned against it because she knew this wasn't a social call, and even if it were, she hadn't seen or heard from Malik in eight years; he didn't need to go any farther than where he now stood three feet from her Christmas tree.

"What do you want? Your partner said she was calling my attorney on Monday. And you saw for yourself that what happened the other night at the club was self-defense, so what? Why are you here?" The real question was why, in the midst of all that was going on in her life, was Malik back? She hadn't thought about him in years, hadn't had the time to think about him or what they'd been to each other, to be exact. And she'd liked it that way—putting work before a pesky love life had seemed like a great plan.

"We need to talk. Alone." He looked good as hell, but that wasn't new.

In high school, he'd played basketball, like most of the guys she knew. But he was really smart, too, which she couldn't say of the other guys. Malik could've gone to any college he wanted to on a full basketball scholarship, but his academics could've also gotten him a free ride. Yet he hadn't left. He'd stayed right here in the city, joining the police academy and now standing in front of her as a homicide detective.

"I'm not talking to you without my attorney, so you might as well turn around and leave." He should leave anyway, because there was obviously a war between her thinking of him as a cop and as a man she'd once thought she loved.

"I'm not here on police business," he replied, locking gazes with her. "I'm here as a friend."

She laughed. Couldn't help it—the word in reference to them was more than foreign.

"What's that for?"

"Friends don't leave." She blurted those words out and then felt like a total ass. The last thing she wanted Malik to know was that she was harboring any type of feelings about how their relationship had ended. Yet, just as she'd decided that night she went to her parents' house, there were some things she just needed to say. "I mean, they don't stop calling or coming around just because things change."

As if he were tired of waiting for her to offer him a seat or even a polite word, he shrugged out of his jacket and walked over to the couch, where he dropped it and sat down.

"When the change comes in the form of you being hugged up with Cory Black, yeah, leaving was the best option. Otherwise, your new boyfriend was gonna be acquainted with my foot going up his ass."

A heavy sigh punctuated the memory in her mind, and she frowned. She also walked over to sit in the chair across from the couch—Draya's spot. "He wasn't my boyfriend."

"You were hugged up with him like he was."

Massaging her temples, she shook her head. "Fine. Whatever. We're not those kids anymore." Although sometimes, Venus felt like she'd been stuck in that time period. She'd been getting good grades then, heading to the college her parents had attended, doing all the right things in her parents' eyes. Yet still feeling like that wasn't enough.

"How've you been?" He shouldn't sound so good and look so fine, and he shouldn't be here in her private space.

"I've been fine." And polite, she'd always been polite. Tonight, she was making more of an effort.

She watched as he moved a hand to smooth down his low-cut beard. "I see you got that fancy job and car you always wanted."

"You wanted an SUV and a single-family home."

He nodded. "I got it."

"Hooray, we achieved our goals." Her tone was bland as she lifted her arm and pumped a fist in the air.

"Still cynical and moody as shit."

Resisting the urge to pout because he wasn't wrong, she crossed one leg over the other. "You haven't told me what you want yet."

"I want you."

Her mouth went dry. Not to be outdone, her nipples also hardened, and she cleared her throat because both reactions were annoying the hell out of her.

"Come again?"

"I want you to be honest with me. Remember, we used to tell each other everything."

She narrowed her eyes at him. "That was about the latest gossip in the neighborhood—who was going with whom and who was planning to fight after school."

"We told each other more than that, V." Yeah, they had, and he'd always called her V.

His deep voice even sounded the same as he'd said it just now.

"I can't keep up with you. First you say you're here for me to be honest with you, then you talk about our past. Which Venus are you here to see, and how do you expect me to react to the fact that you're here in the first place?" Her chest felt tight, and she fought off the thought of having a panic attack. Over what? Malik, the guy she'd given her virginity to, and perhaps a huge chunk of her heart? Or Malik, the guy investigating her boss's murder, who acted like he knew everything she knew about said murder?

He didn't know. Her mind held tight to that thought. There was no way he could know unless she told him.

"I'm here as your friend tonight. And as your friend, I've gotta tell you that you and your coworkers were right to lawyer up."

Damn.

"We didn't do anything." She could profess her innocence without an attorney being present.

"But you're not being honest with me or anyone else asking you questions."

"Nobody else is asking us anything." No lies there. If anyone was thinking that they were hiding something about Rufus's murder, they hadn't said anything to them about it. "And Jackie already gave you a statement."

"She did. But that's all she gave us, and I think there's more. So just tell me what happened. Was the guy harassing you or one of your friends? I can see the three of you stick together and don't hesitate to defend each other. Is that what you and Rufus argued about the night of the party?"

"You're asking questions like a cop." Too many questions, all of which were making her a little nervous. "Besides, don't you have other suspects?" She cleared her throat quickly. "I mean, aren't you investigating other people? Why do you seem so fixated on me and my friends?"

He leaned forward, resting his elbows on his knees. "We've got a few leads on some other possibilities, and we're following them too.

But, V, I'm asking you as a friend to be up-front with me. I can't help you if you don't trust me."

It seemed like years had passed in the time she sat there staring at him. Was he really asking her to tell him everything just because they used to be friends? Well, they used to be much more than friends, but that was then and this was now. Finally, she stood and walked toward the kitchen. "You want something to drink?"

"You got beer?" He got up and followed her.

She opened the refrigerator and took out a bottle of Blue Moon. It wasn't her preference, but Jackie had made more than one crack about her not having anything but bougie drinks in here. He opened the bottle and took a deep drag while she poured a glass of wine. They both leaned their butts against the counter just like they used to do when they were at the playground leaning against the wall.

"I've missed you," he said after another few minutes of silence. "Nobody knows me like you do, V. But you made it clear you were on a different path than me right after graduation. I didn't fit in with your new life."

She took another sip and let the slightly bitter taste of the pinot noir settle on the back of her tongue. "*I* didn't fit in with my new life."

"I thought you were happy."

She shrugged. "I thought I was too."

He set the almost-empty beer bottle down on the counter and turned so that he was standing directly in front of her. With his eyes on hers, he eased the glass of wine out of her hand. She let him. "You used to be happy when we were together."

He was right, and the building heat in his eyes said he knew it. Being with Malik had been the only time she hadn't felt as if she were doing things by an approved checklist. He wasn't her parents' pick for her, something her mother had been perfectly clear about when she found out they were seeing each other. But Venus hadn't been willing to give him up, at least not totally. After Ilene's decree that Venus stop seeing him, Malik had accepted the secret relationship in the beginning, but that acceptance had created a rift between them that led to them being happy one minute and breaking up the next. It was an emotional roller coaster that rode along the edge of her very strenuous relationship with her parents until one day he made the choice to walk away.

Memories assailed her, and she sighed. She couldn't be walking down this path again. This was a mistake for so many reasons, the biggest of which was keeping her ass out of jail.

"I was happy when we were together," she whispered. "But that's not now."

He nodded. "Yeah, it is. Now is right this moment. No questions, no answers. No jobs, just you and me. Just like we used to be."

They used to be combustible. After they'd had sex that first time in her bedroom while her parents had been out at some function, they hadn't been able to keep their hands off each other. For three years before that night, they'd been really good friends, best friends, sharing all the ups and downs of their young lives. When his father used to beat him until he bled and her mother used to yell at her until she wanted to scream, they'd been there for each other. He'd helped her study chemistry, and she'd taught him how to do the Cupid shuffle because line dances weren't his thing. They used to be really good together.

"What are you doing here, Malik?"

He slid his hands up her neck until they brushed past her chin to cup her cheeks. "I wanted to see you again, V. I wanted to do this again."

His lips were warm against hers, that first tentative brush a question while he waited a few seconds for her answer.

The list of reasons why she shouldn't be doing this was still long as hell. She could stop it right at this moment. Push him away and out of her house, then call Jackie and Draya to tell them how truly fucked they were. But she didn't. Instead, her hands found their way to his waist, and her head tilted into his. "Yeah, do that again."

Her request seemed to be his command, because before she could blink again, Malik's lips were on hers. His hands slid back until his blunt-tipped nails pressed against her scalp and his body leaned into hers. Memories were a bitch, and they flooded her with a quickness as she moved her hands up his strong back. He was hard, thick inches of delectable dick pressed into her, and she shivered with anticipation.

What? Hold up? This couldn't be happening.

"Stop me." His voice was husky when he dragged his mouth away and rested his forehead on hers. "Stop me if this is it."

She couldn't think straight—that was the only reason she was hating the fact that the kiss was over. "Is that your way of asking for permission?"

He nodded, and she sighed.

Don't do it. This is a mistake. He's the cop investigating you and your friends.

"It's been so long," she whispered. That was the same thought that'd had her on that pool table the other night with the jerk who ended up getting his nose broken.

"Too long for both of us to keep denying what's obviously been waiting for us to rekindle. I know you felt it the second we saw each other at that massage parlor. And then at the club. I wanted to run back into that club and beat that bastard's ass for touching you." Easing his hands up and down her arms now, as if she were cold and he needed to keep her warm, he continued. "It's strange, I know. And we shouldn't be doing this, especially not under the current circumstances—I know that too. But you've been on my mind since I saw your name on that employee list at BCC."

"We're not what we used to be." That was supposed to come out with more force, more confidence. It sounded like a wimpy line in a love letter.

"That's fine. Then we'll be what we are here and now." He pulled away so he could look into her eyes.

"Horny and desperate?" She cracked a smile, hoping like hell a little humor would break this blanket of arousal she was in danger of being tangled in.

He grinned in return. "I prefer the word *needy*."

"Really? You'd rather be called *needy* than *horny*?"

Grasping her hips and lifting her until she sat on the counter, he eased between her legs. "I'd rather be inside you than chitchatting about needing to be inside you."

And just like that, he had her. The raw edginess to his tone, the candid words that echoed her exact thoughts. When he pushed at her skirt, she wiggled until it was bunched at her waist. While he grabbed the band of her stockings and panties to pull them down, she yanked at his shirt. He stepped back and finished the deed, lifting the shirt up and over his head while she kicked off her shoes and pushed the stockings and panties all the way off.

Touching his bare chest was a must, because he hadn't been built like this when they were teenagers. He was cut like a physical-fitness model; all that deep, dark chocolate-brown skin stretched over taut muscle made her mouth water. He fumbled with his belt buckle, and she took over the job for him. Shifting his attention, he reached into his back pocket for his wallet, pulled out a condom packet, and ripped it open.

"I got it."

"Bossy," he said with a grin and unbuttoned her blouse.

The bra and blouse hit the floor next. She pushed his pants and boxers down and smoothed that condom over his thick erection. Then he was grabbing her around the waist, pulling until her ass almost slid off the counter.

"I really missed you, V." If she was supposed to respond to that in some coherent way, she missed her cue, because the next sound that came from her was a gasp and then a pleasure-filled moan as he thrust all his inches into her.

There was nothing right about this—fucking on her kitchen counter, letting the cop investigating her grip her ass and suck on her tongue, screaming his name like she thought there was somebody out there who would come and save her—all of it was wrong as the day was long. But she couldn't stop. Hell, she didn't want to stop. Right now, she just wanted to come, and with his next thrust, that's exactly what she did.

He finished right behind her, and before any uncomfortable feelings could ensue, he wrapped her legs around his waist and attempted to carry her into the bedroom. Apparently, they were both so caught up in the good-sex bliss that they forgot he hadn't taken his pants and boots all the way off, so right after his first two steps, he stumbled. Her arms flailed until she could grip the refrigerator handle, and he managed to right himself. Laughter erupted instantly, and she unlocked her legs from around him to step away.

"Damn, that was gonna be hard to explain to the paramedics when they came to peel our old asses off the floor." He was leaning forward now, untying his boots and kicking them off.

"Yeah, and they would've been talking about us for the rest of the week, probably. Couple having wild kitchen sex fall and fracture some bones." She laughed some more and then turned away when he stood, completely naked, in front of her.

"Uh, I need to use the bathroom."

She nodded. "Right. So do I." She tugged at her skirt, trying to pull it down over her bare ass. "You can go first."

"Cool," he said and grabbed his clothes before walking safely out of the kitchen.

Venus dropped her head back and closed her eyes, whispering, "Stupid! Stupid! Stupid!" until she heard her phone buzzing from the living room.

Walking barefoot into the other room, she grabbed her phone off the table and read the group text. Sorry if y'all were worried. I'm home now.

With phone in hand, Venus dropped down onto the couch and shook her head. Jackie wasn't the one they should be worrying about. Venus was certain she and what she'd just done now took center stage on their list of concerns.

Chapter 22

Draya

"We've gotta figure out who killed Rufus, and we're going to use this to do it." She reached into her purse and pulled out the USB drive she'd taken from Rufus's office, placing it in the center of the table.

The only thing she didn't like about Miss Shirley's downtown location was the small tables. With all they'd ordered among the three of them and after her insistent request, the server had moved them to a booth just before their mountain of food arrived. She'd finished all she planned to eat of the stuffed french toast she'd ordered and thought now was the better time to discuss the reason for this brunch. Besides, she'd paced the floor in her apartment for most of the night, trying to figure out what she should do—it was either now or never.

"We're gonna use a USB drive to find out who killed a man none of us could stand." Jackie was still chewing a bite of her chicken and waffles as she frowned across the table at Draya. "And why are we doing the police's job for them? I already gave my statement, and they've tested my gun and found nothing. Even though they haven't called my attorney to tell him that, and they're taking a long-ass time to return my property."

Draya had thought about that last night too. In fact, she'd been up most of the night thinking about this situation that, despite their efforts to act normal, still hadn't gone away.

"What's on the flash drive?" Venus seemed skeptical. She pierced the last piece of her Chesapeake omelet with her fork and eased it into her mouth while waiting for Draya's response.

"Look, the guy who was all up in my face last night was Rufus's lawyer. The one I told you has been blowing up my phone since the body was found." Draya looked directly at Venus because she wasn't sure if Venus was really following the conversation or if she was over there judging her yet again.

Jackie picked up her napkin and wiped her mouth. "So Rufus's lawyer gave you this and wants you to find out who killed him?"

Draya sucked in a deep breath and released it slowly. She was about to speak but then decided she needed a drink first, so she picked up the Spicy Shirley she'd ordered and took a swallow. Normally, Bloody Marys weren't her preferred drink. Her great-grandma Jane had loved tomato juice. Draya had hated the sight of it each time she visited. But after her great-grandmother's death, she'd been at a birthday party for one of her cousins, and in honor of Great-grandma Jane, they'd all ordered the drink. Today, she needed Great-grandma Jane's strength to get through what was sure to be the oddest conversation she ever thought she'd have.

"I sent Rufus some pictures while we were together, and he threatened to release them on social media." She knew exactly how it sounded and could probably predict what Venus and Jackie were thinking. That she was a slut, a ho, sending nude pics to the married man she was sleeping with for a promotion. To her ears, all that equated to her being trash, but Draya knew better.

She *was* better, and she'd spent the majority of her life convincing herself of that fact. Now it seemed she had to convince these two as well.

"You did what?" Jackie's eyes widened.

Venus finished chewing and took a sip from her mimosa while giving Draya a nonchalant gaze that only irritated Draya more.

"Look, I've dealt with people like you looking down their nose at me all my life." This wasn't exactly how she'd planned to start the conversation, but since it seemed she needed to prove herself, she kept talking. "Before I hit puberty, the world had me pegged as a statistic. My sixth-grade teacher criticized my too-tight pants and sweater—which were hand-me-downs from my older sister, who's always been twenty to thirty pounds lighter than me. When I told him to mind his business, he said that was no problem; he could just collect his paycheck, since I was probably going to end up strung out on drugs or pregnant before I turned fifteen anyway."

Jackie set her fork down slowly, and Venus stared at her with a mild look of surprise, but Draya didn't want their pity. She only wanted them to understand why she'd done the things she had.

"The lunch lady in the cafeteria didn't give me lunch for a week but instead kept making comments about knowing my mother had received her welfare check so she should've given me money for lunch. And when I was fifteen, my oldest brother, Clifton, overdosed in our living room, just like that nasty old Ms. Mary at the community center told my mother he would eventually do."

The memory left a heaviness in her chest, right where her heart thumped wildly. When she thought her hands were going to shake, she dropped them to her lap and took a deep, steadying breath. "I've been fighting against stereotypes and bullshit predictions all my life, declaring myself smart enough to overcome whatever odds the world placed before me, and I did." She said that proudly, holding her chin up as she met the stares of both the women across from her.

"Yes, I slept with a married man to get a promotion. I'm not ashamed of that fact because there're women out here who were brought up under better circumstances and have done worse. That chick who put her children in a car and pushed the car into the river. Those rich actresses who cheated to get their kids into college. And even Elizabeth Taylor and all her husbands."

"Hold up, Liz just had problems finding love. She tried. Hell, Michael Jackson even proposed to her." Jackie picked her fork up and began cutting into her waffle again.

Venus glanced at her and shook her head before chuckling. "Something is really wrong with you."

Draya agreed and couldn't help grinning as Jackie went back to eating her food. Then she went still when Venus reached out and touched her hand. "They were wrong. All those people who said those horrible things were wrong and should've been fired for overstepping their boundaries as professionals. And you shouldn't have had to spend your childhood thinking about how you would prove them all wrong. No child should have to want validation but only receive judgment and criticism."

The feel of Venus's hand on hers and the way she looked intently at Draya while speaking those words sealed something between them. That space that had always prevented Draya from thinking they could be friends seemed to disappear, and she almost pulled her hand away because she wasn't certain how to deal with that.

"I'm not looking for pity," she said.

"I'm not giving it, because what happened to you wasn't your fault," Venus replied.

"But how 'bout we discuss what's on this USB drive now," Jackie said around chewing her food. "Then we can come up with a way to find all those bastards who said the mean stuff to you, and I'll handle them right quick."

Draya couldn't help it—she laughed loud and hard at Jackie's very sincere suggestion. Venus did, too, as she pulled her hand away from Draya's and sat back against the booth. The tears that had been threatening to fall at the weight of the pain she'd been holding on to for so long stalled, and Draya continued to laugh. She'd never laughed this way with other women before, aside from family members, and that was different. This felt different.

"You might need some anger-management therapy," Venus told Jackie when she was able to stop laughing.

Jackie finished chewing and shook her head. "Nah, I just need for people to stop being idiots, spitting hurtful words at others, then walking away with their heads held high like they're above reproach. I'm tired of that shit. Tired of people thinking it's okay to push their bullshit rules and opinions on everybody else."

Silence fell at their table once more, and Draya sighed.

"I shouldn't have taken those pictures. It was a mistake, and I'm not proud of it." She felt good admitting that out loud.

"Full frontal? Just tits? An ass shot? Spread-eagle? What're we talking here?"

Now, Draya and Venus stared at Jackie in disbelief.

She frowned. "What? They're valid questions. But I'm thinking if ole boy was threatening to go public with them, you must've been showing all your personal business."

"I was showing enough of my business that anyone who knows me would've recognized me." And the double-heart tattoo with her name on the back of her left shoulder.

"What did he want in exchange for not sharing the pictures?" Venus asked.

Jackie cut another piece of chicken. "Nah, bump that, what'd you do to make him want to blackmail you in the first place? Refuse to do some freaky shit? I mean, other than sending nasty pics via text messages."

A couple of hours last night had been spent trying to talk herself out of doing this. To her way of thinking, neither Jackie nor Venus had as much to lose at this point as she did. Jackie had already cleared her name, and the police didn't seem to be looking in her direction anymore, and Venus's only real part in this was due to Draya calling her over to Rufus's house that morning. She was certain if it really boiled down to it, Venus's lawyer could get her out of any criminal charges. But for Draya, even if she came through the one criminal act of not calling to report a murder, once everything came out in the press—which she knew it would—her reputation would be tarnished. How would she encourage young girls to be their best and prove all their haters wrong when she'd done something she was horribly ashamed of?

In the end, she'd decided she had no other choice. If she were going to have any chance of getting out of this mess with a semblance of the reputation she'd worked so hard to craft intact, she needed to tell them everything, and they needed to be on board with this idea or it could all fall apart.

"Rufus was angry because I ended things between us without any discussion or options for reconsideration." She reached for her glass again but stopped and let her hands fall to her lap. "Then Ellen saw me in the parking garage and went back and ran her mouth to him, and that infuriated him."

Venus shook her head. "A dumbass man scorned."

"Exactly." Agreeing with Venus seemed to happen more frequently since the party.

"What were you doing in the garage? Taking more pics?"

This time Draya narrowed her eyes at Jackie in response. Jackie shrugged, and Venus shook her head.

"Well, I'm with her this time. What were you doing in the garage that was so bad, Ellen had to run and tell it all?" Venus's tone was even, no surprise and basically no recrimination.

"I was getting out of Travis's car." When they both looked confused, she continued. "Travis is my new friend. He's also the lawyer representing me—he works in the building."

Jackie sat back in her chair and rubbed a finger over her chin. "Travis Millhouse from the seventh floor? He drives that tan Mercedes truck and wears a diamond stud in his left ear?"

She should've known Jackie would know exactly who she was talking about. "Yes, that's him."

"He's, like, fresh outta law school. In that office with just a secretary and law clerk because that's the only staff he can afford right now." Jackie frowned as she continued with the rundown on Travis.

"He's twenty-six and so what?"

"You're thirty-one," Venus said.

"I know how old I am, dammit! And this is not about Travis. It's about Rufus."

"Lower your voice before everybody in here learns what we're talking about."

"Yes, Mother," she snapped at Venus. "Look, I'm telling you that our best way out of this is to find out who the real killer is and then turn them in to the police. That way the detectives will forget about asking us questions, and justice can be served."

Jackie laughed. "You don't give a damn about justice being served. You're just trying to save your ass and those pictures."

"I'm also trying to save your ass, so don't get cute. You may've given the police an alibi for where you were during the time of the murder, but you were still at that house trying to steal the artwork from his walls." She clapped her lips shut then. This wasn't going the way she'd thought it would. "Okay, all cards on the table. I took the USB drive from Rufus's house before you two arrived. I wanted to find all the pictures he had on all his devices and delete them so they'd never see the light of day. Because if those pictures get out, the plans for my foundation might be over."

Venus paused a second, taking in all she'd just said. "You took evidence from a crime scene?"

"No, Detective McGee. The crime scene was in the foyer where Rufus was lying. The USB drive came from his office."

"The whole house was a crime scene, Draya!" This time Venus yelled. She caught her mistake before any of them could point it out and rubbed shaking fingers over her lips, possibly to keep them closed.

Draya couldn't be so lucky.

"Why're you just telling us about this? You should've said this when we got back to my place that day." Venus's voice was notably lower this time.

"It wouldn't have mattered; I wasn't taking it back."

"Yeah, but we could've started thinking about a way to explain anything missing from the house if we had to," Jackie said. "So again, what's on this thing?" She picked up the USB drive.

"I only looked at the JPEG files, the pictures. That's all I was concerned with," she admitted.

Now Venus was massaging her temples, her elbows braced on the table. "Wait a minute, you've had this flash drive for a week and all you did was check out the pictures on it? Then how do you know we can use it to find Rufus's killer?"

Draya cleared her throat. "Because last night, after Franklin insisted that Rufus had given me something, I got to thinking. Why would Franklin have thought that, and what 'something' meant so much that he had to keep calling me, then practically accost me at a funeral to get it back? My only answer was this USB drive." Jackie still held it in her hand, flipping it between her fingers as she stared at Draya. "So I looked on it again, and this time I saw the folder marked 'Private.' I clicked on it and saw a memo."

"And? A memo and some nude pics. That's not a lot to go on, if we were considering this. Which we're not because we aren't detectives," Venus said.

"It's a supply list."

"I knew it!" Jackie insisted. "This is all about to fall on me and my department. He really was trying to set me up."

Draya leaned in closer to the table and lowered her voice. "The supply list was for equipment that was purchased in the commission of three city contracts. But I'm positive those projects were completed a few years ago."

"Okay?" Venus folded her hands now and left them on the table. "So we have an old memo about a BCC job on a USB drive found in Rufus's office."

Draya shook her head. "The date on the memo was September of this year. Just three months ago, when those projects were done almost two years ago."

Now silence fell over the table as Jackie continued to stare at the USB drive and Venus looked at Draya. "What are you saying?" she asked.

"We all know Rufus was an ass. It stands to reason we weren't the only ones thinking of him that way. What if he was killed because he was jerking somebody around in business? Or what if somebody was blackmailing him the way the bastard was trying to do to me?" She rested an elbow on the table. "I don't have all the answers—I'm just saying that something shady is definitely going on here. Somebody killed Rufus, and since it wasn't any of us, we need to find out who it was. Before the cops settle their sights on us."

"I don't know about this, y'all," Jackie said. As if to punctuate her point, she put the USB back on the table and pushed it in Draya's direction. "Why can't we just delete the photos on the USB and then mail it to the cops to figure out the rest?" She shrugged. "Maybe the last thing we need to be doing is digging ourselves deeper into this hole. Like right now, if those cops walked in here and asked us point-blank if we killed him, we could all say no. If they asked for our alibis, I've already provided one for each of us. But the minute we go sniffing around in Rufus's business affairs, we might start to look guiltier."

"How? We're not the ones who probably stole money from the city. And once I go back and check the archived records in my office, I'm betting that money won't show up on BCC books. So as long as it's not in any of our bank accounts, we're still not guilty. And about your first question, the cops won't immediately know the significance of that memo. The reason I know is because I work in the finance department." Again, she'd thought of all the angles on this, and the only conceivable action for them to take was to look for the killer on their own.

"Yeah, but we're not cops, Dray. We don't know anything about investigating, and who's gonna talk to us about anything, especially something criminal?" Jackie argued.

"I don't see that we have any other choice. It's either sit back and do nothing and continue to be on the cops' radar or get active and prove our innocence. I don't know about you, but I'm sick of waiting for the other shoe to drop. And I definitely don't like being threatened to my face by some pencil-neck lawyer with grimy teeth."

"She's right," Venus said. "Not about the lawyer's teeth, 'cause I didn't examine him that closely. But about the cops. They definitely think we're hiding something, and they're not going to stop until they find out what it is."

"How do you know that?" Now it was her turn to stare at Venus skeptically. She'd been acting reserved since they'd arrived at the restaurant. Even when Jackie had taken a full ten minutes to order three different entrees and two drinks off the menu. Venus hadn't commented, nor had she seemed to react when Draya put that USB drive on the table and described what she thought was on it.

Venus sat back from the table. She lifted fingers to touch her temple again but let her hand fall, as if she'd changed her mind. "Malik, um, Detective Jennings came by my place last night."

"What?" Jackie all but fell out of her chair trying to lean closer to Venus. "We've been sitting here for, like, two hours and you're just dropping that bombshell?"

"She wasn't going to tell us," Draya said, irritation pricking her skin. "She was going to sit there and keep the fact that she hooked up with her high school boyfriend last night a secret." Just like the rest of the bougie Black folk did whenever they did some dirt. Her cheeks heated as she thought about trusting Venus when she should've known better.

"First, it wasn't a hookup," Venus said pointedly. "At least it wasn't planned. I had no idea he was going to show up at my house. And what else was I supposed to do but let him in? He's the police."

Draya pursed her lips and shook her head. "Girl, you know we don't care about no cops showing up at our door. Unless they got a search warrant, they gets no access." Growing up in a neighborhood where cops weren't considered friends, that was one of the golden rules in Draya's household.

"Yeah, you know they ain't never trying to help us," Jackie added.

"He was my friend before he was a cop."

"He was your boyfriend, and you were the one insisting that was in the past," Draya corrected her. "What happened last night? What did you tell him?"

Venus slammed her hands on the table. "I told him nothing, just like we promised to do until our attorneys were present. He asked if Rufus had done something to one of my friends and if that was what we argued about at the party. Like I said, they know we're hiding something."

"Why'd he come see you? I thought his partner was going to call your attorney to set up a meeting tomorrow." Draya wasn't believing shit Venus said.

"She was . . . she is! And I don't know why he came to see me." Venus paused and then cleared her throat. "We had sex on my kitchen counter."

Jackie, who'd just taken a sip from her glass of water, spit it clear across the table. Draya jumped out of the line of fire, frowning at Jackie, then returning her gaze to Venus.

"You fucked the cop who's investigating us?"

Venus arched a brow. "According to you, I fucked my ex-boyfriend."

"On the kitchen counter where I'm never eating again, thank you very much," Jackie said before reaching across the table and grabbing Draya's Spicy Shirley. She emptied the glass and looked at Draya and Venus, who were now staring at her with perplexed looks. "What? I'm not eating from the coochie counter, and you know you're not either."

After that comment, Draya basically felt like their brunch meeting was over. They hadn't formally decided on what they would do next, but she knew what digging she wanted to do. Perhaps after she found something more concrete, Venus and Jackie would be more agreeable to her point of view. In the meantime, getting away from Venus's pretending ass and Jackie's weirdness for a while seemed like a better plan.

Chapter 23

Jackie

On Monday morning, Jackie stepped with a purpose off the elevator onto the third floor where the HR offices were. She wasn't going to be bullied by Ellen any longer. After having some time to think about it, she'd come to the conclusion that the mace incident was a form of assault, and she planned to tell the woman this. Her real reason behind this meeting was to find out what the hell she'd done to get on Ellen's bad side and to see if there was some way the problem could be fixed. Only because it was the professional thing to do.

Otherwise, she didn't give a fuck if the old battle-ax didn't like her. Unlike where her mother was concerned, there was no love lost between Jackie and Ellen. It occurred to her then, too, that she prayed there was no love lost between her and her mother, but truthfully, she didn't know. It had been five years since Clive and Maiselle had made it crystal clear that no daughter of theirs would be openly proud of sleeping with women. That meant Jackie couldn't be their daughter. The pang in the center of her chest burned deep each time she recalled those last moments at her family home.

"Hey, Shell, I need to speak to Ellen for a minute." She greeted the receptionist leading to the HR area and kept walking when Shell—who was on the phone—simply nodded and waved her hand.

Continuing back to the largest office on this floor, she knocked on the partially opened door and then stepped inside.

"Ellen?"

The office was empty. Her computer as well as the Tiffany lamp close to the end of the desk were on, so Jackie knew she was in today. Maybe she just stepped away for a few minutes. Well, Jackie wanted to get this off her chest now rather than later, so she could wait. She walked farther into the office, going to the line of file cabinets across the room. There were a bunch of picture frames on top of the cabinets, snapshots of who she suspected were Ellen's family members in most of them.

"Somebody actually married this bitter woman," she whispered, amazed as she looked at the picture that was so old, she thought it might actually be fading. Well, the guy at least came to his senses at some point and left her evil ass.

Children who looked a little like Ellen and her ex-husband were in other pictures, and she guessed the younger kids were the grandchildren. She had a big family, something Jackie missed terribly.

Besides losing her close high school friends, nobody from her parents' circle of friends had kept in touch with her after she'd come out. And when she'd taken a chance and reached out to some of their kids who were her age, she'd been shocked to learn that they felt the same as their parents. How the hell could so many people be so hateful and ignorant?

On a resigned sigh, she moved away from the file cabinets and walked over to the guest chairs across from Ellen's desk. She'd sit and wait for her and think more about what they were going to do about Draya's suggestion of investigating Rufus's murder. Damn, her life really sucked if thinking about murder was better than thinking about the family who'd rather disown her than accept her.

She was just about to take a seat when a folder on the top of a file stand caught her eye. Actually, it was the address on the tab of the folder that had her moving closer for a better look: "88765 Johanessen Circle."

She knew that address. Stuffing her hands into her front pockets, she stood there for a few minutes just staring at it. Thinking about it, picturing the location in her mind, and then finally nodding. "Yeah, that's it."

Without hesitation, she picked up the folder and opened it to find it filled with receipts. Some for Victoria's Secret, some for Nordstrom and Tiffany's, and an online receipt for what appeared to be a car payment. Why would Ellen have a folder full of bills for Rufus? She knew they were for him, not only because that was his address—she'd never forget it or that house for as long as she lived now—but because several of the receipts had been signed by Rufus.

Okay, there was a simple explanation for this. Jackie tilted her head and thought about it some more. Rufus did have a company credit card—all the high-level executives did. Venus didn't, but if she'd gotten that promotion that Rufus gave to Mike, she would've received one. They could use the card for anything they allocated to a client or for verifiable business expenses.

"Which client was he buying VS stuff for?"

The car payment could've been his. She went back to that slip of paper only to shake her head when it listed the car as a Lexus LX SUV. Rufus owned an Escalade and a Mercedes SLC Roadster. Pam drove a Mercedes S-Class. As far as she knew, those were the only cars he owned. Now, she really hadn't known him all that well outside of work, and she hadn't been to his house frequently like Draya probably had, so he could've had other cars that she didn't know about. But something about this seemed off. It was weird in the same sense as Rufus's lawyer threatening Draya for something she didn't have in her possession.

"Shit!"

She was about to head for the door and hustle back to her office so she could call Draya when Ellen stepped into the office. With lightning-quick action, she put her arms behind her back and tucked the folder under the blue Golden State Warriors hoodie she wore. Today was moving day for a lot of old furniture they'd been storing in the basement, so she hadn't dressed in her normal dress slacks and button-front shirt.

"What are you doing in my office?"

Jackie smiled. "I recall asking you the same thing when you tumbled into my office. You know, when you sprayed me with mace."

Ellen waved a hand in dismissal and walked farther into her office. "I'm an executive at this company. You have no reason to be in my office alone. None at all."

"I'm a manager at this company, and I came to speak to you. Where would you suggest I wait, in the lobby like a visitor?"

With her lips thinning into a straight line, Ellen passed the spot where Jackie stood and went behind her desk.

"Look, I do not have time to go back and forth with you right now. I've got work to do."

"That's cool. I've got work as well. I just think it's time we clear the air." She moved away from the desk, turning so that her back was now to the door. "You obviously have some type of gripe with me. I'm here to see if it can be squashed so we can have an improved working relationship."

She'd rehearsed those words on her drive into work this morning, but now they didn't sound as good as they had in her mind.

Ellen sat with a stiff motion and scooted herself and the chair closer to her desk. "Jacqueline, you must have mistaken me for someone else. I do not have the time or the inclination to develop personal feelings for anyone. So as you so quaintly put it, I do not have any 'gripe' with you on a personal level. My concern, as always, is that the work of BCC be done in an expeditious and professional manner."

"That's my concern as well. But you see, things like denying my vacation time, taking my parking space, and telling the cops that I threatened to kill Rufus—they don't really have anything to do with my job performance. So I'll ask again: What's your problem with me?"

Because if it was just that she was gay, Jackie wanted her to come right out and say that shit. After which time she fully planned to visit an employment-law attorney to see what her options were. Sure, when Draya had suggested this course of action at the party, Jackie had been adamant that wasn't where her head was, but fuck that now. Ellen had crossed the line with the mace attack. Words and exercising her supervisory leverage were one thing, but if any other woman had dared to mace her, Jackie would've beat their ass with pleasure. Only the fact that she was on company property and had the security guards as witnesses stopped her from breaking the old woman's jaw.

Ellen gave a sickly chuckle. "You aren't even worth me having an issue with. I told Rufus we should've fired you and had you arrested after you pulled that gun on him. But no, he wanted you around for some reason."

So he could try to fuck the gay out of her. She couldn't hold back the scowl at that thought.

"But you know he's gone now." Ellen narrowed her eyes at Jackie. "So you'd better be walking a straight line."

Jackie blinked and shook her head. "Is that a threat?"

"Oh no, dear. It's a promise. One that you can bet I'll act on the moment you step too far out of line."

Okay, so they were drawing battle lines. Well, that was cool, because Jackie was certain there was something shady about the receipts in that folder she had tucked under her hoodie. In fact, she was so sure that instead of giving Ellen more clapback to set the woman straight, she only offered a partial smile as she back-walked out of her office.

The minute she was on the elevator again, she dialed Draya's desk. Voice mail. Cursing, she slapped a palm on the *B* button while thoughts ran through her mind about what she should do next. The answer was that she needed proof. One of the sticking points of their brunch conversation yesterday was that right at this moment, Draya didn't have enough proof of anything on that USB drive. That meant if they were really going to start their own investigation, they needed to start gathering evidence, building a case like the detectives always did on *Law & Order*.

Her favorite was the original. She could sit and binge-watch that show an entire weekend, only leaving her couch or bed to get food and drinks. It might be slightly embarrassing how many times in the past year she'd done just that. Anyway, when the elevator doors opened, she stepped off into the basement. The large space had been split into sections, giving some of the other tenants in the building a location to store things. As BCC owned the building, she supervised the space and had access to every part of it.

Walking quickly toward the back where there were half a dozen storage units, she pulled the folder from under her sweatshirt. The three units at the end belonged to BCC, so she moved farther down the line until she was behind the unit for another tenant. She kept going until she was at the back of the unit, where there was a wall with a short ledge, and that's where she dropped the folder and opened it. Flipping through one page at a time, she had to turn on the flash on her phone's camera to get a good picture. Ellen would notice that the folder was gone, so Jackie knew she couldn't keep it forever, or even for as long as it would take to catch up with Venus and Draya. A picture was worth a thousand words, and she snapped three of each document, just in case. When that was complete, her mind shifted to how she was going to get the folder back in Ellen's office without the hag seeing her. She could wait until after office hours and slip back into her office, or she could just slip it into an interoffice envelope and let it arrive on Ellen's desk with the late-afternoon mail. Receiving what Jackie was certain Ellen considered private information through office mail would scare the piss out of her. The thought had Jackie laughing.

She was so busy laughing, she almost missed the sound coming from the other side of this storage unit. At least that's where she thought it was coming from as she stopped walking and focused on the sound. She tilted her head in that direction and frowned at the unmistakable sound of moaning—sexual moaning.

Ah, hell naw. The words floated through her mind as she closed her eyes with indecision. Did she go back there and bust whoever was getting their thing off on company property, or did she keep it moving and make her way back upstairs to figure out what to do with the folder she'd tucked under her hoodie again? Barging in on whoever was just trying to find a little satisfaction made her feel over-the-top nosy like Ellen, while on the other hand, as facilities manager she was paid to oversee the daily operations of this facility. And as that sometimes included the unfair task of asking the homeless guy out front whom she'd become fond of to relocate whenever Louis or any of the other board members were visiting, it probably also meant making sure nobody was fucking on the property.

"Oooooh, Mike, yesssssss."

Granted, Mike was a pretty common name . . . it still had her ears perking up, just as the voice that had said it raised a question. A thumping sound came next, like something falling on the floor, which again was her domain to check out. So without further hesitation, Jackie walked around the storage unit, following the sounds that were growing louder.

She'd just rounded the edge of the unit beside the one that had been hiding her while she'd photographed the contents of the folder when she saw them. There were stacks of boxes outside the unit, which was a violation she didn't have time to note because the woman's body leaning over one of the boxes was a bigger priority. Or rather, the man who was pounding into the woman from behind and the woman groaning his name was the bigger priority. Since her phone was still in hand, Jackie turned on the flashlight app and aimed it in their direction.

All groaning and moaning stopped as Mike Livingston and Robyn the security guard stood frozen like criminals caught in the act. Well, they were caught in *an* act.

"I don't have to tell you how inappropriate this shit is," Jackie said. She took a few steps closer, but not too close.

Like she could clearly see Robyn's bare ass tucked against Mike's bare groin, but she focused her mind and her flashlight on Mike's face.

"Senior Project Manager Michael Livingston." Saying his name like she was announcing a movie star was only a front for the actual disgust she felt at seeing his phony ass in this very compromising situation. "I wonder how Louis would feel if he knew this was how you spent your workday."

"Turn that fuckin' light off," he growled at her.

With a shrug, she obliged, but casting them in the dim shadow of the boxes and storage units didn't mean she hadn't caught them in the act.

"And, Robyn, you deserve better than this wannabe. How disrespectful that he couldn't even spring for a hotel room." Turning to walk away because there was really nothing else she could do, Jackie decided she felt less like Ellen than she'd anticipated.

Ellen would've stood there and continued to judge and criticize a situation that she couldn't have predicted or prevented from happening in the first place. And then she would've—or rather she had when the caught couple was Draya and Travis—run to tell the only person she knew could do something more. Jackie, on the other hand, was satisfied that Mike now knew she had something on his trifling ass. Not that she would resort to any type of blackmail or quid pro quo, as Rufus was known to do, but still it was good to have that ace in her back pocket if ever there was a need.

She'd just gotten to the elevator when she heard footsteps running up behind her. Turning in preparation to fuck up whoever thought they were gonna catch her by surprise, she saw it was only Mike. He'd pulled his pants up and buttoned them, but the tail of his dress shirt was hanging out on one side.

"I don't know what you think you just saw," he said when he was a few feet away from her.

She chuckled. "Then you must not be a good fuck at all."

"I'm not laughing."

Jackie didn't stop. "You should be, 'cause it's kinda funny that the guy Rufus picked to manage a multimillion-dollar project is caught doing something as basically stupid and unprofessional as literally fuckin' around on the job." That shit wasn't funny, it was pitiful, but she figured he got her drift.

"This stays between us."

The elevator door opened, and she turned to step inside, but Mike grabbed her arm. His grip was tight, the look on his face grave with just the barest hint of danger. "I'm serious. You would want to keep your mouth shut about this."

Not only did she yank her arm free of his grasp, but her fingers fisted, and she braced her body as if she were about to throw a punch to this fool's chin. "Don't touch me, and definitely don't toss out veiled threats. You ain't shit, and everybody around here knows it. Rufus might've let you dangle around on his balls, but that shit's over now."

He didn't buck back, not that she thought he would. Mike was a coward, a copycat floundering in the wind now that his mentor was gone. As she stepped into the elevator and held his eye contact until the doors closed, she thought Rufus had groomed Mike to perfection. He was pulling loser-ass stunts like fucking with the staff just like Rufus; she wondered if he'd end up dead like the guy he'd looked up to as well.

Chapter 24

Venus

"Hey, beautiful."

Normally, Venus would've immediately corrected anyone calling on her business phone and addressing her in that way. Today, she clenched the phone to her ear and put on her best professional voice.

"Hi, Terrell. What can I do for you?" It was late Monday afternoon, and she didn't have much time before she needed to leave for the meeting at her attorney's office with the homicide detectives.

"Oh, so professional," he laughed. "I like that."

He continued when she didn't respond. "I had some things come up that I had to deal with personally. My manager for the complex says he's been in constant contact with you and that things are getting started as planned, so there's nothing to worry about on that front."

"That's great to hear. As I stated when we met at your house, we've taken a lot of time to map out what we think is the most time- and budget-efficient plans for construction. You've already approved the architect's design. Our vendors have been contracted, and once we get all our permits in, we'll be ready to break ground." She had a checklist on her computer and a print copy that stayed on her desk, so she was constantly abreast of what was going on with the project.

In the past week, she'd needed all her organizational skills, as she'd also taken on supervising every other project BCC had in progress at the moment.

"Yeah, I knew you'd be on top of everything. That's one of the reasons I wanted you working on the job."

She should say something about Mike—that he was competent and would've worked just fine as lead on the account—but her mouth wouldn't form those lies.

"I'm happy to assist you in seeing one of your dreams come to fruition." That was a genuine statement. She was happy to be on this job and looked forward to seeing the finished product. But she was still wondering what the purpose of this call was.

If he wasn't calling to ask specific questions about the project or to add anything to the plans, then what did he want?

"Cool. Now that we've gotten the business out of the way, I called to see if you were free this weekend. I'm out of town right now, but I'll be back Friday evening. I'd like to see you."

Was he serious? She felt like she was living in a *Twilight Zone* episode where everything in her life had turned upside down. In addition to finding her boss dead, she'd had sex with her ex—the cop investigating her boss's murder—and now her top client was asking her out on a date. What the hell?

"I think we should just keep this professional for now." She spoke the words while simultaneously convincing herself she wasn't saying them because of any memory of Mike's and Ellen's comments regarding her sleeping her way ahead.

"You serious? I mean, we're both consenting adults. If we want to go out and share a meal, what's the problem?" He sounded just as carefree and noncommittal as he appeared to be in public.

None of her basic research on Terrell during his NBA career or about his public personal life had revealed anything other than a friendly, laid-back guy. There weren't any big scandals about him sleeping around and making babies he didn't support. No love triangles or on-court squabbles. He was just a ballplayer with sexy-as-hell lips.

Flashes of Malik's lips covering her nipples the other night had her closing her eyes. That shit had felt so good, and when he'd scraped his teeth over her sensitive skin, she'd come so hard and fast that she swore she'd blacked out for a few seconds.

"Hello? You still there?" Terrell's voice shook her free of the memory of Malik.

"Yes. I'm still here," she said, using her free hand to squeeze the bridge of her nose. "I hear you about us being consenting adults, and I completely agree, we can do whatever we want. However, right now, I'd really like to focus my attention on creating the sports complex you envisioned. I don't want to be juggling personal and business during such an important project. I hope you can understand that."

Did she, though? Was she really worried about Terrell Hopkins being upset that she turned him down for a date? No, but she'd tried her best to make her decision to not go out with him sound as pleasant as possible, because this was her most important project. And besides the business issue, the last thing she needed was to throw anything else into the bizarre mix that was her life right now.

He made a sound like he was chuckling or perhaps just breathing heavily, she wasn't sure.

"I see your point, and I appreciate you being so dedicated to my vision. I guess I can wait until the project's done," he said, and Venus found herself smiling.

That would be at least nine months from now. She had no idea what her life was going to look like by that time. Case in point, she was running late for an appointment with two homicide detectives.

Disconnecting the call with Terrell ten minutes after she should've been on her way to the attorney's office, she had to hustle now to get there on time. Jackie called her cell just as she was walking out of the office.

"Hey. What's up?" she answered.

"We need to talk. I been calling Draya all day, but it keeps going to her voice mail."

"She's been in budget meetings nonstop. I know because I was called in on one of them. But she's fine. What's wrong with you?" Jackie sounded stressed.

"It's been a day, but I don't wanna talk over the phone."

"Fine. You wanna Zoom tonight?" she suggested.

"Nah, it'd be better if we could do an in-person."

"Well, I'm running late for the meeting with my attorney. I can text you when I'm done there. Where do you want to meet?"

"You know Jazzy's Lounge, right? Dinner, music, and free drinks for ladies after nine on Mondays. A leisurely evening out."

Venus shook her head at the way Jackie had said "leisurely," knowing she meant versus the chaotic end that had come to their previous evening out. "Sounds good. I'll text you when I'm done."

"Bet. Be careful."

"I will." Not that she thought she needed to be careful. This was just a meeting—it wasn't an interrogation, and she wasn't about to be arrested. At least she was pretty sure she wasn't. As far as Venus and her attorney knew, the police didn't have any evidence to arrest her.

On the ride to her lawyer's office, she tried not to think too much on that. She'd sent her father a quick text this morning just to give him a heads-up about the meeting. A part of her wished she hadn't needed to do that type of check-in, that she really could be an independent adult and take care of her own business, but she'd known better. If by some off chance the press got wind of her being questioned and her father saw it on the news instead of hearing it directly from her, he would flip his shit. Then the lecture from her mother would follow.

Damn, she was tired of the circle she seemed to be forever running in to appease them. Especially since they did nothing to reciprocate for her. No, she hadn't been physically or mentally abused, and thankfully she hadn't been exposed to the kind of mistreatment and trauma that Draya had, but her life hadn't been all peaches and cream either. She'd mistakenly believed that once she became an adult with a successful career, it would at least get a little rosier, but it hadn't. And she had to figure out how to change that.

Minutes after she'd sent the text to her father, he'd called to give her a complete rundown of what she should and shouldn't say. It was like he was her attorney.

"Don't answer anything affirmatively regarding a timeline of your events. You don't recall every little thing you did and at what times. Don't get roped into any answers about your coworkers either. Just focus on what concerns you." Don had spoken in his stern former-defense-counsel tone. "This is an informal meeting. The detectives are fishing for facts they can hang on to and build their case. Don't give them anything substantial."

"I'm sure Tabitha won't let me get into trouble. I plan to follow her lead today." That had been Venus's polite way of telling her father to stand down. It would've been great if he'd called with some advice like, *Don't worry about a thing, Babygirl. You're innocent, so this will be painless.* But no, Don McGee wasn't really known for encouraging her in things that he wasn't in agreement with.

She parked on the street, used her credit card to pay the meter, and hurried into the building. Once she walked into the office of Green, Betters, and Sloan, she approached the reception desk.

"I'm Venus McGee. Here to see Tabitha Sloan."

"Yes, Miss McGee. They're all in the conference room waiting for you." The receptionist led her down a short hall to a closed door.

She knocked once, then opened the door and ushered Venus inside.

Tabitha stood and came to meet her. "Hey. I was getting worried." She spoke in a hushed tone, and Venus apologized for being late.

She'd known Tabitha for years since she'd worked at the first law firm her father had been at before his transformation into politics. She was a statuesque woman with a golden-brown skin tone and a sprinkle of reddish-brown freckles across her nose. Her wavy blonde hair hung close to her butt, and she wore a sharp-ass burgundy pantsuit.

"Now we can get started," Detective Gibson said when Tabitha and Venus made their way to the conference table.

Venus took the seat next to Tabitha while Detective Gibson and Malik sat across from them. She met his gaze just because she knew it would seem weird if she didn't. This was the first time they'd seen or spoken to each other since Saturday, and it wasn't uncomfortable at all.

All the lies.

"Let's start with how long you've known Rufus Jackson and what your relationship to him was," Detective Gibson said.

Venus looked from Malik to his partner and then to Tabitha, who nodded with permission to answer.

"Seven years. He was a junior project manager when I interned at BCC."

Gibson scribbled on the notepad in front of her. Malik only stared at her. She didn't care what he was thinking. Her goal today was to stay focused on answering the questions that needed to be answered so they could stay away from her from this point on.

"And what's your position with BCC now?"

"I'm a senior project manager."

"Working under Rufus?"

She hesitated. "Yes." That fact still chafed, but she hoped her quick answer hid it well enough. Detective Gibson stared at her as if she could read into each answer she gave, dissect it, and determine its value all before she asked the next question.

"Now, on the evening of Friday, December third, you were in attendance at the BCC holiday party at the Marriott Pier 6 venue."

Tabitha nodded in her direction.

"Yes. I was."

"Was Rufus there as well?" Gibson asked.

"Yes."

The woman barely looked down at the notepad in front of her now, like she'd memorized everything she wanted to say. "Was there a time during that evening that you and Rufus argued?"

Venus had been sitting with her back straight, arms folded on the table. Now she desperately wanted to pull her arms back and drop her hands into her lap. That way they wouldn't see her clench her fingers the way she desperately wanted to do. But she knew if she moved to switch positions now, the detectives would mostly take that as some type of nonverbal communication, and she didn't want that. So she focused on keeping her breathing steady even though her heart was hammering in her chest.

"I spoke with Rufus, Mike Livingston, and Louis Crenshaw that evening."

Gibson stared at her with one brow raised.

"Who are Mike Livingston and Louis Crenshaw?" Malik asked.

She swallowed and gazed at him. "Mike Livingston is also a senior project manager at BCC, and Louis Crenshaw is the executive director of our Baltimore office."

Malik continued. "Had you had the opportunity to speak with these men before?"

"Don't answer that," Tabitha interjected. "We agreed to focus on the night of the party only."

Gibson frowned. "What did you and Rufus argue about?"

"Don't answer that. She didn't attest to an argument." Tabitha was writing on a legal pad, and she didn't bother looking up at Gibson.

If she admitted to arguing with Rufus, the words she'd muttered to him—"If you ever put your hands on me again, you'll regret it"—would come into play. Tabitha had advised they stay away from the details as much as possible. If the police wanted to use that hearsay argument as evidence against her, they were going to have to find more proof to support it.

"But you talked to him that night? Alone. We have witnesses who have already given that account of events." Malik was staring at her now.

His deep brown eyes sucked her in as always. How many nights had she stared into those eyes wondering if they could actually see right through her? That's how it'd always felt with him because he'd been so attuned to what she was feeling or thinking the majority of the time. She prayed that wasn't true now.

"I talked to him," she replied after another nod from Tabitha.

"About what?" he pressed.

"A project we're working on."

"A project you're pissed that Mike Livingston got instead of you," Gibson stated. Her tone was hostile, but her gaze was cool, and Venus met it without hesitation.

"I'm lead on the Terrell Hopkins project," she said without checking with Tabitha, and marveled at the quick glint of surprise in Gibson's eyes.

"Later that night, after the argument that you won't attest to, you left the party with Jacqueline Benson and Draya Carter. Where did the three of you go?" Malik asked.

"To my apartment."

"For what?"

"The after party," she said in a smug tone.

"To plan how you'd kill Rufus Jackson?" Gibson matched her tone.

"Don't answer that," Tabitha instructed.

"How well do you know Draya Carter?" Malik asked. "Did you know she was sleeping with Rufus and that she'd been to Rufus's house? Inside his home office, to be exact?"

Venus opened her mouth to reply, but Malik continued. "We found a fingerprint that matches hers from the bonding records on file with the company."

"That's enough. This meeting is over." Tabitha stood. "If you have questions for Miss Carter, I suggest you contact her attorney. We're finished here, Venus."

Following Tabitha's lead, Venus stood, but not without glaring at Malik. What the fuck was he doing asking her about Draya like that? *His job,* she thought dismally when he matched her heated glare. And she shouldn't have even entertained the thought that he might sit there quietly, considering he'd come to her house for a booty call just two days ago. She walked out of the conference room before Tabitha, hearing her attorney direct Malik and his salty-ass partner to contact her if there was anything else they needed from Venus.

Venus was so pissed, she left the office without staying to speak to Tabitha again. She was headed for the elevators when someone called her name. Spinning around, she was shocked to see her godmother standing in the doorway of the office she'd just come bolting out of.

"Oh, hey, Aunt Carol," she said and walked back to her.

Carol Benning was a slim woman with a heavily-creamed-coffee complexion and long dark hair. The royal-blue wrap dress she wore hugged her body and stopped just beneath her knees, where it met her camel-colored boots. She could easily pass for twenty-five instead of fifty-five, as she was a year younger than Venus's father.

"Hey. You look upset. Did something happen?" Carol asked after they hugged and Venus stepped back from her.

"No," Venus replied with a quick shrug. "Nothing. I just, uh . . . I had a meeting with . . . um, Tabitha." Was that telling too much? The last thing she wanted her godmother to know was that she was somehow mixed up in a murder investigation. It was bad enough her father had to know. "What are you doing here?"

"Oh, I'm meeting Tabitha for dinner. I'm a little early, so I was just sitting in the reception area until she was finished. Are you all right? Is she representing you for something?"

Dammit. Venus had forgotten that Carol and Tabitha had both worked at the same firm with her father years ago. While Tabitha had continued to practice law, Carol and Don had gone into politics. She really should've contacted another attorney, perhaps the one Jackie had suggested. That way, she'd be assured there were no personal ties. As it was, she already suspected her father had called Tabitha to tell her what he expected to happen at the meeting, the same way he'd done with her.

"Oh. That's nice," Venus replied, avoiding her godmother's questions. She inhaled slowly and released the breath, making a conscious effort to appear as unbothered as possible. She didn't want Carol asking her again what was wrong. In fact, she didn't want her to ask her any more questions at all. "I've gotta run. I have another appointment. But it was really nice seeing you again, Aunt Carol."

Venus leaned in for another hug and took a second to revel in how tightly Carol hugged her back. They'd always had a cool relationship, but not a terribly close one. As a councilperson like her father, Carol was just as involved in the community as Don was and thus rarely had time to spend with Venus.

"Oh, it was nice seeing you too, baby." She released her from the hug and ran a hand over Venus's hair. "We've got to make time to see each other more often. Let's schedule something soon so we can catch up."

Venus nodded. "That's a great idea. I'll call your office tomorrow."

"Okay, that's fine. You be careful out there, and I'll talk to you soon."

"I will. Have a good dinner," Venus said but was already walking toward the elevators. She waved at Carol and waited until she went back into the office before breathing a sigh of relief.

Slapping her hand on the "Down" button, Venus willed the car to hurry up and arrive. When it did, she hastily entered, reaching into her purse for her phone. The second Jackie answered, she said, "We definitely need to meet tonight. Draya's in trouble."

Chapter 25

Draya

"Knock. Knock."

Draya looked up to see Travis standing in the doorway of her office. "What are you doing here?" Even though they worked in the same building, she'd made a point to never go into his office, and she thought he'd understood he needed to give her the same courtesy.

"I wanted to see you." He walked in without an invitation, closing the door behind him as a signal that he wasn't leaving.

"Now's not a good time, Travis. I have a lot of work to do and . . ."

He came around her desk and reached for her hands, pulling her up out of the seat. "Make time."

"This is my office, Travis. It's not cool for you to be here—someone might see us." She said all this, but she continued to rest her arms on his shoulders while he laced his hands around her waist.

"I'm not afraid of being seen with my lady. Are you afraid of being seen with your man?"

She'd never given him that title and wasn't sure how she felt about him bestowing it upon himself, but she didn't have time to argue with him. "It's not that. I just have to get these reports finalized before the end of the year." That wasn't a total lie. Her day had been spent mostly in meetings with each department head, going over all expenditures and projected budgets for the upcoming year. But a good portion had also been spent sifting through past reports and saving them onto a new USB drive that she, Jackie, and Venus would go through later.

"I really need to get this stuff done before I leave tonight. How 'bout I call you when I'm done?"

He was shaking his head before her sentence was complete. "I wanted to see and hold you close right now, Draya. Just let it be."

She wished like hell she could, but it did feel good to be held like this. He rested his head on her shoulder, squeezing her tight. For a second, she did try to let everything else go and just experience this moment. She took a deep breath, released it with a heavy sigh, and closed her eyes.

Travis smelled good, and she absorbed every bit of the strength in his arms and this embrace because she definitely needed it right now. Her thoughts had been in overdrive since seeing that memo on that USB drive. Just glancing at some of the old financial reports, she had a sinking suspicion that the more she dug, the more she was going to uncover. The possibility of some of the drama resting on her shoulders as the new finance manager was just another weight she had to bear. It was tiring, and for this moment, she leaned totally on Travis—since he wanted to be here for her and all that.

"That's it. Just holding on for a few minutes is good for both of us," he said as he pulled back from the embrace. "Now, you can't sit in this office working all night. How about we get out of here and grab some dinner?"

"I can't," she immediately replied, because what she needed to do after she left this office was find Venus and Jackie to share with them what she'd learned.

"Baby, I don't like seeing you like this, and I don't like you staying in this office by yourself at night."

"It's only six thirty," she told him.

He tilted his head. "You know what I mean."

"I'm not planning to stay that much longer." It never occurred to her to placate him before, but tonight she wanted to. Easing out of his grasp, she sat back down. "You're not working late tonight? That's a change."

Travis sat on the edge of her desk, ignoring the raise of her brow she'd given at the action. "No. I actually had another reason for coming to find you."

"Oh yeah? What's that?" She turned away from him to look at her screen and make sure she'd minimized all the tabs with financial data on them.

Not that Travis gave a damn about the inner workings of BCC, but it was still her job to protect their financial information. Just the way he was sitting on the desk talking to her could be misconstrued if the wrong person walked in.

"I got a call from a Detective Gibson a little while ago. They want you to come down to the station to discuss a fingerprint they found in Rufus's home office."

Draya's fingers froze over the keyboard, and she turned her head slowly to stare at Travis. "Whose fingerprint?" She knew the answer before his lips formed the word.

"Yours."

She sat back in the chair.

"I need you to tell me all the times you've been in Rufus's house—in every room. If we give them a written statement of dates and times, I can get around the formal questioning. A fingerprint means nothing, because there's no way for them to know when it got there. Also, Rufus was found in the main foyer of the house, not his office. And as far as I can tell from my connections at the police department, Pam didn't report anything stolen from any part of the house."

She pushed the heels of her hands into her eyes and groaned. "I've never regretted an entanglement with any man before now."

"We all make mistakes," Travis said, his tone very professional considering the circumstances.

"I didn't kill him," she said, pulling her hands away from her face. "I might be uninhibited in my dating practices, but I'm not a killer."

He touched her cheek with the backs of his fingers, and she shivered, because she'd never felt anything as soft or as poignant in her life. "I know you're not."

She leaned into his touch. "Thanks for saying that."

"No thanks necessary for speaking the truth. Besides, I'm benefiting from your uninhibited dating practices, so I can't possibly complain about that."

His smile was quick and easy, and she didn't hesitate to return it with one of her own. "You're an anomaly," she confessed.

"Oh yeah? How? Because I'm younger than the guys you usually date?" He let his fingers trail down to her neck, then to toy with her hair.

"There's that." She shook her head and continued to stare at him in a way she never had before. "But there's also something else. You're steady, like a rock. Never bothered by anything I say or do."

"Oh, you mean I don't back down when you try to push me away." He shrugged. "Nah, I've got bossy sisters, so I learned early on how to stand my ground. Besides, whenever I touch you, all those icy words or quick snaps you deliver melt away. You're a lot softer on the inside than you lead people to believe."

"Being soft'll get you killed out in these streets." It was something her brothers had told her when she was young and something she wholeheartedly believed. Until now, because the way Travis had said it held a certain appeal.

"Come home with me, baby. Let me run you a hot bath and bathe away some of your stress. I'll order dinner, and we can spend the night just watching TV or talking. Whatever you want."

That sounded so sweet and so normal. Draya had never fooled herself into believing she'd have a normal life with a man. It wasn't in the cards for the Carter women. Her great-grandma Jane, Granny, and her mother had each been a single parent. They'd all raised their own kids as well as a slew of others in the family or neighborhood, and they'd done just fine. None of them ever confessed to needing a man for more than sex. Granny actually said she only wanted the dick and that they could get outta her face after that. Draya had been seventeen when her grandmother told her that, and she'd laughed each time she'd seen her for an entire week afterward.

"You really want me to come over and help you decorate your tree. Don't try to be slick." She laughed, hoping the sound would break the odd sense of intimacy that had suddenly filled the office.

Travis chuckled too. "Nah, I said we can do whatever you want. I mean, if you'll be okay sitting on the couch looking at that bare-ass tree in the corner by the balcony where you told me to put it, then I'm cool with that."

"Oh, now we're doing the guilt-trip thing." She liked the sound of his laughter, and she had told him to put that tree by the balcony doors.

He lived in one of the condo buildings in Canton and had a fantastic view of the harbor. Christmas lights against that backdrop would be phenomenal. She'd decorated her tree already, so she could go over to his place and hook his up.

Her phone buzzed, and they both looked at it. Draya snatched it up because her screen lit up with the text notification at the top of the screen. While he couldn't see the content, he'd definitely see the name of the person texting, and no matter how good she was feeling around him at the moment, her phone was still private.

Jazzy's Lounge @930

It was from Jackie, and it instantly put Draya on alert.

"I really can't tonight," she said, placing the phone facedown on her desk. "If I stay and get through everything tonight, I can definitely come over tomorrow after work."

He continued to smile, but she noted the shift in his energy. It came with the shadowy look in his eyes. Travis said he believed she wasn't a killer, but did he trust her as his lady? That had been his word, not hers, because as far as she knew, she hadn't committed to anything with him, but the way he was looking at her now made her wonder.

"Sure. Don't forget to send me the list of dates and times you were at the Jackson house. If you can get that to me tonight, I'll email it to the detective, and we can move on from there."

She nodded. "Do you think she'll back off once you send it to her?"

He stood. "If that's all she has on you, she won't have a choice."

"And if they find something else?"

Travis leaned over then, placing one hand on her desk, the other on the back of her chair, his face just inches from hers. "Then your attorney will handle it. That's why you hired me." He kissed her quickly.

Draya reached up and cupped the back of his head, holding him close. "Sort of. I mean, I know you're good at your job. But you're also good at other things."

She licked his bottom lip, then slipped her tongue into his mouth for a quick taste.

He groaned. "Oh yeah? Anything in particular?"

"Oh yeah, your tongue for starters. You're really good at knowing just how to use it."

As if her words were an invitation, he pressed his lips to hers, easing his tongue into her mouth for an instant duel with hers. She tilted her head, loving the second he leaned in farther, taking the kiss deeper. Her pulse kicked up as desire pumped hot and fast through her veins.

"I can use my tongue all night tomorrow if that's what you want," he said, breaking the kiss only long enough to say those words.

Her pussy throbbed from the sound of his voice, and all she could do was moan in response.

A few minutes more of that deliciously hot kiss and Travis pulled away again, this time putting more space between them. “Six o’clock, Draya, and not a moment later. I mean it—if you’re late, I might have to make you pay.”

Pulling her bottom lip between her teeth, she tilted her head. “Really? How so?”

He gripped her chin with his fingers. “I’ll spank that ass once for every minute you’re late.”

She sucked in a breath, not bothering to hide how much that comment aroused her. “Oh, then I’ll definitely take my time.”

Grinning, he leaned in and dropped a noisy kiss on her lips. “Finish your work and don’t forget to email me that list.”

He moved away from her then, heading to the door.

“I will. Have a good night, Travis.”

He opened the door and looked back at her. “Dream about me tonight, Draya.”

As he disappeared before she could respond, Draya leaned back in her chair and mumbled, “Yeah, I just might.”

Chapter 26

Jackie

"So we're definitely doing this," she said, staring across the table at Venus and Draya.

They were sitting in one of the back booths at Jazzy's. The place was dimly lit as always, which provided a great cover for those who needed it. A band was playing their second set of the night, and Jackie was on her second whiskey sour.

"We don't have a choice," Draya replied. She stared down at her empty glass and then up at Jackie.

They both looked at Venus, who'd been folding every napkin on the table into a fan while they'd all shared their developments of the day. "He looked right at me and asked that question like he knew I was hiding the fact that you'd been in Rufus's office that day."

"He's a cop, Venus. What'd you expect? Just because you gave him some didn't mean he was gonna stop doing his job," Draya said dryly.

Venus sat back with a huff. "I know that. I'm not naive."

"Ha!" Draya was loud and unapologetic about making that sound.

"I'm not!" Venus insisted.

"Well, how'd you expect that to go down? I mean, did you two talk about how getting your thing off on the kitchen counter was going to play into this investigation?" Jackie didn't sound as abrupt as Draya, but she did have to ask.

"I don't know," Venus sighed. "And really, it doesn't even matter. We're not dating or anything like that. If we were, then I'd really be in a mess, considering Terrell just asked me out *for real* for real." She looked like she hadn't really meant to say that, and Draya laughed.

"Look at you juggling two men at a time. That's definitely a change for walk-the-straight-and-narrow Venus. Guess my flirty ass is rubbing off on you."

Venus grinned. "Probably so. Like you and your boy toy gettin' busy in your office."

"Unh-uh, that's not what I said happened. He came in and we kissed—that's it. I wouldn't have done anything else in the office."

"But you wanted to, especially when he said he was gonna spank that ass," Jackie said, repeating that part of Draya's story with glee. Because the look on Draya's face had said she'd been ready to cream her panties the minute that young man said that to her. It had been all kinds of comical.

"You mean like Mike and Robyn were doing in the basement? Damn, I would've paid to see that shit," Draya said.

Venus rolled her eyes. "He's such an ass."

"But listen, you can still screw Malik whenever you feel like it," Draya continued. "Just don't give his ass any information about us. If he thinks he's playing you, he's the one gettin' played while you get your thing off. As for Terrell, girl, I'd just go with the flow on that. He seems like he's fickle when it comes to women; plus, he doesn't even live here full-time. There's no point in looking for a happily ever after when there's only a temporary option in range."

Jackie had to nod at the logic in those comments. "Facts."

"Well, what about you? What happened to that lady you were sorta ignoring but then met up with after the funeral? You talk to her lately?"

Venus stopped messing with those napkins and turned her attention to the martini she'd ordered.

Jackie hadn't talked to Karlie since that night, but damn if she'd been able to get her out of her mind. "I don't know if that's a thing or not. I'm not really looking for a thing."

"Girl, I know how that feels. You're just happy being the way you are, and then somebody comes along trying to change the game." Draya seemed to have definite feelings about this subject.

Jackie knew that wasn't due to her personally but probably how that young lawyer was really laying it on thick with her.

"Anyway, we need to figure out how all this ties together." It was better to get off the subject of their personal lives anyway. She wasn't sure confessing all the puzzling thoughts she was having about Karlie was the way to go. Maybe after she had more of a chance to figure out what was happening there, but for right now, they had more pressing issues.

Draya reached across the table to pick up Jackie's phone. She scrolled through the pictures of the documents from the folder. "We should print these out and then delete them from your phone. I can rescan them and put them on the USB drive that I have the financial records on. If I can match these charges to our bank statements, we can prove that they're each linked to Rufus."

"Well, didn't he sign all of them?" Venus asked.

"This car payment is an online receipt. Anybody could've logged into this account and made a payment. But if it was charged to Rufus's company expense account, it's specifically allocated to him. The paper trail is how we'll piece all this together," Draya said.

"Okay, and then what? We create this paper trail that proves Rufus was a cheater in business just like he was in his marriage. How does that help us find his killer?" Venus seemed extremely skeptical of their investigation. "How does it keep them from questioning Draya about why her fingerprints were found in Rufus's office?"

Draya sighed. "I already told you Travis said I should compile a list of the dates and times I was there. We'll submit that to the police, and that answers my fingerprint, because there's no way to time-stamp when the fingerprint was made."

That made sense and sounded like something Jackie may've heard on a *Law & Order* episode.

Venus didn't comment on that again but instead asked Jackie, "How'd you get that folder back in Ellen's office without her knowing it was gone?"

"I don't know if she realized it was gone or not, but I went into the mail room and grabbed an interoffice envelope. Stuffed it in there in time for the morning delivery and went on about my business."

With pursed lips, Draya said, "She probably had a fit when she opened that interoffice envelope and saw that folder."

Jackie nodded. "Probably, but that's what her sneaky ass gets."

"She might circle it back to you, since you were in her office by yourself this morning," Venus added.

"Then that means I've got something on her ass, too, just like I do on Mike. He's such an idiot, and Robyn can do better," she said.

"When you say 'better,' you mean, like, you?" Draya asked with a raise of her brows.

She hadn't even been thinking along those lines. "Nah. I'm still trying to wrap my mind around having somebody in my life again."

"Oooh, so you *are* thinking of sleeping with your text buddy?" Venus asked with a gotcha expression.

Jackie could only shake her head as she picked up her glass and emptied it. There was never a dull moment with these two, and they really did act like they were concerned about what was going on in her life. It'd been a long time since she'd had that.

Another thirty minutes later, and they paid their tab and left Jazzy's. They went to their cars, waiting until they were lined up behind each other at the entrance to pull off and go their separate ways. The instruction to text when they each got home was given again, but after ten minutes of driving, Jackie heard her phone buzz with a message.

She pulled it out of her pocket and read the message: Tell me you both saw that silver Tahoe in the parking lot at Jazzy's.

Venus replied first: What silver Tahoe?

Draya answered: The one that's right behind me now.

Chapter 27

Venus

She felt like crap. All night, plus this morning when she woke, showered, dressed, and came into work, Venus had been plagued by the heavy sensation that she was disappointing them.

Draya and Jackie this time, not her parents.

Why hadn't she just told them about covering for Rufus in the past? Those receipts Jackie had found definitely suggested Rufus was doing some shady bookkeeping and that Ellen was in on it too. And that supply list that Draya had on the USB drive was exactly how Venus had come across the discrepancies on client accounts before. The list was dated just a few months ago, but Draya had said the city projects were completed two years ago. Venus wondered if it was the same accounts she'd already fixed for him.

Dropping her head into her hands, she sighed heavily. How the hell had things gotten this bad?

She knew the answer to that too—because she hadn't wanted to disappoint her parents. Keeping a secret to protect her parents' reputations hadn't seemed like such a big deal until now, when keeping that same secret could help two women who'd come to mean a lot to her. It wouldn't help her either way. If she told Jackie and Draya what she knew and they ultimately uncovered more of Rufus's shady dealings, then the ones she'd covered up from before might still be revealed as well. Rendering her efforts to keep the secret pointless.

If she kept the secret and they didn't find any other proof that Rufus was doing something wrong, then the cops could continue to look to them as possible suspects. They might arrest Draya now that they had her fingerprint at the house. And what if Draya told everything when she was arrested? Then Venus and Jackie would still end up in jail.

It was a no-win situation that she knew she had to change.

Her phone chirped, and she lifted her head to glance at it. "Really? Of all the people." She huffed and grabbed the phone, answering it before she could change her mind about sending it to voice mail. "Venus McGee."

"I need to see you."

"No." Sleeping with the proverbial enemy while being asked out on a date by a client was just the type of love-life stress she didn't need.

"I'm serious, V. I'm right outside."

"Good for you—keep on driving back to Howard County where you belong."

He sighed. "I belong anywhere I choose to be, and right now it's here, waiting to talk to you. Ten minutes."

"You're not the boss of me." She sounded like a child saying that, and even more so because she knew she was going to go down there and meet him. There was no use wasting both their time with the back-and-forth. "Ten minutes."

Disconnecting the call, she grabbed her coat and purse, then left the office. On the elevator down, she told herself she was going only because it would get her mind off the indecision she was wrestling with. Considering Malik was firmly ensconced in the issues surrounding that indecision, he probably wasn't the best person to be around at the moment. Still, she zipped her puffy jacket and pulled on the hood to fight against the brutally cold December wind as she headed out the front door. She didn't know what type of SUV Malik drove, so she just looked up and down the street for any vehicle. When a horn blared, she stared in the direction of the sound and cursed upon seeing him sitting in a police cruiser.

"Are you serious?" She muttered the question while looking around before heading toward the car.

"You're kidding, right?" she asked when she was close enough to lean over and stare into the passenger-side window of the car.

He lowered the window. "It's cold out there. Get in."

"Ohhhhhh, no, you don't." She shook her head. "You are not getting me to climb into that car and then you take my ass to your headquarters and arrest me." She stopped where she stood and folded her arms over her chest.

He was wearing the full police uniform today instead of his usual street clothes with his badge clipped to his belt buckle. She didn't know what that meant, and truthfully, she didn't care.

"Nobody's gonna arrest you if you get in the car, Venus. But I swear if you keep giving me a hard way to go, I'll come over there and cuff your little ass."

And he would too. There was nothing in her memories of him that gave the impression that he was playing about any threat he ever issued. She used to like that about him—that his word was his bond. Now there wasn't anything she wanted to like about Malik, not even the memory of his mouth on her breasts. Okay, maybe she'd keep that one, since it'd been the only thought capable of lulling her into at least a brief sleep these past few nights.

She opened the passenger-side door a few seconds later and sat on the seat before closing the door. "Okay. Talk."

"Not here," he said and started the car's engine.

Panic rose quickly in the pit of her stomach. "You said we weren't going to the police station."

"We're not. Put on your seat belt." After barking that order, he pulled off and didn't speak again until almost twenty minutes later when he'd driven her out of the city and parked the police cruiser behind an abandoned school building.

The car wasn't visible to anyone just passing by on the street, as he'd parked in the back behind a dumpster. She wondered if that meant he was about to pull out his gun and shoot her. If that was the case, she had something she wanted to get off her chest first.

"Why'd you come to my house and have sex with me? Was it to see if I'd tell you more about Rufus? Because if so, that was some low, punk-ass shit!" She unsnapped the seat belt and slid farther toward the door in case she had to hurry up and make a run for it.

"I didn't come to your place expecting to have sex with you."

"Yes, you did. You said it yourself, 'I came so I could do this again' or some such bullcrap!" With every hour that passed since Saturday night, she'd felt used and betrayed by Malik. It was partly her fault because she could've said no at any point, and she knew he would've turned and walked away. Still, she was going to blame him for coming over in the first place.

"I said I missed you. I missed what we had, and yeah, I wanted you again. But that's not the sole reason I came over." He ran a hand down the back of his neck. "The real issue here, Venus, is that you need to tell me everything so your name can stop coming up in this investigation."

She shrugged. "I don't know what to tell you. Maybe whoever is bringing up my name so much is trying to deflect the focus from them. Have you ever thought about that?" She didn't wait for him to respond. "And what are they saying anyway? An argument at a party? Really? Is that what your entire case is hinging on? 'Cause I gotta tell you, if that's true, you're up shit's creek without a paddle."

"I just want your name out of it. Can you understand that? I don't want them even looking at you in that way." He said the words so emphatically, his forehead wrinkled, his gaze burning tiny pricks of heat into her skin.

She waited a beat, wanting to make sure what came next was clear. "I didn't kill Rufus. That's all I need to tell you, Malik. I didn't kill that man."

"Was the argument because he gave Mike the promotion?"

"I didn't tell you there was an argument. Damn! We've gone over this shit before. I'm not about to sit here and rehash it all again."

"Did you know he was sleeping with Draya Carter?"

"I'm not my sister's keeper," she snapped and turned her head so she could stare out the window.

"No," he said slowly. "But you're loyal to a fault."

She didn't reply, mostly because she didn't know what to say. In her book, loyalty was a good thing, yet she was certain by the way he sounded and the sorrowful way he was looking at her that he didn't agree.

"If you thought keeping a secret would protect your friends, you'd keep that secret."

Well, he was partially right. She was keeping secrets to protect her friends *and* her parents *and* herself.

"Just like you suggested we start seeing each other in secret once your mother deemed me inappropriate for you to date."

"I don't want to do this with you again," she said. Rehashing memories was futile; she couldn't go back to the past and redo a damn thing.

"But you wanted to be with me back then. And I wanted to be with you. We were young and in love and good for each other, but your mother thought differently."

"I'm her only child. Her only daughter." And the last guy Ilene wanted her falling for was the son of a drunk and a mother who worked as a bus driver.

"Don't do that!" he shouted. "Don't defend her, not to me. Because if anybody knows better, I do."

Venus rubbed both her temples now, praying she didn't get a headache as a result of all this stress. "I said I didn't want to do this with you."

"You don't want to do anything your parents don't approve of—you never have." He drummed his fingers on the steering wheel for a few seconds, the sound annoying her to no end.

"I did a little research on your attorney before our meeting. I like to know who I'm dealing with in an interview. She used to work at the same firm as your father fifteen years ago."

She looked over at him. "So?"

"So you would pick an attorney who your father approved of. Or did he select her for you?"

"I'm an adult—I can call my own lawyer."

"And then your godmother was there. Councilperson Benning also used to work at the firm with your father and Tabitha."

"Malik, where is all this going? You don't care who my attorneys are or where they used to work."

"But I do care about you, V. I've never stopped caring about you. That's why I want you to be honest with me."

"I can't." The words slipped out before she could stop them, and she gritted her teeth.

"Is your father involved? Is that why you can't talk to me?"

She gasped and glanced in his direction. "Why would you say something like that? My father is not involved with murdering someone."

The rise in her tone hadn't fazed him in the least—he was still looking at her with that calm but exasperated way he used to a long time ago. A muscle twitched in his jaw—his patience was wearing thin. But then he closed his eyes for a couple of seconds. When he opened them again, they seemed softer, his jaw more relaxed, and when he spoke, his tone was lighter.

"The only times you ever stopped talking to me was when your mother forbid us to be together and after your father caught us together that last time. You said I walked away and didn't look back, but do you want to know the real reason why I did that?"

She didn't and yet she did. Mourning the loss of Malik as a friend and a lover had taken years, and she'd never been as close to another man since then.

"I'll take your silence as a yes," he said with a light chuckle. "I couldn't stay with you and watch you continue to try and choose between me and your parents."

"I wasn't doing that."

"You were. Our senior year, when your mother told you to, you said it was over."

"But then I came to your house and we got back together."

"In secret, and I agreed to that. But then when your father saw us at the museum, you broke it off again."

She sighed because he was right, and just like the time before, she'd gone to his house days later and they'd gotten back together. But it hadn't been the same after that.

"You started college, and I was working at the bar, and you changed. It seemed like it was a lot easier for you to brush me off then with excuses about needing to be at the church or in class or whatever else your parents thought up for you to do. You were never going to choose me over them. I knew it, and you knew it too. So I walked."

Fumbling with the button on her coat pocket, she said quietly, "I never pegged you for a coward."

"I always knew you were their puppet."

Her head jerked up. "What did you just say to me?"

"You heard me. You were always their puppet, doing whatever they said regardless of how you felt. When you were living under their roof, I respected that, but once you'd moved into the dorm and were on your own, I expected something different. I wanted you to stand up to them, to be your own woman."

"I am my own woman. I do what I want, when I want."

"Then tell me what you're keeping from me. Tell me so I can help you."

Rage bubbled inside her now at his audacity. How dare he practically kidnap her in this police car just to call her names? "I'll tell you something that you and your partner seem to be ignoring. Rufus was an egotistical bastard known for being an asshole in all its gruesome formations. He thought his community dick was a gift to every woman walking, even those who didn't like dick at all. His wife allowed his transgressions, and the money and power he wielded from working at BCC afforded him the lifestyle to be the city's biggest and best-dressed asshole on a daily basis. But I didn't kill him," she said again, solemnly. "Now, can you take me back to my building, please? I don't much like sitting in parked cars behind schools."

"You used to like it," he said quietly after a few seconds had passed.

"As we've both stated, we're not teenagers anymore." He didn't respond right away, and again she figured now was as good a time as any to speak her mind. "I'm not gonna be your ass on the side or whatever you might want to call it."

"You know I'd never consider you that."

Venus shook her head. "What I know is that you had to bring me back here to talk in private. Not *Hey, V, let's go to lunch,* or *How 'bout I grab some Mission BBQ and bring it by your place for dinner tonight?* Those are things that people who're dating do. This right here and the come in and slam my ass on the kitchen counter, that's that secret-affair-type shit that Rufus was into. But I'm not."

"I know that's not your thing. You want forever after. That's what you always told me."

"I don't know what I want anymore." She sounded as tired as she felt. This entire situation was running her ragged, and she needed to find some peace.

"You should figure that out. What *you* want, how *you* want to live, what matters most to *you*. Stop letting them be a part of your equation,

Venus. As you just told me, you're an adult now. Your parents don't have the authority to dictate your every move."

He was right, and that's why she didn't counter his words. Every one that he'd just spoken was true, and admitting that made her feel pathetic and weak.

After a prolonged silence, he sighed heavily. "I'll take you back now."

Once again, they drove in silence—her looking out the side window and Malik staring through the windshield. He parked behind a UPS truck, and she released her seat belt and grabbed the door handle.

"I shouldn't have to tell you this, but whoever is hell-bent on pinning this on me, Jackie, or Draya is probably somebody you should be looking at more closely."

"I am." She opened the door, but before she could step out, he grabbed her arm gently yet possessively, and she paused.

"I've never stopped wishing I could give you forever after, V."

Her heart thumped with that statement, and warmth spread through her. There'd been a time in her life when she'd dreamed of living happily ever after with Malik. They would get married and have children, go on vacations to the beach or Disney World. They'd build a life of love and respect, treating their children as individuals and respecting their opinions. It was going to be perfect. And then it was over.

"Wishes don't come true," she said softly. "Not even at Christmastime."

Chapter 28

Jackie

The annual Tubs of Toys fundraising gala presented by the combined prosecutors' offices around the state was on Saturday at the Marina Golf Club in Annapolis. Rufus always purchased two tables for the event, and this year, Venus had declared it was her task to hand out the tickets in Rufus's absence. That little stunt had almost caused Ellen to suffer a cardiac event as she blustered and complained straight to the top. Louis's email to every employee of BCC naming Venus the temporary VP of operations had shut Ellen all the way down. And of course, it had given Jackie, Draya, and Venus tickets to this formal, high-profile event.

"This couldn't have worked out better," Draya said as they walked into the ballroom. "Louis practically telling the world that you're temporarily in Rufus's position means that whoever Rufus's contact at the city was might try to rekindle their dealings by talking to you."

To her right, Draya was wearing a black off-the-shoulder sequin dress that hugged her like a second skin and draped down to the floor. Her hair was a wavy wonder hanging past her shoulders. On her left, Venus held a silver clutch in front of her one-shoulder, velvet-and-taffeta, floor-length navy-blue gown. Jackie held her head high as she stood between her two beautiful friends wearing the coolest burgundy velvet tuxedo with a black silk shirt. Karlie had sent her a kissing-face pic after she'd impulsively texted her a pic asking how she looked. She'd saved that kissing-face pic to a folder marked "Favorites" and had looked at it twice on the forty-five-minute drive down here.

"I honestly don't think anybody's going to confront me. Especially not at a party like this," Venus said.

"Your cop might," Jackie said. "He's over in that corner staring like he's itching to come over right now."

Venus stared straight ahead. "I don't even know why he's here, but I'm just gonna ignore him."

Jackie noted how big the ballroom was—ignoring a person was definitely possible. There had to be more than four hundred people here. There were tables draped in white linen cloths, red flowers pouring from tall vases on each. The red-and-white theme continued throughout the space with at least a dozen trees decorated with red bulbs and white lights. Under each tree were red plastic tubs, all filled with gifts wrapped in red-and-white wrapping paper.

"Can we just focus?" Draya insisted, and Venus nodded.

"Okay, well, even if someone from the city approaches me, how am I supposed to know what to say to them?" she continued, her face already forming that frown she'd been wearing much too often this past week.

"You just go with the flow. They're not going to outright proposition you here tonight—just take note of who from the city approaches," Draya said.

"But wait, I thought you found some entries in the financial records that indicated Rufus might've been stealing from projects he'd done in other counties too."

Draya nodded. "Exactly. That's why this is the best place for us to be tonight. City and county politicians will be here."

"And hundreds of prosecutors, some of whom might actually be thinking of the case they'll present against us," Jackie added.

Waving a hand, Draya stepped out of the formation they had going and headed toward one of the company's two marked tables. "Look, we talked about this. We just need to get some more names to match to these transactions. If Rufus was still billing the city for projects that had been completed a long time ago, somebody at the city had to be helping him."

"I agree," Jackie said. "Somebody at the city would've caught it if they were paying for supplies twice, or even after a project was completed."

"Somebody like a congressman who was known for getting Ted Billings city contracts," Venus added quietly.

Of the three of them, Venus was the only one who had a relationship with her father, and Jackie thought they seemed close. Instead of being upset when they'd first brought up her father's possible involvement while sitting at the table in the lunchroom the other day, she'd been an active participant in the discussion. It'd been Draya's decision to eat there at least once a week instead of going out so it didn't appear as if they were changing their routine too much. Most people coming in and out hadn't paid them any attention. Ellen had ventured in and eyed them until she'd purchased her food and walked out. Jackie had almost thought the woman was going to come over and say something stupid to them. Instead, she'd just given her death glare and walked away.

Tonight, since they were on the topic again, Venus continued. "I could just ask my father."

"Hell no!" Draya immediately responded. "We don't want to tip our hand too soon. We have to line up all these ducks in a row."

They were at the table now, the first ones to actually take a seat at the second table—since the first one was full. When she was seated, Jackie watched as Draya and Venus set their purses on the table and then maneuvered all the extra material of their gowns before sitting.

For a few minutes, they just sat there, each of them looking around the room. "I feel like we're casing the place, working up some type of master plan. But I look too good to be getting into any fights tonight." Jackie brushed imaginary lint from her lapel.

Draya shook her head. "No, you keep your inner Creed on lockdown for tonight." She grinned and pulled her phone out of her purse to check the time. "It's still early, so people should continue trickling in. I don't see anybody of note right now."

"Of note?" Jackie asked, wondering when they'd started talking in this TV crime-show lingo.

"They're not here yet," Draya replied with a roll of her eyes. "Nobody we talked about being a possible suspect is here yet. Well, except for Mike, who just walked out with Robyn. I can't believe you gave his ass a ticket."

Venus and Jackie followed Draya's gaze across the room.

"It would've looked bad if I hadn't," Venus replied. "But wait, he only had one ticket, so Robyn can't be his date."

"She's probably working security," Jackie added.

"Maybe we should go over the list of people we came up with again, just so we'll recall who to be on the lookout for tonight." Venus leaned in close and spoke in a hushed tone.

"That's a good idea," Jackie replied. "I'll start. Mike, because Venus said he mentioned that he and Rufus had gone to a strip club after the company party."

Draya had started rocking to The Jackson 5's version of "I Saw Mommy Kissing Santa Claus." "Doesn't jive. Rufus was Mike's meal ticket at BCC. Killing him wouldn't help Mike's situation."

"Ellen," Venus said, even though everyone knew that was Jackie's first go-to contender. "We've long wondered about the sickeningly close relationship she had with Rufus. Even if she were forty years younger, she wouldn't have been his type, so why the hell did he keep her around? And why was she hiding those receipts for him? Maybe she knew about the bogus city deals and was protecting him. In return, he was allowing her to stay on the job harassing all who walked through those glass doors."

Draya drummed her fingers on the table. "Again, he would've been her meal ticket, so why kill him?"

"To clear a space to get one of her children a job. Two of her sons were laid off earlier this year," Venus said.

"She's right. I heard that too," Jackie added.

"She stays at the bottom of the list. Pam is at the top. She stands to lose the most if it comes out that Rufus was crooked, because everyone will look at her as if she knew what he was doing, and then they'll speculate about her." Draya mouthed a few lines of the song and then continued. "Besides that, what wife wants to meet the woman her husband was screwing so she can ask if that woman killed the dumbass husband? That shit don't even make sense."

"None of this makes sense, if we're being real," Jackie said. "But I'm hungry so I'm 'bout to hit the buffet."

By the time Jackie came back with a plate of food and a second plate full of desserts, Venus and Draya were whispering about something and staring across the room.

"What's up?" she asked. "What happened while I was gone?"

"Look who's here and enjoying the bar already," Draya said and pointed.

Jackie followed the direction where she was aiming and saw Lynette Frost, Rufus's administrative assistant. She would've been a cute girl with her hair in a shoulder-length wrap, caramel complexion, green eyes, and plump lips, but her attitude was pure trash. That knowledge was enough to have Jackie even dismissing how good that strapless red dress looked on her.

"Oh. She always gets a ticket to come to this, right? I mean, I'd think Rufus would give his assistant one even though he didn't deem it appropriate to give all the managers in the company one." Her comments sounded salty, but really, she'd been okay with not being required to attend too many work functions. Being around Ellen five days a week was enough.

"Yeah, she's usually here, so I kept her on the list this year," Venus said. "But I don't recall ever seeing her this twisted so early in the evening. We should talk to her, see what she knows."

Draya was already nodding her agreement before she waved a hand in the air. "Hey, Lynette, there's space over here at our table."

Jackie had shifted her focus to her plates, wondering if the mini éclairs would be tasty—sometimes they were just a bunch of pastry and not enough cream inside. She hated that.

"Hey, y'all." Lynette spoke when she arrived at the table.

"Hey," Venus replied.

Jackie only looked up to give a slight nod. Lynette barely acknowledged it before taking the seat closest to Venus. That put three chairs between her and Jackie, and Jackie tried not to laugh.

It was no secret that Lynette didn't like anyone who wasn't her version of normal, and it was also true that Jackie didn't give two fucks about who Lynette liked or didn't like. But she was interested in hearing whatever Draya and Venus could get her to say. Probably not much, because Lynette was nothing if not loyal to Rufus—like, to an annoying fault, the way she did that man's bidding. And as far as anyone in the office knew, they weren't sleeping together.

"So what've you been up to, Lynette? I haven't seen you around the office much." Venus tried to look nonchalant, but Draya's insistent gaze said she was eager to hear anything and everything Lynette might have to say.

Lynette nodded, her hair moving like sheets of black silk along the sides of her face. "I've been packing up Rufus's office and getting boxes ready to be shipped to his wife. So, so much stuff. Especially in that safe—you know, the one beneath that painting of the two suns."

"Um, yeah, the safe under the paintings," Venus said and then shrugged when Lynette looked over her shoulder as if she thought somebody had come up behind her.

Obviously, Venus hadn't known about any safe in Rufus's office, and of the three of them, she'd most likely been in there the most. Jackie hadn't known about it either, even though it was probably something the facilities manager should've known.

Lynette emptied her glass and touched a hand to her throat. Jackie didn't know what the woman had been drinking but suspected it wasn't something she was used to burning as it went down.

"Lots of papers and stuff. I guess things he didn't want to keep at his house. So many numbers and canceled checks. I asked Ellen where I was supposed to put it." Lynette shrugged and frowned. "She didn't have an answer, just said to put it in a box and she'd take care of it."

"And did she take care of it?" Venus asked.

Lynette hiccupped and then picked up her glass again. She turned it over and frowned once more. "It's empty."

"I'll get you another if that's what you want," Draya said and reached for the glass.

But Lynette held on to the glass and extended her arm across the table. "I want *her* to get it."

Jackie looked up, a Korean barbecue chicken wing on its way to her mouth. All eyes were on her. "Who?" she asked.

"You." Lynette slurred the one word. "Pretty please."

This trick was twisted. Venus and Draya were giving Jackie expectant looks, Draya going so far as to wiggle her eyebrows and nod in Lynette's direction, signaling they wanted to keep plying the woman with drinks so she could keep talking. It was a decent plan, but Jackie didn't like her part in it, especially since Lynette barely spoke to her on a regular basis. Grumbling under her breath, she snatched the glass from Lynette.

"What are you drinking?"

"Absolut." Another slurred word, but Jackie knew what she meant.

"Straight?" she asked without hiding her shock.

Lynette nodded very sharply and repeatedly until Venus grabbed her chin to stop the motion.

"Damn, no wonder your chest's on fire." Walking away, she went to the bar and got the drink.

When she returned to the table, she extended her arm to set the drink down in front of Lynette. The woman was still talking and now apparently using hand and arm movements to express her drunk-slurred words. Her arm bumped Jackie's, and some of the drink spilled onto Jackie's hand before she could release the glass.

"Ooops," Lynette squealed seconds before she grabbed Jackie's arm and licked the back of her hand.

Venus made a hurling sound while Draya's face scrunched in disgust. Jackie yanked her hand away so hard, she accidentally hit Lynette in the face.

"Owwww. She hit me." Another hiccup and then Lynette reached for the glass.

Jackie went to her seat and seriously considered going to the bathroom to run scorching hot water over her hand. Instead, when Venus recovered and thankfully didn't throw up all over the table, she reached into her purse and found a bottle of hand sanitizer that she passed to Jackie. "Use all of it," Venus said.

She really didn't have to say that, because it was exactly what Jackie planned to do.

"And you know he was nasty." Lynette resumed talking after another swallow from the glass. "Well, you probably already knew that." That was directed at Draya, and Jackie grinned behind her hand as she resumed eating.

The Korean barbecue wings were fiery and delicious.

"He had all kinds of nude photos in that safe."

All their eyes widened and their ears perked up.

"Really?" Draya cleared her voice. "Were they of anyone you recognized?"

Lynette nodded so hard this time, it looked like her head might pop off. She was gonna be so sick tomorrow morning. As soon as Jackie got Venus and Draya alone, she was gonna ask whose idea it was to get the poor girl drunk, then pump her for information.

"Yep, I sure did," Lynette said.

"Who?" Venus and Draya asked simultaneously.

Lynette didn't nod this time; instead, she pointed, and the three of them followed the direction of her wavering finger. "He had lots and lots of pictures of her."

"Oh shit," Venus whispered.

"Damn," Jackie said.

Draya smirked. "I knew it!"

State's Attorney Leslie Drake had just arrived at the party.

Chapter 29

Venus

It was one wild weekend.

Lynette showing up already drunk had been a godsend that she and Draya had immediately pounced on, and the information she'd ended up giving them had been golden. They left the party shortly after Leslie arrived because Jackie insisted they needed to take Lynette home. Which they did, and then the three of them had another conversation while sitting in a Burger King parking lot because of course, Jackie was hungry again. It was a wonder that woman wasn't three sizes bigger, the way she ate.

"So Rufus had more nude pictures. Does that mean he was blackmailing more women?" Draya asked from the back seat of Venus's car, since Jackie had insisted they switch spots after the ride down.

"Probably," Jackie replied. "That man really was a funky hot mess."

"He was that indeed," Venus said with both her hands still clenched on the steering wheel. She hadn't been able to let it go even after putting the car in park. Her heart was still thumping wildly at having learned all they had from Lynette and seeing her own father huddled close with her godmother as they'd been on their way out. Draya had immediately pounced on that, making not-so-subtle comments about the two of them having hooked up in the past. Venus didn't want to believe that. For one, she couldn't put her father in the same infidelity category where Rufus roamed. And two, Carol was like family. Still, she hadn't been able to shake how closely they were standing together, whispering about something so intently that neither of them had seen Venus and the others when they walked right past them to get to the entrance of the ballroom. Now, not only was she doubting the credibility of the man who'd raised her, but she was also doubting his loyalty to her mother. It wasn't something she thought she'd ever get used to.

"Those pictures give Leslie motive to want him dead, too, so she's going on the list. And when Lynette gives us a list of all the other women who had pictures in that safe, we'll have more suspect names to add."

Jackie turned sideways in the passenger seat so she could look back at Draya. "You really think she's gonna remember anything that happened tonight when she wakes up? That girl is fucked up; she probably won't remember her name for a day or two."

"She was pretty drunk," Venus said. "I feel kinda bad for doing that to her."

"Nonsense, we didn't do that to her. She came to the party drunk. Pissed off because now that Rufus is gone, her job isn't guaranteed. And because things he promised her, like assistance getting her mother free rent in the new senior building we just built, are out of the question now."

"What kind of hold did this guy have on people? It's like women thought he was some type of god. Young women like Lynette, successful women like Leslie, and even dried-up old women like Ellen, they all fell to their knees to do his bidding. I just don't get it." Jackie sounded truly befuddled.

Draya cleared her throat. "We didn't all fall to our knees. I got exactly what I wanted from that dude and kept it moving."

"Everybody's not that good, Dray." Venus meant that as a compliment, but she wasn't sure if Draya had taken it that way.

"Look, I don't set out to use men. I just don't allow myself to be used first," Draya snapped.

No, she definitely hadn't taken that as a compliment.

The conversation lasted another fifteen minutes after that before Venus got tired of sitting in the car and wasting her gas to keep it warm. So she drove everyone home and then returned to her apartment, where she sat contemplating all the things she'd learned in the past few days and what she could do to get ahold of the situation. There was no doubt in her mind that the time had come for her to tell Draya and Jackie what she knew about Rufus's previous shady financial dealings, because she was almost positive those incidents were connected to the information Draya and Jackie had found. But they still needed proof, and Venus thought she had a good idea of how they could find it. She thought about it for hours while sitting on her couch, staring at the lights on her Christmas tree until her head started doing the church nod.

Now it was Monday again, five days before Christmas. As she stepped off the elevator onto her floor at work, she felt a little anxious about calling Draya and Jackie to tell them about what she'd found. She sent up a silent prayer that this would all turn out the way she hoped, but she wasn't sure. At this point, she didn't think she'd ever be sure about anything again.

Her attention was snatched away from her personal thoughts as she noticed that the small number of staff members who were in the office this early were huddled together around one cubicle whispering as she approached. She didn't care what they were talking about as long as their work was done when it needed to be. The last thing she wanted to get in on was more office gossip, so she continued to walk until one person turned to her.

"Did you hear Mike's dead?"

Everything in her stilled at those words. "What did you just say?"

It was Avis, another administrative assistant in the department, who spoke next. "It's been all over the news this morning. They found him in his car parked over by the Science Center. He'd been shot in the head."

Mike was dead. Found in his car. Shot in the head. The words replayed in her mind. He was dead, just like Rufus. What the hell was happening?

Venus pushed past Avis and hurried to her office, where she slammed the door. Dropping her bag and purse onto one of the guest chairs, she dug in her pocket and found her phone. Pressing the saved number, she paced the floor, heart hammering in her chest, mind whirling with thoughts.

"Hey?" Draya answered.

"He's dead." The words tumbled out of her mouth as if she'd been too afraid to say them before.

There was a pause and then a question spoken very slowly. "Who's dead?"

"Mike!" She knew she'd yelled, and she clamped her lips shut before turning and pacing in the other direction. "I just got to the office and everybody's talking about it. They say it's all over the news, but I didn't turn my TV on when I was getting ready this morning. I listened to Christmas music instead. Then when I got in the car, I had my playlist on, so I didn't get news there either."

"Okay, wait a minute. Calm down. Let me turn on my TV."

She could hear rustling in the background and was now clenching the fingers of her free hand for lack of anything better to do with them.

"Shit!"

Venus was behind her desk now, and she dropped down into her chair. "It's true, isn't it?"

"Yeah. It is."

"Shot in the head just like Rufus."

"Don't say that."

"Why not? It's true."

"Still, just don't jump to conclusions. I'll call Jackie, and we'll be in your office in twenty minutes."

Venus nodded. They'd be here soon; there were several different scenarios she could come up with in that time, but she knew she'd keep returning to the same one. What if Mike had been killed by the same person who'd killed Rufus?

The thought had her fingers shaking as she logged on to her computer and immediately went online to pull up the local news station. Watching the story they ran and then heading over to Twitter to see what the other local reporters were tweeting kept her occupied until Draya and Jackie showed up.

"The reports are all the same. Single gunshot wound to the head. Found in his car, which was parked on a very public street." She relayed that information in the time it took Draya and Jackie to enter her office, close the door, and take a seat.

"Fuck!" Jackie wasn't any happier about that news than Venus was, but Venus doubted it was for the same reason. "Just like Rufus except for the location of the body. Why didn't they kill him in his house and leave him there? He's single—it would've taken days for someone to find him."

"Maybe that's why, because they wanted him to be found sooner." Venus sat back in her chair and rubbed her eyes. Her temples throbbed; the headache had already arrived and was causing so much pain, she wanted to scream. "Plus, Mike lives in those new apartments over on Park Avenue. They would've had to use a silencer to kill him there without anyone in the building hearing the shot."

"So there *are* some differences. Meaning they probably weren't killed by the same person." Venus knew that Draya wanted to sound hopeful, but none of them was buying what she'd just said, not even Draya.

"Mike worked for Rufus. He and Rufus went to a strip club the night of the party—who knows who they could've met up with there or pissed off. Maybe both deaths are just a random guy who didn't like two pompous, scandalous bastards and decided to get rid of them." Dropping her hands to the arms of the chair, she blew out a breath and said what she'd been thinking since she first heard the news. "Or maybe it's closer to the theory we've been considering for Rufus's killer, that Mike could've been involved in some of Rufus's shady deals."

"We just talked about this at the gala the other night," Jackie said.

Tilting her head so she could run her fingers through today's long, straight tresses, Draya sighed. "Yes, we did. And Mike was at the gala. So when was he killed? Yesterday?"

"Or after the party, just like Rufus." Venus had been running all these details through her mind as she waited for Jackie and Draya to get here. She'd tried to be optimistic and to find more reasons not to believe this was connected than reasons it could be. It was a losing battle.

"I have another theory," she said, resigning herself to the fact that now was the time, regardless of this new shock of Mike being killed.

Jackie shook her head. "Let's hear it."

Venus was still sitting behind her desk. She sat up taller in her chair and looked at Jackie and Draya, who were seated across from her in the guest chairs. She took a slow breath and said a silent prayer for forgiveness.

"Two years ago, I came across some invoices for supplies that had been misplaced in another file. I knew the reference code on the invoices as two projects that Rufus had managed." She paused and reached into the drawer, removing the folder she'd retrieved from a locked box at her apartment and stuffed into her purse. "They were city projects," she said and set the folder on the desk.

With her hands on top of the folder, Venus looked down at her fingers. Long fingers that her music teacher had once said would be good for playing the piano. She wore a pearl ring on her right ring finger, a gift to herself for her thirtieth birthday last year.

"What's in the folder, Venus?" Jackie asked, and Venus looked up to see her staring pensively at her.

Venus cleared her throat and continued. "I couldn't figure out why the invoice amounts were so high. The projects had been completed, so we should've only been billing for the final contract payment. When I pulled the correct files, I could only find the preliminary contracts, not the signed ones. At any rate, I could still verify the payments we expected to receive. All other invoices in the files had been paid. The two invoices I found were for 'previously unbilled' supplies, but those supplies weren't necessary to the project, even before the project was completed."

"So Rufus was cooking the books long before this new supply list I found on that USB drive," Draya said. "That bastard! And I wouldn't have caught it as a discrepancy because our department only logs in the receivables—we don't validate the invoice."

"No," Venus said. "That's my job."

She let those words linger in the air for a few seconds and prepared to do what she should've done years ago. "Since I caught the invoices before they went out to the city, I fixed them to reflect only the final payment request for a completed job. I removed all the supplies that were listed as 'previously unbilled.'"

"That's what you were supposed to do," Jackie said, but Venus could tell by the crinkling of her brow that Jackie wasn't so sure.

"Yes and no. In validating the final invoices on any project, I'm supposed to check the files for each to make sure we're capturing all outstanding expenditures. The ones noted on the invoices weren't outstanding; they were added purposely."

"Rufus added them on to the invoice so the city would make a bigger payment to the company," Draya said. "Then he gave himself large bonuses and charged personal expenses to the company without regard because he knew he was bringing in extra cash. I always wondered how his bonuses were calculated, and now I see. He knew what was coming in, so he could easily ask for that amount. Louis gave him free rein, so he'd sign off on whatever Rufus put in front of him."

"That slick bastard," Jackie said.

"But wait a minute," Draya continued. "You said you changed the invoices. What did Rufus say when he found out you did that?"

Venus clasped her fingers together; then she pulled them apart, all while keeping eye contact with Draya. "He hit the roof and threatened to say I was involved in the plot if I told anyone. Right after that, Mike was given the duty of checking the final invoices."

"You covered for him and he threatened to claim you were complicit—" Jackie was saying before Draya interrupted her.

"And you're just telling us this now."

Venus could see Draya's fury rising in the way she sat forward in the chair, her hands clenching the arms.

"You should've told us about this before, Venus! All this time we've been talking about what we all have to lose and everything we knew about Rufus, and you kept this to yourself."

"Maybe she had a good reason for not telling us," Jackie said hopefully.

Venus appreciated Jackie's efforts, but thinking back on it now, she wasn't sure her reasons were good, so much as she believed they were necessary. "Everything I do reflects on my parents. No matter how old I am when someone says Venus McGee, they immediately think of Donald and Ilene McGee." She sighed. "So I didn't say anything about what I knew Rufus was doing because they were city projects, and I didn't want it to circle back to my father."

"You don't know if that would've happened, though," Jackie said. "And not telling just made you look as guilty as Rufus."

"I know it would've happened," Venus told them and then offered the folder.

Draya jumped up from her chair and grabbed it. After giving Venus a scathing gaze, she opened it and began reading.

"Draya's right," she said while Draya continued to read and Jackie stared at her. "I should've said something before. I just kept thinking that all of this was going to blow over and I wouldn't have to tell. But it was always in the back of my mind, especially when the police wanted to question me. I was so afraid I'd have to tell and my father would be implicated and—"

"And you can't please everybody," Draya said with a heavy sigh. "I don't know how many times I have to tell you that. Especially when the person you're trying to please is knee-deep in this shit just like Rufus." Draya passed the folder to Jackie.

"Just because your father's name is typed on these contracts with three other city officials doesn't mean he was the one working with Rufus," Jackie said after looking at the papers.

Venus sat back in her chair and sighed. "I can't find the signed contracts. Only one rep from the city is required to sign regardless of how many may have worked in negotiating the deal. But his name's still on there, so he still would've been implicated in some way."

Jackie stood then and began pacing. "So wait, what's happening now? What are we going to do? Send her father to jail?"

"That's all the paperwork I had in a separate file. I didn't want to shred the original invoices just in case Rufus ever really got out of hand. He insisted I wasn't bold enough to blackmail him, and he was right—I never would've done that, but I wanted him to always know that I could." She'd wanted to have a little bit of power over him, and thinking that now made her feel sick.

"I knew we couldn't trust you," Draya said, still staring at Venus with an angry gaze.

Venus rubbed her temples. "Don't do that. I've been in this with both of you since the start. You're the one who called me, remember? I could've continued lying in my bed, sleeping off all that liquor, but no, I got up and came out in the cold to help save your ass! So don't stand here and make it seem like I've betrayed you." Even though a part of her had felt that way for the past couple of weeks. "Should I have said something sooner? Yes. But I didn't, and all I can do now is apologize for that. But don't you dare act like I'm not trustworthy."

"You're a self-righteous—"

"Stop it!" Jackie said, cutting Draya off. "She's right. She could've continued to keep this to herself. She could've not come when you called, and she could've easily told her cop boyfriend everything, but she didn't."

"We don't know what she's told him," Draya said, folding her arms over her chest.

"C'mon, Dray, you know if she'd told him, they would've already hauled all of us out to the precinct for questioning. Hell, they may've even had grounds to arrest us, considering you took that USB drive from his house, leaving your fingerprints all over the place."

"Well, you pulled a gun on him; let's not forget about that," Draya countered. "You're not innocent in this."

"None of us is totally clean in this," Venus said and stood from her desk. "That's the point. If there's nobody else we can trust, we've gotta be able to trust each other. So I'll say it again: I'm sorry I didn't tell you both this sooner. But here it is now. My father may really be involved in this." That was still blowing her mind. Although they'd talked about it before, Venus had considered it a long shot. She'd prayed it was a long shot.

Draya sighed. "Okay, let's think about this clearly. What does any of what Venus just told us prove? I mean, how does it help clear us?"

Venus walked around the desk. "It could give the police information to look in another direction. Malik said they're investigating other people."

"I don't believe that." Draya frowned.

"It's true—Robyn told me that night when Ellen maced me. She said the cops had been back and forth in the office talking with different people. And speaking of Robyn," Jackie said, scrunching her face like she'd just remembered something, "she left the party Saturday night with Mike."

"How do you know that?" Venus asked.

"When I went to get that drink for Lynette, Robyn was at the bar. I told you she was probably working security. She was grabbing a drink, since her shift was over. She said she'd been there from early in the afternoon checking out the facility because the mayor was expected to be in attendance as well." Jackie shrugged. "Anyway, she was looking down at her phone, so she didn't see me approach. Then, after I spoke, she was acting all nervous, like she didn't know how to face me after the basement sexcapade." Leaning forward to rest her elbows on her knees, Jackie nodded. "I knew something was up with her, but I wasn't trying to get all into her business. Especially not if it involved that asshole Mike."

"She just came out and told you they were leaving the party together?" Draya seemed more bothered than worried, the way Jackie and Venus were.

"Nah, I gave her a piece of advice—told her not to let a guy like Mike bring her down by having her do things to jeopardize her job. She agreed the basement was stupid and said it was their first time doing it there."

"But not their first time doing it?" Draya frowned.

Jackie shook her head. "He texted her while I was standing there, and that's when she said she had to go. She said he was taking her to a nice hotel this time, and they were going to spend the night down there in Annapolis."

"What? She was the last person to see him alive? I wonder if the cops will figure that out." She really did wonder, because the way Malik stayed on her back, she was beginning to wonder how good he was at his job. Chasing after her on such a small thing as an argument with the guy at a party didn't seem overly productive in her book.

Draya sighed heavily and shook her head. "Okay, so if we take all the paperwork we've discovered to the police right now, what does that prove? Not enough," she said, answering her own question. "Like Venus just said, there may be multiple names of city reps on that contract, but the one who signed it is most likely the one who worked one-on-one with Rufus. So the person who signed it could've been pissed off at him for stealing money on their watch and killed him. We need that person's name, because we can't go to the police until we have enough evidence to really prove somebody else had a motive to kill. And we can't keep slinking around here like undercover cops. Because we're not. I mean, we don't carry guns, so we can't just pop a fool in the ass for following us."

This was a total shift in all that Draya had been saying since this began. Staring at her now, Venus realized how tired she looked, how that spark she normally had whenever she entered a room had been dull and listless when she came in today. They were all getting tired of this mess.

"Nobody's following you, Dray." It was Jackie's turn to recite those words to her. "You're being paranoid because we're running around here like a bunch of inexperienced cops."

"To be fair," Venus said while holding up a hand, "we haven't done anything except pull some reports and make some connections."

"Not true—we . . . or rather the two of you . . . actually interrogated a very drunk Lynette at the party." Jackie looked way too pleased to place that part of the investigation at their feet.

"True. But we also confirmed Rufus was sleeping with Leslie. And I don't care if we don't learn anything else—that was a bombshell that definitely makes me consider her a suspect." With an elaborate motion, Draya flipped her hair over one shoulder and crossed her legs.

Venus's computer dinged with an incoming message. Seeing it was from Ellen and marked urgent, she groaned. "It's not even ten in the morning and this woman is sending emails."

"Who?" Draya asked.

"Who else?" she replied with a smirk. "The BCC Busybody."

"Bitch," Jackie murmured.

"Oh. My. Goodness." Venus couldn't believe what she was reading now that she'd opened Ellen's message.

"What now? Is the Grinch about to take away our Christmas bonuses?" Jackie asked.

"She better not," Draya said.

"She's retiring," Venus told them. "Effective immediately."

Today had been one hell of a day, and Venus couldn't wait to get into her bed. She wasn't cooking anything, so dinner would have to be some leftovers or a ham-and-cheese sandwich. She didn't have the strength or forethought for anything else. It took her less than fifteen minutes to get through the door, use the bathroom, and then change out of her work clothes and into a Grinch nightshirt. Seeing the familiar green villain on the front made her smile as she recalled Jackie's reference to him earlier today. The reason she'd referenced him did not make her smile.

Ellen's office had been cleaned out completely, her name had been removed from the door of her office, and her administrative assistant went off on vacation. The office was abuzz with the news about Mike and Ellen for the duration of the day. Little to no work was done, even by Venus. Sure, she'd sat at her desk for the full eight hours she normally worked, but she hadn't gotten anything done other than reviewing emails on the sports-complex project and answering Draya's call when she told her she could request digital copies of the signed project contracts but it would take a day or two for her to receive them.

Groaning, she walked into the kitchen, telling herself not to think about work, murders, cops, or anything else that gave off unhappy vibes for the rest of the night. Her spirit couldn't take it. She stood with the refrigerator door open, surveying the contents as if she expected something new to appear.

Why don't you take a picture and stop wasting my electricity?

That's what her mother would've said if she were here. Venus slammed the refrigerator door shut and moved to the cabinet to grab a bag of plain chips and a butterscotch cake. Then the doorbell rang.

Leaving her dinner on the counter, she walked her bare feet into the living room and took a peek through the peephole. Her heart thudded and paused, then thudded again. She opened the door and asked, "What are you doing here?" The last time she'd seen Malik had been at the gala on Saturday. They'd only glanced at each other then. Before that, it had been last week, when he'd practically kidnapped her.

"It's dinnertime. I picked up food and thought you might like to share." He held up a brown bag, and she almost smiled as she saw the Mission BBQ logo.

"You're not cute." Yet it was taking everything in her to bite back the smile that desperately wanted to form.

"No. I'm hungry. So can you let me in so we can eat?"

Saying no just wasn't an option, since she was hungry too. She stepped aside so he could come in, but after he took the first step, she placed a hand to the center of his chest. "I do not want to talk about the murders of Rufus Jackson or Mike Livingston or anything else that relates to BCC or your job. If that's a problem, you can turn yourself right around and take your food with you."

With his free hand, he eased her hand from his chest, bringing it up to his lips to place a light kiss on the back. "It's no problem at all."

Chapter 30

JACKIE

She couldn't believe she'd actually done it, but it was too late to undo it.

Jackie stood in her apartment and stared at the floor-length mirror leaning against the wall in her bedroom. The decision to leave work early had been a no-brainer. Today had been an overload of thoughts, conflicts, possibilities, and fears. All rolled into one huge snowball that she was afraid would steamroll right over her. At three thirty, she'd tapped out, sending a text to Venus and Draya that she'd had enough for the day and would catch up with them in the morning. They'd both responded that they understood, and she'd walked out of the office, sending another text to Karlie before she'd made it to her car.

Feel like hangin' out with me this afternoon?

Her answer had come quickly, and Jackie grinned at the yes followed by a kissing emoji. Feeling refreshed and energized for the first time all day—well, to be honest, in weeks—she'd hurried home to shower and change. Now she stood to the side, admiring her side view.

Butt was definitely a little bigger this year than it had been last year, but that was fine; she still held on to her athletic build, and the black jeans with dark-gray button-front shirt gave her a slick, casual flair. She loved watches and today wore a silver Movado with black Nike boots and the diamond stud in her left ear sparkling. Friday had been her day at the barber, where her sides were trimmed and neatly shaped, and she'd pulled her locs back from her face, holding them with a black band. A quick application of some lip balm and a spritz of Versace Eros cologne and she was ready for this date.

Turning so that her front now faced the mirror, she stared at herself long and hard. She was going on a date—one year, three months, and two days after the breakup with Alicia. Rolling her neck on her shoulders and brushing a hand down the front of her clothes, she gave herself a reassuring nod that she was ready for this and walked out of her bedroom. Grabbing her black leather hipster jacket and pushing her arms through the sleeves, she picked up her keys and headed for the door. "No turning back," she whispered as she closed and locked the door behind her and ran down the stairs.

The second she stepped out onto the front steps, she checked the time on her watch: 5:15. She'd told Karlie she'd pick her up at 5:30, so she was right on time. Yet she didn't proceed down the steps right away; instead, she looked up one side of the street. The line of row homes on her block continued, some with fronts painted white or other odd colors like pistachio green, but the majority were redbrick with cement steps and narrow double doors that always made her feel like they belonged on a Victorian-style home instead.

On the corner, three guys stood wearing hoodies, hands pressed into the front pockets of jeans that hung too low on their hips. One smoked, while another called out to someone on the other side of the street. Cars whizzed by, and in the distance, the all-too-familiar sound of police sirens sang through the air.

She looked the other way to the corner with the traffic light, a street where a woman walked across with two kids running and laughing ahead of her. These were the sounds and sights of inner-city life, and

Jackie loved it. She could've moved out into the county like Draya had or at least into the up-and-coming business-centric area of downtown like Venus had, but her heart would always be in the city, on the streets where every bit of her Black culture had been molded.

The traffic light had just turned red when a silver Tahoe sped right through it, almost hitting one of the children and causing the mother to scream in panic. Jackie ran down her front steps, about to head to the corner if someone should need help, when she turned back to stare at the truck still speeding up the street. It was the exact make, model, and color of truck Draya said she'd seen following her last week.

There were probably thousands of those same trucks in that same color on the streets in Baltimore alone. There wasn't anything special about this one—she was certain. With another check to make sure the kids and their mother were safe, she shrugged and waited until the traffic cleared to jog across the street and climb into her car.

Karlie lived in South Baltimore on a narrow street that seemed more like an alley. She came to the door seconds after Jackie sent her a text that she was close, and for a moment all Jackie could do was stare at her. Five foot seven, round hips and ass, slim waist, perfect breasts, and a smile that she swore would light up the night . . . the punch of lust was definite and immediate. But this time it was also filled with something else.

Her hair was parted down the middle and pulled into a ponytail that she'd let hang over one shoulder. She looked like a young Jennifer Lopez with her dark-blue jeans, skinny-heel brown ankle boots, and cream-colored turtleneck beneath a brown jacket. Jackie couldn't hide her grin when Karlie opened the passenger-side door and slid onto the seat.

"Hey, you," she said and leaned over the console to kiss her lightly on the cheek.

"Hey," Karlie replied with a smile. "I was surprised but happy to hear from you today."

Jackie pulled off, driving down to the end of her block and turning. On one side of the street was Carroll Park, where she used to play softball, and on the other were more row homes. She took in the sights, still a little nostalgic about her city life, before answering. "I needed a break and thought it'd be cool just to do something fun for a change."

"Oh, okay, so I'm considered fun."

She glanced over to see Karlie was grinning. "Yeah, you are."

"Well, I'm just glad I didn't have work or class tonight."

Karlie was a manager at one of the clothing stores at the outlet mall. She was taking evening classes at the community college and was on her way to receiving a degree in medical coding. Her parents had died in a car crash years ago, and she lived in their family home with her two younger sisters and her niece.

"I'm glad too." It occurred to Jackie at that moment that she hadn't even considered that Karlie might not be available for this impromptu date.

When they were back in the downtown area and she was hunting for a parking space, Karlie asked, "Where are we going?"

"Since this was all last-minute, I just thought of somewhere I hadn't been for a while and figured that would be cool for a first date."

She'd parked the car and opened the door for Karlie when Karlie took her hand and said, "This is our first date."

Jackie nodded, sure in what she was doing and saying at this moment. "It is."

They walked the short distance before going into the National Aquarium. Karlie chuckled as they came up on the first exhibits of the stingrays. "I can't even remember the last time I was here. Oh, wait, I do. My niece, Dominique, had a school trip, like, two years ago, and my sister couldn't get off to go with her, so I came."

"Did you like it?"

"I loved it. Here, come on—let's go over here so we can touch one."

Jackie let herself be dragged through a circle of kids until they came to the touching pond. "I'm not touching that," she said with a frown.

"What are you, a chicken?"

Tucking her hands up under her arms, Jackie made the clucking sound without hesitation, and Karlie laughed loud and long. Jackie laughed, too, in a way she hadn't in a very long time. An hour later, they were walking through the rain-forest exhibit when Karlie once again took her hand.

"You know it's their loss, right?" she said, her voice almost too quiet for the humid air filled with bird screeches and some other weird sounds.

"Whose?" Jackie looked over their heads, trying to find the red bird that was pictured on the sign they'd just passed.

"Your family and Alicia. They don't get to spend fun moments like this with you anymore, and it's too bad, because this time I've been with you has been fantastic."

Warmth engulfed her, and it had nothing to do with the tropical climate that was being mimicked in this area. She'd shared bits and pieces about her past with Karlie, and Karlie had done the same with her. Their pasts were different, yet kinda the same in that they both were looking for something. Jackie wondered briefly if she'd found it.

"On one level, I know that." She shrugged. "But it still hurts. I mean, I'm not in love with Alicia anymore. She wanted to move on, to live in DC and follow her dreams without me. It took me a minute, but I came to grips with that. But my family . . ." She let her words trail off as they walked.

"My family called me a bum magnet. If there was a no-good, lying, cheating, broke-ass dude within a ten-mile radius of my house, I was in his face. Then, when I brought home a girl, they were like, *Oh, she's just trying something different.*" Karlie shook her head. "In the end, it doesn't matter. They have a right to their opinion, and I have a right to live my life. That's how you gotta look at it."

She was right; Jackie was entitled to happiness, and at this moment, amid everything going on, Karlie was her happy. Releasing her hand, she stopped walking and pulled Karlie to her.

"I'm just gonna look at you right now," she said. "'Cause that makes me feel really good. You okay with that?"

Karlie's grin spread fast and wide. "I'm okay with that."

"Good," she whispered, leaning in closer to touch her lips to hers. "That's real good."

The perfect date moved on to dinner at Phillips Seafood, which used to be the spot when Jackie was a teen but tonight had just been okay. It didn't matter—being with Karlie had made it better. In fact, being with her these past few hours tonight had been exactly what Jackie needed, and when it was time to take Karlie home, she'd taken a chance and asked a question she hadn't planned to ask. "Wanna go back to my place and chill for a while?"

When Karlie didn't immediately respond, she got nervous and followed up with, "I'm not talking about sex. I just . . . I really liked being with you tonight, and I'm not ready for it to end."

Karlie stepped to her, cupping the sides of her face. "I would've been okay with sex. But we can keep taking it slow if that's what you need."

Jackie grinned. This woman was something else. Pretty, smart, intuitive, and she was into her. How long had she been walking around thinking that something had to be wrong with her that the people in her life she cared most for couldn't wait to be away from her? Yet here Karlie was, not only telling Jackie she'd wait if that's what she needed but showing her she was down for doing just that by not giving up all those weeks when Jackie had been ghosting her.

"Cool. I'm in the mood for Christmas movies," Jackie said as they started walking back to her car. "You like Christmas movies, don't you? I mean the good ones like *Home Alone* and *Gremlins*."

"Wait. What? *Gremlins* is not a Christmas movie," Karlie argued.

Jackie made a face and then laced her fingers with Karlie's. "You wild! It's definitely a Christmas movie. Remember, Gizmo was a Christmas gift."

"Yeah, a gift gone horribly wrong."

"That's the best part." Jackie laughed as they crossed the street.

The debate continued, with Karlie agreeing to watching only the first *Gremlins* and the first two *Home Alone*s. "That third one was trash," she said as they stepped onto the curb and walked the last steps toward the car.

It wasn't until Jackie was walking around to the driver's side and had reached for the door handle that she felt the urge to look around. She always paid attention to her surroundings—that's just something she was trained to do, living on the streets of Baltimore. But tonight, what she was looking for felt different. What she was afraid of started to be more real than she'd anticipated, and it took a good few minutes and Karlie calling her name to snap her out of the feeling that maybe someone was watching not only Draya, but all of them.

Chapter 31

Draya

"Hey. I was just thinking about you, and I wanted to call to see how you were doing."

She was doing terrible. Draya didn't say that; she couldn't. Admitting that type of weakness to Travis wasn't an option. As it turned out, the words didn't matter—silence had been a snitch all by itself.

"Draya? You there?"

"Yeah, I'm here." She cleared her throat. "I was just lying on the couch watching TV." She was lying. The TV wasn't even on and hadn't been in the hours since she'd come home from the office. Her landing spot had been on the couch after she'd changed into sweatpants and a T-shirt, but her house was dark except for the Christmas lights blinking on the tree. If it were too bright in there, somebody might see her.

"What's wrong? Did something happen?"

"You mean something other than another one of my coworkers being murdered, one abruptly retiring, and the headache I came home with because everyone in the office was talking about both things all damn day? No, nothing happened at all."

Okay, that may've been a tad dramatic, and she needed to bring it down a notch or two. Sitting up on the couch, she held the phone firmly to her ear and cleared her throat. "Really, I'm good. What's up with you?"

"I'm about fifteen minutes away from your place. I can stop by."

Why was this guy so damn nice? Perhaps a better question would've been, why did she assume all guys were less than nice? Well, she knew the answer to that—her father, who'd only ever appeared when her mother wanted him in her bed but disappeared whenever she mentioned a bill needed to be paid; her brothers, who had kids by too many different women and squawked about paying fifty dollars a week in child support; and then there was Rufus, the married man who felt it was his duty to fuck every other woman on earth until somebody put a bullet in his forehead.

She had to close her eyes at that point, 'cause she was beyond extra tonight.

"I don't think that's a good idea. I'm not in the mood for company."

"Then you need to get out. It's a beautiful night. A little cold but still nice." When she didn't respond, he continued. "I'll come pick you up. We can go see the lights on 34th Street."

Now that did get a small smile out of her. Draya loved driving down that street every year to see the light displays on each house on the block. It amazed her how all the neighbors came together every year, each of them decorating their homes with thousands of lights, some even stringing them from one house on one side of the street to another on the other side of the street. It was a magical experience that for the last few years she'd done alone.

"I'm about ten minutes away from your house," Travis prompted.

"If I come out, I want hot chocolate from Starbucks and a brownie from Gladys's Bakery." A quick glance at the clock on the Blu-ray player across the room said it was just a little after eight at night, so both places were still open.

"Anything you want. Be there in a few."

Travis ended the call, and Draya sat on the couch holding the phone for a few more minutes. If she went outside with Travis, she would be safe. Nothing would happen to her, and nobody would be near her but him.

"Fuck!" The word was loud and echoed throughout the otherwise-silent room.

This wasn't her. She wasn't scared of anything or anyone—she'd never been able to afford that luxury. In her world, it had been fight or flight, and running wasn't something Dot Carter would tolerate from any of her children. So Draya had stood up to naysayers—teachers who didn't think she was smart enough; mothers who told her she wasn't good enough for their sons; doctors who half-ass listened to any complaint she'd ever had because they'd been too quick to assume her symptoms were either from being overweight, an STD, or a possible pregnancy; even wives, who gave her the stank eye because they knew their husbands were checking for her. She'd held her ground and relished proving them all wrong.

Yet today, for the first time in her life, she'd run home from work and locked herself in this apartment because she'd been afraid she would be next. If it was open season on BCC employees, was her name on the hit list? What did Franklin really think she was hiding? Who was that person driving the silver Tahoe that she knew without a shred of doubt she'd seen in the parking lot at Jazzy's and then again following her after she'd left the lounge?

Sighing heavily, she stood up from the chair and walked into her bedroom. "This shit's gotta stop."

Second-guessing herself, looking over her shoulder, acting like a private investigator, and ducking the police—all this shit was out of character for her, and it just needed to end. Tonight, it could, even if for just a little while.

She changed into a purple velvet jogger this time, slipped on her sparkly lavender UGGs, and ran her fingers through her own wavy hair. After she'd removed her wig when she came home, she'd thought about washing her hair, so she took out the braids that were required for the wig to lie right but then had changed her mind and let her natural tresses be. With no energy to do anything other than apply lipstick and mascara, put on earrings, and spray on a bit of perfume, she had on her coat and was planning to meet Travis downstairs in the lobby when he rang her doorbell.

"Hello, gorgeous," he said when she opened the door.

"Hello yourself, handsome." He was fine as hell, and he was good to her too. Those thoughts stayed with her as she locked her door and they walked to the elevator. When he reached for her hand, she let him hold it, and when they stepped into the elevator car and he pulled her close for a tight and warm-as-hell hug, she let him do that too. Because it felt damn good. She deserved to feel good for a change.

The holiday lights, hot chocolate, and the brownie put her in a great mood, so after they'd been out for an hour and a half and Travis suggested they go back to his place, she'd agreed without hesitation.

"Come here—sit down and let me make you feel better."

Yeah, sex would make her feel better, so Draya followed him to the sofa. The tree she'd helped him decorate last week was gorgeous, those lights as lovely against the backdrop of the harbor as she'd imagined. He turned on the electric fireplace and came over to join her. It occurred to her that he might be setting some type of mood, but she didn't need that. She was ready.

But instead of Travis coming back to the sofa and sitting next to her to start the foreplay with a kiss, he sat beside her and lifted her legs onto his lap. She was about to ask what he was doing, but he was already removing her boots. After pulling off her socks, he began rubbing her feet. Her mouth opened to protest when a bolt of pleasure—not sexual but of the purely blissful, relaxing type—soared through her. "Okay, you sure know how to do all the right things." She really hadn't expected him to answer as she adjusted the pillows on the sofa to fit beneath her head and lie back with a sigh.

"For you, Draya, I'd do anything."

Those words were also unexpected, or rather the feeling of sincerity that laced them had caught her off guard. "Why?"

He smiled; she could see him through the slits of her eyelids that had lowered of their own accord.

She continued. "I really want to know why you put so much time and energy into me. I mean, you gotta know that's not what I'm in the market for—at least I thought I made that clear when we first started hanging out." She always made the parameters of her affairs clear from the start. Entanglements and drama weren't her thing, which was why she'd started wishing Rufus dead in the first place.

"I believe that when you search for love or true emotional connections, they become more elusive." Okay, he was going to give one of those deep type of answers when a simple *I like you a lot for real* would've sufficed. "You aren't looking for anything serious, and neither was I. Remember, we talked about this that first night we spent together."

"Mm-hmm. At the Westin after we'd talked in the elevator and had drinks at Mo's." Why she remembered that night three months ago, she didn't really know. It was a simple, impromptu date that had led to some mind-blowing sex. She and Travis had been a casual thing since then.

He was pushing up the legs of her pants now, massaging her calves with his magical hands.

"That was a good night. I remember thinking, *This woman is fine, can hold a good conversation, and is phenomenal in bed. Not to mention, she isn't aiming for me to put a ring on it.* I'd hit the jackpot." He chuckled. "And then that changed."

"What changed? My conversation or my sex?"

"You, Draya. You changed me and what I thought I wanted from a relationship."

She let her eyes close all the way then, as if doing so would stop the warmth spreading throughout her each time he spoke or the spike of fear that nagged at the back of her mind.

"That wasn't my intention." None of this was her intention. Not with Rufus, not the night of the party, and certainly not this thing with Travis.

"And therein lies the perfection in this moment."

She hated when he talked like a lawyer.

"Look at me, Draya. I want you to see me when I tell you this."

Nope. No. Not a chance in hell. She didn't want to see what she didn't want to feel. But what she felt next was him taking her hands in his, rubbing his fingers over hers, while he waited patiently for her to stop acting like a child and open her damn eyes. She did, slowly, and found him staring directly at her.

"I like you," he said softly. "A lot. I need you to know that now and to let it sink in, because I don't foresee it stopping."

"I'm not what you think you want, Travis."

"You're everything I know I need."

She sat up then, the action bringing their faces closer while her legs remained on his lap. "I don't have a clue what I need right now." It was as honest as she'd ever been with a man—hell, probably as honest as she'd been with herself in a very long time.

He grinned. "Well, that's where I come into play. Me and this thing that's blossomed into a relationship. See, this is the part where I recognize all that you're going through, and I provide what you need before you even accept that you need it."

"Like tonight's outing and foot massage?"

"Right. And the trust and support you feel you don't have enough of right now. Things are uncertain in your work life. The police backed off after I submitted your list of dates and times you'd been at Rufus's house, but you're afraid that won't be enough. I'm here to tell you that even if it isn't, I'll still be right here, holding you in private and defending you with my zealous representation in public."

She touched her fingers to his lips then, because it was all too much. He was saying too many of the right things, hitting all the perfect notes, and she couldn't take it. She couldn't believe it because she was smarter than that. Her mother and grandmothers had raised her better. No man could be this good and this perfect. It had to be a sham.

"Let's back up to that holding-me part. What would it take for you to make that happen right now? For us to be naked and in each other's arms in the next two minutes." This was what Draya knew. It was what she could relate to and how she reconciled the harsh realities of her world with the basic need for satisfaction.

Travis didn't waste any more time with words, something she would forever be grateful for. There was nothing else to say at this point, nothing she wanted to say, because at this moment, all she needed to do was feel.

After he'd stripped her of all her clothes and forbade her from helping him do the same with his, she lay back on the couch, and he began to touch her. First with his hands on each of her shoulders, slowly moving down her arms, where he once again brought her fingers to his lips, this time sucking each into his mouth, one at a time. That shouldn't have been as erotic as it felt, but when he placed her now-damp fingers around his rigid dick, she gasped at the immediate warmth that started in her palms and spread quickly throughout the rest of her body.

While her fingers were wrapped securely around him, he drove his hands into her hair until he cupped the back of her head. He tilted her face so she could look up at him instead of staring at the lovely tip of his erection. "I told you I'd give you whatever you needed," he whispered before licking his lips slowly.

It was instinct that had her doing the same, then glancing down at his erection and considering licking there. He must have read her mind and decided that wasn't what he wanted, at least not at this moment, because he eased out of her grasp. Removing his hands from her head, he lay her back on the sofa and cupped her breasts. Sucking each nipple into his mouth was only a small amount of torture, but running his teeth along those nipples ramped the arousal meter up more than a few notches. His attention moved from there to her belly, where he kissed and dipped his tongue into her navel, then lower until he was sucking the plump folds between her legs.

Screaming out in pleasure wasn't new to Draya. She had no problem letting her lover know when he was doing a good . . . scratch that, a damn good job. But now her body pulsed with a deeper need, a more potent satisfaction that she knew only one way of achieving. Easing her legs down and noting the surprised look on Travis's face when she did so, she said, "Let me show you what I really need right now."

Without hesitation, she stood from the sofa and grabbed his pants. His wallet was in the back pocket; she found it and a condom and sheathed him in the next few seconds. He probably expected her to want to ride, since that was her preference, but no, not this time. Instead, she lay back on the sofa, propped one leg up on the back of it, and let the other dangle off the edge.

"Now," she told him, and waited until he obliged her.

Draya had no idea when they'd moved from the sofa, or rather when Travis had carried her into the bedroom, because surely after that orgasm, she hadn't been able to think, let alone walk. And now she was turning over in Travis's bed, a place she'd been before but not all night. Cracking her eyes open a little wider, she glimpsed the wavy red numbers coming from the alarm clock on the nightstand. It was a little after one a.m. Good, she had time to get up and go home.

She was just about to push away the sheets that covered her and climb out of the bed when flashes of their conversation came back to her. Particularly the parts when he'd been thrusting deep inside her and he'd whispered, "I'm so glad I found you. So fuckin' glad you're here with me."

Draya had felt a definite shift in his tone with those words. Sure, they weren't the infamous *I love you*, which she hated to hear during sex because she certainly didn't believe them coming at that time. For clarification, she probably would second-guess them coming at any time. Anyway, the seconds after he'd said it, she'd tensed and then amazingly had warmed all over again. Shaking her head now reiterated her exact reaction then—she didn't know what the hell was going on here, with him, tonight. And until she did know, she needed to get away from him.

This thing between them had changed fundamentally. She'd first sensed it last week when she was here decorating his tree, but with all the other things going on in her life, she'd been able to push the nagging feeling to the back of her mind. Tonight, the instant she'd opened her door and seen him standing there, the feeling was resurrected, and she should've stayed her ass home and sent him on his way. But no, she'd wanted that feel-good sensation. She'd wanted him to make her laugh, to show her the Christmas lights, and to buy her that delicious brownie and hot chocolate, because if she was doing all those things, she wasn't thinking about people assuming she might be responsible for one of those killings. Now she realized she'd made a big mistake . . . again.

Gingerly, she eased the sheets away and then slid out of the bed in some great contortionist feat until her body landed on the floor. That action wasn't quiet, but luckily it wasn't loud enough to rouse Travis from his sated slumber. She crawled until she was out of the bedroom and found her clothes scattered about in the living room. Hurrying to dress, she just pulled on her pants and shirt, stuffing her underwear in her purse. Grabbing her coat, she headed for the door. If he came out of that room right now, he'd ask her too many questions, and her answers right now wouldn't be what he wanted to hear. This was for the best.

After she'd made it out the door, she vowed to really take the time to think about what she wanted where Travis and men in general were concerned. But that would be later. Now she headed to the elevator, using her phone to call an Uber. Once she was down in the lobby, she zipped her coat and put on her gloves as she prepared to go outside and wait for her ride. Stuffing her phone into her pocket, she pushed the door open, and then stopped. It only took a second for her to see it—the silver Tahoe parked across the street.

Her heart sank, her mouth gaped open, and the scream that should've come was stalled. Draya turned back into the building, running through the lobby like someone was chasing her. She passed the empty receptionist's station and ran to the first door she saw. Yanking it open, she stepped into the stairwell and leaned back against it, breathing heavily and praying that whoever was in the Tahoe hadn't found his or her way inside.

The doors to this building were locked after six p.m. Tenants had a security code and key card to gain entrance. The place was monitored by security cameras, but there was no on-site guard, so if the driver had shot her where she stood, it would've taken a while for somebody to see the video link and call the police.

"Fuck!" She was on her own, at least for the time being.

Her thoughts flipped between going back upstairs to tell Travis or finding another way out of this building. If she called or went back up to Travis's place, he'd jump out of bed and spring into action. First, going out front to see the Tahoe for himself; then, if it was gone, he'd call the police. He'd insist she stay at his place for the night, during which time he'd want to talk about why she'd snuck out of his bed in the first place. Most importantly, and why she finally decided not to call or go back up to Travis's place, was that if she did, she'd feel like she needed him. And Draya didn't want to need any man for anything.

With shaking fingers, she reached into her pocket for her phone to call the one person she knew wouldn't leave her here and would understand completely the fear streaking through her chest. She dialed the now-familiar number.

"Hello?"

"Venus, you gotta get over here quick!"

"Draya? What are you talking about? Where are you?"

"I'm at Travis's place and I was leaving and that silver Tahoe is out front. You gotta come get me right now!" She prayed Venus wouldn't go into the part where she told Draya what to do instead of just doing what Draya asked of her. She really didn't feel like dealing with the mother hen right now.

Yet she'd been the one she called without hesitation.

"Venus, I'm scared. Please, you have to come now."

"I'll be right there. Text me the address."

Chapter 32

Venus

"This is like déjà vu all over again!" Jackie yelled as soon as she'd climbed into the passenger seat of Venus's car. "Why does shit keep happening to her?"

"To be fair," Venus said, "shit happens to us too." The fact that she'd had sex with Malik again came to mind.

"Where's her car? Why can't Travis drive her home or call the police? Both might be smart at this point." Jackie talked a lot when she was upset.

Venus, on the other hand, tended to get extremely quiet before the ultimate emotional explosion occurred. She wasn't near that point yet, but her hands were gripping the steering wheel very tightly, and her heart was thumping loud enough for Jackie to hear—if she wasn't talking so much.

"I don't know the answer to any of those questions. What I do know is that it's not normal to think someone's following her. Like, who would it be? The killer wouldn't follow any of us if we're the cops' top suspects." But now, she wasn't even sure how true that was. Not that Malik had said anything while he'd been at her house tonight.

He'd actually been true to their agreement and hadn't spoken about any of the things or people she'd warned him not to when he first showed up. That could be because they were too busy talking about her validation issues with her parents and how he'd learned to let go of trying to prove himself to people who couldn't care less. Venus was torn between figuring out whether her parents were as concerned about her personal well-being as they always were about how she represented them.

"Venus! Are you listening to me?" Now Jackie was talking a lot *and* talking loudly.

"Yes, I hear you, Jackie. I'm less than three feet away from you, so there's no need to yell."

"Well, you were staring off into space."

"Driving. That's what it's called. Keeping my eyes on the road because it's dark and I don't want to get into an accident. Is that all right with you?"

Jackie slouched down in the seat like either a sullen child or a woman trying to hide from someone. That thought had Venus looking up and down the street twice at the four-way stop before driving through.

She'd just turned onto the street where Travis's building was located when Jackie raised up enough to look out the window. "Do you see the truck?"

"No." She hadn't really expected to. "I told you I think she's overreacting."

"I don't know, Venus. She might be for real."

"Why would you say that? The other night when we were at Jazzy's, you didn't see a truck in the parking lot either." She was focusing on the numbers of the buildings now because there were a few apartment towers on this street.

"But I saw one tonight."

Her head whipped around to look at Jackie, and her hands must've, too, because a loud car horn blaring caught her attention, and she had to swerve to keep from having a head-on collision.

"Shit!" she huffed. "Are you serious?"

Jackie shrugged. "It sped up my street while I was standing on the steps. Almost hit a woman and her kids."

"And you think that was the same one Draya saw."

"I don't know. I mean, logically, there are thousands of those trucks in the city alone, so what are the odds? But you gotta admit it's a big coincidence. Oh my . . . What the hell is she doing?"

Venus sighed when she saw Draya peeking out of the door to the building coming up on her right. Then she waved her hand over her head and yelled Venus's name.

"Well, if somebody was following her, she just made herself and me a target." Draya was so over-the-top with every damn thing she did. And here they were again, driving into who knew what type of situation because of a phone call from her.

Slowing down until she came to a stop, Venus hit the button to unlock the doors and then waited while Draya ran across the street. Was it a coincidence that she was wearing yet another—albeit a different color—velour sweatsuit?

"I don't know where it went," Draya said the minute she was in the back seat and had slammed the door. "It was right there in that spot."

Looking through her rearview mirror as she pulled off, Venus could see Draya pointing to an open parking spot on the other side of the street.

"Well, it's not there now," she said dryly.

"You don't believe me?" Draya's tone was combative as always. "Why the hell did you come if you don't believe I was in danger?"

"Because that's what friends do, apparently. We get up in the middle of the night and drive all over the city to pick up the other friend who is probably close to losing her damn mind." Venus was in a precarious mood.

All the events of earlier today combined with her dinner and sex with Malik, and she couldn't get a grasp on any sense of calm—or normal, for that matter.

"I am not losing my mind!" Draya yelled.

Jackie had turned so she could stare into the back seat. "Your shirt's on backward."

Venus looked through the rearview mirror again. "Shit!"

Draya huffed. "It's not that big a deal, Venus. You're not the fashion police, you know."

"I don't give a damn about your shirt—I was talking about the silver Tahoe that just pulled up behind us." She'd blinked twice as she looked through the mirror, hoping she was wrong. This street was pretty well lit between streetlights and lights left on in the buildings. The color could've been white, but she was fairly certain it was silver, and she knew the model because her father used to own one years ago.

"See, I told you!" Draya yelled.

"Shit! Speed up, Venus!" Jackie jumped on the yelling bandwagon as well.

Venus pressed on the gas, even though she was strongly opposed to speeding. She was even more opposed to being killed or whatever the driver of that Tahoe wanted to do with them. She flew through the next red light and turned down a side street she knew would lead to an alley that she could go through quickly and turn around again, hopefully losing the truck. With all the turns, the car was moving fast and swerving all over the place, and Jackie and Draya were yelling about not being ready to die and acting even more dramatic with each one.

"Put your damn seat belt on," she told Draya and kept on driving.

The Tahoe was close on her bumper. The driver had switched on the truck's high beams, so they were practically blinding her each time she tried to look back. She didn't know if it was a man or a woman driving, but whichever it was, they were good at chasing. Venus was determined to be better at eluding.

Swerving into the lane of oncoming traffic to avoid slamming into the back of two cars waiting on another red light, she said a silent prayer that they didn't end up dying tonight.

"I can't believe this shit," Jackie said, holding on to the door handle as if that was going to save her life. Well, it might keep her from being ejected from the car, but if whoever was chasing them was doing so with the intent to kill them, then neither that nor wearing a seat belt mattered.

"Who the fuck is it?" Jackie yelled back at Draya. "Did you see the driver when you came out earlier?"

"No!" Draya yelled again as she slid across the seat when Venus took another sharp turn.

"Didn't I tell your ass to put on the seat belt?"

"How can I when you're driving like you're on the Dover racecourse instead of city streets?" Draya argued but managed to right herself and pull the seat belt around her waist to clasp it.

She was right; Venus was driving recklessly, but she was also trying to save their lives.

"I didn't see the driver earlier either," Jackie announced.

The car hit a bump, and Draya bounced up and down in the back seat. "You saw the truck earlier?"

Jackie nodded and pulled her phone out of her pocket. "I'm calling the cops. This is what we should've done before."

"And tell them what? That we're being chased by a truck with an unknown driver. This isn't a Stephen King movie," Draya snapped. "That's why I didn't call them before."

"You didn't call them before because you never think beyond your self-interests, which I'm betting is the reason why you didn't just go back upstairs and get Travis." Venus was irritated as hell and no longer in the mood to sugarcoat things.

"Hold up! You don't get to judge me, Venus McGee. I know you think you're all perfect and shit, but you don't look down your nose at me when you're doing more scandalous shit than I am."

"How is that even possible, Draya? I mean, be real."

"Will you two shut the fuck up! I can't hear myself think, let alone hear the 911 operator." Jackie's voice rang loudest.

The truck clipped the bumper of her car this time, sending it into a tailspin across the two lanes. Jackie dropped her phone. Draya screamed something that sounded like a scripture but ended with her asking forgiveness for coming out with no underwear on, and Venus held on to the steering wheel, trying to retain control even as she fought to keep from wetting her pants.

She managed to turn the wheel enough so that when the tires stopped spinning, they followed her direction and made a peeling sound as they drove back down the street they'd just come up. Turning down a darker residential street now, Venus kept going until the road split in one direction going toward the harbor and the other toward the highway. Could she lose the driver on the highway? There'd be more traffic there. It was worth a shot.

But it wasn't meant to be. The second she was about to turn onto the ramp, the Tahoe hit them again, this time sending her car over the guardrail to rest in a ditch.

◆ ◆ ◆

Venus's face burned like hell, and blood streamed down the left side to drip on her jacket. Her nails were filled with dirt after she'd tried to climb out of the ditch but slid and had to hold on to something to keep from tumbling back down. Draya and Jackie were right behind her, the three of them coming to a stand on the side of the road seconds apart.

"What the fuck is going on?" Jackie yelled.

"Where's the Tahoe?"

"For the love of all that's holy, please stop talking about that damn Tahoe," Jackie said and then cursed again. "My back!"

"Don't tell me to stop talking about the truck that just tried to kill us. The same truck I've been telling you both was following me. Especially not now that we're out here in the cold." Draya's voice sounded a little different now. No longer was she screaming nervously at the top of her lungs, tossing out directives in a fear-laced screech.

Jackie didn't sound the same either. It could be the cold wind blowing and feeling as if it cut straight through her clothes to rattle the bones beneath. Or more than likely, it was the fear that had filled the interior of her car as they'd been riding in a high-speed chase like something they'd see on television instead of ever imagining they'd experience in real life. Her vision blurred as she lifted her head higher and tried to look to see if that truck was still in the area.

It wasn't. Another car whizzed by, not even noticing the three women standing on the side of the road freezing their asses off in the dark of night. Three insane women who were apparently in over their heads.

There were so many things whirling through her mind at this moment that Venus felt nauseated and light-headed. Her arms shook as she pushed a hand into her jacket pocket and pulled out her phone. Taking a deep breath and releasing it on a shaky moan didn't really help to clear the sensations, and she turned on the phone, pressing the button for the recently saved contact. With shaking fingers, she brought the phone to her ear and heard his voice seconds after the first ring.

"Hey," she said in what she thought was a casual tone. But then her throat clogged on the next word, and she paused a second to try and get herself together. "We were just run off the road by . . . by . . ." She couldn't finish the sentence.

"Where are you?" Malik asked.

She blinked back tears and gave him their location. After a string of curses, he disconnected the call.

"Did you just call that cop?" Draya seemed a lot closer than she had just a few moments ago, her voice echoing in Venus's head until it throbbed some more.

Jackie limped around to stand on Venus's other side. She'd pressed her hands into the pockets of the sweatpants she wore while Draya tried to pull that little hipster fake-purple-fur jacket she was wearing closer over her chest.

"Yes. I called Malik." She put her phone back into her pocket and cursed at that annoying feeling of something rolling down her skin again. Lifting the hem of her T-shirt up as far as she could without flashing everyone with the sports bra she wore beneath it, she had to lean her head over a little to wipe off some of the blood streaming down her face.

Groaning with the pain, she mumbled, "Do you want to stay out here all night and freeze?"

"No. But I don't want to go to jail either," Draya snapped.

"Didn't you just yell at me for *not* calling the cops?" Jackie's tone was loud and tinged with exhaustion.

Venus swayed as she tried to stand up straight again. She felt arms going around her shoulders and leaned into them.

"Whoa, I got you," Jackie said.

Draya huffed. "I yelled at you because that's what I do. I yell when I'm upset, and dammit, I'm pissed right now."

"Yeah, well, join the club," Jackie replied.

Draya didn't seem to be hurt; she was walking just fine and talking as much as she normally did. Jackie, on the other hand, had winced as she stood close to Venus.

"You should sit down," Venus told her. "You sound like you're in a lot of pain."

"You're bleeding," Draya told Venus and then reached into her purse that was crossed over her body and pulled out a tissue. She closed the small space between them and pressed the tissue to the gash on

Venus's head, and Venus tried like hell not to yell out as the pain almost blinded her.

"Okay," Draya said, tossing that first tissue and handing Venus another one. "Your guy is coming. He'll call an ambulance, too, 'cause that's what cops do. We're gonna be all right, y'all."

Draya laced an arm around Venus's waist. "We're gonna be just fine," she continued as if she were trying to convince them all that was true.

"Yeah. We're gonna be fine," Jackie repeated.

Venus didn't echo the words because she wasn't so sure. This whole ordeal had just taken an unexpected turn, and she didn't know if life as they'd known it was ever going to be fine again.

Flashing lights and sirens sounded in the distance, and she whispered, "Thank you, Jesus," before putting the tissue to her forehead again.

Moments later, a black SUV and a police cruiser pulled up. Malik was running toward them in the next seconds.

"Are you ladies all right? The ambulance is on its way." He looked at all three of them, his gaze moving quickly from Draya down the line to Jackie before he turned back and yelled, "Call for another medic!"

Two uniformed officers had gotten out of the cruiser, and one came running up to them, going to Jackie and putting his arms around her so she could turn and lean into him. Draya stepped away, saying, "I'm fine. But she needs to see a doctor. That gash on her head looks serious."

Malik stepped up to her then, one arm going around her waist, while he touched a finger to her chin to tilt her head back. "Yeah, it's serious." He spoke through clenched teeth. "What the fuck were you doing? You could've been killed!" He gave her a little shake, his gaze burning into her with fury.

She opened her mouth to speak, but he shook his head. "Shut up. Just shut up. We'll talk after you've been looked at."

He took over holding the blood-soaked tissue to her head, cursing again when she winced.

"There was a silver Tahoe," Draya said from where she now stood a few feet away from Venus with the second officer. "It was outside when I came out, and then it followed us when Venus came. The driver was chasing us and ran us off the road."

When Venus met her gaze, Draya stopped talking. The officer had given her his jacket, and she was pulling it close around her body. "I didn't get the license plate, but I've seen the truck before," she finished.

In the next moments, the ambulances appeared. Venus was already being put on a stretcher when she glanced over to see Jackie lying down on one, too, and Draya standing beside her. Malik took her hand and walked alongside the paramedics until he had to release her and she was loaded into the back of the ambulance. He surprised her by climbing into the back with her to take her hand again.

"You're gonna be fine," he said, as if he were trying to convince both of them. "Just fine."

Venus closed her eyes because they were getting too heavy to try and keep open any longer. She could hear the paramedic asking her questions, and she felt her lips moving, so she must have been answering him. The ache in her head was so bad now, it became a blur of pressure, and she started to tremble. Malik didn't let go of her hand—that's what she remembered most about the ride to the hospital. He'd come to help and he hadn't let go of her hand.

Chapter 33

Jackie

"I can't believe you called your new girlfriend—the one you're not sure you're getting serious about—to come and pick us up at two in the morning." Draya was sitting in the chair against the wall about four feet from the hospital bed where Jackie was now resting.

"We need a ride, don't we?"

Draya hadn't stopped talking since they'd climbed out of that car. A part of Jackie knew it was because she was scared as hell, and Jackie could certainly relate to that. That saying about life flashing before your eyes had been true as the car tumbled off the side of the road—she'd seen snatches of her life like a movie preview, and it had left her shook.

"Yeah, I guess we do. But I could've called us an Uber." Draya's hands clutched her purse, Jackie's hoodie still on her lap.

The nurses had given it and the rest of Jackie's clothes to Draya when Jackie came into the emergency room and they rushed her back to get X-rays and blood work. That was more than an hour ago, and the doctor had since come into the small room to tell her nothing was broken, just a few sprains. They'd given her some pain pills and prescriptions and now she was ready to go.

"They're keeping Venus overnight for observation." Draya cleared her throat after making that statement.

Jackie sighed. "That's probably a good thing. The gash on her head looked bad. Did she call her parents?"

Draya shook her head. "No. I saw her for a few minutes while you were in the back, and she said she didn't want to worry them if it's just a concussion. Her cop was still there with her."

"That's good," Jackie said.

"Is it?"

Draya looked at her nervously, and Jackie was about to tell her she didn't want to hear no shit about their situation with the cops right now. It definitely wasn't the time. But Draya kept right on talking.

"I mean, they broke up before. 'On-again, off-again,' as Venus put it. What if it doesn't work this time? He's all by her side now, coming to her rescue. Knowing her, she's gonna be thinking some romantic shit is brewing just for him to turn around and break her heart again."

Jackie slid off the bed and went to stand in front of Draya.

"I'm just sayin' that's how guys do. They come back when they feel like it and go when they please. If he hurts her, I might have to catch a charge for punching him in the throat."

Kneeling in front of Draya, Jackie took her hands and waited until Draya met her gaze. "We're all going to be okay, Dray. Whatever happens between Venus and Malik, Venus is going to be okay because she's got us." When Draya gave a slow nod, Jackie smiled. "I mean, she's got me breaking noses for guys and you ready to punch a dude in the throat for her, so I think she's pretty protected."

Draya laughed. "Yeah, you with your wannabe Creed ass. Take this hoodie so we can get out of here."

Jackie stood and put on her hoodie. Draya stood, too, brushing down the front of her clothes and taking a deep breath. "Malik told me to give my statement to those other officers while you and Venus were being examined. So I told them everything from the time I almost came out of the apartment building and then ran back in to call y'all."

They were walking toward the curtain that gave minimal privacy in the crowded emergency room. "Yeah, I gotta stop following Venus when she says she's going to pick you up. It's too damn dangerous." Draya playfully nudged her, and Jackie grinned. "Seriously, though, I'm glad the police are involved now. I mean, in something that's on our side."

"Yeah," Draya said. "Me too."

◆ ◆ ◆

They stood just outside the emergency-room doors minutes later, waiting for Karlie to pull up.

"You sure your girlfriend's coming? We could've had an Uber by now."

"You sure do talk about calling Ubers a lot, but we always end up in a car speeding to come and get you," Jackie replied. "And she's not my girlfriend."

"Ha!" Draya shook her head. "Keep telling yourself that. And go over there and sit on that bench. Just because the doc said you didn't have to stay doesn't mean you're not still sore."

Jackie shook her head. "Nah, I'm good." She was still sore, but the pain meds were starting to kick in.

"Whatever you say." Draya shook her head and shivered from the cold. "What're you going to tell your girl about what happened?"

Jackie hadn't really thought about that. Once the doctor had said she was fine to go home, she'd just asked Draya for her phone and called Karlie, who'd answered quickly, although the sound of her voice said she'd clearly been asleep. There was no hesitation when Karlie agreed to come and pick them up, and Jackie had simply felt good talking to her and knowing she'd see her again.

"Well, she doesn't know we're the Black Charlie's Angels out in these streets investigating murders and being chased by psychos, so let's not talk about any of that when she gets here," Jackie told her, and before Draya could give another smart-ass remark, Karlie pulled up.

Minutes later, after quick introductions, they were settled in Karlie's car for what ended up being a quiet ride all the way to Draya's condo building.

"Thanks for the ride, Karlie. Wish we could've been meeting under better circumstances," Draya said as she opened the door to get out.

"It was no problem," Karlie told her. "I'm just glad everyone is okay."

"Yeah, me too," Draya said. "Call me in the morning, Jackie."

That was different from the *"Text when you get home"* they'd been used to saying to each other. "Will do," Jackie replied.

When they were alone and she'd pulled away from the building, Karlie reached a hand over the console to lace her fingers with Jackie's. The warmth that spread through her was unbelievable and so comforting, Jackie completely forgot about the pain in her back. That could also be due to the painkillers, but she settled back in the seat feeling good about thinking the woman sitting beside her was responsible. Karlie hadn't asked any questions, except if everyone was okay, when Jackie called her, and when she'd pulled up at the emergency room and hopped out of the car, she'd hugged Jackie immediately. "I'm so glad you're safe," she'd whispered.

"Yeah, me too. Thanks for coming out at this time of night. I really appreciate it."

"Of course I was coming to get you. I mean it—I'm glad you thought to call me."

She *had* thought to call Karlie first. Draya had said that was because Karlie was her girlfriend, but really, who else was Jackie going to call? She had no family who spoke to her or would even care what happened to her, and her only other friends had taken that tumble off the road with her. Still, she hadn't felt depressed about any of that at the time; she'd simply felt grateful that she was alive and able to call somebody in the first place.

But on the real, was Karlie her girlfriend? The pleasant pain-free haze that hovered over her at the moment kept her from delving deeper into that issue, and she lay her head back against the headrest for the duration of the ride.

When Karlie finally pulled up in front of Jackie's place, she stopped the car and looked over at her.

"Need some help? I'm gonna be a nervous wreck thinking about you in pain for the rest of the night. So I'd probably keep texting you anyway."

Jackie grinned because she didn't doubt that for one minute—Karlie loved to text. "Sure, park over there." Another decision made without her prerequisite worry or contemplations about relationships and giving Karlie the wrong impression about where this was going. Jackie knew they were so far beyond that part now.

Minutes after Jackie totally embarrassed herself by creeping up the steps like she was a ninety-year-old, Karlie followed her into her apartment and back to her bedroom. Again, another decision made without thought, because even though the pain had substantially ebbed, she wasn't even going to try and sit on her tiny couch after all she'd been through tonight.

"Here, let me help you," Karlie said.

Jackie sat on the bed and did as she was told while Karlie removed her shoes and her jacket.

"Where's your heating pad and medicine?"

"Both are in the bathroom, in the linen closet. But they gave me some meds at the hospital. There's some more in that bag, and I got a prescription."

"Okay, good. I'll just grab the heating pad."

While she was gone, Jackie reached for a pillow and turned her body so she could lie flat on the bed. She couldn't believe the shit they'd just gone through. This outrageousness had to stop. Her thoughts shifted again when Karlie returned with the heating pad in hand.

"This has to go in the microwave, right?"

Jackie nodded. "Yeah. I picked that up last year, and it's the best invention. They're so much better than the ones you have to plug in. Only problem is eventually they cool off, but you're not really supposed to keep the heat on you that long anyway." She sounded like an infomercial for the heating pad, but she didn't know what else to say at the moment. It had been a long time since there was someone to take care of her.

"I'll be right back, and I'll bring you a glass of water in case you're thirsty."

Jackie watched her walk out of the room. She lifted an arm and dropped it over her eyes. A few hours ago, Karlie had been sitting in the living room with her watching *Gremlins* and laughing her ass off at the ugly little creatures. She'd made microwave popcorn and sat with her legs tucked beneath her on the couch as if that's how she spent every night. Jackie had loved every moment, and when she'd had to take Karlie home, she'd kissed her longingly in the car, wishing like hell she felt ready to take things further with her.

"Here ya go," Karlie said when she returned. "Sit up so you don't choke."

Jackie eased into a sitting position and accepted the glass of water, taking a few gulps. She was way thirstier than she thought.

"Now let's get this hoodie off and we'll put the heating pad right at the spot where the pain is."

Karlie grabbed the hem of Jackie's hoodie at the same time as Jackie, and their hands collided. They both paused and stared at each other before a nervous grin spread on each of their faces. Slowly, Jackie lifted her arms and let Karlie pull the hoodie up and over her head. She wore a white tank top under it because that and her boxers were what she normally slept in. Karlie's gaze dropped down to her chest and the thin material of the tank top.

Clearing her throat, Karlie reached around Jackie and positioned the heating pad. "Here, lay down."

Again, Jackie did as she was told.

Standing, Karlie removed her own coat and grabbed the remote from the nightstand to turn on the TV. She walked across the room and turned off the bright light they'd switched on when they came in, casting the room in the hazy blue glow from the TV screen. When Karlie returned, she sat on the side of the bed and took Jackie's hand.

"You probably shouldn't go to sleep just yet if you hit your head—at least that's what my mother used to say. So we'll just watch some television and chitchat until I feel like it's safe for you to rest."

Jackie laced her fingers through Karlie's and pulled her hand to her lips to kiss them. "Thank you so much. For real, you don't know how much I appreciate everything you've done tonight."

Watching the genuine smile that spread across Karlie's face sent another flood of warmth through her, and Jackie swore it took the pain away just like Karlie's touch had in the car. Now, she wasn't on some delirious shit about supernatural healing powers or anything like that. It was just that Karlie's touch, and having her so near when things had gone straight to hell, was a comfort Jackie hadn't realized how much she missed.

"Come here," Jackie said, her voice thick with emotion.

Karlie leaned down to her, and their lips touched. Gently at first, as if they were just getting to know each other. When in fact, they'd been kissing a lot since that night in the parking lot at Jazzy's. Jackie liked kissing Karlie. She adored how soft Karlie's lips always were, especially since it was winter and the brutal Maryland winds could crack lips the way they did sidewalks. And each time their tongues collided, she released this light moan that sent waves of pleasure throughout Jackie's body.

Tonight was no different. Amid the tightness in her back and the steamy warmth of the heating pad was that pleasure that circled into every part of her body because she was kissing Karlie. When Jackie looked back on this moment, she was sure she wouldn't know how to explain the second she decided that Karlie's shirt had to be removed as well. But when that T-shirt was gone and there was only a burgundy bra covering the most perfect titties she'd ever seen, she let out a breath she hadn't known she was holding.

"You sure?" Karlie asked. She looked so pretty tucking her bottom lip between her teeth, her hair a wild mass around her shoulders.

Jackie braved any pain that might come from the move and sat up again. She wrapped her arms around Karlie and unsnapped the hook of the bra, pulling back to watch it fall away, baring—to her delight—big dark-brown nipples. "I'm sure," she whispered, her mouth a little drier than it had been before.

Clasping her hands to Karlie's cheeks, she took another kiss, this one with more intensity, more desire than she'd known she had stored inside her. Karlie grasped her arms and tilted her head to lean into the kiss. Jackie's teeth scraped along Karlie's lips, their breathing heavy and loud as Karlie reached up to pull Jackie's hair free and run her fingers through it. Jackie wanted to do so many things at this moment. She wanted to lay Karlie on her back and suck on her titties until she could no longer think straight. She wanted to lay her naked body against Karlie's and hold her there until . . . whenever. She wanted Karlie's screams of pleasure, to see her pretty eyes cloud with desire, to feel her orgasm take them both to a higher place.

What she did was a little different. Grabbing her by the waist, she lifted Karlie off the bed and lay back while positioning Karlie to straddle her.

"Careful," Karlie said as she adjusted herself on top of her. "I don't want to hurt you."

Jackie grinned. "Baby, wanting you so badly is starting to be more painful than any injury." She pulled Karlie down. "Now bring those pretty titties to me."

She tasted like honey. Straight-up, no jokes or fanciful thoughts, just pure sweetness as Jackie ran her tongue over a puckered nipple. She held both heavy breasts in her palms, kneading them and groaning at how pliant and erotic that shit felt. Sucking one nipple completely into her mouth, she closed her eyes to the powerful punch of lust. Karlie had her hands on the pillow on either side of Jackie's head, holding herself up while Jackie sucked to her delight. She couldn't get enough, making a rude-as-hell snorting sound as she greedily went from one tit to the other.

"Yes, baby. Yes, suck it just like that."

Damn, her sexy voice sounded as good as her normal tone. Jackie needed more. Pushing one hand down Karlie's body, she unsnapped the button of her jeans and eased the zipper down. When her fingers slipped under the material of Karlie's panties, she groaned at the silky warmth of her shaved pussy.

"Shiiit!" She moaned the word, dragging it out the way desire slowly filled her.

Karlie raised her hips a bit to allow more access, and Jackie silently swore this woman could get anything and everything she owned . . . and shit she didn't even have, for that matter.

Parting her damp folds was like opening a treasured gift on Christmas morning. Touching the tight bud of her clit and feeling Karlie's instant quiver was like hitting the lottery. She released the hold on her breast and cupped that hand around the back of Karlie's head, bringing her down for a kiss full of tongue and teeth, while her fingers sank deep inside her. Karlie moved her hips with Jackie's motions, both of them moaning and panting, waiting for that precious moment and needing it like they needed air. And when it came and Karlie bucked over her, Jackie whispered in her ear. "That's it, baby. This pussy's all mine now."

Chapter 34

Venus

Holding her phone to her right ear because on the left side it pressed against the edges of the big-ass bandage that had been applied to the gash on her head, Venus listened as it rang two times.

It was eight thirty in the morning—there was no way she should still be asleep.

"Hello?" Draya sounded groggy as she answered.

"Hi," Venus said, not sure she sounded much better than Draya, thanks to all the pain meds they'd pumped into her last night. "It's me. I need you to come and pick me up."

"What? Pick you up from where?"

Irritation flared. "From the hospital, Dray. Where do you think? That is where you left me last night." The slight rise in her voice made her feel a little dizzy, and Venus frowned.

She'd been diagnosed with a mild concussion, and the contusion on her head had received five lovely stitches. Dr. Lancken had been a very pleasant gentleman who looked like he could've been fresh out of high school with his dimpled chin and startlingly blue eyes. When he'd made his rounds this morning, he'd told her she was clear to go home but that somebody needed to pick her up because he didn't want her traveling alone.

"Oh. Venus. Wait a minute." There was some rustling in the background that sounded like Draya was rolling around in the bed instead of jumping right up and telling Venus she was on her way. "Hey. Okay. I'm back," she said.

"I'm being discharged from the hospital in the next half hour or so, but they're not going to give me the paperwork and send me on my way until somebody is here to pick me up."

"How're you feeling? Are you sure they said you can come home?"

Draya had a million and one questions all the time. Venus swore she just liked to hear herself talk. "I'm groggy. I still have a headache, although not nearly as bad as it was last night, and the sight of that oatmeal they brought me this morning made me want to hurl. Can you please come and get me?"

Draya actually chuckled. "You sound like a seven-year-old."

Venus tried to drape an arm over her forehead, but that was a little painful, so instead she dropped her arm down to the bed and clenched her fingers in the sheet. "Well, I'm not, but I would like to go home sometime this morning. So get your butt up out of bed. It's your turn to come and pick me up."

The silence that came next told Venus the irony of this phone call hadn't been lost on Draya.

"I'm sorry," Draya said in a soft tone. "I'm sorry I ever got you and Jackie involved in all this. I was so upset last night about how things have turned out that when I came home, I took two Ambiens and prayed for some peace."

Venus gasped. No wonder she was still asleep and sounded like she'd been under the bed when she finally answered. "Draya. You can't take two of those. On second thought, maybe I should call an Uber, 'cause you don't need to be driving." Venus's heart raced at the thought of what type of peace Draya may have actually been searching for.

"Girl, please. I've done it before. It just relaxes me for, like, a day or two. I hadn't planned on going into the office for the rest of the week anyway. I'm just really sorry that I got us all into this mess."

"We each made our own decisions, Dray. Don't blame yourself for somebody else's actions."

"I know what you're saying is right, but I can't help but feel guilty. And don't make your headache worse by trying to talk me out of it. I need to wallow in it so I'll learn the lesson."

"What lesson?"

"Just sit tight—I'll be there to get you in a little while."

Draya hung up the phone before Venus could say anything else, and for a few minutes she did exactly as Draya had said. She lay in that hospital bed, thinking about all the things that had happened over the last week and wondering if she'd perhaps been living somebody else's life for that time. If that were possible, she was ready to get out of it now, even though going back to her old life didn't seem as attractive as it had before.

Lying in this room last night with the lights out because they only increased her discomfort, she'd thought about all that had happened since the holiday party and the things that had been going on in her life before. The contrast was there, but the one thing that was constant throughout was how unhappy she'd been. Before the party, she'd been unhappy at the job; complaining about Rufus had become an almost daily activity, whether she was doing it in the privacy of her own office or home, or the occasions that she'd sat at the lunchroom table with Jackie and Draya. The other parts to a trio she'd never imagined being a part of.

Then there was Malik. He'd thought she was sleeping, but she knew he was sitting in that chair beside her bed. That's where he'd spent the night, leaving sometime around six this morning when the nurses came in to check her vitals. She recalled how intensely he'd scrutinized every minor thing the nurse had done to her, his brow wrinkled, lips pressed tightly together.

"You do know she wasn't causing me any pain," she'd said when they were alone again. "So you can go home now. I'm fine."

He hadn't replied for a few moments, and she'd thought he was going to completely ignore her, but instead he'd stood and come closer to the bed. Taking her hand again, he'd held it tightly before leaning over to touch his lips softly to hers.

"You scared the crap outta me, so don't tell me when to go home." His words were softly spoken while his face was still close to hers, and her heart ached.

Amid all the other bumps and bruises on her body at the moment, that particular part of her throbbed in a way it hadn't in a very long time.

"Now, I am going to run home, grab a shower, and check in with BCPD to see if they've found anything on that Tahoe, but then I'll be back." He used the pad of his thumb to trace along the line of her jaw. "I'm not walking away this time, V. I'll be back."

She closed her eyes to the memory now, feeling that same pang in her chest that she had when he'd been here. In addition to everything else that was going on, now she needed to figure out what she was going to do about Malik and these feelings he'd awakened. For now, she sent him a text telling him she was being discharged and that Draya was already on her way to pick her up. With that in mind, she put the phone on the table they'd rolled over to the bed, and then she held on to the side rails to raise herself up.

An hour later, Jackie and Draya walked into the hospital room. Venus had already made her way to the bathroom, cleaned up, and dressed, so she was sitting in the chair that Malik had occupied all night when they arrived.

"Awwww, look at you," Jackie said as she rushed in, coming over to the chair and wrapping her arms around her.

"Damn, do I look that bad?" Venus hugged her back, glad to see that she wasn't wincing in pain the way she had been last night.

"No. No, not at all," Jackie said.

"Well, they could've been a little neater with that bandage," Draya said as she came to sit on the edge of the bed across from Venus. "But at least you don't look like you're about to pass out anymore."

Venus smirked and then chuckled. "Thanks, Dray. That means a lot coming from you."

In fact, it did. The two of them showing up here to get her did mean a lot, just as it had when they'd crowded around her last night, holding her up because it absolutely felt like she was going to faint in those moments before Malik and the ambulances arrived.

"So we ready to get up outta here? I can't stand hospitals; they give me the creeps," Jackie said.

Draya rolled her eyes. "You weren't saying that last night when you were chillin' in the emergency room."

Jackie stood close to the chair like she didn't want to leave Venus. "That's because they were giving out those fantastic pain pills last night."

Venus smiled. "Yeah, I got a few of those myself. But I am ready to go. I just need to let the nurse know you're here, and she'll come around with the wheelchair to cart me out of here." She stood and walked over to the bed to push the "Call" button.

"Before she comes, I need to say something," Draya said.

Venus stopped and was about to walk back to the chair again, but she felt a little woozy.

"Here, sit down." Draya pulled her on the bed next to her. "You sure you should be going home?"

She nodded. "The doctor said I'd still feel a little dizzy and nauseous for another day or two but that if it got too bad, I should come back. It's much better than it was last night, and I really don't want to stay here."

"Then it's a good thing we both took off from work. We can stay with you all day to make sure you don't fall on your face once you get home." Jackie stood in front of them. She wore joggers and another hoodie, all gray this time with pristine white tennis shoes. Venus was really glad to see her.

"That's right. But I'll take care of the cooking because we know somebody doesn't know how to act in the kitchen," Draya said.

"Who? Me or the one who likes sex with her meals?"

Venus blushed at the memory and told them both to be quiet. They shared a quick laugh, and the feeling of unity surrounded her.

"After I sent my email to HR saying I wouldn't be in for the rest of the week, I checked my other messages. There was an email from our digital-storage department saying the files weren't as difficult to find as they'd originally thought and that the signed contracts were attached. I didn't even open them, just wanted to tell you both and to say it's time for us to go to the police."

Jackie locked her hands behind her back and nodded. "I agree. This shit is gettin' too serious now."

"Shoulda, coulda, woulda," Venus said with a very slow shake of her head. "I don't know how many hours I spent last night thinking of what we should've done or could've done instead of all the things we did that landed us where we are now. It was a futile effort, so I definitely agree—it's time to go to the police. And I know you probably won't believe this," she said, more to Draya than Jackie. "But I don't think Malik believes we killed Rufus. I think he wants us to tell them what we know so he can prove it."

The nurse came in before they could talk anymore. Venus thought that might be for the best. She wanted to go home and get a hot shower, put on some clean pajamas, and climb into her bed. If Jackie and Draya were going to be her nurses for the day, so be it, but they were gonna have to keep it quiet, sit in her room, and watch all the Christmas movies she wanted. They could discuss going to the police tomorrow—today, she just wanted to rest.

She slept during the ride to her place, and Jackie helped her out of the car, carrying the discharge bag and Venus's purse as they entered the building. She could've carried that stuff on her own, but she wasn't going to complain about the help. They were at her door when she was trying to dig into her purse while Jackie held it to find her keys.

"You know this place isn't all that bad. I actually like the refurbished look," Draya was saying as she ran her hand over the crown molding around the doorframe.

"I don't like the chunk of change they charge for it," Jackie replied and then shrugged when Venus looked at her. "What? I checked it out last year to see if I wanted to move. But nah, I'll stay where I am, where I'm not expected to pay a grip for a two-bedroom apartment."

"It is expensive," Venus said, finally finding the key and moving to slip it into the lock. "I have it listed in my five-year plan to buy a house—" Whatever she was going to say next died in her throat as she didn't need to put the key in the door at all.

They all watched as the door to her apartment opened slowly, and a man came into view.

"Gifford." Draya gasped. "You bastard."

Venus recognized him from the funeral home. He was Rufus's personal attorney, and he had awful taste in clothes, as evidenced by the wrinkled khaki pants and dingy white shirt he wore.

"Just get inside," he instructed, and when none of them moved, he pulled the hem of his shirt back to reveal the gun tucked in the waist of his pants.

Jackie moved closer to Venus, putting an arm around her, encouraging Venus to lean into her. When Venus did, she felt what she thought might be a gun tucked in the waistband of Jackie's joggers. She didn't know when Jackie had gotten her gun back from the cops, but for just a second, she felt a tinge of relief.

"Go," she whispered and glanced over to Draya with what she hoped was a be-cool glare. Urging Jackie to walk in ahead of her gave Venus time to ease her phone out of her pocket and turn the recorder on. She didn't know what was about to happen, but she knew one thing for certain—she wanted to have proof for the police to use later.

They walked inside, and she jumped at the sound of him closing the door behind them.

"Have a seat," he said, urging them into the living room.

The three of them stood in front of the table where the three Wise Men still stood, flashes of their first night after the party in this very room shooting through her mind. Look how far they'd come since then. "We'd rather stand," Venus said and then cleared her throat. "What do you want?"

Franklin looked her way and smirked. "Venus McGee, the only woman I've ever known to scare Rufus."

His words meant nothing to her. Whomever or whatever Rufus may've been afraid of meant nothing to her, not anymore. "So you've been following us all this time? You were driving that Tahoe, weren't you?"

Laughing, he walked across the room to stand in front of her tree. Easing the gun from his pants, he used the barrel to tap one of the silver bulbs hanging from a branch. "Bingo. Give the lady a prize." Gifford had a bizarre look on his face—his nose was crooked, probably from being broken before; his dull gray eyes were wild like he could possibly be high; and his five-o'clock shadow was in the range of looking as unkempt as his clothes.

"I've been watching you three since you left Rufus's house that Saturday morning. Oh!" He feigned surprise, lifting the hand holding the gun to tap it against his temple. "I forgot. You didn't tell the police about that, did you? They don't know how you stood over Rufus's dead body and then walked out without calling to report his death to anybody."

"If you know we were there, you must've been there too. And you know we didn't kill him," Draya said.

Franklin pointed the gun at the bulb on the tree again, this time whacking it until the bulb broke and the pieces fell to the floor. The tree shook, and Venus sucked in a breath. "That's not what the fingerprints on the gun are going to prove," he said.

"You can't possibly have all our fingerprints," Jackie said. "Draya's the only one that's been bonded, and none of us have a criminal record."

"Yet." Franklin grinned. "And don't underestimate me, girl."

Jackie bristled and took a step forward. "Oh, I got your girl, all right."

Venus grabbed one arm, and Draya had the other as they pulled her back to stand with them.

"What do you want?" Venus asked him.

He was staring at Jackie, grinning. "He was never gonna get you, huh? Nah, you would've given him hell, just like Venus over here. But you, Draya, you gave Rufus everything he wanted. At least for a while."

"Look, you didn't come here for entertainment or to speak ill of the dead," Draya snapped. "So what do you want from us?"

"If you'd given it to me when I first asked, we wouldn't be in this position right now," he said before knocking another bulb off the tree. "But now we're at the point of no return."

Venus's heart beat so fast, she could hear the echo and struggled to hang on to her composure.

"Where's the flash drive and all the other papers you've managed to compile? And don't bother to lie to me because I know you have it. This one over here was even smart enough to figure out how to get more of a paper trail." Franklin forgot about the tree and snarled in Draya's direction. "But you ran into a snag—gotta wait for the storage people to deliver those signed contracts to you. Too bad you'll be in jail by the time that happens."

How did he know all of this? Venus looked at Draya, but she was staring at Franklin, probably trying not to look as confused as Venus felt.

"Did Ellen tell you that?" Jackie asked and then shook her head. "That bitch! She did, didn't she? I bet she was standing right outside Venus's office door listening to our conversation just like she was doing at my office week before last."

"I don't know what you're talking about. Last I heard, Ellen Pierce retired. I believe she's moved to Florida to be with her grandkids," Franklin said, an evil grin spread across his face.

But Ellen's retirement email had come right after they'd been having the conversation about the contracts in Venus's office. She remembered because that was the moment it felt like they were caught in a funnel of mayhem with all that was going on.

Draya surprised them by pulling the flash drive from her purse. "It's all on here. Where's the gun you say has our fingerprints on it?"

What the hell was she doing?

"Oh, it's in a safe place. But before we get into that, I've been authorized to sweeten the deal for you."

Venus's head felt like it was going to explode as she tried to grapple with what was going on. Last night she'd been run off the road, she had a freakin' concussion, and now this insane lawyer was in her house holding a gun on them. Whatever she'd done to deserve all this drama, she hoped the physical and mental stress she was now enduring would be enough of a punishment. She didn't want to die—not here and definitely not at the hands of this crooked lawyer.

"No. Give us the gun you've found a way to put our fingerprints on and we'll give you the files. That's it. That's our deal." Jackie quickly fell into step with whatever ruse Draya had going, and Venus struggled to stay alert. If these two were cooking up something, she had to be prepared to do her part, whatever that was.

"Not so fast, little miss." He looked Jackie up and down with disgust, and Venus silently prayed she didn't pull her gun out and shoot him between the eyes.

"If it were up to me, I would've gotten out of my truck and made sure each of you was dead last night. Meddling bitches!"

Draya sucked her teeth. "Just get on with it, Franklin. We don't have all day."

He moved with lightning quickness, closing the distance between him and Draya to press the gun right up to her temple. "You're on my time now. I'm not Rufus. I don't give a damn how well you suck dick; I'm not losing my mind over you."

Venus was trembling all over now while waves of adrenaline seemed to pour from Jackie as she stood poised to strike beside her. Draya, on the other hand, appeared the epitome of calm, cool, and collected as she stared directly at Gifford.

"Don't pull a gun unless you plan on using it, Frankie."

Was she taunting him? This was getting out of control. No, Venus sighed, it had been out of control from the start.

"Bitch," he muttered and took a step back.

Draya didn't say it, but Venus glimpsed the sag of relief in her shoulders.

"I've been authorized to offer you each a million dollars to go somewhere and forget about whatever financial improprieties you learned Rufus was involved in." The unmasked grimace on Franklin's face emphasized how much he disliked making that offer.

"You don't have that kind of money," Draya said.

But whoever was in on this with Rufus does. A hunch had her thinking that other person might be the city official who'd signed those contracts. Venus didn't think her father had that type of money, and she definitely didn't believe he'd have someone hold three women—including his only child—at gunpoint just to keep his name clear. At least she prayed with every ounce of her being that he wouldn't.

"All you need to know is that I have the money and I'll give it to you, each of you, with the gun that killed Rufus, if you turn over those files and get the hell out of Baltimore for good and keep your mouths shut." He backed up and extended his arm, pointing the gun at each of them one at a time. "Or, make no mistake about it, I will use this."

At that moment, a battle cry ripped free from Draya, and before Venus could stop her, she lunged for Franklin, wrapping her hands around the guy's neck. Her action took the man by surprise, and he stumbled back. Venus kept her focus on the gun in his hand as she ran for him, grabbing his arm and keeping it pushed upward.

"You simple bastard!" Draya yelled as she continued to choke Frank.

His face was beet red as he used his free hand to slap at Draya. The three of them tumbled back, knocking over a table before hitting the floor. With Draya still holding tight to his neck and Venus slamming his arm down to the floor like she'd seen cops do on television to get the suspect to release the gun, Jackie yelled, "Get outta my way!"

Venus turned just in time to see her raising her arm, gun in hand. "No! Jackie!"

"Hush, Venus! Y'all get outta my way so I can get a clean shot!" She was moving her arms back and forth, trying to find a way to shoot him.

Venus screamed. "We don't need a real murder charge. Stop!"

"Kneecap him!" Draya yelled. "Or I'm gonna choke the life outta him."

Franklin thrashed beneath them, and Venus finally just grabbed for the gun in his hand. He wasn't trying to let it go, and she was afraid their exchange would end up in a flyaway bullet soaring through her living room. But none of that happened because in the next seconds, the door flew open and "BCPD—put your hands up!" sounded throughout the space.

Venus froze. Draya yanked her hands away from Franklin's throat. Franklin gasped, and Jackie dropped her gun to the floor, raising her hands slowly into the air.

Chapter 35

Draya

They were separated, each in their own interrogation room, she supposed. Drumming her fingers on the table, she tried not to appear as nervous as she really was. What she wanted to do was scream in frustration at how unfair and ridiculous this entire situation was. They weren't killers; they were three normal women trying to live their best lives without the bothersome boss who still managed to annoy the hell out of them, even in death.

There'd never been anything in her life that Draya had regretted doing. Not one man she'd slept with or one teacher she'd cursed out for something foul they'd said to her. She'd been proud of every step she'd taken to pull herself up out of the situation she'd been born into, despite the odds. And then came Rufus. She regretted every moment she'd spent with him now. To hell with the promotion, the higher salary, her condo, all of it—if she could take back sleeping with that trifling asshole, she would. In the blink of an eye, she would.

The door opened, and she stopped moving, sitting up straighter, prepared for whatever. Again, that was way more bravado than she actually felt. They'd let her call her lawyer when she first arrived at the precinct. Travis had been in his office, and his secretary had put Draya directly through to him. Seconds after she told him where she was, he'd said he was on his way. She hadn't spoken to him since sneaking out of his apartment last night, so she wasn't sure what terms they were on right now. That's why there was a spark of surprise when she watched him walk into the room, close the door, and take a seat across the table from her.

Now she let her hands fall into her lap where he couldn't see her clench and unclench her fingers. "Hi." The one word sounded woefully insufficient and pitiful as hell.

He set his briefcase on the table, flipped the gold latches on the top, and opened it to take out a notepad and pen. Pressing the top of the pen against the notepad until it clicked, he cleared his throat and began. "You haven't been officially charged with anything at this point. Howard County homicide detectives and Baltimore City officers want to question you with regard to what happened at Venus McGee's apartment today. My suggestion is that we prepare a statement, make it, and unless they come up with some charges at that point, you walk out of here."

So professional, so matter-of-fact, so different from how she was used to dealing with him. Regardless of what had happened between them last night, he'd come here dressed in a dark-brown suit, white shirt, and butter-yellow tie that highlighted his deep mocha skin tone. And for the first time since he'd come into the room, he made eye contact with her.

"Based on everything we've ever discussed about this situation, here's what I think your statement should be." He turned the notepad so that it was right side up for her to read and pushed it across the table toward her.

Draya had never been through any of this before, but she'd heard plenty of stories from her brothers, other family members, and friends of the family who'd visited BCPD often. Leaning forward, she read what Travis had written. His handwriting was really neat, and she found herself focusing on the schoolteacher-perfect *I*'s he made throughout.

I, Draya Carter, acknowledge having a sexual relationship with Rufus Jackson.

I also acknowledge visiting the home of Rufus Jackson on multiple occasions, previously outlined in a document provided to the Howard County Police Department.

I also acknowledge . . .

She looked up at him. "I was wrong."

"Excuse me?" His brow furrowed and he continued. "If there's something that's inaccurate, we can change it. This was only a draft, and it should actually be in your handwriting. You'll sign and date it, and they'll add that to their report."

Placing her palms flat on the table, Draya took a deep breath and released it. She stared directly into Travis's dreamy brown eyes. "I was wrong about you. About us."

He sat back in his chair with a jerky motion, as if she'd reached over there and pushed him. "Draya."

"No, let me finish." Because if she didn't, she might never have the guts to do this again. Her heart was beating faster than it had been when she was trying to kill Franklin a little while ago or when she'd climbed out from that ditch last night. "I was wrong not to tell you that I was feeling the change in things between us too. That the casual affair I'd insisted we have from the start had already begun to feel like something a little more serious."

There was no response from him; he just blinked like he was seeing her for the first time. That could be true, because she believed she was actually seeing him—the honest, compassionate, and loyal man he was—with more clarity than ever before.

"I don't know how to do committed relationships because I've never wanted to. I never believed in them. And I'm not saying I wholeheartedly believe now—I'm just admitting that this thing between us feels different from anything I've had before." There, she'd gotten it out. Her plan had been to think about things between them more, to rehearse how she planned to break off the affair, when all the craziness in her life settled down. But the moment she'd heard his voice on the phone telling her he'd be right here and then showing up for her, regardless of how she'd treated him—and especially because she'd never formally paid him a retainer to represent her—everything changed.

"Now's not the time or place for this," he said before rubbing a hand down the back of his head. "We have to prepare a statement before they walk in here at any minute, tossing questions at you. This is a very serious situation. However, I think we're in good shape."

"Are you talking so much and so fast because you really want to kiss me?" He wasn't wrong; this was an extremely serious situation—her freedom was on the line, so she should be totally focused on fighting whatever charges the police might throw at her. But hearing Travis's response to everything she'd just said was important. Reaching for something in life she never thought she'd have no matter how hard she worked was important too. It was detrimental to her emotional stability, and it would save her from the flush of embarrassment that heated her skin.

He leaned forward and stretched his arm across the table until his hand covered hers. "I can't kiss you in an interrogation room."

Relief soared through her, coming out in a gasp as she smiled. She looked down at their hands and turned hers over to entwine their fingers. "Right. I'll give you a pass."

"Thank you." He winked at her. "Now let's get this statement completed."

Chapter 36

Venus

She knew it was him without having to turn around.

"I'm not saying anything until my attorney arrives," she said while her head throbbed with the worst headache she'd ever experienced.

Her arms were folded across her chest to ward off the chill she'd been feeling since being escorted out of her apartment building like she was a criminal. No, Malik hadn't put cuffs on her. He'd actually been very gentle after he'd pushed past the Baltimore City officers to get to where she was still lying on the floor. Franklin's gun was a few inches away from her.

Neither of them had said a word as he'd reached for her. She'd accepted the help up, then slid her hands out of his grasp, letting them fall to her sides. He'd touched her arm then, directing her out of the room and into the front seat of his car. She'd buckled herself in and stared straight ahead until they arrived at the station.

She hadn't known the words to say then, hadn't known how to express all that she'd been thinking and feeling. With every second that ticked, every day that passed, she learned something else about the man she'd answered to, the father she'd looked up to, the people she worked with, so much until she didn't think she could keep it all straight. Emotions tumbled around inside her until she thought she might literally explode from the buildup. This moment was the first time she and Malik were face-to-face since arriving at the precinct.

"Why didn't you tell me you were being followed when I was at your apartment?" That same deep voice. It had changed when he'd turned fifteen, and over the years it had just grown sexier. She knew she'd never forget it.

"Why didn't you tell me you were following me too?" Taking a breath, she forced herself to turn around at that point. "While I was in and out of a medically induced sleep at the hospital, I wondered how you'd managed to get there so fast. It was because you'd been following me. Just like that night at Chino's. You didn't come into the city just to hang out at that club. And the spa, you followed me there too."

During the ride here, she'd had ample time to piece things together, all while he sat a couple of feet away from her.

He leaned against the wall close to the door, pushing his hands into the front pockets of his slacks. He didn't wear a tie, and the top two buttons of his dress shirt were undone, but he still wore the suit—a gray one with faint pinstripes that looked really good on him.

"I would've been there before you called if I hadn't gotten cut off by some tractor trailers just before you got onto the ramp. I was trying to protect you, but I failed. You got hurt, and I won't ever forgive myself for that." He sighed. "You wouldn't tell me the truth, but I knew something was going on. I knew Jackson had done something to you or one of your friends, and I was determined to find out and to keep the three of you out of jail if you were innocent."

"If?" Her brow raised. "You never believed I wasn't involved in his death, did you?"

"I told you I knew you weren't a killer. Dammit! I was trying to do my job, V."

"No." She stopped that immediately. "You don't get to call me that anymore. My name is Venus."

He frowned. "I asked you to trust me."

"But you never trusted me, Malik. That's the problem here. You came waltzing back into my life because Rufus Jackson, the asshole supreme, was killed. Not in the years prior, when you could've easily found out where I lived, the same way you ended up doing as a result of this investigation. At any time before all this, you could've come to me and given me that bullshit about wanting to be with me again, but you didn't."

"You're blurring the lines." He spoke slowly, not moving a muscle, all while she raged on the inside.

"No, you blurred them when you came to my apartment and fucked me on my kitchen counter. How do you think the rest of the officers out there will react to that little piece of evidence? How would your superiors back in Howard County react?" He'd be in a lot of trouble—she already knew that—and she'd never do that to him. She'd never sacrifice her personal business just to get back at him.

"If you had just told me everything from the start. Hell, I'm still trying to piece this shit together. Who in the hell is that sleazy attorney, and why was he at your apartment? You were found with a gun. Do you have any idea how that looks? If you're trying to prove your innocence, you don't do it by committing another crime!"

"Don't talk to me like that." She took a step toward him. "Don't ever talk to me like that again. I told you I didn't kill Rufus. Finding out who did was your job. I shouldn't have had to do any of the shit I've done." She snapped her mouth shut then. "I'm not saying another word until my attorney gets here, and as for what you and I were doing . . ." Her voice cracked, and she clamped her lips shut.

She'd begun to feel something for him again; there was no doubt about that. But could she trust what that was? Did she even want to?

"I don't know what that was, and I don't even want to think about it right now. I don't want to think about what we had in the past, because I'm not that person anymore. I'm not going to be that person anymore," she said adamantly. Strength and confidence filled her now, seeping into all the gaps that had formed over the years while she did everything that was required of her, instead of everything that would feed her.

Watching him walk quietly out of the room hurt more than she'd expected it to. Actually, at this point, Venus didn't know what the hell to expect. Her life had been on one wild-ass roller coaster ever since that party.

Minutes later, her father and Tabitha came in, and she sat down, ready to do whatever her lawyer told her to do.

"I want you to tell Tabitha everything, and she'll figure out where to go from here," Don said when he sat across the table from her.

He hadn't hugged her like he normally did when he saw her, and surprisingly, that didn't even sting. She'd disappointed him—she could tell by the way he was being so formal and distant—and she no longer gave a damn. Because he'd disappointed her too.

"You don't have to be here. I can talk to my attorney alone." Those words sounded formal and distant too. She was proud.

"Venus." That was the stern tone he used when he was about to chastise her for something, but Venus was no longer a child living under his roof.

"No, Daddy. I can do this by myself. And in the future, when I hire an attorney, I'd rather you not go behind my back and speak to her." That she directed at both him and Tabitha, because Tabitha should've known better than to allow him to be involved in her case.

"We must make sure your statements are carefully worded. Everything you say and do from this point on will be documented in case files. The press will snatch up any tidbits they can. We have to be on point with how this is handled," Don continued.

"I have to tell them what I know," Venus said, staring directly at him. "Everything I know. That's how I plan to handle this. Whatever the press reports is out of my hands."

Don—because he wasn't acting like a father should—leaned in, placing his hands on the table as he glared at his daughter. "You will not mess this up for me."

All the years of lectures and reprimands, of being cloistered in her parents' world like she was a pawn in their game instead of a child in their life, came flooding back. But instead of drowning her in guilt and obligation, this time the memories strengthened her. They steeled her spine and tilted her chin as she spoke. "You will not continue to dictate my every move. My life is my own, and I don't need your validation anymore."

"Don," Tabitha said with a hand to his arm. "I think you should go."

He clenched his fists at his sides and looked like he could strangle Venus at that moment, but Tabitha continued insisting that he leave.

When he was gone, Tabitha offered Venus a tentative smile. "Let's take this slowly," she said. "I want you to start from the beginning and tell me everything. Then we'll decide how to proceed from there."

Venus nodded. She took a deep breath and released it—along with all the strain and stress from her past—slowly. Then she told Tabitha her story.

Chapter 37

Jackie

This house was warm as hell again, but she smiled as she slipped off her coat and then turned to reach for Karlie's. Different from the last time she had been at Aunt Dot's house, it was crowded in here this evening. Then again, Christmas dinner tended to bring family together.

"Coats go upstairs!" Bo yelled from the other side of the room.

Jackie half expected him to still be mad at her for stabbing his friend in the hand, but Draya had assured her he knew Levi could be a jerk most of the time.

"Cool. Merry Christmas!" she said.

Bo nodded in response and then continued to talk to whomever it was standing closest to him.

"I'll be right back," she said to Karlie. "You'll be fine right here."

Karlie frowned playfully and gave Jackie's shoulder a push. "Girl, go on. I know how to act around people."

Yeah, she did. In the few days since Jackie had been ready to shoot Franklin Gifford with the new gun she'd purchased because the police had been so slow to return her old one, she'd been spending a lot of time with Karlie and her family. Karlie and her sisters loved to cook and eat and watch some gross-ass show called *Dr. Pimple Popper*. Her niece was cute and guaranteed to be a heartbreaker when she grew up. Being with them had felt as comfortable as if Jackie had known them all her life. Similar to the way she felt whenever she was around Venus and Draya.

Speaking of those two, they were standing in the bedroom on the second floor where all the coats were being piled on one bed when Jackie got up there.

"Hey, Merry Christmas, ladies!" Jackie dropped the coats and went to hug each of them.

They'd all taken the rest of the week off from work, so they'd just been communicating via text and the Zoom call Jackie had insisted on when she felt it had been too long since she'd seen their faces.

"You're looking particularly happy. Was Santa good to you today?" The wiggle of Draya's brows after the question had Jackie laughing and blushing at the same time.

"We're good. She's downstairs. You sure your mom's okay with her coming?"

"Did you see all those people downstairs? My momma probably don't even know who's in this house right now." Draya looked happy too. Jackie figured the young lawyer had something to do with that.

That and the fact that their attorneys had struck a deal wherein they each made full statements about the morning they'd found Rufus's body and turned over all the evidence they'd accumulated to document Rufus's fraud scheme with the city in exchange for no obstruction-of-justice charges being filed against them. And since the evidence they'd provided the police had opened a full investigation into a couple of city employees, starting with Carol Benning, who'd been the one to sign all the BCC contracts, they'd each also agreed to testify to how they found the documentation.

Even after learning of her godmother's connection to this case and ending the hookups with the sexy detective, Venus looked relaxed in her jeans and black knee boots. "I'm glad both of you made it. You were taking forever."

"We had to spend some time with her family first. I bought Dominique this Barbie plane that's better than any doll toy I ever got for Christmas." And she'd felt like a million bucks when Dominique's face lit up with a smile. "I called my parents this morning too."

"How'd that go?" Venus asked.

Jackie shrugged. It hadn't gone well, but she wasn't going to dwell on it anymore. She'd done what she felt she needed to do. The next step would have to come from them. "It is what it is," she said simply. "What about you two? How's it going since . . . you know?"

Draya sighed heavily. "That's what we were up here talking about. Can you believe Carol Benning was arrested for killing Rufus? Not only because he was stealing from her while both of them were supposed to be stealing from the city but also because he'd tried to blackmail her with some nude pics too. I mean, I knew he was a bitch ass, but I had no idea how nasty he really was."

"What really blew me away was that the classy woman I knew as my godmother was also sleeping with that slovenly and despicable Franklin Gifford. That's how he ended up doing her bidding by trying to frame us and then eventually get us out of the way. My father is still pissed about that." Venus tucked a few braids back behind her ear. "But I'm glad Lynette came forward with all the pictures she found in that safe. All the ones except for what she returned to you," Venus said, glancing at Draya.

Covering her face and shaking her head, Draya groaned. "I told Travis he ain't nevah getting a nude pic from me. He better look his fill in person. And I confirmed my meeting with the bank two days after the New Year, so I'm one step closer to getting the foundation off the ground."

"That's what's up," Jackie said with a nod and a smile toward Draya. "Whatever you need, I'm down for helping out. I bet there'll be some young ladies I can probably help out too."

"She's right," Venus said. "We're really proud of you, Dray. And of course I'll be there, too, doing whatever you need me to do."

"Trying to be in control, I'm sure," Draya joked. "But yeah, thanks. I'm glad you'll both be there. This is going to be good; I can feel it."

Jackie felt it too.

"And the very best part is when we go back to work next week, we won't have Ellen to deal with." Venus raised a hand and looked up. "Thank you."

Jackie clapped her hands. "Franklin was right—old girl got on a plane to Miami to live with her daughter quick, fast, and in a hurry after she told him about our conversation. Whatever else she was hiding for Rufus, she knew it was about to be revealed when I sent her file through interoffice mail."

"Facts." Draya nodded and pointed at Jackie. "And now, come spring, our new permanent VP of operations will break ground on the Hopkins Sports Complex."

They both looked at Venus, whose grin was so big and bright.

"Yasssss, sis. Congrats," Jackie told her.

"Thanks. Terrell called to congratulate me yesterday. We're having dinner to celebrate tomorrow." Venus looked a little nervous about that admission.

"Awww, look at you. I swear I rubbed off on you in the dating department," Draya said.

Venus rolled her eyes. "I hope not."

They chuckled, but Jackie couldn't help adding, "What's really wild is finding out that Robyn was the one who killed Mike."

"Yeah." Venus nodded. "Men gotta learn to stop pushing women over the edge. She thought they really had something going until they were at that nice hotel in Annapolis and she saw texts and pictures from one of those strippers from the club he and Rufus had gone to."

"And then did you hear, he told her she wasn't shit and he was gonna have her fired before he tried to throw her out of the hotel room wearing just her underwear?" Draya added.

Jackie blew out a breath and shook her head. "All I know is if I'd had my gun in my purse like she did, I'd have pulled it out and shot his ass too."

"Oh, we know you're trigger-happy," Venus said.

"Absolutely." Draya laughed so loud this time around, they both joined in, and Jackie knew she'd finally found the place where she belonged. Yeah, it still hurt that her parents didn't want to be part of her life, but she was coming to terms with the fact that it was their loss, not hers. She had a new family now—Draya and Venus and the peeps downstairs. She couldn't wait to do the gift exchange with Aunt Dot and Granny.

"But seriously, though," she said when their chuckling died down a bit, "I gotta say something."

They tried to get it together, but Draya was still laughing and almost fell over onto the pile of coats. Venus managed to grab her arm and looked at Jackie. "Go on—we're listening. You know she's had a drink already and don't know how to act now."

"Oh, y'all started this party without me, huh?" Jackie grinned. "But I'll make this quick. I just wanna thank the two of you for coming into my life and being just what I needed, when I needed it. I mean, who would've imagined having drinks at a party would lead to the after party at Venus's house?"

"And a dead man the next morning," Draya said dryly.

"Yeah, that too," Jackie agreed. "But look how far we've come since then. In just a few short—but long as hell at the same time—weeks, we've grown closer and leaned on each other in ways I know I hadn't done with anybody in a long time. And I'm just grateful for that. I'm happy to call you two drama queens my friends."

"Did this trick just call me a drama queen?" Draya asked playfully.

"Awww, we love you, too, with your greedy-ass self." Venus went to her and hugged her, and Jackie held on so tightly, she thought she might break her.

"Don't forget about me," Draya said and joined in the hug.

"See what I'm sayin'? Drama queen." But Jackie loved them; she loved the friends who had come to her through a stressful-as-hell time in her life. When they finally broke the hug, she moved to the bed where she'd dropped her coat and pulled out the bottle of Hennessy from her inside pocket. "Now, who's ready to get this Christmas party started right?"

"Oh no, not again," Venus groaned. "You and that bottle are how this all started."

Draya stepped up and took the bottle from her. "Ignore Mother Hen, and let's go get us some glasses. Merry, merry Christmas, y'all!" She was singing and walking out the door with the bottle when Jackie looked at Venus. They both shrugged before following her and singing along, "Merry, merry Christmas!"

"Y'all up here smokin' those funny cigarettes?" Granny came up the stairs just as they stepped into the hallway. She had one hand on her hip, the other pushing her glasses farther up on her nose. "We're down in the kitchen waiting to do our gift exchange, and Bo said y'all was up here having a private party."

Draya laughed even more, but Jackie stepped forward, wrapping her arms around Granny for a big hug. "Merry Christmas, Granny." When Granny's arms came around her to hold her tightly, Jackie closed her eyes at the feelings of comfort, acceptance, and peace. "I've got your gift right downstairs," she continued when the connection broke.

"Good. I got yours too, and you're gonna love it. I ordered it online and Dot wrapped it, so all I had to do was put one of those tags on it and write your name."

Granny talked as she turned to walk down the stairs. Jackie followed, with Venus and Draya still singing behind her. After going back into the living room to grab her bag of gifts, Jackie made her way through the dining room and into the kitchen, where Aunt Dot was taking hot rolls out of the oven.

"It's time to open the gifts!" she yelled, holding her bag up in the air.

Venus and Draya must've already known to bring their gifts in here, because festively wrapped boxes were across the room on top of the washing machine.

"All right now," Aunt Dot said, wiping her hands on her red apron. "Can't wait to see what's in all those boxes. This was a fun idea."

"It was all Jackie's idea," Draya said and smiled in Jackie's direction.

"Then she should open hers first," Granny announced and walked to the washing machine to grab a box. "Here, this one's from me."

How long had it been since she'd opened gifts with anyone? While Christmas was about so much more than presents, Jackie had always loved the looks on her parents' or her friends' faces when they opened a box to see something she'd purchased especially for them. Today, she was surrounded by a roomful of people who accepted and cared about her, so it didn't matter what was in the box. They were the greatest gift she could've asked for this year.

Then she finished ripping the paper off the box and yelled with glee. "Hell yeah! Five gift cards to all my favorite restaurants! After I eat here tonight and take home some leftovers, I'm gonna eat well for the next week!"

While Venus and Draya shook their heads and grinned, Jackie walked over to Granny again, this time kissing her on the cheek before snagging another hug. "This was way over the amount we agreed to spend," she whispered.

"Don't tell me what to do with my money," Granny snapped and pulled back to look Jackie in the eye. "Take it and enjoy yourself with that nice young lady out there in the living room."

Touched beyond measure, Jackie could only grin and say, "Thanks so much, Granny, for everything."

"No thanks necessary," Granny said with a wink. "We're family now."

Those words resonated in Jackie's mind throughout the night. Everything she'd been through had been worth it, since in the end, she'd found her family.

ACKNOWLEDGMENTS

I'd like to thank Laura Bradford for believing in this story from the moment I left that rambling paragraph in her in-box and for continuing to believe even on the days that I doubted. Lauren Plude for joining in and championing our vision. Angela James for her unflinching honesty and expertise, which helped make Jackie, Draya, and Venus shine.

I would also like to thank my beta readers—Deborah, Matysha, LaSonde, and Kelly. My very special author friend, Odessa Rose, for listening to me whine and talking me off the ledge. Genell Collins and Manu Velasco for helping me make sure that Jackie was her best authentic self. Keisha Mennefee and Honey Magnolia PR for their invaluable advice and support.

Finally, I'd like to thank Mr. A. and my girls (The Queen and The Princess) for listening to me ramble about scenes, characters, and deadlines and knowing it was best to remain silent until it was over. I love you for your unwavering support.

ABOUT THE AUTHOR

Photo © 2012 Lisa Fleet Photography

A. C. Arthur has worked as a paralegal in every field of law since high school, but her first love is and will always be writing. A multiple-award-winning author, A. C. has written more than eighty novels, including those under her *USA Today* bestselling pen name, Lacey Baker. After years of hosting reader appreciation events, A. C. created the One Love Reunion, an event designed to bring together readers, authors, and other members of the literary industry to celebrate their love of books. A. C. resides in Maryland with her family, where she's currently working on her next book, or watching *Criminal Minds*. For more information, please visit www.acarthur.com.